ROCK ADDICTION

NALINI SINGH

NEW YORK TIMES BESTSELLING AUTHOR

For detailed descriptions of these books, as well as additional titles, visit Nalini's website: www.nalinisingh.com.

ROCK ADDICTION

COLLIDE

HER SMILE SMASHED INTO HIM with stunning force. He heard nothing of the party around him, saw no one but her. God, that smile, the way she cupped her sister's face with such open affection before the two of them hugged. Really hugged. No fake bullshit, no playing up for the journalists in the room.

They weren't paying attention to anyone else, happy simply to see one another.

Then she laughed as she drew back and the sound was chains around his heart, a thousand guitar strings pulling tight. It hurt and it was beautiful. For an instant, he almost forgot where he was, he wanted so badly to have that unguarded smile turned in his direction. He could imagine her warm brown eyes looking up at him as she ran her fingers over his jaw and rose on tiptoe to slide one hand around his nape to haul him down for a kiss.

Fucking hell.

When was the last time a woman had done that to him the instant she walked into a room? Never. Not even when he'd been a hormone-drunk youth. And the fact he knew she was exactly as she appeared to be, that she wasn't out for fame or money? Yeah, that just made her sexier. No way was he leaving this party without her, the raw need to possess her a violent craving in his gut.

He didn't believe in fantasy shit like destiny or fate or the biggest con of all—love—but he knew himself. And he knew what he wanted: to tug her to him with his hand fisted in her hair, brand her with his mouth, warn every other male in the room that she was off-limits. But the instant he did that, he'd make her front-page news when he wanted her all to himself.

Private.

Alone.

No cameras.

No lights.

No fucking interruptions.

PART ONE

CHAPTER 1

S HE WANTED TO BITE his lower lip.

Wanted to tug on the silver ring that pierced one corner of that delicious, toe-curling mouth.

But mostly she wanted to bite down with her teeth, taste the badness of him.

"Um, Molly?" A hand waved in front of her face. "Molly?"

Blinking, she forced her gaze away from the man who made her want to do bad, bad things and toward the petite form of her best friend. "What?" Her skin flushed until she wondered if her fantasies were visible to everyone in the room.

"You mind if I bug out?" Charlotte took a last tiny sip of her pomegranate martini before placing it on one of the small, high tables scattered around the room. "I want to spend tomorrow making sure all the files are in order for the new boss."

Molly scowled, all embarrassment fading. "I thought you were trying to take it easy on weekends?" The fringe of the black flapper-style dress she'd pulled out of her closet in a moment of whimsy swirled just above her knees when she

3

shifted to give Charlotte her complete attention. "Isn't making sure everything's up to standard Anya's job anyway?" It was Anya who was personal assistant to the CEO; Charlie officially worked in the records department, but Anya had a way of treating Molly's best friend as her own assistant.

"New boss has a rep," Charlotte said. "I don't want to be fired because Anya didn't bother to do what she should." Narrowed hazel eyes behind fine wire-rimmed spectacles made it clear Charlotte had no illusions about the other woman.

Nodding, Molly considered the cherry that decorated her nonalcoholic but very pretty cocktail. "Let me get my coat." Disappointment whispered through her veins, but really, what would've happened if she'd stayed longer? Zilch. Zero. Nothing.

Okay, maybe another blush or two inspired by the rock god across the room, but that was it. Even if he, for some wildly inexplicable reason of his own, decided he wanted her, the one thing Molly would never *ever* do was become involved with someone who lived in the media spotlight. She'd barely survived her first brutal brush with fame as a shocked and scared fifteen-year-old; the ugliness of it had left scars that hurt to this day.

"Oh, no, don't." Charlotte put a hand on her arm, squeezed. "I'll order a cab. You're having too much fun staring at Mr. Kissable."

Molly almost choked on the cherry, lush and sweet, that she hadn't been able to resist. "I'd say I can't believe that came out of your mouth"—cheeks burning, she fought not to dissolve into mortified laughter—"but you have been my friend for twenty-one years and counting."

Charlotte grinned as she took out her phone and texted a cab company. "You know who he is, don't you?"

"Of course. He's only one of Thea's most important clients." And on the cover of every second magazine that came across Molly's desk at the library, all sleek muscle and tattoos and a sexy smile curving those dangerous, bitable lips. If she couldn't resist reading the articles and sighing over the photos, that was her guilty little secret.

"You two talking about me again?" Her sister's sultry voice sounded from behind Molly, followed by her slender body—currently clad in a tight red designer sheath.

"About your raking-it-in client," Charlotte clarified.

"That's *über*-client to you." Raising her champagne flute, Thea clinked it against the glass that held Molly's frothy concoction. "Here's to rock stars with voices like sex and bodies like heaven."

Molly felt her stomach clutch, and even though she knew it was none of her business, said, "You sound like you're speaking from personal experience," grateful her voice came out steady.

"Molly, m'dear, you know I never mess around with money." Her older sister's uptilted eyes, a burnished brown, were suddenly dead serious. "And Zachary Fox, known to his gazillion and one fans as Fox, and to any woman with a functioning sex drive as hot with a capital *H*, is serious money. As are the other members of Schoolboy Choir." Putting down her empty champagne flute beside Charlotte's cocktail glass, she said, "Come on, I'll introduce you both to him."

Charlotte shook her head. "No thanks. You know me and gorgeous men—I turn into a Charlie-shaped statue." Having

5

kept her phone in hand, she now looked down as the screen flashed. "That's a message from my cab driver. He's downstairs."

"You're sure about going home alone?" Molly couldn't help but worry about her best friend. Charlotte was fierce and strong and the only person who'd stood by her when the scandal broke, but she knew Charlie's own past had left invisible wounds that had never quite scarred over.

"Yes—I use this driver a lot for work stuff. He always waits while I unlock the door to my place and disarm the security." She hugged Thea good-bye before doing the same to Molly, leaning up to whisper, "Live a little, Moll. Take the hot rock star home, then tell me all about your night of wild monkey sex."

Molly's breath caught at the idea of it, foolish and impossible though it was. "If only." Over an hour into the party and Fox hadn't even looked in Molly's direction, that's how high she registered on his radar.

"Fox knows who you are," Thea said after Charlotte had left. "He saw a photo of us in my L.A. office—the one from after we went through the caves."

Molly groaned. "You mean the one where we both look like drowned rats, have giant black inflatable rings around our waists, and dented helmets on our heads?" The trip through the waters of the underground cave system had been fun, but it did not make for alluring photos. "Let's not forget the ancient gray wetsuits that made it look like we were molting."

Choking on her laughter, Thea nodded. "He was interested in doing the black-water rafting thing when I told him where we took the photo. I'm sure he'd love to talk to you about it."

Molly fought the temptation to get close to him any way she could, and it was one of the hardest things she'd ever done. "No thanks," she said, her mind awash in visions of what it would be like to meet him in a much more private setting, run her fingers over the firm lines of his body... bite down on his lip. "I'd like to keep standing over here with my fantasies." Distance or not, the needy, achy feeling in the pit of her stomach continued to intensify, her response to the rock star across the room scarily potent.

Thea raised an elegant eyebrow.

"If I meet him," she added through the shimmer of heat that licked over her skin when he laughed at something one of his bandmates had said, the sound a rough, dark caress, "and he's an arrogant snob or worse, a stoned-out idiot, there go my fantasies."

"Fox is neither a snob nor a stoner." Thea's lips kicked up. "The man is the whole package: intelligent, talented, and a nice human being unless you piss him off by pushing too hard about his private life—and I don't think there's any chance you'll go paparazzi on me."

"That just makes it worse," Molly pointed out, trying not to watch as Fox bent his head to speak to a bombshell brunette in a dress the size of a handkerchief. "How can I fantasize about him ripping off my clothes in a moment of reckless passion if he politely shakes my hand and says it's nice to meet me?"

Molly had learned her lesson about reality versus dreams as a teenager—once destroyed, some dreams could never be resurrected. And for some reason, she couldn't bear for this silly, unattainable dream to be splintered by reality.

"If you change your mind," Thea said with a shake of her head, "speak up soon. Fox never stays long at these things." She picked up a cobalt blue cocktail from the tray of a passing waiter. "I'd better go make nice with the other guests."

Watching her publicist sister expertly work the room, Molly smiled in quiet pride. Though they'd joyfully connected after a lifetime of not knowing the other existed, the bond was yet new, fragile, and no one who wasn't aware of their family history would ever guess they were related. Twenty-nine to Molly's twenty-four, not only was Thea naturally slender in contrast to Molly's curves, she had the smooth golden skin of her Balinese mother as well as Lily's eyes, but she'd gained her height from Patrick Buchanan, topping Molly by a good five inches.

Their shared father had put his stamp on Molly in a far stronger fashion, giving her the black hair she constantly fought to tame, creamy skin that burned easily, and eyes of deepest brown. Every time Molly looked in the mirror, she remembered what Patrick had done, and each time she wrenched her hair into a tight twist—as she'd done tonight— it was in silent rebellion of the shadow he threw over her life even from the grave.

Patrick Buchanan, "family values" politician and vicious hypocrite, was the kind of man who'd have taken a stranger home for a night of uninhibited passion.

Fingers tightening on the stem of her glass, Molly made the deliberate decision to turn away from the rock star whose presence made her body sing. It was just as well that Fox was oblivious to her existence, because should he turn those smoky-green eyes in her direction, Molly had the heart-thudding sense that she might break every one of her rules and give in to the other Molly who lived inside her. That dangerous woman was Patrick Buchanan's irresponsible seed, someone who might well wreck everything Molly had built brick by brick after her world fell apart.

Releasing a shuddering breath, she wandered over to the plate-glass window that functioned as one wall of the exclusive penthouse suite Thea had hired for the party. The bright lights of New Zealand's biggest city sparkled in front of her, a cascade of jewels thrown by a careless hand and bordered by the black velvet of the water that kissed its edges.

"Stunning, isn't it?"

She glanced at the man who'd spoken. "Yes." Rangy, with eyes caught between gold and brown, he was only a few inches taller than Molly, but there was a contained energy to him that made him seem bigger.

"I'm David."

"I know." She smiled. "David Rivera—you're the drummer for Schoolboy Choir."

"Wow." David rocked back on his heels, hands in the pockets of the tailored black pants he wore with a stone-gray shirt. "You actually recognize the drummer. Big fan?"

Her smile deepened. "My sister's your publicist." Based in L.A., the only reason Thea even had an "office" in New Zealand was because of Molly. That fictional office had alleviated some of the pressure during their first nervous meetings, making Thea's flights to the country about something other than the relationship they were trying desperately to build.

"I didn't know Thea had another sister." David's eyes skated to where Thea stood with Fox, the lead singer's arm around her waist, and all at once, he wasn't the charming, well-dressed man who'd been talking to her, but one with a stiff jaw and rigid shoulders.

"Thea," she said softly, as the rich darkness of Fox's hair caught the light, "has three very specific rules."

Sharp interest, David's attention snapping back to her. "Oh?"

"One: never sleep with clients." The words weren't only for David's benefit—the idea of her sister in bed with Fox caused her abdomen to clench so tight it hurt.

"What's the second rule?"

"Never sleep with clients."

"Why do I get the feeling I know the third one?" Thrusting a hand through the deep mahogany of his hair, he blew out a breath. "She ever made an exception?"

"Not as far as I know." Having forced her gaze back to the multimillion-dollar view in a vain effort to control the visceral pulse of her physical response to a man who could never be hers, she followed the path of several blinking lights in the distance, a plane en route to the airport.

"You want another drink? I definitely need a beer."

Molly shook her head. "No, I'm heading off." She didn't trust herself to stay any longer, didn't know what she might do; every cell in her body continued to burn in awareness of the rock star on the other side of the room.

Putting her glass on a nearby table, she dipped into her little black purse to find the keycard Thea had handed her that morning. The card gave her temporary access to the building's parking garage.

"Thanks for the advice on Thea's rules," David said with a rueful smile.

"Don't mention it." Molly wondered if her sister had any idea of the drummer's feelings. "Will you be flying home soon?" Schoolboy Choir had played a sold-out concert three days ago as part of a new outdoor music festival that had attracted bands from around the world.

"No, we're staying in town for a month."

Molly froze.

"It's been a tough year," David continued, "and we need downtime before the tour we have coming up. We liked it here, figured what the hell, we'd just stay on instead of flying somewhere else for a vacation."

It made perfect sense… and Molly knew she'd spend the next month obsessing over whether she might run into Fox again. Her cheeks heated at the sheer ridiculousness of her response. God, she had to go home.

"I hope you enjoy your time here," she said as she turned away from the view. Of course, her gaze went straight to Fox. A leggy blonde was currently whispering in his ear while several other women looked on grim-eyed. It was a stark visual reminder of the gulf that existed between them, regardless of her body's potent response.

David's voice broke into her thoughts. "I'll walk you to your car."

"No, that's okay." When he frowned, she added, "There's a guard on duty in the garage. It's safe." Smiling her good-bye, she began to tunnel her way out of the packed room.

Skirting around the tall form of the guitarist for Schoolboy Choir, an almost too-handsome blond male in the midst of charming an actress Molly recognized from a local soap opera, she managed to snag Thea for a quick hug. "I'll call you later in the week," her sister said in her ear. "I'm staying in the country with the band for the first part of their vacation."

"Oh, that's wonderful." Molly loved spending time with her older sister now that the initial awkwardness had passed. "If you're in the city anytime, come into the library and we'll sneak out for a coffee."

"Deal."

With that, Thea returned to her guests while Molly continued on to the exit—where she gave in to the inexplicable ache inside her and craned her neck for one last glimpse of the man who'd turned her blood to molten honey. Fox, however, was nowhere to be seen. "Not exactly a surprise," she muttered under her breath, recalling the gorgeous women who'd been buzzing around him.

More than likely, he was in a shadowy corner of the building, pinning one of those women to the wall while he pounded into her. The image poured ice-cold water on her fantasies.

Stabbing the button to summon the elevator at the end of the corridor, she tried to think of anything but Zachary Fox's muscled body flexing and clenching as he drove himself into that nameless, faceless woman.

Her pulse fluttered, her breathing choppy.

"Thank God," she said when the elevator arrived and, stepping inside, scanned her keycard over the reader before pressing the button for the garage.

"Hold up!"

Automatically pressing the Open button until the other passenger had ducked inside, she turned to give him a polite smile. It froze on her face.

Because there in the flesh stood the sex god whose lip she wanted to bite. All six feet four inches of him. Masculine heat, golden skin… and smoky, sexy dark green eyes focused on her mouth.

CHAPTER 2

PATIENCE WASN'T FOX'S STRONG SUIT, and he'd almost killed himself with it tonight. Then he'd just about killed David for getting close to her while he kept his distance. Now, finally, he was alone with Molly and all he wanted to do was mess up her hair, kiss her until her lips were swollen and wet.

Then he wanted to do it again. And again.

Fighting the gut-wrenching need that threatened to turn him inside out, he forced himself to lean back lazily against the elevator wall. "You're Molly." It came out a rough purr.

Her eyes widened, fingers curling into her palm. "Yes."

He wanted those fingers on him—any part of him. "Would you mind giving me a ride?"

A large percentage of the women at the party would've taken that as the invitation it was and been all over him in one second flat. Molly, however, took a tiny step back. "Don't you have a driver?"

Abdomen tight, he continued to keep his tone playful, easy, though he was feeling close to feral. "I gave him the night off."

"A taxi?"

If she took another step back, Fox wasn't sure he'd be able to restrain his need to put his hands all over her sweetly feminine flesh, taste her with his mouth. "I don't know the address I'm going to."

The elevator dinged at that moment, and he waited as Molly stepped out into the parking garage before following. The skin at her nape looked like cream; he wanted to lick it up, close his hands over her breasts from behind as he did so, press his rigid cock up against her. Yeah, he wasn't in a patient mood.

"Oh?" It was a husky question. "If you don't know the address, how do you plan on getting there?"

Unable to resist any longer, he bent to the soft, subtle, maddening scent of her and whispered, "That's why I need a ride, Molly," his lip ring brushing the shell of her ear. "I don't know where you live."

She dropped her keys.

FOX BENT AND PICKED THEM up, the chocolate silk of his hair sliding over his forehead. "Here." Putting them gently into her hand, he closed her fingers over the cool metal, his touch callused from playing the guitar.

Goose bumps broke out over her skin.

Blood rushing through her ears, Molly squeezed her fingers until the edges of the keys dug into her palm. "Are you always this…" She waved her free hand, realizing for the first time that he'd come to a cocktail party wearing black jeans and a black T-shirt. Yet he'd undoubtedly been the most charismatic person in the room.

"I'm making an exception for you."

Molly knew it was a line... and she didn't care.

That terrified her. But not enough. For the first time since her world had imploded when she was fifteen, danger tempted more than it scared. Looking up into Fox's face, his beauty holding a hard edge that said he'd break all kinds of rules, push her past her comfort zone, she knew she was about to give in to the other Molly, the one who'd been in a cage her entire life. "My car's in the second row."

Opening the driver's side door for her when they reached her sporty white compact, Fox said, "I haven't driven on the left before, but I like driving."

It took her a second because that teasing grin, it had stolen her breath, the lean dimple in his left cheek devastating her senses. "You can like driving in your own car." With the rest of her night about to spin heart-thuddingly out of control, she needed to be in charge of something, even if it was only the wheel of her car.

"It was worth a try." Sliding into the passenger seat, he pushed the seat all the way back to accommodate his legs.

"Would you allow me to drive your Porsche?" Pulling out of the garage, Molly battled the need that urged her to stop the car and tell the rock star next to her that he could do anything and everything he wanted to her... just so long as he let her bite down on that pierced lower lip.

"I don't have a Porsche." He shifted in an attempt to stretch out farther before realizing it was a futile effort. "I have a Lamborghini Aventador. Hot red, and baby, she's a sweet ride."

Molly had no idea what kind of car that was, but it sounded fast and dangerous and sexy. Like Fox. "So," she said, her toes curling, "would you let me drive your Lamborghini?" Her voice came out a little breathless, her heartbeat slamming against her ribs.

"Sure, Molly. If you promised I could do hot, dirty things to you before, during, and after."

Squeezing the steering wheel, she stared out at the road, the city center vibrant with groups of young males trying to make time with club-going girls in tiny glittering dresses and strappy tops—clusters of laughing wildflowers unworried by the autumn chill. Molly had never been that young, that carefree, had never stepped foot in a club after that first time in college—when she'd come face-to-face with the girl who, as a naïve and love-struck underage schoolgirl, had been photographed naked in the backseat of Molly's father's car.

She'd certainly never had a one-night stand.

Except now she had a rock star in her passenger seat, and they weren't planning on ending the night with a cup of tea and nice, polite conversation. "We need to stop at a pharmacy or a convenience store," she said, trying to act like the sophisticated woman he no doubt expected her to be, even as her hands threatened to tremble.

"Sure."

"You're going in." Molly wasn't ever going to be sophisticated enough to brazenly walk into a store at ten at night to buy protection.

"Okay."

Molly asked herself what she was doing. Really, *what was she doing?* The idea of Fox in her bed, his strong hands, his mouth—that delicious, delectable mouth—on her flesh, it stretched her nerves to breaking point. Fantasy was one thing, but to take the next step? To make it real? Especially when she *hadn't exactly done any of this before?* It made her throat dry up, her skin go alternately hot then cold.

"When did you pick me?" The words just tumbled out, her normal filters shredded by his proximity.

"Pick you?"

"For tonight."

A small, charged silence, the car turbulent with smoldering male energy. "That's an insult, any way you cut it."

Her cheeks burned. "You're right," she said, knowing she'd just blown all chances of pulling off any kind of sophistication. "I'm sorry."

That gritty purr was gone from his voice when he said, "Hey, I'm a musician. We all sleep around."

"I'm a librarian," she blurted out, unable to take the sexual tension entangled with the biting edge of male fury. "Everyone knows we're repressed old ladies with too many cats."

A chuckle. "Clever, Molly." Again, he stretched out his legs, or tried to. There was simply too much of him to fit in her little car. "You know, if I go into a store and buy condoms, it'll be all over the tabloids tomorrow that I fucked a local."

She felt her cheeks heat again. At this rate, she was going to have third-degree burns by the time they got home. "Wear a disguise." She fought to keep her breathing shallow, but it was no use—Fox's scent had bonded with every molecule of air in the car.

"Where am I supposed to get a disguise, Miss Molly?" The teasing question was abrasive silk over her skin.

Biting down on her lower lip, she told herself to *focus.* "There's a cap in the backseat, sunglasses in the glove compartment."

He found the items, tried them on before ripping off the sunglasses. "I wear these girly things and my cock will shrivel up." It was a growl. "Cap'll do. Long as they don't notice the ink."

"Just act shady," Molly said, her breasts straining against the lace of her bra, the fabric rasping against the taut tips. "The clerk will be so worried you're planning to shoplift or do something else nefarious"—*Nefarious?* Really, Molly!—"that he won't notice anything else." As long as the clerk wasn't female.

No woman would *ever* miss a single tiny detail about Fox.

"You think I can look shady?" A single finger traced the line of her jaw.

Her body wanted to whimper. "You have five o'clock scruff," she managed to say past the sheer want choking her, "you're dressed in black with a ball cap pulled low, and your left arm is covered in scary tattoos." In truth, she found the ink beautiful, wanted to explore the artwork slowly and in intricate detail. "Yes, I think you can do shady."

A chuckle, deep and low. "You're mean under the blushes. I like it—I'll also like licking up that blush from every inch of your body... after I use my tongue to get you off."

Molly forgot how to breathe.

When she didn't respond, he said, "Not even a little peek? I'll start to think you don't like the look of me."

Instinctive self-defense had her saying, "You know exactly how gorgeous you are."

She caught his shrug out of the corner of her eye.

"It's a face. It's mine. I don't want to kiss my own face. I want to kiss yours—while we're skin-to-skin and I have my cock balls-deep in you."

Heart ricocheting against her ribs and fingers bone-white on the steering wheel, she pulled into the convenience-store lot. "Go."

He left without another word, jogging to the door. She wondered if he really was that hungry for her. As hungry as she was for him. Until she had to convince herself not to simply drive to the darkest part of the lot and crawl into the lap of the beautiful, dangerous man she'd never expected to touch. It would take less than a minute to undo his zipper, nudge her panties aside, and—

"Jesus, Molly." She pressed her forehead to the steering wheel and squeezed her thighs together.

It only intensified the ache between her legs.

They were taking precautions, she thought, trying to rationalize what she was about to do. She wasn't drunk. Neither was he. They weren't being stupid about it… but it was still going to be a one-night stand.

She took a deep breath to settle her frantic thoughts, but the lingering scent of Fox, hot and dark, seeped into her, derailing any attempt at coherent thinking. Undoing her seat belt, she opened the door and stepped out into the cold chill of the night, the soft breeze causing the layers of fringe on her silly, pretty dress to sway softly.

Could she do this and look at herself in the morning?

The answer was scarily easy. Every woman was allowed a Fox in her life, allowed one night of unrestrained passion… wasn't she? This would be hers. When it was over, she'd put the wild, unruly part of her away forever—the part that came from her father and would otherwise destroy her life, as Patrick Buchanan had destroyed their family.

At least she was single, wouldn't be breaking anyone's heart by sleeping with Fox.

The convenience-store door opened on the heels of her decision, to reveal a man with a sinful smile and a body made to give a woman decadent pleasure. "Ready?"

"Yes." *Yes.*

The rest of the drive home passed by in what felt like seconds. Parking her car in the underground garage of the low-rise building in which she had her apartment, she walked with Fox to the elevator.

He put his hand on her lower back as they entered it, sending a jolt up her spine, but his attention was on their surroundings. "You need better security." Narrowed eyes scanned the darkened parking garage. "It wouldn't be that hard to bypass the scanner to the garage."

It startled her, the edge of concern in his tone. "How do you know that?"

Hand still on her lower back, his lips curled up in a teasing half smile. "You'd be surprised what a boy can learn at boarding school."

Molly couldn't imagine him as a boy. His every action shouted strong, confident, *adult* male. "This is me." Stepping out on the third floor, she headed down the hallway, her heels clicking on the uncarpeted surface and her nerves doing a stuttering dance.

"You know your neighbors?" He leaned against the white-painted wall as they got to her door at last—the one right at the end.

Unlocking the door with fingers that wanted to tremble, she pushed it open and flicked on the light to reveal the spacious entryway that flowed into an open-plan living room and kitchen-ette. "Yes," she said, dropping her purse on the wooden bench where she usually sat to slip on her shoes. It was an effort to find words through the haze in her brain. "We keep an eye on each other."

Fox came in behind her. "Fuck, yes." The sound of the door being kicked shut on that harsh exhalation, strong male hands on her hips, hot breath against the curve of her neck.

She went motionless, her pulse in her mouth.

Tugging her hair free from its twist, then nudging the heavy wildness aside to bare her nape, Fox said, "I can't wait to taste you," in a voice that was pure whiskey and sex and hard rock.

Then those lips, that divine, delectable mouth, was on her. She shivered as he slid one arm around her waist, crushing her to him. His lips were firm and demanding on her, his stubbled jaw scraping deliciously over her skin. And that ring, it brushed against her in cool strokes that made her imagine what his kiss would feel like in other, more private places… places no other man had kissed.

Fox thrust a jean-clad thigh between her own at that se-cond, forcing her to keep her legs spread. The denim was abrasive against her sensitive skin, the flex of his thigh threat-ening to send her over. *"Fox."*

Making a sound of pleasure deep in his throat, he sucked on the curve of her neck and tightened his grip. He was pure muscle and strength underneath skin tanned a golden brown, his erection pushing against her lower back in a blatant de-mand that made it clear who held the reins. There was nothing of softness about Fox. When he moved onstage, it was all coiled power and deadly grace.

And now he'd focused that aggressive intensity on Molly.

"The dress," he said, biting gently at the skin he'd sucked. "Take it off."

Her fingers shook as she lifted them to undo the hidden zip at the side. "It—" Clearing her throat, she tried to speak past the arousal and nerves strangling her vocal cords. She had no idea what she was doing, Fox utterly out of her league. "It has to come over my head," she managed to get out.

He caressed her hip before releasing her. "We'll go slower the second time around."

The second time around?

She'd barely processed the thought when his hands were gripping the bottom of her dress, gathering up the liquid-soft fabric in strong hands. He bared her so fast she had no time to worry about the fact she wasn't built anything like the tall, slinky models and actresses who usually buzzed around him.

"I can't wait to have you naked and wet beneath me." His hand rose up, closed over the heavy mound of her lace-covered breast.

A little shocked at his bluntness, she gasped and arched into him, wordlessly begging for more. But he left her. Trembling, she blinked, tried to find her senses.

"Why the hell do they wrap these boxes in indestructible plasti—"

"Here." Turning on legs that threatened to crumple, she took the small box in an effort to give herself time to think, to catch up with what was happening... and became hotly aware of Fox taking the chance to rip off his T-shirt. Breathing became impossible as he revealed a chest she'd never actually expected to see on a real man, the taut ridges of his abdomen inviting her to touch, to pet and kiss and suck.

"You're supposed to open it." He tugged the box from her grasp with a slow smile, one that said he knew exactly what he did to her—and that he planned to take brazen advantage.

As she blushed, he tore open the box and flat packets exploded around them.

She glanced down reflexively... and that was when Fox closed his hand over her nape, tilted back her head, and kissed her full on the mouth.

His lips... his lips should've been illegal.

Vaguely aware of him undoing her bra and tugging it down her arms, she moaned into the kiss as he pressed her closer with one big hand on her lower back, her bare breasts crushed against the tensile muscle of his chest. She whimpered, sensation prickling through every nerve ending in her body to pool between her legs.

"Yeah, just like that, baby," he said into the kiss, his lip ring rubbing over the wetness before he gripped her jaw to hold her in position and thrust his tongue into her mouth.

The audacious intrusion startled her, made her realize once again that she'd taken on more than she could handle. *Far* more. Then Fox licked his tongue over her own, his hands sliding down her back to squeeze her lower curves, and reason fractured under a wave of pure, unadulterated pleasure that drove her to the edge of sanity.

She bit down on his lower lip.

"Fuck!"

A second after that single brutal word, she found herself lifted up as if she weighed nothing and pressed against the hallway wall, her legs around Fox's waist, her ankles crossed at his lower back, and her arms wrapped around his neck. Then he was kissing her again. And again. And again. Each kiss was as open and as sexual as the last, one of his hands fisted in her hair, the other molding and squeezing her breast.

Gasping when he released her just long enough that she could suck in a breath, she fell back into a kiss that made it obvious her paltry experience of men had in no way prepared her for being taken by Zachary Fox.

CHAPTER 3

A LICK, A SUCK, AND Fox lost it. Breaking the kiss, he reached down between them to undo his belt buckle. The goddamn zipper threatened to cut his cock in half, but he got it down, sheathed himself, his fingers trembling. If he wasn't careful, he'd come on the first thrust.

That was when Molly pushed at his shoulders. "Wait, wait."

Fox froze, his chest heaving. "You want to stop?" He couldn't think of a worse hell.

"No"—her throat moved as she swallowed—"but I have to tell you something."

Fingers tightening on her thigh, he bent until their foreheads touched. "What?"

"You"—a jagged breath that rubbed her nipples against his chest—"may need to go in a little slow. I'm not... hugely experienced."

He shuddered. "Are you a virgin?" Fox didn't do virgins; he didn't have the patience for it... but he'd make an exception for Molly. Fuck, he'd make every exception for Molly.

A pause before she nodded. "Sorry."

"Baby, you don't ever have to be sorry in bed with me."

Kissing her hard and deep and long, he squeezed her nape. "I won't hurt you." He wanted Molly with him all the way, and he suddenly realized he goddamn *liked* the idea of initiating her into sex.

Addicting her to it, to him, sounded even better.

So, even though his brain was hazed by lust, he kissed her until she grew soft around him, her breathing erratic and the juncture of her thighs liquid with heat. Shoving aside the gusset of her panties as he broke the kiss with a suckling taste of her lower lip, he circled the sensitive flesh around her entrance with a callused fingertip. She shivered, muscles fluttering and pupils hugely dilated.

Loving the unmistakable honesty of her response, he kissed her again, then nudged one finger just inside her. She clenched tight and slick around him, and he wanted more. He wanted everything. "Yes?" A question asked against lips swollen from his kisses.

Fingers digging into his shoulders, she simply nodded.

"Say it, baby." He didn't want any doubts in Molly's mind about their first night together, now or later.

"Yes." Throaty and breathless, the single word threatened to snap the ragged leash around his instincts, but he'd promised not to hurt her and Fox didn't break his promises.

He pushed deeper, slow and relentless, adding a second finger when she moaned. Sweat breaking out over his skin, he spread his fingers inside her, moved gently... and she began to rock instinctively on him. "Yes," he said, his voice rough. "Move on me." Withdrawing without warning, he pushed his fingers back into her in a single thrust, her body slick enough to take it.

She cried out his name, burying her face against the side of his, her breath a burn over his skin. Hauling her back with his free hand in her hair, he ran his lips down her jaw to her throat, pumping his fingers into her the entire time.

Her muscles fluttered around him, her nails cutting tiny half-moons into his shoulders, her breathing soft pants.

Groaning, he continued to plunge his fingers in and out of her, even as he placed his thumb on the plump, slippery bud of her clit. "Open for me, baby." He bit her lower lip as she'd bitten his, caught her startled whimper in a kiss. "I want in."

He flicked her clit.

Back arching, she came in a shocked spasm that left her melted and ready in his arms. He kept his hand where it was, pressed his body close to kiss her again. Seduce her. That orgasm had been beautiful, but he knew she had more inside her, his sexy little librarian. And he intended to see it, coax it out of her.

His cock throbbed.

Gritting his teeth, he reined in the driving need to pound into her. That would come. Right now Molly was back with him, that first short, sharp orgasm having left her ripe for another, this one darker, deeper, tighter. Her body twisted on his, her nipples pebbled points he fully intended to bite.

Later.

The wet sound of his fingers plunging into her body, the scent of desire thick in the air, her muscles clasping him with a sensual greed he fully intended to feed. "Don't you come again, Molly," he warned, sliding his fingers out of her, to her moan. "I want to feel you squeezing my cock this time, not my fingers."

Lace tore, her panties in shreds in two short seconds.

"Open your eyes." Holding the eye contact when she obeyed the harsh order, the possessive drive inside him a primitive thing, he luxuriated in the way she dug her fingers into the heavy muscle of his shoulders as he circled the broad head of his cock against the nerve-laced skin at her entrance.

A soft, feminine sound, her body going taut as a drum, her skin flushed a luscious pink. "I can't—"

That was when Fox tightened his hold in her hair, his other hand gripping the softness of her hip, and pushed in an inch. Molly stiffened, her body rippling around him in a way that had nothing to do with pain. Growling in his throat, he kissed her again. "*Don't.*"

"Now," she whispered. "Before I—"

He was buried in her the next instant.

Molly cried out into his mouth as he fought for control. Kissing her with every ounce of skill at his disposal—and yeah, he had a lot of skill—he licked his tongue against hers, stroked and sucked until she shifted restlessly.

He clenched his jaw so hard he could hear his bones grinding against each other. No way in hell was he going to last much longer. "Does it hurt?" She was stretched tight around his thickness.

A shake of her head, her fingers curling in his hair as she asked for another kiss with a sweet, hot brush of her lips against his. Willing to give her anything she wanted, he opened his mouth over hers at the same time that he began to move. Slowly. It took furious self-control.

Molly began to move with him on his fourth stroke, impatient and needy. *"Fox."*

Thank God. Shifting both hands to her hips at that broken cry, her head falling back to expose the delicious line of her throat, Fox pounded into her, deep and relentless and ruthlessly fast, his chest rubbing against her nipples with every movement.

Wanting more, wanting *her*, he curved his hand around her throat and drew her down to his mouth. His ring pressed into the softness of her lower lip, his chest crushed her breasts, but she held on tighter instead of pushing him away, her pleasure-swollen tissues providing erotic friction against the aching hardness of his cock. "Wet and tight and so good." The words came out a growl. "I might just fuck you forever, Molly."

She orgasmed on a gasp, her body gripping him with such feminine strength he was the one who felt taken, possessed, owned. Sliding his hold to her jaw, he kissed her throughout her pleasure, and then he pinned her to the wall and took his own.

"YOU FOUND THE BEDROOM."

Fox looked at her from where he lay beside her on his stomach, his eyes lazy and satisfied in the muted light of the bedside lamp. "Not difficult." One big hand stroked down the line of her spine to splay on her lower back, fingers just brushing her buttocks.

Molly's own fingers curled in the sheets. "Only one bedroom." It was a nonsensical statement, but she was having trouble thinking past the heavy afterglow of unadulterated pleasure… and the bite of a fear that said maybe she'd made a terrible mistake. This had been meant to be her one wild night, something to carry with her as she walked into a safe, calm, happily *dull* future, except it had felt like more than sex, more than a single moment of madness in a life lived by the rules.

It had felt like a branding.

"I might just fuck you forever, Molly."

He'd used her name, that's what got to her. Right at the end, when she could've been any warm, willing female, he'd called her by her name, made it crystal clear he remembered exactly whose body he held against the wall. And she'd never forget his, never forget the man who'd taken such rough care with her. His entry had burned, the pressure intense, but that had faded into a pleasure that blinded.

"So many thoughts in those big brown eyes," Fox said, playing his fingers over her hip.

Drawing in a long, quiet breath, she turned onto her side and shook her head, a knot of worry in her chest. "Nothing important." It had been her first time, she told herself, with a man who knew exactly what he was doing. No wonder she was off-balance.

The fact was, Zachary Fox might've taken her as if he meant forever, but this one night was all they'd ever share. There was no cause to worry she'd started something that held the potential to devastate the life she'd so painstakingly built for herself.

"Did you say something about a second time?" she asked when it looked like he might follow up on the implied question—though she wasn't sure her body could handle Fox and what he did to her again.

His smile was pure sex, his hair falling over his eyes as he shifted over her, pressing her onto her back. "You'll be even more sore than you're already going to be."

Molly could feel her skin coloring, but she said, "I can handle it." It panicked her a little to know their time together would end with the dawn, but that was the reason it *had* to end. Even should Fox lose his mind and decide he wanted to start up a relationship with a librarian who couldn't pull off sophisticated no matter how hard she tried. "Please."

Dimple creasing his cheek, he dipped his head to her breast. "Since you asked so nicely"—a playful lick—"I'll even give you a reward."

The second time around was delectably slow and astonishingly instructive. Molly might've been inexperienced, but she was smart, read a lot. She knew there were endless nuances to what men and women got up to behind closed doors. But when Fox lowered his head to between her thighs and put his mouth on her, when he showed her exactly what that ring felt like against her most delicate flesh, she realized some things required practical application.

And, when it was over and he tucked her close to the hard planes of his body, she stayed. For this one night, a night that would never be repeated, she could trust a man to hold her.

"YOU WORK EVERY SATURDAY?" Fox asked the next morning as they walked toward her car.

Molly nodded. "The library opens seven days a week, rain or shine." Her work-week started Tuesday, ended today.

"When will you finish?"

She felt her stomach dip, shook it off with pure strength of will. The night was over; wild, dangerous Molly with her taste for rock stars and bone-melting pleasure put permanently under dustcovers, leaving sensible Molly in charge. "Around five," she answered. "Can I drop you off somewhere?"

Her heart stuttered with the effort to keep her voice steady. Even she knew there were certain unwritten rules of behavior after a one-night stand, chief among them a calm, mature morning after. No blushing, no thinking about how Fox had wakened her an hour before her alarm had been set to go off, his fingers between her thighs.

She *was* sore. It had been worth it.

"The library where you work," he said now, "where is it?"

"City center." Realizing she was staring at his lips, her skin flushing and breasts aching, she wrenched her gaze away and unlocked the car.

"I'll get off there," he said after sliding into the car with an audible groan at having to fold his body into the compact space. "It's an easy walk to the apartments we've taken on the waterfront."

Molly's hands clenched on the steering wheel as she drove out of the garage. "I thought you'd be on one of the private islands?" Safely beyond her reach, where she couldn't give in to the temptation to ask him for just one more night.

"Nah, that's not our style, but one of Thea's minions did also book out a small hotel for us on the island with the wineries."

"Waiheke." The vibrant island was a short ferry ride across the water, though she guessed Fox and his bandmates had their own transportation to a no doubt private beach.

"Yeah, that one." He tugged at a tendril of hair that had escaped the twist at the back of her head. "Fancy."

Damn her skin and its inability to be mature, but at least her voice only sounded a fraction husky when she said, "Professional." It was getting harder and harder to breathe with him so close.

He looked her up and down. "Boots, skirt, slinky top. Nice."

Having stopped at a traffic light, she resisted the urge to tug at the soft coral-colored wool of her thin V-necked sweater. "It's not slinky. It's warm. The air-conditioning's high at work." As for the skirt, it was tailored but not tight; she needed to be able to move freely.

"I bet you give all the teenage boys hot flushes."

"I don't give anyone a hot flush."

"Yeah?" A single word full of sensual challenge. "I seem to recall having several heat waves hit me. Four times, wasn't it?"

Molly had never been teased this way. "Do you always keep score?"

"Hell yeah." He leaned back in his seat, hands behind his head, biceps taut. "You sore?"

Molly was fairly sure he wasn't supposed to care after a one-night stand, but since he did, she fought her embarrassment to say, "Nothing major." Except that she'd feel him inside her with every step she took today.

"Good." He tugged on the curl again. "Anyway, four times in the span of less than eight hours is excessive, even for me. Especially since right now, I'm fighting the urge to push up your skirt to see if you're wearing pantyhose."

Mind scrambled, she stared straight ahead. "No."

"So if I slid my hand up, I'd touch—"

"Unloading zone." She came to a hard stop on the street kitty-corner from the commercial parking lot where she usually

34

left her car. "Out before I get a ticket." Or before she turned the car around and spent the day letting him make her even more deliciously sore.

"Mean, Molly. That was mean." Undoing his seat belt, he reached over to clasp his hand over her nape, kiss her on the lips. A full kiss. A kiss that made her want to play with that ring, suck on his lip, lave her tongue against his, her hands in his hair instead of locked to bone-white tightness on the steering wheel. "I'll be seeing you, Molly Webster," he murmured with a final nibbling taste of her lips.

"Yes, see you." But as she watched him walk away, a rock god burnished by the morning sunlight, she knew that was the last she'd ever see of Zachary Fox outside of music videos or Schoolboy Choir concerts. His life and her own, they might as well have been on different planets.

Swallowing the thickness of emotion in her throat, she pulled away from the curb.

The fantasy was over.

CHAPTER 4

EXITING ON THE TOP FLOOR of the serviced apartment complex on the waterfront, Fox went not to his own apartment but to Noah's. He knew the band's guitarist, who also played bass like a pro, would be in; Noah might bed a different woman—often women—every night, but he didn't stay the night with any of them, and if he brought them back to his place, it was only for as long as it took to have sex.

Fox knew why the other man couldn't sleep with anyone else in the room, but they never discussed it. Not like women discussed shit. They simply had each other's backs—Noah knew if he felt himself sliding too deep into hell, he just had to reach out a hand and Fox would haul him out. Not that Fox was sure the stubborn bastard *would* reach out. Didn't matter. Fox would never allow Noah's demons to swallow him up.

He knocked lightly and wasn't surprised when a rumpled Noah opened the door soon afterward. The other male looked like he'd rolled out of bed a second ago, his jeans hanging low on his hips, stubble on his jaw. It was an illusion—Noah rarely slept past dawn, regardless of his nighttime activities.

"You got coffee?" He walked in, leaving the door open. It was only the four of them up here, with the elevator locked to their personal keycards and service personnel instructed to come up only on request. It was one of the first things they'd realized after Schoolboy Choir's first album went triple platinum—that if they wanted any privacy at all, they'd have to fight for it.

"Check this out." Noah pointed to a machine that looked like it had escaped the deck of a spaceship. "Looks worse than the monstrosity you have at your place back home."

"I know how my monstrosity works." Fox scowled, kicking himself for not having properly checked things out before the party last night. He'd just thrown his gear inside his own apartment, the band having been at a nearby hotel till then. "Damn it, I walked right by the coffee place next door because there was a line."

Dark gray eyes glinting, Noah found a mug, thrust it under one of the many spouts, and pushed three buttons of the thousands on the spaceship coffeemaker. Half a minute later, Fox was holding some kind of cinnamon-scented coffee so frothy he could feel his testosterone levels dropping just looking at it. "What the hell, Noah? You want me to drink this?"

"You have to drink it," the blond male snarled. "It's the only crap I've figured out how to make on this thing."

Fox took a sip, got mostly foam. He tried again, shuddered. "Give me another mug." When Noah handed it over, he started slotting in the shiny pod things that sat in a basket beside the coffeemaker and pushing random buttons.

Three pods later, he hit on the right combination for plain black coffee. "Clearly, I'm the brains of this outfit."

"Gimme that." Commandeering the coffee, Noah took a long drink, groaned. "*This* is coffee. Now show me what the fuck you did."

Fox successfully made a second cup and, taking it, followed Noah out onto the balcony, both of them leaning their forearms on the balustrade. The view of the harbor was spectacular, the sparkling blue-green water busy with countless watercraft. Close to the city it was mostly commuter ferries, though there was also a tall-masted racing yacht and a boat that looked like it might be taking tourists out to see dolphins. Farther out, Fox could see sailboats and small personal fishing craft as people headed out to enjoy the brilliantly sunny—if cold—fall day.

"You had breakfast?" Noah asked as they watched a kayaker set off for one of the islands, his muscular arms and smooth pace as he rode the waves created by bigger craft making it clear he was no amateur. "I can scramble some eggs. Or we could wake David up and hold him upside down over the balcony until he agrees to feed us."

Fox grinned at the reference to David's superior culinary skills. "I already ate." Finishing off his coffee, he dangled the mug from his fingers and thought of the delicious armful of woman who'd kicked him out of her car.

"You have a look that says 'I not only got laid but had my mind blown.'" Noah froze in the act of grinning. "Shit, Fox. I saw you leave the same time as the woman Thea pointed out as her sister. If you've touched her, Thea will make your life a living hell, probably schedule you to appear on a Japanese game show."

Damn right he'd touched Molly. And he planned to do it again. "She's mine." Sex usually worked women out of his system; it had only worked Molly in deeper.

Noah angled his body to stare at him. "What?"

"Molly. She's mine." This was no longer about anything as simple or as easily handled as physical attraction.

"I need more coffee." It was a groaned-out statement from his bandmate. Grabbing Fox's cup as well, Noah went back to the machine, returning a few minutes later to say, "You're serious?"

"Deadly." Fox drank from the full cup the other man had handed over. "You know when you get the whisper of a melody in your head, or the murmur of a song? And you have the gut feeling that if you could just *hear* the rest of it, just capture the music"—the need an ache as frustrating as it was piercing—"you'd have something fucking amazing?"

Noah nodded.

"Yeah well, that's what it feels like with Molly." The most compelling whisper of his life. "I'm not about to walk away from that."

"Could just be lust," Noah said bluntly. "It can hit hard, leave a man seeing stars, and then it's over."

Fox thought of Molly, of what her body, her scent, her taste, did to him.

His own body hardened at the memory. Yeah, their physical chemistry wasn't in question; he could've happily stayed in bed with her all day today and been greedy for more. The things he wanted to do to Molly Webster... But despite their erotic connection, sex wasn't the first thing that came to his mind when he thought of Molly.

It was her smile.

Eyes glowing from within as her whole face lit up, that smile had knocked him sideways at the party. Then had come her blushing smile in bed when he made a very dirty suggestion midway through their second time around, followed by her smart and funny response as her self-protective shields fell enough that he'd caught a glimpse of the heart of her.

Each glimpse had only deepened his craving to know more. He didn't only want to fuck Molly; he wanted to talk to her, wanted to hear her use words like "nefarious" and discover what else might come out of her beautiful mouth. And he wanted that brilliant, *real*, full-body smile turned in his direction.

"It's not just sex," he said into the silence that had fallen between him and Noah. "It's something else." A thing for which he didn't have a name, but that he knew in his gut was important, rare. The idea of turning his back on it made every cell in his body scream "*Hell,* no!" "I have to hear the whole song, learn the entire melody." Figure out if this was a song with staying power... or one that would fade into history without leaving a mark.

His shoulders grew tight.

Thrusting a hand through his hair, the blond strands glinting in the sunlight, Noah raised an eyebrow. "She good with that? Being involved with you isn't exactly going to be a picnic for her once the media gets hold of the news."

"Molly thinks we had a one-night stand." Not that he could blame her. It wasn't as if he'd made his intentions clear—but he had a feeling those intentions would make Molly run hard and fast in the opposite direction.

So he just wouldn't tell her.

CHAPTER 5

WORK KEPT MOLLY BUSY, THE library buzzing with a mix of adults and children as well as keen university students after some of the older material held in the archives. And if parts of her body twinged and throbbed in unfamiliar ways, they'd settle soon enough, erasing any lingering physical trace of Fox's possession and leaving behind only memories—memories she had no intention of smothering.

Her dream of a stable, happily boring life hadn't changed, would never change. It made her stomach lurch to even think about the horror that had been the unforgiving glare of "fame" after her high-profile father was found with that underage girl, the constant whispers and stares.

No, she didn't want excitement. What she wanted was blissful normality: a job she liked; a steady, faithful man; a house on an ordinary suburban street; a sedate minivan with room in back for the slobbering family dog. But… when she was living that safe, stable life, the memory of her night with a smart, sexy, roughly tender rock star would be a hidden treasure, a quiet acknowledgment of the other Molly. The Molly who might've lived a life more adventurous and less ordinary in another time, another place… a Molly who, in this world, was a little too broken to ever again be permitted to hold the reins.

FOX HADN'T BECOME THE LEAD singer of one of the best-selling rock bands in history by being a shrinking violet. No, he went after what he wanted, no holds barred. And the raw promise he could feel between him and Molly? He had to know where it would lead, the need so strong he hadn't felt anything like it since the day he'd figured out that music was his escape, the air in his lungs.

Which was why he was leaning against the wall beside Molly's apartment at five that afternoon, a guitar by his side.

The elevator doors opened at a quarter after the hour, Molly going motionless two steps outside of it, the doors closing silently at her back. Yeah, she hadn't expected him, but Fox was ready to work with that. Waiting patiently as she took a deep breath and completed the trek down the corridor, he drew in the scent of her, his gaze lingering on the fluttering pulse in her neck.

"How did you get past security?"

Fox smiled slowly at the blurted-out question, wondering if Molly knew how bad she was at hiding her emotions. He liked it, liked that he saw the real Molly, not an illusion she'd created to tempt him—not that she had to do anything but smile to tempt him. "I told you the security sucks."

Unable to resist, he reached out to run his finger down one creamy cheek flushed with a mix of surprise, passion, and, he was certain, sweet, hot feminine anger. His guess was borne out when Molly unlocked her door with jittery hands and put down her handbag on one corner of the bench, her fingers trembling before she curled them into her palms. "You're breaking the rules."

"What rules?" Closing the door, he leaned back on it and willed her to face him. Much as he loved the shape of her from the back, he liked watching those expressive eyes whisper her mood to him.

Shoulders tight, she turned. "This was supposed to be a one-night stand."

"Ah." Folding his arms over the plain black of his T-shirt, he said, "How about a one-month stand instead?" He knew he had to play this exactly right. Molly was wary of him, and yeah, he could understand why. To have her in his life beyond a fleeting instant, he'd have to win her trust.

She jerked up her head. "What?"

"Why not? I like you. You like me." He smiled—because the reason Molly had needed to jerk up her head was that she'd been staring at his chest. "Admit it."

Sitting down on the bench, she began to unzip her boots, very obviously *not* looking at him. "You're okay for a rock star."

He wanted to bite her, then pet her until she was limp and languid in his arms. "We burn up together." Deliberately modulating his voice—his instrument—for maximum effect, low and bedroom rough, he saw her fingers stutter on the zipper. "I'm here for a month. It's an easy equation."

When the words "Let me think about it" fell from her mouth, he thought she might've been as startled as he was, her lips parting on a slight gasp—as if to call back the declaration.

Crouching down, he began to tug off her boots, distracting her from her thoughts. He had no intention of playing fair. There were very few things he'd ever truly hungered for in life, and he'd never been given any of them. He'd claimed each through sheer, unrelenting will and the grim refusal to surrender.

Now... now there was Molly. "Are you kicking me out?"

"Don't you want a different woman each night?"

He heard the tremor she tried to hide, and knew she'd said words similar to those that had lit a spark under his temper the previous night on purpose. Molly Webster was trying to scare him off because she was finding it difficult to say no.

Gut tight and blood hot, he got rid of her remaining boot. "You really have a high opinion of me." Expecting warm, supple skin under his hands when he slid them up below the hem of her skirt—because he was more than happy to use her physical response to him to tie them together—he found an unexpected barrier instead. "You said no stockings." The material under his touch was silky and soft and smooth.

"They're tights."

Body hardening even further at her breathy response, he traced the fine fabric another fraction past the hemline of her skirt, kept going. "Thigh-high tights." Suddenly, they were the sexiest things he could imagine. "I want to see." See the rich cream of her skin against the frame created by the deep gray and blue pattern, kiss every satiny inch.

She put her hands on his, halting him when he would've pushed her skirt up to her thighs. "I haven't said yes yet."

"Yes, you have, Molly." Fox held her gaze, sweeping his thumbs slowly across the delicate skin above her tights. "I can feel it in the pulse under your skin, hear it in your voice, scent the damp heat of you on my tongue."

Maybe, *maybe* he'd have found the strength to walk away from the intoxicating intensity of the pull between them if Molly had been indifferent to him—though far more likely, he'd have done everything in his power to change that, because he wasn't the walking-away type, not when it came to the things that mattered. But Molly wasn't indifferent.

Skin coloring on the heels of his words, she tried to squeeze her thighs together. He blocked her by wedging his body between them. "Don't be embarrassed, baby." Shifting position slightly, he caught her lips in a teasing, coaxing kind of a kiss. "You have no idea how unbelievably hot I find it that I make you so wet."

When her hand came to rest on his shoulder, her fingers just brushing his nape, he had to exert steely control not to deepen the kiss, not to pull down her panties and take her then and there. That would leave him in the same position he'd been in before she let him in tonight, Molly skittish and unsure.

He had to be smart about this, coax her as he'd coax a difficult chord from the guitar. With sweet patience and hard-eyed determination. "You make the rules." Pressing a kiss to the hollow of her throat, he stroked his thumbs over her skin again. "Tell me what you want."

MOLLY SWALLOWED. FOX WAS RIGHT; she wanted him as much now as she had during the hours they'd spent tangled in the dark. But a single night she could justify. Anything longer threatened to take this beyond a moment of wildness and into far more perilous territory.

"One month," she whispered near soundlessly. "After that, you leave and never contact me again." It was a stipulation born of the pain inside her, a pain so old it had its own heart-beat, a dark heaviness that was a terrible ache.

"That's clear enough." A kiss on her jaw, the movement of his thumbs on the sensitive skin of her inner thighs radiating pleasure that pooled in the throbbing bundle of nerve end-ings between her legs.

"And," she rasped, "we're exclusive for that month."

His hands tightened on her flesh. "No one else, I promise." Another teasing, tormenting brush of his thumbs, the callused pads scraping erotically over her flesh. "Come here, baby." The seductive invitation in that whiskey-and-sin voice stole her will, threatened to destroy everything she'd worked for in life.

Dangerous, he was so dangerous. Still, she dipped her head that final inch and kissed him. Her control of the contact lasted approximately two seconds. Gripping her nape with one hand to hold her in position, Fox kissed her, not raw and deep as she'd expected, but with a slow attention that had her entire body aflame, the ring on his lip a hard accent. He slid his other hand higher up her leg at the same time, making her stomach flutter, her inner muscles clench.

"Such pretty, soft skin." It was spoken against her mouth, his lips curving in a smile as he licked playfully across her own. When she shivered, his eyes darkened, his kiss deeper but just as slow, as if this rock god had all the time in the world to kiss and caress Molly Webster. His hand gently squeezed her nape.

Warning bells clanged in her mind. It felt as if she were drowning, kiss by slow kiss, Fox coaxing her into deeper and deeper waters. "The bedroom—" she began on a slightly pan-icked breath.

Eyes lazy, hooded, he kissed away her words before glanc-ing down at her legs. Her heartbeat was in her mouth as she watched him push up her skirt to expose the pale skin of her upper thighs.

"You make my mouth water." Lowering his head, he pressed a single wet kiss on the inner curve of her right thigh, his stubbled jaw rubbing against her flesh.

She clutched at his hair, the strands dark silk against her palms. "Fox, we—"

Shifting his grip to under her thighs, he pulled her for-ward on the bench, her hands falling to the leather seat cushion to brace herself as he altered her center of gravity. "Hmm," he murmured, the green of his gaze holding her own for a second that stole all the air in her lungs. "What's the rush, Molly Webster?" He bit down over the tendon in her neck.

Hands back in his hair, her fingers spasmed into a tighter hold, her breath a tremor.

"Bad Fox." Licking out, he soothed the sensual hurt with his tongue. "There, I'm behaving now."

She shuddered, surrendered under the gritty seduction of his voice, sought his mouth with hers. It was clear she wasn't the one setting the pace tonight, but she no longer cared. Not with Fox's strong body between her legs and his hands on her own, his kiss-es drugging her to a languorous pleasure that made her want to explore him as slowly as he was exploring her.

Groaning, Fox shifted one hand into her hair, unraveling the twist, but didn't take over this time. No, he let her kiss him, let her play with the lip ring that fascinated her. Molly felt oddly shy as she went to—

Her home phone rang.

She ignored it, her lower body melting at the way Fox continued to stroke his thumb over her skin as they kissed. No rush, no hurry, nothing but pleasure, her bones heavy with it.

The phone kept ringing.

And ringing.

Finally, the answering machine kicked in. Molly was a mass of helpless flesh by that point, couldn't have cared less who it was. But the worried female voice, familiar and beloved, intruded more effectively than a scream. Sudden panic slicing through the sensual haze, she pushed at the wide shoulders in front of her. "I have to get this."

Fox released her without argument after taking one look at her face, and she ran to grab the handset on the counter that separated her living area from the kitchenette. "Charlie, what's wrong?"

"Oh, you're home." Her friend's voice, a low whisper, broke on the last word. "I just..." A deep inhale. "There's someone else in the office, and there shouldn't be. I came back from the bathroom and heard them moving around."

"Leave," Molly said, her fingers rigid on the handset.

"No." Charlotte took another shaky breath. "It's probably only the building security guard doing an unscheduled round, but could you stay on the phone with me while I go check it out?"

Molly bit back her instinctive negative reaction to her friend's plan, knowing how important it was to Charlotte that she not crumble under the weight of what might be an imagined fear. "I'm right here."

Having circled to the other side of the counter, Fox, his expression grim, caught her eye and mouthed, *Problem?*

Maybe, she mouthed back, hoping she was wrong. That was when a scream sounded from the other end of the line, followed by a thud, as if the phone had hit the carpet. "Charlotte! *Charlie!*"

Scrabbling, rustling sounds, then Charlotte's voice, a little breathless and holding a taut tension. Not fear though; this was excruciating embarrassment. "I'm fine." A pause, a deeper voice murmuring in the background before Charlotte returned. "I just met my new boss," her best friend groaned into the phone. "Or more specifically, I threw an industrial-strength stapler at his head."

Knees trembling in relief, Molly braced her elbows on the counter as Fox reached out to tuck her hair behind her ear. Catching the intent lines of his expression, she touched his wrist, let him see everything was all right. He didn't know Charlotte, but he'd heard that scream, too.

Maybe she'd imagined the protective concern in his expression... No, she didn't think so. Every instinct she had said this man would never stand by while a woman was hurt. Neither would he ever hurt one. Not physically. Now he rubbed his thumb over her lower lip before dropping his hand and moving to pick up a delivery menu she had on the counter from a neighborhood restaurant.

"Oh God, Molly, what if he fires me?"

Molly wrenched her attention back to her best friend. "He's not going to fire you," she reassured Charlotte as Fox turned the menu toward her. "You were in the office being a diligent employee, remember?" Not sure how she felt about the fact she was about to have dinner with the rock star who'd been meant to be a one-night stand, Molly nonetheless pointed at her favorite dish and Fox pulled out his phone to place the order.

"Right, that's right. I—" Charlotte broke off as the deep male voice returned in the background. When her friend came back on the line, she sounded half-strangled. "He just said we're going out to dinner so I can bring him up to speed on 'certain issues.'"

Molly decided she liked the new boss. "Go." *Make Anya look bad*, she added silently. It infuriated her that Anya—all gloss and impeccable style—dumped her work on Charlotte, then took the credit, with Charlotte too shy and reserved to push herself forward. "Order the most expensive thing on the menu."

"I'll probably throw it up," Charlotte said morosely. "I better go—he said five minutes."

"Good luck." Hanging up, she stared at the gorgeous man who'd made her bones turn to honey with his kiss and felt the butterflies in her stomach take flight again.

Terror, anticipation, near-painful desire... Molly wasn't sure what she was feeling, what she was *doing*, but when Fox turned to look at her with a half-smile on those bitable lips, she knew she wasn't going to renege on their agreement.

One month. A single, passionate month out of a lifetime. Surely fate wouldn't begrudge her that?

CHAPTER 6

OX SAW SECRETS IN MOLLY'S eyes. His instinct was to demand she share them, demand she let him in, but he knew damn well that would never work. For this battle, he'd need patience when patience was the one trait he'd never been accused of possessing. Putting away his phone, he walked over to take her hand, tug her to the door he'd found while he'd been placing the order.

A single push and it slid open to showcase a minuscule balcony—but one with a clear view of the city skyline. The fall air was crisp, the temperature having dropped since he'd entered the building. It cooled his skin, did nothing to chill the heat in his blood. Allowing Molly to go first, he waited till she turned to face him, then pinned her against the railing with his hands on either side of her body. "Food'll be here in about fifteen minutes."

"Oh. Good." Her voice was a touch husky, her eyes not quite meeting his.

Fox fought the urge to haul her to the bedroom, strip her to the skin, take her deep and long until all distance was erased. Sex was easy. He didn't want easy. He wanted Molly.

Deliberately pressing so close she had to tip up her head to look at him, he said, "Was that your friend from the party? The tiny blonde with glasses?"

Her eyes widened. "You noticed us?"

"I noticed every damn thing about you." Giving in to temptation, he kissed the line of her throat, her jaw, suckled on her lower lip.

Molly's heartbeat had accelerated under his caresses, her pulse thudding beneath her skin. Yeah, sex might be easy, but he had no problem using it to tie Molly to him while he worked on what he really wanted. "How long have you been friends?"

Her chest rising and falling in ragged breaths, Molly's eyes lingered on his mouth and on the lip ring he'd figured out she loved. He felt his mouth curve. "Molly," he said, pitching his voice low and deep, his entire body primed for her until it was only his grip on the cold metal of the railing that kept him from petting and stroking and seducing her right on this balcony.

The color on her cheekbones darkened, her lashes coming down to shade her eyes. "Since nursery school," she said after almost half a minute. "We should go inside. It's cold."

Wrapping her up in his arms, he spoke against the shell of her ear. "Is this better?"

Molly didn't answer, but her arms came around him a few seconds later.

It felt... right.

Rubbing his cheek against her temple, he suddenly re-membered his stubbled jaw. "Sorry. I don't want to mark up your skin." Not quite the truth. He liked seeing her creamy flesh reddened by his kisses, his touch, intended to rub his jaw along the sensitive inner skin of her thighs in bed tonight before he tasted her.

"I don't mind." A quiet murmur, her breasts pressed against his chest, her hip dangerous temptation under his hand. "Do you want to—I mean, should we—" Her fingers clenched in his T-shirt. "I suck at this."

Enjoying his soft armful of woman, Fox stroked her from the top of her spine to the sweet curves below. "I think you're perfect." Natural and unaffected and with an open desire that made him her slave, if she only knew it.

"So, should we…"

Fox knew she was attempting to wrench this night back under control, push them into the bedroom where it was safe. He could even guess at the reasons why she didn't want to become any further involved with him. Hell, he wouldn't date himself. Not with the reputation he'd earned as a young musician, a rep that had never quite worn off—and that didn't take the relentless media attention into account. No sane, intelligent woman would want to be caught up in his world, her every action scrutinized, her life put under a microscope.

Fox had nearly punched out a reporter last month, and he'd been living this reality for years. So yeah, he understood. He just didn't plan on allowing any of that to get in the way of his pursuit of Molly and the nameless but increasingly powerful thing between them—because he'd protect her. She wouldn't be thrown to the wolves, would be safe with him and the band.

"Takeout," he reminded her instead of speaking his thoughts aloud. The instant he did, Molly would realize he'd never actually agreed to her one-month time limit and pull away. He couldn't allow that; he needed the time to coax, cajole, and pleasure her into trusting him. Enough to give them a real shot.

AN HOUR AND A HALF later, Molly found herself uncertain of what to do. She'd never had a passionate affair before, felt gauche and lost.

Closing the distance between them, Fox took her hand, led her into the bedroom. "Such big brown eyes." He cupped her face between those rough-skinned hands that felt so exquisite against her skin. "What're you thinking?"

That *voice*. Hard rock and pure sin, it made her breath catch, her stomach somersault. "That I don't know what to do," she admitted, since he already knew the exact breadth of her experience.

Fox rubbed his thumb over the plump flesh of her lower lip. "We do what feels good" was his simple answer. "First"—his eyes intent on her face—"you tell me if I need to wait till tomorrow."

It took her a second. Then, fingers curling on his T-shirt, she shook her head. "No, I think it'll be okay." Her muscles ached, but there was no pain.

"You just say stop if it isn't." His mouth was on hers as soon as she nodded, his kiss intoxicating.

By the time their lips parted, her hands were under his T-shirt and on the hot skin of his back, her nipples rasping against the fabric of her bra. She was acutely aware of his hands on her backside, the hold blatantly sexual. When he shifted to undo the button and zip on her skirt, she allowed the black piece of clothing to drop to the carpet, the style loose enough that it didn't catch on her hips.

Nudging away her hands, he tugged her sweater over her head himself. "Beautiful."

Molly knew she wasn't beautiful, not like the starlets and models who lived in his world, but he made her feel that way, his voice gritty with appreciation. Clasping his hand over her nape again, he drew her in for a kiss as wet and as demanding as the need between her thighs. "Take off your bra for me, baby."

Shivering at the sound of that voice meant for sex and sin, she pulled the straps down her arms, then undid the hooks to drop the black lace bra on top of her skirt. It left her dressed only in matching panties and the thigh-high tights Fox looked at with a smile of pure male approval. It set her skin afire with nerves.

His hands on her. No warning, no hesitation, his palms covering the bare mounds of her breasts. Shocked into a moan, she arched into him, shuddering at the feel of his rock-hard body against the softness of her own. When he released her needy flesh after a single squeeze, she wanted to whimper, beg for more.

Tracing the top edge of one leg of the tights, his other hand flat on her lower back, he said, "Funny how these make me have the dirtiest fantasies." He nipped at her kiss-swollen lower lip, his statement making her want to squirm. "In the bed."

She had no motivation to disobey that order. Slipping under the sheets, she watched him strip with clean efficiency.

The T-shirt went over his head to reveal a chest that had her hands fisting on the bedspread, shoes and socks were nudged off, jeans ripped off... underwear, too.

Her body twinged, reminding her she'd had that muscled male body on her, *in* her. And was about to again. Sucking in desperate gulps of air, she swallowed as he got into bed and leaned on his elbow beside her, his erection pressing against her thigh.

"There go those thoughts again," he said, tugging the sheet down to expose her breasts. "I should've had you naked an hour ago, shouldn't I?" He rolled one nipple lazily between thumb and forefinger.

Biting back a whimper, Molly nodded. "Yes." Any time to think and she began to wonder what in the world she was doing. "I never thought I'd be here, like this." Naked in bed with a rock god.

"I'm damn glad you are." A smile so smoldering it devastated her senses, then his cock thrusting against her abdomen as he came over her after shoving the sheet totally aside. "It's just you and me in this bed." He braced himself on one muscled arm, tattoos bright in her peripheral vision. "Outside world doesn't exist. So give in and enjoy."

"Give in and enjoy."

There were so many things wrong with that statement when it came to the life Molly wanted to live. "I'm not sure I can do that. I'm not a rock chick. I'm a librarian."

"Stereotypes, Miss Molly?" The eye contact searing, he slipped his fingers under the waistband of her panties. "Tut, tut."

Her hand clenched on his arm, muscle and tendon moving under the golden silk of his skin as he slid those long, strong fingers through her slick folds, the callused tips lusciously abrasive. Unable to hold the dark intimacy of his gaze as he cupped her with sexual possessiveness, she shifted her attention to his mouth—but her view disappeared the next second, chocolate-dark strands of hair in her vision.

Heart rabbiting against her ribs and body primed for the hot, wet suction of his mouth on her nipple, she waited. She should've known Fox would never be predictable. He ran his tongue leisurely up one breast, then the other—as if she were his favorite flavor of ice cream and he intended to take his time and enjoy her lick by lick. Her skin was sheened with perspiration, her hand fisted in his hair by the time he closed his teeth over part of one breast, biting down just enough that it was pleasure, not pain. *"Fox."*

Raising his head at the breathy sound, he released her breast to take her mouth, his tongue stroking aggressively past her lips in a kiss that smashed right through her boundaries and insisted she respond.

Out of my depth, I am so out of my depth.

It didn't matter, not here, not now, with his body on hers, his mouth demanding. Stroking her tongue against his own, she tried to hold him to the kiss, but he broke it to say, "We haven't finished our conversation," his tone making it clear that was about to change.

"Anyone ever tell you," Molly managed to say, "that you like to have control?" It took extreme effort to get the words out, her brain completely scrambled with what he did to her.

"Why do you think I'm the lead singer?" A smile with just enough arrogance to be irresistible.

Molly was unable to take her eyes from the masculine curve

of his mouth, the piercing having its usual wicked effect on her senses.

"I like to be the boss."

She'd already figured that out and part of her, the part that had been forced to become an adult at fifteen, the part that had driven her to carve out a better life for herself through merciless determination and absolute discipline, said she should protest.

Except, the thing was… she was tired.

Tired of being always responsible, of never permitting herself to let go in case she went too far and ended up right back in the hell that had killed her parents and splintered her life. Being with Fox couldn't fix her past, couldn't eradicate the fear and need inside her… but maybe she could surrender the reins for a fragment of time and not feel guilty about it. After all, this gift-wrapped box would vanish in a month.

Perhaps that was why she said it, why she confessed one of her deepest fears. Because he was safe, would forget her and her secrets as soon as the month was over. "I worry."

Fox brushed strands of hair off her face. "About what, baby?"

Heart aching at the tenderness she hadn't foreseen, she said, "Of who I'll become if I give in."

Fox didn't break eye contact at the uninvited emotional intimacy, though theirs was meant to be a strictly physical relationship. She was the one who lowered her lashes. "Addiction runs in my family." Gambling, alcohol, women, *love*. It was the last, most dangerous addiction of all that had destroyed her mother.

Tipping up her chin, Fox sucked her upper lip into his mouth, then shifted his attention to the lower one. Breasts deliciously crushed against the taut wall of his chest, she shivered and curled her fingers around his neck, unable to get enough of his kisses.

"Do you think you'll become addicted to mind-blowing sex?" A teasing question except there was no humor in the eyes that locked with hers.

This was getting too serious, too fast, but she was the one who'd opened the gate. "If I give in to this," she whispered, "what other boundaries will I break? What other addictions will I develop?" That was the fear that haunted her always, shaping each and every one of her decisions.

"Have faith in yourself." He pressed his lips to the shockingly sensitive spot below her ear, her shiver reflexive. "I do."

Molly knew Fox was sweet-talking her to get her to do what he wanted in bed, his sexual experience apparent in the way he played her body like he played the crowds while onstage. None of that altered her unexpected, dangerous desire for him. "You were meant to be a one-night stand." The biggest risk she'd ever taken. "Look where I am now. It's a slippery slope."

Fox's answer was a kiss that took over her mouth, enslaved her senses. Her body attempted to rise toward his in a luxuriant wave, was halted by the weight of him pinning her in place.

When he broke the sumptuous intimacy of the kiss to look into her eyes once more, she was lost in the deep green. "Have faith, Molly," he said again, and she crashed.

Drowned.

CHAPTER 7

MOLLY STRUGGLED UP INTO A sitting position some time later, tucking her no doubt wildly tumbled hair behind her ears and pulling up the sheet to cover her breasts. Just in time. Fox walked into the bedroom the next instant, holding a plate of cheese and crackers in one hand, a bottle of wine in the other. She exhaled at the sight of him.

He was naked.

Except for the tattoos. A jagged tribal design in black ink ran along his left shoulder and licked at his neck before continuing down the left side of his back to his hip, the design sleek rather than bulky. His left arm, in contrast, was covered by a gorgeous stylized dragon in brilliant color, its body wrapping around Fox's arm multiple times. Around the dragon were hundreds of tiny leaves—shaded from spring green to autumn brown—all in motion, as if the dragon had disturbed them in flight.

It truly was a piece of living art.

Those two were the biggest pieces, but on the right of his ridged abdomen fell three vertical lines of fine text that she'd read last night. They were from Schoolboy Choir's first hit song, penned by Fox and Noah, with David and Abe providing the hard rock tempo that had helped shoot it to the top of the charts.

"We all have this tat," he'd told her before he left the bedroom. "Different locations on the body."

"Even David?" The drummer always looked so elegant and urbane.

Fox had grinned. "You'd be surprised what David has under those Ar-*mani* suits he likes to wear."

Now, as Fox bent to put the bottle of wine on her dainty bedside table, she glimpsed the intricate pattern of black ink on the top of his right arm that he'd told her had been created for him by a friend who was a tattoo artist. Incorporating musical notes and hidden words, it was a puzzle that could be unraveled only by someone who really knew Fox.

That arm was otherwise bare of ink, except for a horizontal line of characters directly above his pulse point.

"What language is that?" she said, brushing her fingers over the characters, still not quite believing she had the right to touch him.

"Move your hand to the left and down and I'll tell you."

Heat in her cheeks as she saw he was semi-aroused. "How can you…" She waved in the general direction of his groin.

"Because you're built and I have a high sex drive." Grinning at her renewed blush, the lean dimple in his cheek devastating, he passed her the plate and got into bed. Or onto it.

"Under the sheet," she ordered, trying to retain some sense of control when she knew it was far too late where Fox was concerned. "I can't focus with you naked."

A very male laugh, a hand in her hair as he drew her to him for one of his slow, drugging kisses.

"You know how to touch a woman." It came out throaty, soft.

"I've had a lot of practice." His smile didn't disappear, but there was a sudden, disturbing falseness about it.

Molly knew she'd be fooling herself if she believed she knew anything of Zachary Fox, the man behind the rock god, but she couldn't stay silent when every instinct she had screamed at her to speak. Fighting her discomfort at discussing such an intimate thing, she said, "I'm not going to turn on you because you are who you are." She'd known exactly who it was she'd invited into her bed and that his sexual experience far outweighed hers.

"Especially," she added, fingers curling into the sheet, "when I'm the beneficiary of all that practice."

His smile became vividly real again, gorgeous and of a man who was enjoying being with her. It troubled her how quickly he could do that—withdraw from a situation while appearing involved... but that was only something she'd have to worry about if they were on the road to a relationship. That simply wasn't in the cards, even had Fox not been seriously out of her league.

The media, tabloid and otherwise, was fascinated by him.

After having been savaged to shreds during her father's ignominious fall from grace, any kind of media attention was Molly's worst nightmare. It had been endless, article after article, whisper after whisper, innuendo after innuendo. She'd fought and fought, refusing to allow the agony of it to crush her, to give the bullies at school the satisfaction of seeing how badly she was bleeding inside, but then a policeman with a solemn face had come to tell her she was an orphan, and she'd broken.

The fractures had never quite healed right.

But it wasn't Fox who'd caused the teenage girl she'd been such terrible hurt, and at that instant, she couldn't forget the pain she'd sensed behind his earlier words. "Did a woman hurt you?" She knew she'd crossed another line as soon as the words were out, couldn't find the will to fill the air with others in order to call them back.

An unreadable expression on Fox's face. "No, it wasn't a lover." With that inscrutable answer, he leaned across to claim a tender, suckling kiss before getting his lower body under the sheet as she'd asked and reaching for the food. "Here." He popped a bite of cheese into her mouth and she understood the topic was closed.

Chewing, she swallowed and told herself it was better this way. Because the more she saw of the real Zachary Fox, the more she liked him. "Those characters aren't like any Asian language I've seen," she said, focusing on his body instead of on emotions that had no place in a temporary relationship, "though they're close."

"Hmm." He fed her another piece of cheese.

Molly scowled, though she wanted to trace the curve of his lips with a fingertip. "Are you going to tell me?"

"What? And ruin one of rock's greatest mysteries?" He ate a cracker with cheese on it, a wicked smile in his eyes. "What the fuck is that on Fox's body? Was he stoned when he got the tat? Did he just get a drunk tattoo artist?" A raised eyebrow. "Or is the bastard pissing with everyone for the fun of it?"

"I won't tell anyone," Molly cajoled, feeling young and playful in a way she'd never expected, in a way she'd never been. "Cross my heart."

"Do I look like a sucker?" Tapping her nose with a single finger, he reached over for the fancy wine Molly had bought in case Thea had time to come over, her sister being a wine buff.

Leaning down over the side of the bed to snag a Swiss Army knife from his jeans, Fox used the corkscrew to pop the cork, then drank straight from the bottle. She must've made a sound, because bringing down the bottle, he winked. "I'll replace it with something better." Holding out the wine, he said, "Bet you've never done that before."

Molly shook her head. "I don't drink."

"So this is all mine?" Fox grinned. "Excellent."

Having braced herself for questions, she blurted out, "Most people ask about the not-drinking," then wanted to slap herself for making it an issue. Why couldn't she keep her mouth shut around Fox?

"It's bad musician manners to bring it up," he answered, "'cause you never know who might be in AA or detox." Wrapping an arm around her shoulders, he hugged her close. "But since you already did, and also since you don't show any signs of an alcoholic jonesing for a drink, I'm guessing you've been around someone who drank?"

"Yes." With that, she took a cracker, loaded it with a big hunk of cheese, and bit down. She might've made a mistake in her surprise, but the idea of discussing her mother with Fox had her chest going tight, her lungs strained—it was one thing to let go, another to trust him with the vicious pain that had shaped her. "Why didn't you bring the grapes?"

Fox set aside the wine. "So you'd have to walk nude to the kitchen and get them."

Relieved he'd taken the hint and dropped the subject of her aversion to alcohol, she shook her head. "Not happening."

"Why not? You have an amazing body." A bite on her shoulder, his hand sliding along the inside of her thigh. "Like that old painting of the redhead rising from the clamshell."

The Birth of Venus.

Utterly undone at being compared to the sensually beautiful artwork, she thrust a cracker between his lips. "Shh." His body might be so hot it should be illegal, but she was beginning to learn it was Fox's mind that was his most dangerous weapon. Add that to his voice and it was no surprise women fell into his lap at the crook of a finger.

He ran his thumb along the inner seam of her thigh. "Want me to behave?"

Sensation curling through her body, Molly paused, not sure she *did* want him to behave—and he threw back his head. His laughter pleased every one of her senses, made delight bubble through her veins.

"I like the way you think, Molly," he said, but stopped tormenting her, settling for claiming a kiss anytime he felt like it.

Fox, as she'd learned tonight, was a man who enjoyed kissing. It was an unexpected and wonderful discovery, and it made Molly realize she liked kissing, too. Especially the way Fox did it, with an exquisite patience that made her feel terrifyingly cherished.

It was only later, the bottle of wine still almost full—Fox had decided it was too sweet for him—and her lips wet and tingling, that he dragged on his jeans, held out a hand, and said, "Come on. I'm starving. Let's go finish the takeout."

Not hungry, but willing to keep him company, Molly said, "Pass me the robe on the back of the door."

He picked up and threw her his T-shirt instead. Molly tugged it on, the scent of him a glove around her body. A deep warmth inside her, she got out of bed and took his hand, conscious all at once of exactly how tall he was.

"Did I tell you how hot you look when you're dressed up all professional with your hair prim and proper?"

Molly certainly didn't feel prim and proper now. "You just did."

A slow smile that caught at her heart in a way that set off those warning bells again, but she didn't want to listen. Not tonight, not when everything had been so wonderful.

"You ever wear those skinny skirts that go past the knee?" Fox ran his hands up and down her hips, the T-shirt moving softly against her skin. "The ones that look strict and professional and sexy at the same time?"

"Those"—she swallowed to wet her throat—"are called pencil skirts."

A rumbling sound of pleasure when she shuddered at the kiss he laved on the curve of her jaw. "Yeah, you ever wear one?"

"No." The shape hugged her body too closely.

Dropping kisses along the line of her neck, Fox shifted his hands to her backside. "I get hard just thinking about your ass in one of those skirts." He nipped at her sensitive flesh. "Wear one for me?"

Molly thought she should probably refuse but couldn't figure out a reason why when he was so close, the masculine scent of him short-circuiting her brain. "Okay."

"Hot damn." A groan, hands squeezing her lower curves. "I can't wait to see your body in the skirt I'm buying for you."

"Wait." Molly pushed at his chest. "You didn't say anything about buying it."

"Semantics." A hard kiss, one hand rising to grip her nape. "Be kind, Molly. Let me enjoy my fantasy."

Her knees went weak at the rough appeal.

Molly had never been anyone's fantasy, couldn't find the willpower to stand strong against a rock god who saw something in her that she didn't see in herself. For this one month, she'd be that woman, be that other Molly, the one who'd accept a rock star's gift and who'd rise on tiptoe to tug on his lip ring. Yet even as she thought that, even as she fought the clawing echoes of memory, the panicked voice of the woman she'd spent years becoming yelled at her to stop, to *think*.

FOX HAD FELT MOLLY SLIPPING away over the past half hour. Frustration gnawed at him with every nonanswer she gave from across her round little kitchen table, the Molly who'd spoken to him with such vulnerable honesty in bed nowhere in evidence. *Patience*, he reminded himself as he finished eating, *have some fucking patience*.

He knew exactly what was wrong, knew that in some part of her she'd begun to realize what he already understood. That this, what they were doing, it wasn't just sex, wasn't just an affair—people who simply wanted to fuck didn't talk about hidden hurts, didn't treat each other with tenderness.

"I'm not going to turn on you because you are who you are."

Her words continued to reverberate in his mind, so damn beautiful. She had no idea what her promise meant to him—he'd seen the truth of it in those eyes that couldn't lie, felt it in the way she touched him. He wanted the right to that tenderness every day of his life and he'd fight dirty to get it.

"I saw an ad for a horror flick that's on TV tonight," he said after drinking the glass of water she'd poured him earlier. "Want to watch? You can pretend to be scared, and I can take the opportunity to slip my hand inside that cute fluffy robe of yours."

Tugging on the belt of the robe she'd slipped into a quarter of an hour earlier in another damn sign of retreat after leaving his T-shirt on the bed, she straightened her shoulders. "I want to be up and going before eight tomorrow morning."

"I thought you had Sunday and Monday off?"

"I do, but I want to go to the market to get fresh vegetables, dig around in the antique stalls."

Fox stared at the woman who was turning him inside out. "You're skipping sleeping in to get vegetables?"

Eyes sparking, she glared at him. "It's fun. Even if the antiques are mostly fake."

"Shit." He laughed. "Now I have to come."

Molly hesitated.

And Fox stopped laughing. "You want to keep me confined to the bedroom." Anger kissed his bloodstream.

Throat moving, she bit down on her lower lip. "People will recognize you."

Shit. He wrenched his angry response under control. "I'll make sure they don't." Reaching across the table, he ran his fingers down her cheek, and when she appeared uncertain, he pushed the advantage. "Show me a little of this city I'd never otherwise see."

"All right." A husky whisper that caused a fierce exultation inside him.

"But," she added quickly, "you can't stay tonight."

Fox gritted his teeth, consciously dropping his voice to the edgy purr that always made her blush, melt. "Molly." He'd happily seduce her back into bed if that was what it took to keep her in his arms through the dark hours of night. Because sleeping together was a whole different ball game than sex, and the woman he wanted as his own knew it. That was why her breathing was ragged, her arms wrapped tightly around herself. "It's already late"—he slid his hand down to cup the side of her neck—"and you said we have to get up early for the market."

Pushing back from the table in a jerking move, she broke contact and rose to her feet. "Stop," she said when he got up and began to move toward her. "I want you gone. I'll call you a cab."

The flat rejection lit the fuse on Fox's temper.

•

CHAPTER 8

"**D**ON'T BOTHER," HE GROWLED, STRIDING toward the bedroom to pull on the T-shirt she'd discarded. "I have a car." It was a good thing he hadn't ended up drinking more than half a glass of that damn wine.

His fury roared even more wildly when he emerged from the bedroom to see that she'd unlocked and opened the door, ready to throw him out. Fox wanted to slam that door shut, force her to face the reality of what pulsed between them, growing stronger with every second they spent together, but the small part of him that remained rational told him he'd lose her the instant he did.

Allowing her to simply shut the door on his back, however? Not ever going to happen. Fisting his hand in her hair, he kissed her startled taste into his own mouth. "I'm not the kind of man who likes to have the woman running the show. I made an exception for you, but it's not working."

She pushed at his chest, eyes glittering. "That's the most arrogant thing I've ever heard."

"Yeah? I'm not done." Backing her up against the wall, he bent his knees so they were eye to eye. "The sex between us is mind-blowing, and I want to have a whole hell of a lot more, but I'm not letting you blow hot and cold."

Even as he spoke, he knew he was fucking up his grand goddamn plan to slowly seduce Molly into his life and his world. It had been a pipe dream from the start—he wasn't the kind to mess around when he made up his mind. "So decide." He held the eye contact, made her see him. "You either want me in your bed *and* your life for the month, or you don't. I won't play your sex toy."

Molly's gasp followed him as he released her and, slinging his guitar on his back, walked out the door. His blood was a pounding rush in his ears, his jaw rigid. The sane part of him knew he was overreacting, but he couldn't stop the response any more than he could stop playing music. The scar ran too deep.

Molly was the only lover who'd ever torn it open.

And she'd done it on their second night together. It slammed home the fact that he was already in far too deep for this to be any kind of a brief affair. Not that he'd needed the fucking reminder. He'd never, *never,* reacted to a woman this way. And her stubborn blindness to the truth of what burned between them aside, the more time he spent with Molly, the deeper he fell.

Honest and smart and with a sweet tenderness to her that cut him off at the knees, she pushed buttons he didn't even know he had.

"Stop." A breathless demand. "You're the one who proposed a one-month stand."

Turning, he stalked back to her doorway just as another door opened down the hall. "Molly?" said a heavyset man wearing black sweatpants and a navy tee. "You okay?"

Fox shifted instinctively to protect her from the view of the other man, her body clad only in that silly fluffy yellow robe that drove him crazy. She flushed and looked around his side. "Yes, I'm fine."

The stranger gave Fox a long, suspicious look before saying, "Just yell if that changes," and shutting his door.

Fox waited until Molly's eyes were back on him to speak, his voice harsh and his arms braced on either side of the doorway. "I might have proposed a one-month stand," he said, "but I didn't expect to be used and shoved out as soon as I'd served my purpose." It infuriated him. "Or should I say as soon as my cock had served its purpose?"

Molly flinched, but she didn't back down. "What? You expect me to let you move in for the month?" Her words came out in a furious whisper, her hands clenched to bloodless tightness even as her cheeks flared with hot spots of color. "I never did anything to make you believe I'd be fine with that. There are boundaries."

Gripping her jaw, he said, "You don't get to treat me as disposable."

Shock rippled through the anger in the dark brown of her eyes. "No, I—"

"You can't use me for sex," he interrupted, too pissed to hold back the words, "then put me away until the next time. I will not be your fucking dirty little secret." Not when it was brutally clear their relationship had already crossed the line from sex to a far more demanding, far more passionate bond. "Decide, Molly."

"I can't." The words were shaky, the anger draining away to leave her expression stark with pain. "I can't become entangled in you."

"You'd rather live half a life?" he asked without mercy, knowing he was pushing her too hard, too fast, but unable to stop himself, his response to her a violence inside him. "Always with one step backing away, ready to run to safety?" Sensing his temper was about to slip the leash totally, Fox pushed away from the doorjamb. "Make sure you can live with that choice."

THIS TIME WHEN FOX TURNED and walked away, Molly didn't call him back. Closing the door with fingers that trembled, she slid down to sit with her back to it, the robe he'd teased her about bunched around her thighs and her eyes on the bench where Fox had kissed her until he melted her bones.

"You'd rather live half a life? Always with one step backing away, ready to run to safety?"

The knuckles of one clenched hand pressed against her mouth, Molly shook her head. That wasn't what she was doing. She was living life on her terms—she supported herself, had a job she truly enjoyed, a best friend she loved, and a sister she'd embraced. More, she had a plan for her future and if that plan wasn't bursting with excitement, that was exactly what she wanted.

You're also twenty-four years old, another part of her whispered, *and the only two relationships you've had, if you can even call those fiascos relationships, have been with men who were... comfortable. The first was married to his job, the other in love with his ex-girlfriend. Neither one tried to get anything more than a kiss. And you didn't really care. You don't think something might be wrong with that picture?*

It was a pitiless indictment of the life she'd built out of nothing. A safe, careful, content life. Rather than a strong, purposeful plan, it suddenly sounded unutterably sad.

A tear trickled into her mouth, the taste of salt hot.

Knuckling it away, she got up and found the phone as well as the chocolate-fudge ice cream and took both back to the couch

Thea's sleep-slurred voice came on the line two rings later. "Hello?"

"Thea, it's me." Normally, she'd have called Charlotte, but if her smart best friend had one area of total cluelessness, it was on the subject of men.

"What's the matter?" Instant wakefulness.

Thea listened, not saying anything until Molly had poured it all out. "I guess it's too late to warn you against getting involved with someone in the industry?" Not waiting for an answer, she continued. "Here's the thing, Molly, Fox isn't the type of guy you can be with and expect to hold the reins. That vibe he gives off? It's not an illusion—he really is that intense."

Sipping sounds, Thea drinking the herbal tea she'd made while Molly talked. "I've worked with him for over two years," she continued, "and never once has he delegated control of any aspect of his private life to an assistant, manager, *anyone*. You have no idea how rare that is at his level of success."

Molly swirled her spoon in the melted ice cream, emotion a rock in her throat. "It was meant to be one night."

"You're the only one who can decide if you want more," Thea said, "but speaking professionally, if you had to pick a time and a place to have an affair with a man like Fox, this is about perfect. You can stay off the radar if you're careful, and he'll be gone in a month."

The idea should've comforted her. It didn't. It... hurt. It really hurt. "What if I can't maintain the distance?" she said on the heels of that staggering realization, her eyes burning. "What if I fall for him?" The agony and humiliation of being in love with a man who didn't love her was her worst nightmare.

She'd grown up watching her mother drink away her pain, Patrick Buchanan's infidelities acid on her soul, until by the time Molly was seven, her mother was a stranger, an alcoholic so accustomed to the effects that she was permanently drunk yet appeared sober. Molly had always known the truth, had hated seeing the distant ghost of the mother who'd once read her bedtime stories and promised her Daddy would be home soon. Daddy, of course, had no doubt been banging his aide or another young staffer at the time.

"Molly," Thea said, breaking into the agonizing slap of memory, "you said it yourself—that bastard who donated sperm to make us did a real number on you." Blunt, unexpected words. "The real question is, do you want him to manipulate the direction of your life from the grave?"

Long after the conversation with Thea had ended, Molly sat staring at nothing. Was her sister right? Was her whole life not a life at all, but rather an *anti*-life, as she did everything in her power not to repeat the mistakes of either her father or her mother?

"You'd rather live half a life?"

Fox's words circled in her brain, smashing and crashing into what Thea had said until she couldn't think. So she did what she'd done since she was a child alone in a large air-conditioned mansion, the nanny new and unfamiliar again because her mother didn't want her daughter to grow attached to another woman: she called Charlotte.

Her friend was up reading.

Too confused and upset to talk about Fox anymore, she just told Charlie of her conversation with Thea, of her sister's final, piercing question.

"I don't think," Charlotte said softly, "Thea knows how strong you are, how brave. She never saw you handling the bullies when you were fifteen."

"But she's right, too, isn't she, Charlie?" Abdomen tight and shoulders tense, Molly dropped her head against the sofa-back. "I make all my choices based on what happened back then." The shock, the disbelief, the public degradation followed by a screaming loss that had left her numb for months.

"If you're happy with your life," Charlotte replied, sweet and intelligent and perceptive, "what does it matter how it came to be?" The slightest pause. "*Are* you happy?"

It took Molly a long time to answer, to be honest about it. "No," she whispered. "Sometimes the rules I've made feel like a straitjacket." Squeezing until she couldn't breathe, her chest compressed by the weight of the expectations she'd placed on her life.

"Then be brave again." A quiet, powerful statement, followed by a fierce one: "Be that fifteen-year-old girl who told Queen B-face to shove her snotty nose in a dark, dark, place."

Unanticipated laughter bubbled in Molly's throat. "You mean Queen Bitchface?" she teased her friend affectionately. "I notice you still can't repeat the words I actually said that day."

"Sometimes, when I'm alone really late at night, I try to say bad words out loud," Charlie said with the sharp, self-deprecating humor very few people were ever lucky enough—or trusted enough—to witness. "Once, I even said the 'F' word behind Anya's back... very quietly."

Molly's smile deepened. "You degenerate."

"Thank you." Charlotte's voice turned solemn again with her next words. "If you don't want the same dream anymore, it's okay, Moll. You're allowed to change your mind."

Her heart aching, Molly said, "I still want that dream. So much." The white picket fence, the suburbs, the blissful ordinariness of being normal, she hungered for it so badly. "Only... maybe I can relax the rules, stop simply surviving and start living."

Never again would she come into contact with a man as talented, as dangerous, and as fascinating as Fox. While they could never exist in the same world, his life lived on a wild, Technicolor stage that caused her veins to fill with pure terror, he was hers for this one month out of time.

Molly didn't want to give up that month, not for anything. Especially not because of scars formed by the actions of two people so messed up their toxic relationship had eventually killed them.

FOX POWERED THROUGH THE CITY streets until he hit the winding road that went along this part of the Auckland coast. The yachts and other seacraft had been moored for the night, but the area was vibrant with life as a result of the myriad restaurants clustered in the central section. Frustrated by the slow vehicle in front of him, he throttled back the speed—just as well, because right around the corner was a cop car.

That'd be perfect, getting his face splashed over the papers for racking up a speeding ticket after he'd told Molly he could keep a low profile. Teeth gritted at the reminder of why he felt like a powder keg about to blow, every muscle and tendon in his body stretched to snapping point, he continued to drive until he'd ground down the serrated edge of his temper.

Fox had never had any intention of allowing Molly to see that part of him, but he hadn't counted on the effect she had on him. He couldn't keep his distance. The only good news was that Molly hadn't been the least afraid of him, despite the way he'd snapped. Grown men had backed down before him when he got that pissed, but Molly? She'd stood strong and fought.

He was proud of her spirit even as he was infuriated with her.

Now he had two options: return to his waterfront apartment, leaving the ball in Molly's court, or drive back to her place and use sex to get what he wanted. He could, of that he had no doubt. Their chemistry was a thing of erotic beauty, his sexual experience a weapon against which she had no defense. Except if he did that, they'd repeat this cycle again as soon as her mind cleared.

And he had no intention, *none,* of ever again being kicked out of Molly's bed.

Option one, however, carried with it a good chance she'd run scared. Fox wasn't about to let that happen. Because their fight didn't change the reason she'd said yes to a one-month stand despite her fear of addiction—the same reason she'd thrown him out and he'd blown up at her tonight.

And what they got up to between the sheets had nothing to do with it.

Eyes focused on the road, one hand on the wheel, the other on the stick, and his mind on the stubborn woman whose taste still lingered on his tongue, he decided on option three.

His body settled into the bucket seat, anticipation uncurling in his gut.

CHAPTER 9

SEVEN FORTY-FIVE THE NEXT morning and Molly's fingers trembled as she looked up the number Fox had input into her cell phone the first night.

"In case you ever need a musician," he'd said with a smile that had made her want to straddle his hair-rough thighs and claim kiss after kiss while his hands roamed over her. She hadn't been confident enough to act on that impulse, but she wasn't going to stay silent this morning.

Regardless of the stuttering beat of her heart.

Initiating the call, she readied herself to wait while he woke up, but it was answered on the first ring. "If you're a telemarketer, I'll be supremely pissed," was the growled warning.

"Fox, it's me," she said, then winced. As if he didn't know a thousand women who had his name on speed dial.

She'd just opened her mouth to identify herself when he said, "Molly Webster," turning her name into a purring caress. "You often prank-call strange men on Sunday mornings?"

Goose bumps broke out over her skin. "I wanted to invite you to the market," she said before she could lose her nerve, twisting her fingers in the thin cotton scarf she'd wrapped around her neck because she liked the indigo color against the raspberry of her cardigan. "If you still want to come."

"Baby, I always want to come."

Face red-hot, though her nerves eased at the sign he wasn't still furious, she laughed. "I can't believe you said that."

"How soon can you be ready?" he asked, and she could hear the smile in his tone.

"I'm pretty much done, but I can drive over and pick you up. It'll take me about ten minutes at this time of day." The roads would be all but dead, even in the city. "Is that enough time?"

"Man who needs more isn't a man, but I don't even need that."

"I'll start driving now." The butterflies took flight again, her need to see him a scary, beautiful craving.

"Or you could come downstairs to the surface parking lot."

Eyes widening, Molly ended the call and grabbed her purse. When she left the elevator on the ground floor to step out through the main doors, it was to find a low-slung beauty of a car parked near the exit from the underground garage. A bright, sleek yellow, it was a sexy, powerful intruder in amongst the compacts and sedans. Just like the man who prowled around the car to put his hands on her, her own on his chest a heartbeat later.

"You were so confident I'd call?" Her violent pleasure at his presence slammed up against annoyance at being taken for granted.

"Hell, no." Smoothing his hands over her hips, his touch proprietary, he said, "But while I might possibly have a temper—"

Molly couldn't maintain her annoyance in the face of his blunt response. "Possibly?" she said with a small smile, happiness dancing in her at having the heat and power of him so close, his scent in her every breath.

"Possibly." He nudged her closer between his spread thighs, his hands moving to her butt, the green of his irises brilliant under the morning sunlight. "I'm not a man who gives up when I want something, and I want you, Molly. Under me, on top of me, with your luscious mouth on my co—"

Damp heat between her thighs, she pressed her fingers against his lips. "Stop. We're going out." Not back inside and to the bedroom where words weren't necessary, pleasure and sensation their vocabulary.

A slow smile that turned her knees to jelly. "Yes, ma'am." Squeezing her butt, he dipped his head, his lips flirting with hers until she wrapped her arms around his neck and opened her mouth. He stroked his tongue deep, the rhythm languorous and she had the thought that if she hadn't made him leave last night, he'd have moved in her with the same unhurried patience this morning.

"Come on," he said when their mouths parted, that sexy dimple creasing his cheek and his hand cradling her nape in a way that felt breath-stealingly protective. "Let's hit this market before I take you up against the wall there." His forehead touched hers. "I'm not sure your neighbors would approve."

Cheeks blazing, Molly shot a nervous glance around the parking lot. It proved empty of all other life. *Phew.* "Aren't you worried about photographers?"

"I fucking love this country." He placed one hand on her lower back, nudging her toward the car. "Even your paparazzi are polite and don't bother people until after ten."

"Ha-ha," she said, trying not to think too hard about how

incredibly good it felt to be with him. "And wow, look, you picked such an inconspicuous car."

"Smart-ass." He lightly spanked that ass, to her renewed blush. "The rental company only delivered it yesterday, and as far as anyone knows, it was hired by a corporation."

"Where's your disguise?"

"Wait and see." Leaning down to open the door, he said, "Into my chariot."

Molly bit her lower lip and wondered if she should warn him about the parking situation at the market. Then the devil in her, long stifled, grinned and said why not give him the full local experience? "Is this a Lamborghini, too?" she asked, sliding into the buttery-soft leather bucket seat with a sigh of pleasure.

"Baby," he said, after getting into the driver's seat, "we need to have a serious discussion about your lack of knowledge of the most beautiful machines on this planet." Closing a hand on her thigh, high enough up that her breath caught, he slipped on mirrored sunglasses with the other. "This is a Ferrari Spider."

She widened her eyes, unable to tone down her awareness of that hand on her thigh... or of how possessive it felt. "Gosh, what a rookie mistake." Faux embarrassment. "I mean, what ordinary person can't tell a Ferrari and a Lamborghini apart on sight?"

"A certain librarian clearly wants to be in trouble today." Shifting his hand from her thigh to grip the back of her neck, he held her in position for a patented Fox kiss. Deep, wet, lusciously sexual.

He didn't stop until she was squirming restlessly in her seat. A final lick across her lips, a warning squeeze of her nape. "You'll get the rest of your punishment later."

"You—" Shaking her head, she pointed to the street—and if his grin kicked her in the heart, she'd already made her decision, already decided not to be a coward, to embrace this month no matter the consequences.

"Busy place," Fox said fifteen minutes later, the area around the outdoor market a hive of activity, cars and pedestrians intermingling as the early birds made their way to the entrance.

The Ferrari received more than a few hoots and hollers, especially when the tiny paved parking lot proved full even so early, and Fox was waved into the overflow lot—a grassy field that also occasionally functioned as a racetrack.

"Molly, you have some explaining to do," Fox muttered when the car's undercarriage almost scraped a raised section of earth during their turn into the "parking space" pointed out by the orange-vested teenage boy acting as an attendant.

"Were you expecting valet service?" she asked innocently, enjoying playing with him in a way she could've never predicted that first night. "I heard they have that at the malls in L.A."

"Oh, your punishment is going to last a long time." He turned off the engine. "I think I'll need to hear some begging before I show any mercy."

His growled warning, voice holding that edgy roughness that had turned him into a megastar, had her clenching her thighs together as he reached into the miniscule backseat to grab a baseball cap and what looked like a sticker. Confused, she watched him peel off the backing and apply it to his cheek. Suddenly, he had an impossibly realistic-appearing tattoo of a knife-edged starburst on his face.

"Wow," she murmured, running her fingers over the "tattoo." "That's incredible."

"I have a friend who's a makeup artist." He tugged on the cap, the brim shadowing his sunglasses. "She fixes me up with these—people focus on it and don't bother with the rest." He pulled on a gray hoodie that covered his arm tats, and suddenly, he wasn't Fox the rock star but Fox the gorgeous, intelligent, fun guy who was going to the market with her early on a Sunday morning.

Feeling her heart twist in a way that heralded trouble, she didn't resist when he put an arm around her waist once they'd stepped out of the Ferrari—even though it wasn't safe, wasn't sensible.

She already knew that in a month, when he left, it would *hurt.*

"That is a smokin' car," the attendant said, having wandered over to admire it.

Fox halted. "You have a license?"

"Yeah."

"Keep an eye on it and I'll let you drive it around the block."

"Man, thank you." Shocked awe on the teenager's face. "Man, shit. I'll make sure no one touches it."

Sliding his hand into the back pocket of her jeans as they left the lot, Fox allowed her to set the pace of their exploration. She'd worried the lip ring would make him noticeable, but no one seemed to pay him much mind even when he ditched the sunglasses, asking her to keep them in her purse. Of course, he attracted plenty of admiring female glances, with more than one envious one leveled at Molly, but none of that had to do with his rock star status. No, it was Fox's raw sexual appeal.

"This is my favorite section," she said, leading him to the dubious antiques while wondering how any woman stayed sane in a relationship with a man so desired by others. The idea of Fox with another woman—

Strangling the thought before it could ruin their day, she went to the best stall. "Some of it is actually real. Like this." She picked up a teacup and saucer in beautiful condition. "See the mark on the bottom?" she whispered. "And they're selling it for only five dollars."

Fox pulled out a five and handed it to the stall owner before she could go for her wallet. Opening her mouth to protest, she saw the glint in his eye and knew he was expecting it. "Thank you," she said instead, giving the cup and saucer to the stall owner's son so he could wrap it up in cushioning newspaper.

"Good choice, baby." His breath warm against her skin as he leaned in, one hand on her lower back, he said, "Don't you feel guilty fleecing these nice people?"

She pointed to another similar set as her nipples grew tight and sensitive against the lace of her bra. "I saw that at our version of Walmart last week for seven bucks. He's selling it for twenty. Trust me, they make their money."

Fox carried her purchases for her as she rummaged for treasures. He was unexpectedly good-natured about the time she spent, even found an old metal lighter he thought David would get a kick out of. "He doesn't smoke anymore, but he collects these."

A fun two hours later, Molly picked up the fresh vegetables she wanted and they headed back to the horse-racing track turned parking lot where Fox's car sat unmolested, the teenager on stern guard. Seeing Fox, he grinned and shoved his hands into the pockets of baggy camo cargos belted so low on his hips Molly half expected them to fall off. "So, we're sweet, right?"

Fox fist-bumped the boy in answer. Glancing at Molly after he'd put the shopping in the trunk, he said, "You mind riding in the back?"

"That's not happening." A five-year-old would have trouble squeezing in there. "I'll grab a coffee and wait while you two go for your ride."

Kissing her to the kid's wolf whistle, his hand cupping the side of her face with a tenderness she was coming to expect from her hard-rock lover, Fox said, "I'll be back soon."

Happiness floated in her blood, tiny bursts of starlight.

Fear attempted to take hold on its heels, but Molly locked it out. Not today, not this month.

She'd have endless time for regrets after Fox was gone. And though she knew it could never be any other way, for a piercing instant as she watched Fox laugh with the excited teenager, the sound entangling her heart, she wished it could. Wished her life had been different. Wished she was the kind of brave, strong woman who could give a man like Fox what he needed not just for a single month, but for a lifetime.

FIFTEEN MINUTES AND SURELY MORE than a single block later, loud cheers told her the car was back. It prowled into the parking lot in Fox's hands a few minutes after that, and she knew he must've stopped where the attendant's friends could admire the vehicle. "Did you have fun?" she asked, getting in when he reached across to pop open the passenger door.

"Not as much fun as I have with you." Tapping her cheek, he pulled out. "Breakfast?"

"My place. Your reward for pretending you enjoyed the shopping."

"I do like shopping."

"Liar." She'd glimpsed the telltale twitches.

"Well, I liked watching your ass when you bent over to do your shopping."

The butterflies in her stomach swirled and dipped in dizzying flight. "You're impossible." She threatened to peel off the sticker he'd told her needed to come off with water.

"I think you want to be naked over my lap."

Throat dry and thigh muscles going tight at that deep-voiced response, she sat on her hands, not sure of her impulse control where he was concerned. They made it as far as the kitchen table—where she found herself bent over the smooth wood, her jeans and panties around her ankles and her fingers clawing at the tabletop as Fox pounded into her in a single powerful stroke.

CHAPTER 10

HAND IN HER HAIR, HE tilted her head to the side and bent over to bite down on the spot where her neck flowed into her shoulder, his chest pressed against her back. "You are so fucking sexy, Molly."

Fracturing within and unable to do much of anything in this position, Molly gave in to the experience of being taken by a man who made no bones about being turned on by her body and who said low, hot things that made her want to whimper and beg for mercy.

Fox, however, wasn't in the mood to draw things out. Pushing into her after five deep, fast thrusts, he pinned her in place for a long, slow minute as his body shuddered, before coming down to kiss her neck. He'd shaved this morning, his jaw smooth against her skin. "Give me a sec and I'll take care of you."

Molly shivered at the way he said that, the blatant sexual promise in his voice. "That's okay," she whispered, though her breasts ached, her body on the brink. "You took plenty care of me last night."

Pulling out to her gasp, he said, "That's not how I work. Stay in place or I really will spank your sweet ass."

Molly set herself to rights the instant he disappeared into the bathroom, the idea of giving him that particular view mortifying. Fox took one look at her when he exited, sans facial tattoo and T-shirt, and backed her straight onto the table. Where he flipped her around and, pulling down her jeans and panties, proceeded to make good on his threat, his hand caressing each cheek before he delivered four light swats that almost pitched her into orgasm.

That was only the start.

His body a muscled wall at her back, he tugged her head to the side again, his voice deliciously low in ear. "I told you I was going to punish you." His fingers slipped between her thighs from the back, the callused tips rubbing the engorged tissues of her entrance with torturous subtlety. "And"—a lick along the edge of her earlobe—"I don't think a naughty woman who teases her man all morning should get to come without earning it."

Her man.

Molly barely had time to process what he'd said before Fox did something with his fingers that arced sweet white fire through her nerve endings, the pleasure a lightning storm.

HALF AN HOUR LATER, SHE tried desperately to catch a breath where she lay naked on the sofa, one of her feet flat on the floor, the other on the cushions. Part of her wanted to hide in red-faced embarrassment at her splayed position, but that part was buried under the exhaustion of a pleasure that had turned her bones to noodles.

A very satisfied-looking Fox, his jeans still on, knelt on the floor beside her. Placing his hand on her abdomen, he touched his lips to hers, his tongue owning her mouth. "How about I make breakfast?" Self-assured fingertips around one of her swollen nipples, a nipple he'd sucked until she begged.

It wasn't the only thing he'd sucked.

She slapped at his shoulder, her aim off. "Be quiet." Another ragged breath. "I'll make breakfast—soon as I can move." Right now, her muscles were jelly. "I think I might be dead."

Chuckling, Fox kissed her again, stroking his hand up and down her body until she wrapped an arm around him, loving the sensation of being petted by that strong hand. Her stomach chose to growl right on cue.

Breaking the kiss on a blush that made him dip his head, lick along the upper curve of her breast as if to taste the color, she said, "I need my robe." Before he made her forget everything.

Once again, he grabbed his T-shirt. "Raise your arms."

He bit teasingly at the side of one of her kiss-reddened breasts before tugging the soft gray fabric down over her head. Padding to the bathroom to tidy herself up a bit, she returned to the kitchen a few minutes later, her feet stuffed into fluffy purple slippers shaped like monster claws that Charlie had given her as a joke gift, her hair corralled into a loose braid, and fresh panties on under the T-shirt.

Fox was sprawled on the couch, the remote in hand while a cartoon played on the television screen. Stomach dipping at how right he looked there, how painfully good this felt, she forced her gaze off him and put on the coffee, then began to gather up the ingredients for omelets.

Since that would hardly fill Fox up, however, she put out some bread to be toasted, then went hunting to see what else she had. "Fox, do you want fried potatoes?" It wasn't like he had anything to worry about in the weight department—the man was pure firm, strokable muscle, the energy he burned onstage brutal.

He also, her body reminded her on a ripple of remembered pleasure, burned energy in other ways.

"Hell yeah." A grin over his shoulder that cut through the afterglow to hit her straight in the heart. "Come kiss me."

"Not risking it while I'm starving," she said, using humor to bury her worry at how fast she was falling for a man she could never hope to claim. "Next thing you know, I'll be naked again."

"I'll never say no to naked Molly." He prowled up off the sofa to take a seat on a stool on the other side of the counter, pouring himself a cup of coffee while she quickly peeled and sliced the potatoes, the pan already heating up.

"What do you think about Sydney?" he asked without warning.

Disappointment pinched at Molly at the idea of losing even a tiny part of their month together, but she wasn't surprised he was interested in a visit. The Australian city was only a three-hour flight away.

"I visited with Charlie last year and loved it. We were total tourists"—she laughed softly at the thought of how much fun they'd had—"even did a cruise around Sydney Harbour." Putting the potatoes in the pan, she looked up to meet the dark green of Fox's gaze, hoping he couldn't see how much she was already missing him. "You can book flights easy enough, even at short notice."

"I'm going over end of the coming week." He grabbed a piece of the green pepper she'd diced for the omelets. "Favor for a friend. He set up a charity concert, but the entire band he booked just went into rehab."

"What?" Molly turned around. "*All* of them?"

"Might be a publicity stunt, but yeah, it does happen. Except for those premade boy bands"—a smirk—"a lot of us were friends first, and friends get into bad shit together." He ate another piece of the pepper. "Who else are you going to shoot up with but the people you trust most?"

Molly had never heard even a whisper of drugs attached to Fox, wouldn't have been attracted to him if she had, but she couldn't not take this opportunity to make certain. "Have you—"

An immediate shake of his head. "No, not my deal. Music's my addiction."

Relaxing, she whipped up the first omelet. "I didn't realize bands as big as Schoolboy Choir could move so fast."

"Normally no, but like I said, Marc's a buddy, and he's raising money for a children's charity. It would've been a problem if we were already doing a concert in the city, but since that isn't the case, there's no bullshit red tape."

She poured the omelet into a second pan. "So he'll refund the people who wanted specifically to see the other band?"

A nod. "He figures he'll make that up with the increased ticket sales." Fox shrugged, his shoulders rippling with the lithe muscle that felt so beautiful under her touch. "Plus, we're here, and it's a low-stress outdoor gig."

Putting the fried potatoes on a couple of thick paper towels to drain, she flipped the omelet. "I'm sure you'll draw a huge crowd." The words "legendary" and "iconic" were already being used in connection with the band's name—

Schoolboy Choir's sheer, raw talent was as obvious as their love of music.

"You could be a part of it."

Air was suddenly hard to find. "Are you asking me to go with you?" she said at last.

"It's on Saturday night. You could leave work a little early if you don't want to take the whole day off, be there in plenty of time."

Molly bit the inside of her cheek, her throat thick. The fact was, since she usually never requested unanticipated vacation days, her boss wouldn't quibble about either a half-day or a full day. "You'll take this the wrong way," she said when she could speak, turning to face Fox with her breath painful in her lungs, "but I don't want to be known as the woman you're sleeping with."

His lashes lowered to hood his expression. "Yeah, how else should I take it?"

"You'll go," she said, gripping the counter behind her and fighting back tears. "After a month, you'll go. But I'll still be here, living my life. Being famous, even by association... I can't handle it, Fox." Already, her stomach churned at the idea of being known as "Fox's Secret Lover," the headline sure to be splashed across the magazines.

Molly might have decided to break out of the box into which she'd wedged herself at fifteen, but fame was the one thing she'd never touch, not for anything or anyone.

Not even a man who made her wish for an impossible dream.

Heart aching and throat raw from holding back her emotions, she turned back to the stove and plated the omelet, then poured in the other one while pushing down on the toaster lever to start the bread. "Don't be angry," she said quietly, aware it'd be difficult for him to understand the depth of her aversion to the idea of fame without knowing the ugly background responsible for her gut-deep abhorrence.

Yet she couldn't tell him, couldn't bear to see pity—or even worse, disgust or speculation—in his eyes. She understood she wasn't being rational, that Fox wasn't like the teenagers who'd alternately shunned and tormented her after the scandal broke, but this was the one point on which she simply couldn't be rational. It hurt too much.

FOX FLEXED HIS HAND ON the counter, his eyes on Molly's back. "I get it." Shoving a hand through his hair, he blew out a breath. "Shit, yeah, I get it. I once walked a girl home from a bar in London because she was drunk and the next day, she sold her story to the tabloids." It had been early on in the band's career, but Fox had never forgotten.

"Turned out we had a 'mad sex romp' in the seconds it took for me to make sure she got safely inside her place." He'd felt like such an idiot for falling for what had obviously been a setup, given that the tabloid had pictures of him in her doorway. "That was her claim to fame and she milked it for all it was worth."

The second omelet done, Molly put it on a plate then came over to wrap her arms around him from the back. "Well, whatever happens"—she rubbed her cheek against his skin, the open warmth of her affection a powerful drug of which he couldn't get enough—"I promise not to sell the videos I made of our mad sex romps."

He half-turned to tuck her under his arm, realizing his librarian was trying to make him feel better. The tenderness he felt for her dug its tendrils in even deeper, the emotion a punch to the gut. "Funny." He scowled. "Not."

Rising on tiptoe, eyes laughing, she rubbed her nose against his.

He was fucking undone. Just gone.

"Do you have a real one of those?"

"What?"

"A sex tape?"

"There was this time with an entire professional cheerleading team…"

Her expression was priceless.

Shoulders shaking, he claimed a hard, fast kiss. "Gotcha."

"Funny. Not." She pulled his hair in a retaliation that just made him want to haul her into his lap and mess her up with his mouth, his hands. So he did. It was the best damn breakfast he'd ever had.

THEY DROVE OUT OF THE city and down the coast that afternoon, the stark autumn scenery stunning through the windows of the low-slung car as it ate up the road. Stopping for ice cream at an isolated corner store, they took seats on the grassy verge of a windswept beach. Low tide as it was, the sand seemed to go on forever, smooth as sugar and sprinkled with minerals that made it glitter under the sun.

Despite the beauty, the cool temperature meant there were only three other people on the beach, and they were far out near the water's edge—a bundled-up toddler and his parents.

Nearby, there was only a long piece of driftwood worn smooth by time and water and the occasional seagull pacing the sand for tiny crabs and mollusks.

"This is the best date." The unsophisticated words spilled over Molly's lips, she was so happy.

Picking up her hand, Fox kissed her palm, the caress unexpectedly sweet. "Yeah, it is."

She curled her fingers around his, let him taste her ice cream, took a big bite out of his, which made him cry foul and attempt to claim it back in a laughing kiss. There would, she thought as he wrestled her giggling form to the grass, be no forgetting Fox. It wouldn't only hurt when he walked away, it would be brutal.

Strong, intelligent, and talented, he'd marked her deep inside.

That talent was in haunting evidence later that night, when—having picked up his acoustic guitar on the way back from the beach—he played for her. Lying curled up naked under the sheet in bed, a jean-clad but otherwise undressed Fox in a chair facing her, Molly listened and felt her entire body ache at the harsh beauty of his music, the edgy sound distinctively Fox.

"I can't figure out how you create something so extraordinary from a few strings and your fingers." She could listen to him forever. "Play it again, please."

Fox's smile was quiet, the look in his eyes unreadable as he complied. "It's not finished yet."

"Will you," she began, hesitated, took the plunge. "Will you play it for me if it's done by the time the month is over?"

A long look. "Yeah, baby. I promise."

For some reason, she believed in his promise, despite the fact she'd spent a lifetime learning not to trust. "Thank you." Then she lay silent as he moved his fingers over the strings with a grace that astounded and compelled. When he added his voice, keeping the volume low to avoid disturbing her neighbors, she felt her heart stop beating.

A fallen angel might have a voice like that, she thought, hard and pure and with an unashamed sexuality to it that invited the listener into sin. It made her eyes burn, tears roll down her face.

Setting aside his guitar as the last note faded from the air, Fox walked over to kneel beside the bed. His hand slid into her hair, his lips touched hers... and Molly felt herself fall, her shields crashing in splintered shards at her feet.

CHAPTER 11

FOX HELD MOLLY IN HIS arms after she fragmented in pleasure. He'd touched her with all the tenderness he had in him after she cried while listening to the song he'd been working on for weeks, the final pieces coming only today. Because of his beautiful Molly who did things to him he didn't understand, who spoke to him without lies, who made him wish he were a better man. It didn't matter. He wasn't going to give her up.

Brushing back her hair when her breathing quieted, he looked down. "Hey."

A shy smile before she snuggled back down against his shoulder and traced the song lyrics on one side of his torso. "Was this your first tattoo?"

"No, that was the inner-wrist characters."

"Did it hurt badly?"

"Like a bitch." He laughed at the memory. "But I was with the guys—all of us decided to get inked to celebrate our first number one—so none of us could make a sound. Afterward, we went and got drunk and whined like pussies."

Molly's laughter was music he knew he could never capture with chords and notes.

"I have something for you," he said after they'd lain in warm silence for several minutes. Reaching down to snag his jeans, he tugged out the folded piece of paper he'd put in the back pocket this morning. "Here."

"What's this?"

He knew the instant she found the answer to her question. Her cheeks went bright red, but he knew she was listening when he said, "I'm clean, Molly, and I haven't been with any-one but you since that medical report. I wanted you to have the info before I asked you if we can ditch the condoms." Even young and stupid, he'd never taken chances, but he wanted to be skin-to-skin with Molly, brand her from the inside out.

Yeah, it was primitive as hell. Fox didn't care.

"Oh." Molly carefully folded the report back into a neat square and gave it to him to put on the bedside table. "Why—" She coughed to clear her throat. "Why did you have this done?"

Fox thought about how to answer that without betraying something it wasn't his business to tell. "Friend needed to go get checked after he did something idiotic, and I went with him. Moral support."

"This was done a month ago," Molly said a little hesitantly, and he knew what she was asking.

"Fact is," he said, shifting so that she was below him, her eyes looking up into his as he braced himself above her, "I haven't been with anyone for a hell of a lot longer than that. It's been almost a year."

Her pupils dilated. "But you're so…"

"I have a high sex drive, but I got over the stick-my-dick-in-anything-hot-and-female stage a long time ago," he said and, when she didn't flinch away from the unvarnished answer, decided to lay it all out. He hadn't been an angel and he'd rather tell her that than have her wonder or get the twisted version from the tabloids.

"At first, it was like having candy thrown in my face, women waiting wet and willing wherever I turned." He'd been a nineteen-year-old suddenly drowning in money and women, with no parent to put a brake on things, and the label happy to use his exploits and those of the others to further build their hard-rock image. "I took the candy, fucked around."

He gripped her chin to turn her back toward him when her eyes glanced away, wanting her to see he was dead serious about his next words. "These days, however, I prefer to take my time, choose a lover I enjoy in and out of bed."

Molly knew and accepted that Fox was no kind of virgin, his sexual experience simply a part of him, but she found she didn't like hearing about his conquests. It made her wonder if he'd done the same things with them that he did with her. If he'd cupped a woman's face so tenderly while he kissed her slow and sweet, if he'd spent a lazy Sunday morning petting a lover until she turned boneless, if he'd wrestled with a woman over ice cream, his laughter filling the air.

It took conscious effort to push away thoughts that betrayed so much about the kind of trouble she was in. "Y...you know I haven't been with anyone else," she said, trying to sound as practical as he'd done and failing miserably, "and I had a physical for medical insurance four months ago. It was all clear." She rubbed her foot over the sheet, this conversation so far outside her realm of experience that she had to think about every word. "I'm protected against pregnancy...

so I think we could." Her doctor had prescribed the Pill to regulate her cycle.

Fox brushed her hair off her face. "You okay with it? Because if you're not, we go on like we've been doing. I'm not an asshole who'll make you feel bad about your choice."

Molly thought of having Fox inside her, no barriers, all hard heat and power, and knew she wanted the intimacy. "Yes. I can show you the insurance report if—"

"It's okay." His hand curved gently around her throat. "I trust you."

She stroked her hands over his shoulders. "Not very smart of you."

Shifting, he thrust his thigh between hers, the crisp hairs on his skin a deliciously coarse abrasion against her flesh. "I didn't say I trust every woman, only a certain librarian who loves to play with my lip ring." A more serious look. "But if the contraception fails for any reason, you tell me."

Molly's throat dried up, the discussion suddenly too intense, too much more than it should be for a fleeting relationship. Pushing at Fox, she would've left the bed, but he wouldn't let her go. Instead, flipping over onto his back, he tumbled her on top of his body. "Hey, hey, what's the matter?"

She raised her head, her breath hoarse and choppy to her own ears. "The idea of a child coming out of a relationship with an end date," she said, speaking around the lump of ice that was her heart, "it's terrifying."

His pupils jet-black against vivid green, he nodded. "I get it, and baby, if anything does happen, I *will* be there for you." Words potent with a raw emotion she couldn't identify. "Don't shut me out."

All at once, she remembered an article she'd read about Fox, back when he'd simply been a darkly beautiful rock star she'd sighed over from afar. "You never knew your father." She knew she was crossing another line, but Molly had realized she didn't know how to compartmentalize sex and emotion.

Fox was no longer just that fantasy rock star; he was a man whose touch made her ignite and whose smile made her breath catch in her chest. He could cook a single fancy dish that he'd promised to make her the next time they had a night together, was talented, had a temper, and a fascination with fast cars. All those pieces and so much more made up the person he was... a person who'd begun to matter to her in a way that could have no happy ending.

"I promise I'll tell you if it happens." She was the one who brushed back his hair this time, suckled a soft, sweet kiss from his lips. "I'm sorry if I brought up bad memories."

A crooked smile, his fingers spreading on her lower back. "What am I going to do with you, Molly Webster?" Running his hand up her spine, then back down, he surprised her by adding, "My mom was drugged out of her mind at the time I was conceived, couldn't have picked the guy out of a lineup, and she certainly wasn't ready for a kid. She dumped me with my grandparents the week after I was born."

Her heart broke; she knew what it was like to be abandoned by your parents, but she'd been a teenager at the time, not a defenseless child. "I'm sorry."

"Don't be—I loved living with Gramps and Grammy." Deep warmth in his tone. "I grew up digging in the garden, even had my own plot. My best harvest was seven carrots when I was six."

Fascinated at this glimpse into his childhood, she hugged the moment to her heart. "What did you do with them?"

"I made my grandmother put carrots in the soup, and we also had to have them in our sandwiches."

"Sandwiches?"

"Absolutely. Carrot and cheese sandwiches."

Unable to resist that grin, she traced his lips with a fingertip, laughed when he pretended to bite. "How did your grandparents cope with an active little boy?"

"By tiring me out until I couldn't cause trouble."

As the night softened and went still around them, he told her stories of being allowed to go wild on his kid-sized skateboard while his grandparents watched over him, of playing stickball with the neighborhood kids, of cooking with his grandmother and learning carpentry with his grandfather.

It sounded like an idyllic childhood, but there was something beneath, a dark pulse of anger. Molly wanted to ask about it, wanted to learn every piece of him, but knew instinctively that it would be too profound an intimacy. She didn't want to put him in the position of having to push her back, of fracturing the painful beauty of this instant when it was only Molly and Fox talking to one another.

No past that had altered the course of her life. No present where he lived in a world in which Molly simply couldn't survive. No future where he'd be only a heartbreaking memory.

Keeping her silence and stifling her hunger to know this complex, talented man both in and out of bed, she fell asleep to the rhythm of his voice, only to wake to the unadulterated demand of his kiss.

GOING BACK TO WORK ON Tuesday felt like stepping into a different world. She and Fox had spent the whole of Monday together as well, the day a lazy, playful one.

Her rock star had no inhibitions in bed and coaxed the same openness from her. "That's it, baby," he'd say, encouraging her to taste, to explore, to indulge and be indulged, his voice a finely honed instrument of which she couldn't get enough.

"Earth to Molly."

Molly jerked when a slender hand waved in front of her face. "What? Sorry."

"It's okay." Her colleague laughed. "Must've been some weekend—you were on another planet."

Flushing guiltily, Molly reined in her wayward thoughts and focused on work. Three hours passed before she checked her phone—a deliberate act of willpower on her part—to find a message from Fox inviting her to the island hotel Schoolboy Choir had booked out, for a casual dinner with "the boys."

Just meat on the grill, forget the greens, he'd added. *And Noah lost a bet with Abe, so he's making his (in)famous passion fruit cheesecake.*

Molly's fingers trembled. Putting down the phone before she dropped it, she went to help at the desk as the seniors' book club came en masse to check out their selections for the week.

It wasn't until forty-five minutes later, while she was on her lunch break, that she picked up the phone again. She didn't know what to say, what to do, but she did know it was dead certain at least one aggressive member of the paparazzi had to have followed Schoolboy Choir to the island. Lusted after

105

by millions of women and idolized by as many men, Fox, Noah, Abe, and David were too good for business to leave alone.

Wanting to be wrong, to be proven needlessly paranoid, she opened a browser window on her phone and input a news search for the band's name. It took a split second for the search engine to show her several images of the villa-style hotel Schoolboy Choir had booked, as well as a couple of shots of two of the band members—Abe and Noah—throwing a football around on the beach.

Below that was a photograph of David diving into the undoubtedly freezing water.

The final image was of Noah and Fox leaning on the balcony railing of a waterfront apartment, the image clearly taken from somewhere on the ground. Molly recognized Fox's T-shirt; it was the one he'd worn the first night at the party.

The caption made her tongue go dry, her breath coming so fast she knew she was in danger of a panic attack: *The local female fans are apparently extending a warm welcome—Noah was spotted returning to his apartment around four in the morning, while a source tells us Fox spent the entire night with a lucky mystery woman!*

CHAPTER 12

SCREWING HER EYES SHUT, MOLLY ignored the roaring in her ears and concentrated on doing the breathing exercise the school counselor had taught her back when the scandal first broke. It took several minutes, but she was eventually able to read the article associated with the apartment photo.

A wracking shudder of relief.

The article was pure fluff, the "source" probably created in the reporter's imagination in order to spice up the photo editorial, which was heavily focused on Noah's shirtless upper body.

Did you know, she messaged Fox, *there are already photos online of the band on the island—and at your apartment building?*

Grill's out back in an enclosed space the paps can't get at, came the reply. *I'll pick you up at eight.*

The message was so Fox, confident and take charge, and if Molly was honest with herself, she liked that about him... but some risks she couldn't take. *No,* she wrote back, *I'll see you another night.*

The phone rang in her hand a second later. "I'm not changing my mind," she said, before he could charm her into exactly that.

"Don't worry, baby." The grit and sex of his voice made her body ache, but more dangerous was the effect he had on her heart. "We know how to avoid the cameras when necessary—it's why we give the paps an easy shot now and then, so the bastards stay lazy and don't dig."

She couldn't bear to miss even a single night with him, wanted badly to give in, but her stomach churned at the idea of her past being dug up by the voracious media, of the nightmare beginning again. Sweat broke out along her spine. "No, Fox. I can't risk it."

"You're being overcautious." Edgy frustration, a kiss of the temper she'd already come up against once. "Even if someone snaps you from a distance, it won't be a huge deal."

Fingers clenching on the phone, she said, "It would be to me," and hung up. A lump choking her throat as she fought the tears, she stared unseeing at the wall in front of her. Maybe he didn't know her history, but she'd *told* him how much it meant to her to stay out of the spotlight.

And he'd said it didn't matter.

Despite her angry hurt, she couldn't help checking her phone an hour later, a cold tightness inside her. There were no further messages from Fox.

EXITING THE ELEVATOR OF HER apartment building at six that night, Molly found herself searching for a tall male form leaning against the wall, guitar by his side. Her gut-wrenching disappointment when Fox wasn't there offered an agonizing preview of exactly how much it would hurt if she never saw him again. Pushing through the door after unlocking it, she dumped her stuff and sat down on the bench to take off her shoes—and remembered what Fox had done to her in this spot.

"Stop it," she ordered herself, but it wasn't that easy. Fox had left his mark on her entire apartment.

She lasted an hour before she couldn't stand the memories anymore. Picking up the phone, she called Charlotte. Her best friend was working late but fell in happily with the idea of dinner down at the Viaduct, that section of the waterfront always vibrant with life.

"So," she asked, after meeting Charlotte in the lobby of her building, "how's it going with the new boss?" Maybe the jagged knot in her chest would unravel if she just didn't think about Fox.

"Honestly, after that disaster over the weekend, I've tried to stay out of his way." A groan at the mention of a dinner she'd described in a text message as *Silent Charlie-mouse waiting for the growling, bad-tempered predator to eat her.* "He's causing carnage in management. Two new firings today."

"Wow."

"I know, right? Anyway, enough about T-Rex."

"What?" Molly laughed at the look on her friend's face, Charlotte's cheeks pink at having been caught out. It eased some of the tension in her body, though it did nothing to ease the ache deep inside her. "T-Rex?"

"He's big, scary, and people run when they see him coming." With that succinct description, Charlotte slipped her arm through the crook of Molly's as they walked out into a night that actually wasn't as cold as it could've been. "Do you want to get ice cream first and find a good spot to watch the water? Radio said there's a super yacht coming in soon. Might be fun to see some gazillionaire's fancy boat."

"Dessert before dinner?" she said, forcefully ignoring the horrible sense of loss that continued to grow within her. "I'm in."

Ice creams in hand an easy stroll later, they decided to sit on the wide, shallow steps near the ornate ferry building that was a piece of history amongst the steel and glass so prevalent in this section of the city. Hand-holding couples on dates, businesspeople on their way home, night runners with their earbuds in, the surrounding area was electric with activity.

"So," Charlotte said after they'd taken their seats, "what's the matter?"

Molly looked out over the harbor, the dark slick of water colored by the lights of nearby businesses. Even now, she could get on a ferry and be on the island in under forty minutes. "Why do you think anything's the matter?" she asked, quashing the dangerous impulse that could destroy her.

A shoulder bump. "How long have we been friends? Spill. Are you still worrying about what Thea said?"

"No. But... there was a reason I had that conversation with Thea." Taking a deep breath, Molly told Charlotte what had happened after the party.

Her best friend's mouth fell open. "You—with Zachary Fox—" Throwing one arm around Molly with a cry of wild glee, she smacked a big kiss on Molly's cheek. "My hero!" She pulled back her arm a second before her ice cream would've toppled over. "At least one of us will have outrageous stories with which to shock any grandchildren we might or might not have."

Startled into a giggle, Molly leaned against her petite friend and shared the rest. Not the private memories, the ones that meant the most, but the reason why she'd be alone in her bed tonight. "Do you think I'm being ridiculous?" she said at the end. "About not being caught by the media with Fox?"

"Of course not." Charlotte finished off her cone, balled up the napkin it had been wrapped in, and took Molly's to the trash as well before coming back. "I was there, remember?" She closed her small-boned hand over Molly's. "Did you tell Fox about what happened? So he knows it has nothing to do with him?"

Shaking her head, Molly pointed out the gleaming super yacht that had appeared in the distance. "I'm falling for him," she whispered, admitting the truth to the one person she knew would never betray her trust. "I can hardly bear to think about the end of our month together." If Fox even wanted to continue their affair after today's fight. "If I let him in any further... it'll be agony."

Charlotte didn't respond for a long time, the two of them watching the sleek progress of the yacht built to be a dream on water, golden light pouring through every window. Someone had also put up tiny colored lights along the railings, adding a sense of mischief and whimsy to the regal craft, the colors pretty against the silky deep blue of the night.

"I'm scared, Molly," Charlotte said at last, her voice quiet. "All the time. You know why."

Molly hugged her close. "We don't have to talk about it." It hurt her friend to discuss the events that had devastated her first year of university, causing internal scars that had

111

never faded. Because while Charlie had been shy her whole life, she'd also always had a sparkling fire inside her, which that brutal year had all but doused.

"No, it's okay." Her friend turned to face her, soft blonde curls escaping the knot at the nape of her neck. "I miss out on so much because I'm scared—and the thing is, I'm intelligent enough to know it. That just makes it worse."

"You're selling yourself short." Molly wouldn't allow it. "You said I was brave, but I wouldn't have made it through high school and foster care without you." She didn't know how many times she'd cried in Charlotte's arms, or turned toward her for silent moral support when the taunts threatened to break her down. "You were my rock."

"You were mine, too." Charlotte shook her head, her eyes full of quiet power behind the transparent shield of her glasses. "Don't let that tough, strong, fifteen-year-old girl down, Molly. Don't shortchange yourself like I do."

Heart breaking for what her friend had been through, Molly turned back to face the water before she started crying. "Is it worth it," she said when she could speak without her voice cracking, "for a single month?"

"That's for you to decide—but I vote for breaking the bed with Mr. Kissable." Charlotte fanned her face.

Molly burst out laughing, grateful once again for her best friend. She only wished she could help Charlotte conquer her own fears, convince her to put away the shapeless, unflattering clothes that swamped her tiny frame and let down those pretty curls. But if Molly's rules were her security blanket, Charlotte's clothes were hers. "Maybe you need a rock star of your own."

"No way. I'd rather go to bed with T-Rex."

Molly's antennae shot up. That was the second time Charlotte had mentioned her new boss—*and* she'd linked him to sex, however tenuously. "What's he look like?" she asked casually.

Scowling, her best friend shrugged. "What most carnivorous monsters look like."

"*Charlie.*"

A sigh, pointed chin propped up in fine-boned hands. "The name Gabriel Bishop sound familiar?"

Molly gasped. *"No?"* Gabriel Bishop, known on the field as "the Bishop," was a former pro rugby player turned corporate genius. Tall, with wide shoulders and heavily muscled, he was certifiably hot in a hard-sex-and-hard-play kind of way. "Hey! Didn't you once say you wanted to rip off his shirt and sink your teeth into his pecs?"

Charlotte spluttered at the reminder of her cocktail-induced sigh at the TV screen during a game where Gabriel Bishop had been roped in as a guest commentator. "I swear," she said, "you have the memory of an elephant!"

"So?" Molly waggled her eyebrows, fingers discreetly crossed and hope a bright, bright flame in her heart.

"That was before I realized he wasn't human." With that pert comment, her friend shifted her attention toward the restaurant section of the Viaduct. "I'm starving."

Luck was with them and they snagged an outdoor table with an amazing view of the water, yachts and other pleasure craft berthed in neat rows in the marina. As they ate, Molly thought of everything her friend had said, everything she herself had decided about stepping out of the box in which she'd lived for so long, and sent Fox a message: *Search for Patrick Buchanan and scandal.*

CHAPTER 13

FOX NARROWED HIS EYES AT the phone screen when Molly's name flashed up. He was still pissed at her for hanging up on him, enough that he needed to wait a bit longer—get his boiling temper down to a smolder—before he went after her and got to the bottom of this. Stubborn as he was learning his Molly could be, he hadn't expected a capitulation.

Tapping to open the message, he frowned, then did the search. "Fuck!" He barely controlled the urge to throw his phone.

Noah, who was sitting on the steps leading down to the sandy beach, while Fox was on the porch above, stopped strumming his guitar. "Care to elaborate, oh articulate one?"

"You know how I said Molly was mine?" He dropped his legs off the railing to hit the deck. "That I planned to convince her to enter into a real relationship?"

"Tough thing to forget."

"Yeah, well, I was an arrogant prick." Not just then, but today, when he'd told her it wouldn't matter if she was snapped. He'd had *no* fucking idea who and what he was dealing with;

what he'd just learned told him Molly was the last person in the world who'd ever want to be in a relationship with a man whose life was dogged by the prying lens of paparazzi cameras.

CHECKING HER PHONE AGAIN AS she entered the apartment after dropping Charlotte off at her town house, Molly felt her stomach drop at the continued lack of a return message from Fox. He was likely busy with his bandmates, she told herself, not the kind of man who'd have bothered to go immediately online to follow a cryptic message from a woman he'd known less than a week.

Or maybe he'd done the search, realized how messed up she really was, and decided to cut his losses.

A stabbing pain in her chest.

Swallowing past it to release a trembling exhale, she kicked off her shoes and wandered into the bedroom to change into flannel pajama pants and a faded gray T-shirt. That done, she shoved her feet into her silly purple slippers and, pulling her hair back into a ponytail, went into the bathroom to wash off her makeup and brush her teeth. Smoothing in some moisturizer at the end, she settled into bed and picked up a romance novel she'd been looking forward to finishing.

She'd forgotten she'd stopped right before a love scene.

Her breath caught, her mind seeing not the words on the page, but the erotic scenes that had taken place in this bed a day past. *This* was why she hadn't wanted to get involved with a man like Fox—that addictive gene in her body had kicked into high gear where he was concerned, until she could smell him all around her. Impossible, since she'd changed the sheets while he was in the shower this morning.

Blood hot at the reminder of *why* she'd changed the sheets, she looked back down at the novel, determined to read on. Five minutes and one incomprehensible paragraph later, she put the book on the bedside table and got up to make a cup of chamomile tea. She'd just taken the tea from the pantry when there was a knock on the door.

Jumping, she froze.

The short, hard knock came again, and this time, she moved, padding over to the security peephole to see a rock star on her doorstep. Her throat dried up.

"Molly." Quiet, sexy, a little rough. "Open up."

Heart slamming against her ribs, she looked down at her pajamas, thought about her washed-clean face... and realized none of it mattered. Not when she'd just given him the key to her greatest vulnerability.

She unlocked and opened the door.

Fox, his arms braced above the doorjamb, his white T-shirt taut against his biceps, said, "I had to steal a boat for you."

Toes curling in her slippers even as she stood there feeling exposed, raw, she somehow managed to say, "According to a certain celebrity magazine, you're worth a cool kazillion or two—you probably bought the boat."

"Noah wouldn't be too happy. He's become attached to the thing." A dawning smile, but his eyes were serious. "Let me in."

Realizing she'd been blocking the doorway, Molly stepped back and Fox came in, pushing the door shut behind him and flicking the deadbolt. The sound was loud in the silence, seemed to signal an intent to stay that had her stomach in knots.

"You look good enough to eat," Fox murmured, his hands going to her hips.

She found her own against the firm warmth of his chest.

Fingers brushing the side of her breast through the soft fabric of her T-shirt, he ran one hand up over the skin bared by the scoop neck to close his fingers around her throat. "I got your message."

Feeling vulnerable in a way that had nothing to do with the fact he was bigger and stronger, she looked away. "Did you do the search?"

"I'm sorry, baby." Rubbing his thumb over her jaw, he tugged back her head with the hand not around her throat and bent to take her lips. "Open, Molly." When she obeyed, he kissed her with an unhidden male hunger and a harsh tenderness that stole another piece of her.

Lost, she rose on tiptoe and linked her hands behind his neck, her taut, aching breasts crushed against his chest. He groaned and squeezed her neck a fraction, just enough to get her notice.

"Fox?"

"I want you in my lap." Nipping at her lower lip, the ring rubbing over the kiss-swollen flesh, he drew her not into the bedroom but to the sofa.

Sprawling there, he crooked a finger. Molly really, really wanted to find that arrogant, but the sight of him aroused and ready for her made her breath catch, her body melt. Kicking off the slippers, she straddled him, and because he was her own personal piece of insanity, leaned in to tug on the ring that had led her into trouble in the first place.

His lips curved, and the painful happiness inside her grew bigger, threatening to crush her ribs outward.

"Kiss me, Molly."

It was one demand he'd never have to make twice. Burying her hands in the thick silk of his hair, she indulged herself in the taste of Fox, having missed him until it hurt.

PLEASURE THICK IN HIS VEINS, Fox ended the kiss on a soft suck of sound and looked into brown eyes that held a pained vulnerability. He felt something tear inside him, the need to take care of her a violent craving. "Come here." Kissing her with all the tenderness he had in him, he brushed his hands up and under her T-shirt to caress the lush cream of her skin.

Touch by touch, kiss by kiss, he gentled her, seduced her, the raw sexual possessiveness he always felt when it came to Molly tempered by a vicious protectiveness. By the time he pulled off her T-shirt, she was liquid honey around him.

Easing her down onto the sofa on her back, he bared her lower half then rose to strip, conscious of the way she watched him.

"You're so beautiful." It was a husky feminine whisper as he came down on top of her.

Fox drew up her thigh and, pausing only to check she was ready for him, pushed into the welcoming heat of her body. He needed to be inside her, needed to reclaim her. Molly gasped, her neatly cut nails digging into his arms and her thighs wrapping around him.

God, she felt good, felt like his. Pulling her hands off his arms to place them on either side of her head, he wove his fingers with her own, their eyes locked as he rode her slow and deep; Molly moved with him, sensual and natural and fucking perfect.

Fox had done plenty of debauched things in the twenty-seven years he'd been on this earth, had treated sex as a bodily need, found pleasure before... but this... "Look at me, baby," he demanded when her lashes fluttered down, her body an erotic song below his own.

Deep brown eyes met his own. "Fox."

His name was the last word either one of them spoke as they rocked together to a pleasure that was a passionate kiss that engulfed both their bodies. And through it all, they held the eye contact, their hands clasped.

It was the most starkly intimate moment of Fox's life.

"HOW WAS DINNER?" MOLLY ASKED a long time later, cradled against Fox's chest.

He'd sat back up after his breathing evened out and taken her with him, her legs on either side of his and her head on his shoulder. It was an unquestionably sexual position with both of them nude, but this felt affectionate... as the sex had felt like so much more. Now, from the way Fox was running his hand slowly over her back, it was clear he was pleasing himself as much as he was pleasing her. That did things to her she didn't want to accept, didn't want to think about.

"Bullshitted with the guys," he said in answer, the vibration of his voice against her another small but potent intimacy. "Played some music. It was good."

Molly went to speak, closed her mouth, afraid she'd break this moment. The way Fox had touched her, possessed her; the way he'd held her gaze to the very end; the way he'd so gently kissed her cheeks, her nose, her closed eyelids after the pleasure caught them both in its relentless current; it was more than she'd ever expected. Warm and strong and protective around her, he was everything, *everything* she'd never dared dream of. Why did he have to be from a world she could never survive?

Throat thick, she pressed a kiss to his collarbone, staying tucked up against him. "Thank you for stealing Noah's boat." For coming to her.

"You always let strange men in at night?"

Molly's lips kicked up at the corners, the terrifying emotion that threatened to rip her apart woven through with a playfulness Fox alone seemed to awaken. "Only rock stars I'm banging."

His laughter rumbled against her, his growling bite at her throat making her smile deepen. She was *so* happy. "It's my turn to help close up the library tomorrow," she said, trying not to worry about the inevitable flip side to this painful happiness, "so I have a later start. We can have a nice breakfast." She didn't want him to go, wanted to hold on for every minute, every second that he was hers.

Fox brushed aside her hair to bare her cheek. "About your father." He stroked his other hand over the bare curve of her hip. "I'm sorry you went through that."

Molly had been hoping he wouldn't want to discuss the topic, though she'd known the hope was a foolish one. "It happened a long time ago." She'd quietly begun to use her mother's last name at eighteen, instead of her father's, closing the chapter on that part of her history.

"You turned me down for dinner today because of it. It matters." Wrapping his arms around her until she felt warm and safe and shielded from the cruelty of the world, he said, "You matter."

Her barriers shattered. "It was all so sordid." Swallowing the jagged rock in her throat, she fisted her hands against his chest and lifted her face to his. "All my life, I grew up with people idolizing my father—youngest politician ever to hold such a critical post, part of the ruling party, landslide victor of a major seat he continuously held through multiple elections, active in charities, smart, handsome, witty."

Molly, too, had adored him—until she'd grown old enough to see through the illusion and her mother's desperate fantasies, begun to understand that Patrick Buchanan cared only about himself. "Then he was busted with that girl my age, from my own *school*, in the back seat of his car, and I saw the other side of fame."

Patrick Buchanan had been charged with statutory rape, though the girl, the *child*, had insisted it was consensual. "They released him on bail because he was a 'pillar of the community,' but the press hounded him." She'd often wondered if her parents would both still be alive if the judge had made a different decision. "They camped out in front of the house night and day."

Fox's arms tightened. "Ah, hell, baby."

"At least he deserved it, but they also hounded my mother. Asking her how she felt. How did they think she felt?" Her voice rose as old anger, old pain, had her thumping her bone-white fists against his chest. "I was in the car one day when a reporter shoved a microphone through the window as we left the drive and asked her if my father made deviant sexual requests in the bedroom." Molly had almost thrown up.

Fox muttered some brutal words, cradling the side of her face with one big hand, his other arm steel around her.

"I was protected from any direct questions by the fact I was a minor," she continued, the words shoving to get out after having been suffocated for nine long years, "but everyone at school knew." Name suppression had been pointless when the photos of her father with the girl had been plastered across the Internet, the original images taken by a jealous boy who'd followed his fifteen-year-old girlfriend to the assignation.

"That's when I learned how cruel people can be." The boy who'd originally posted the photos had ended up in serious trouble, too, for distributing sexual images of a minor, but the damage was done. "I didn't defend myself at first—I knew it was that poor girl who continued to stick by my father, saying they were 'in love,' who was the true victim." Instead, Molly had taken blow after blow in penance, her soul bruised black and blue.

"Then"—she took a shuddering breath and buried her face against his shoulder, the memory vicious—"someone set up a page about me on a website we all used, calling me a slut and a whore and saying I'd probably had something going on with my father." Nauseated, she'd curled over in the computer lab, dry heaving as her classmates stared... or sniggered. "I'd never even been kissed, but boys I didn't know started posting that I'd done sexual things with them, that I was a 'freak.' I knew I had to fight back then or they'd break me."

"Hey." Fox's hand on the back of her head. "The shitheads don't matter."

Shaking from the ugliness of the memories, she tried to curl impossibly deeper into him. "It wasn't the bullies who did the real harm, it was the way the people I'd thought were my friends joined in." The exclusive all-girls private school her father had insisted she attend, because that was where the child of a man of his "stature" should go, had turned overnight into a toxic hothouse.

Furious her tears wouldn't stop falling, she swiped her hands across her cheeks. "Suddenly I wasn't being invited over for sleepovers and birthday parties, and even the people who didn't join in with the bullies looked uncomfortable when I walked by." Charlotte alone had never turned her back, Molly's small, fierce, loyal defender.

"I heard the other students gossiping about how I groomed my friends for my father, even though I didn't know the girl at the center of it all." The two of them hadn't had a single class together. "Then the media reported children's services had been to the house to see if I needed to be removed, and it was read as confirmation of the rumors. It was ugly."

"Fuck, baby, you must've been strong as hell to stick it out," Fox said, his voice holding a taut, angry tension. "Most kids would've left school for home study."

"I did that later, when I was told I was being transferred to a public school." Traumatized from her parents' deaths after a horrific year, she'd had no resources left to deal with a whole new set of bullies. To their credit, children's services hadn't argued with her decision, instead helping her enroll in an accredited correspondence course.

"But back at the start," she continued through a throat that felt as if it had been shredded by a steel grater, "I was determined to show them all." It was teeth-gritted rage that had driven her. "Now I look back and wonder why it was so important to me when I hated most of my schoolmates by the end of the first week after it began."

"No, I get it." Fox kissed the side of her face, his embrace a living barrier against the darkness. "Part of the reason I raised so much hell as a teenager was to show my mother I didn't give a shit."

CHAPTER 14

FOX NEVER SPOKE ABOUT HIS mother beyond the obvious, but when Molly raised her head, wiping the backs of her hands over her eyes to rid herself of the remnants of her tears before touching her fingers to his face, he knew she was about to ask for more. He would answer. After the brutal honesty of what she'd shared, to do anything else was unthinkable.

"Your mother, you were mad at her because she left you as a baby?" Her own eyes were yet bruised from the ugly memories of her teenage years, but her voice was painfully gentle, as if she was afraid of hurting him.

Fuck, what the *hell* was he going to do about this? Because no damn way was he walking away from Molly. "That was the best thing she ever did for me," he said. "My mother was young, couldn't handle a child." He shrugged. "Gramps and Grammy might've been old-fashioned, not overly expressive, but I was safe, healthy, happy."

One of his earliest memories of his mother was of her telling him to "Behave," because his grandparents had been very good about putting off their retirement plans to look after him. So he'd always known he wasn't a choice his grandparents had made—but that hadn't mattered. Not when they'd never treated him as if he was just a responsibility.

"My mother used to come by now and then." His muscles tensed, anger a dark burn beneath his skin. "She'd bring me gifts, play a game or two, then be gone." For days afterward, her perfume—floral and rich—would linger in the house. That was how he knew she came to visit other times, too, while he was at school or with friends. He hadn't been jealous about that. "I knew she was my mother," he told Molly, "but to me, she felt more like a distant aunt, so I never felt neglected or treated unfairly. Gramps and Grammy were my parents."

Molly pressed a gentle kiss to his cheek, her hands stroking his nape—as if she knew what was coming was going to be bad.

Holding her close, he opened the doorway to the echoes of a lost little boy's grief. "When I was seven, my grandmother died, and my grandfather followed three weeks later." It had destroyed his world.

Molly hugged him tight, her tears quiet. Burying his face against her neck, he breathed in the warm, sweet scent of her and told her the rest. "I went to live with my mother and her family."

Molly sucked in a breath.

"Yeah," he said with a twist of his lips, "she'd pulled herself together a couple of years after she had me, married into money and had another child, a girl three years younger than me." He clenched his hand against Molly's spine. "Turned out she'd never told her Ivy League husband about me, and the prick refused to bring up 'some piece of trash' she'd had off a stranger in a club."

"Prick is too nice a word." Molly pulled back to look him in the eye, her expression livid in a way he'd never seen, not even when they'd fought. "Who *says* that in front of a grieving child? He deserves to be horsewhipped, the useless waste of space."

Fox found himself grinning, the last thing he'd ever have expected. "Trust me, I've had a few fantasies along those lines—before I realized the limp-dicked fucker wasn't worth it."

Kissing him in that way she had of doing, one that always made his grin deepen, Molly said, "I'm sorry you had to live with such ugliness," and brushed her fingers through his hair.

Fox's smile faded. "I didn't—to cut a long story short, the prick told my mother it was either him or me, and she chose him. I was placed in a boarding school in another state and left there to rot." No way to dress it up and he'd stopped trying to convince himself otherwise a hell of a long time ago. "It was an expensive place, a sop to her conscience I guess. As she led me inside, she said, 'I love you, Zachary,' and it was the first time in my life anyone had ever spoken those words to me."

Hearing the way he bit off the declaration, Molly knew the damage done that day had been brutal. Fox likely never again wanted to hear those words, wouldn't trust them if he did.

"I was never invited back to their house," he continued in the same harsh tone, "spent my vacations at the school and, later, at Noah's house. My mother visited about twice a year, when I suppose she could sneak around the prick—or when she could be bothered." He leaned back against the sofa, his fingers digging into her hips as his grip tightened. "When I was ten, I told her I didn't want to see her again."

Molly's chest throbbed with an ache that made her eyes hot, but she didn't allow her sadness for the boy he'd been to

127

show. Fox, she knew instinctively, was too proud to accept that. Instead, she ran her hand down to tug at one of his, twining their fingers together when he allowed her to take it. Neither did she ask him if his mother had listened to what had been a desperate cry for love disguised as anger—his face told her the truth.

"Thank you for trusting me." Grazing the rigid line of his jaw with her fingertips, she rubbed her nose gently against his. "I know that can't have been easy."

"It's not exactly a secret." He thrust his free hand through his hair. "The tabloids and gossip sites dug up every dirty detail of my life as soon as Schoolboy Choir hit the big time."

"Mine wasn't secret either," she pointed out. "It still hurts to talk about it."

His brow darkened. "I'm a man. I don't have feelings."

"Ha-ha." A deep tenderness in her veins that she knew was going to get her into bad, bad trouble, the kind of trouble that could permanently scar, she kissed him on a wave of heartbreaking emotion. The contact helped heal the torn-up places inside her, at least a little.

She hoped it did the same for him.

His hands warm on her lower back, he pressed his forehead against hers afterward, their breath mingling. "I have a plan for Sydney."

Molly stifled her immediate negative reaction, unable to back away after the emotional honesty of the past few minutes. Fox, she thought, wouldn't be so tender with her, only to disregard her deepest fear. "Tell me."

"You're going to be a roadie."

Blinking, she stared at him. "I am?"

"Yep. Stick a Schoolboy Choir crew cap on your head, give you a pair of big, black-framed glasses and a clipboard, and you'll become invisible to the media." A coaxing kind of a kiss, his hand cupping her nape. "Say yes, Molly." Wickedness in the smoky green.

Molly felt her heart catch; she'd much rather see him this way than angry and hurt.

His next words were as wicked as his gaze, as his smile. "I don't think my cock will survive a weekend without you."

It wasn't the most romantic invitation, but that did nothing to alter the fact that he was planning to go to a lot of trouble to have her with him. *Her*, Molly, when he could have any woman for the taking at the concert. Inhaling a deep breath, she seriously considered his suggestion. No one would ever mistake her for a starlet or supermodel, especially with the crew accoutrements Fox had suggested, and if she dressed down as she assumed the crew did.

It wasn't as if she'd run the risk of a reporter spontaneously recognizing her from the old scandal. Molly Buchanan had been a late-blooming and gawky teen with braces whose breasts had barely budded. Molly Webster was a twenty-four-year-old with a rock star for a lover, a rock star who loved her curves. So long as she didn't do anything to make someone pay specific attention to her past, no one would ever connect the girl with the woman. Her colleagues at the library certainly hadn't.

"I think," she said, adrenaline pumping through her veins, "I like the idea of being undercover."

"That's my Molly." This time his kiss was unashamedly sexual, his arousal long and thick against her inner thigh. Breathing in shallow pants when he broke the kiss, she watched his mouth as he spoke, his lip ring an outward sign of who he was: Fox wasn't a bad boy—he was the harder, more demanding, grown-up version.

"We'll fly out on different flights," he told her. "That'll make sure no one connects the two of us." Hands on her thighs, he smiled *that* smile, the one that dared her to do naughty, naughty things. "Ride me."

"I...I've never..." Sucking in air, heat rising up her body in a lush pink wave that made Fox cuddle her closer, she admitted the truth. "Not on my own." He'd always helped her. "Teach me how."

He used the hand he had on the back of her neck to haul her down to his mouth, his tongue thrusting aggressively between her lips. "You're gonna kill me," he said afterward, cheekbones painted with a red flush. "I never was into the whole professor-student deal, but I've changed my mind."

"Fox." She tugged at his lip ring in retaliation for the sensual teasing, playfully threatening to pull it off.

Smile deep, he positioned her until the blunt head of his cock nudged at her, but he didn't allow her to push down. "Use your hand to guide me." He cupped her jaw, holding her in place for what she'd come to think of as a "just because" kiss, indulging himself in her.

It made her melt.

"Professor Fox," he said against her lips, "promises to grade you fairly."

"You," she said, a wild sensual joy within, "shouldn't be set loose on unsuspecting women."

An unrepentant look. "Class is in session, Miss Webster."

So wet it would've been embarrassing if she weren't with

Fox, with whom nothing was taboo, she reached down between them to close her hand over his thickness.

"Ah, damn, that feels good."

Her breasts aching at that masculine growl, Molly discovered a long-hidden streak of wickedness within herself. "Enough for an A?"

"The exam"—the tendons in Fox's neck strained taut—"is ongoing." He hissed out a breath as she took the first inch of his rigid length inside her, her tissues stretching deliciously.

"Oh." Removing her hand, she pushed down, eager to feel all of him.

Fox shuddered, one strong arm locked around her upper back, his other hand on her thigh. "Move on me, baby."

He kissed her endlessly as she rocked on him, his free hand shifting to lie on her butt, urging her into a faster rhythm. She might've been the one on top, Molly thought before thinking became a vain hope, but Fox was in charge. The insight only made her wetter, needier, and soon the only sounds in the room were those of their rasped breaths and of skin slapping on skin.

When she came apart in his arms on a breathless scream, her vision hazing, he held her close and whispered, "My beautiful Molly."

Another piece of her heart splintered away.

A second later, he thrust deep, holding himself there as he came in an intimate pulse inside her. One hand in his hair, her other arm around the width of his shoulders, she held him through his pleasure, emotion a knot inside her chest... and spluttered with surprised laughter when he pressed an open-mouthed kiss to her throat and said, "We need to schedule a retest as soon as possible—it appears Professor Fox has difficulty grading and fucking at the same time."

MOLLY SPENT THE REST OF the week attempting to come to terms with the fact she was about to fly off for a secret weekend with Zachary Fox, rock star, and the most intriguing, complex, and gorgeous man she'd ever known. Charlotte, when they met for lunch on Thursday, dragged her off to a designer lingerie shop. "You have a smoking-hot man who wants to do you six ways to Sunday. I say this calls for ridiculously expensive French lingerie."

A fluttering sensation in her abdomen, Molly spent the next ten minutes touching the rich fabrics and laces, buttery and soft. "I can't afford most of this." She kept her voice to a whisper so the sales assistant wouldn't give them the evil eye.

"Liar." A poke in the ribs. "You might not be rich, but you hoard any extra money you have."

That was the trouble with having a best friend who knew her so well. "What's the point of buying lingerie that'll stay on for five seconds at most?" she muttered instead of thinking about why it was so important to her to have a nest egg tucked away.

"Five *seconds*?" Charlotte put a hand over her heart with a dramatic sigh. "Wait while I have an orgasm."

"What, you still haven't jumped T-Rex? Even now that you two are attached at the hip?" To her best friend's shock and Molly's glee, Charlotte had been promoted to T-Rex's personal assistant without warning.

Anya, meanwhile, had been given her marching orders.

Charlotte made a face at her. "Why would I want to jump a man who yells at me one minute and leaves chocolate cake on my desk the next?"

"What?" Paying for the decadent bra-and-panty set she hadn't been able to resist, Molly pointed a finger at her best friend. "You've been holding out on me."

"Hah! More like I've been protecting you from the madness," Charlotte said as they walked out, her eyebrows drawn ominously together. "This is only my second day in the position, but he's already driving me insane. Yesterday he made me work till ten at night, caused me to miss a date with Ernest—"

Not giving herself time to second-guess her reaction, Molly said, "What you and Ernest are doing isn't called dating, Charlie."

Charlotte folded her arms, a mutinous expression on her face. "So maybe he hasn't made a move—"

"After a *year*." Molly didn't normally push Charlotte on this topic because she knew why her friend made the choices she did, but Charlotte was definitely reacting to T-Rex, and it was the first positive sign of deep healing Molly had seen in her. She'd be no kind of best friend if she didn't nudge that healing along. "Doesn't Ernest spend the whole time telling you about his model-airplane collection?"

A glare. "I admit he's a bit obsessed with his models, but he's small like me, kind, and he doesn't raise his voice at me."

"You know I like Ernest; he's a lovely, sweet man." She bumped her shoulder against Charlotte's. "I understand why you *want* to be attracted to him"—the reason a heartbreaking one—"but the truth is you aren't."

Charlotte ducked her head, not saying anything.

Refusing to give up, Molly said, "You convinced me to be brave. I think you can be, too."

"I'm not like you, you know that."

"Do I?" Molly shook her head. "You said you were in awe of me for standing up to Queen Bitchface, but I remember you telling off the worst clique in the school until they crawled off with their tails between their legs." Her best friend had been a tiny blonde fury that day.

"It's different when it's someone I love. When it's me..." Charlotte swallowed, her next words a rasped whisper. "He scares me."

Her hope for Charlotte flickering under the sudden cold front of her friend's words, Molly drew Charlotte to a bench in the nearby square, the falling water of the fountain quiet music in the background. "T-Rex?" Receiving a nod, she put her hand over Charlotte's. "Are you afraid to be around him?" If her instincts had led her in the wrong direction and this guy was—

"No," Charlotte said before Molly's mind could continue along that disturbing path. "No, not like that." She checked her watch. "We better go—we'll be late getting back to work."

"I'll make up the time." This conversation was too important to abandon. "And since T-Rex didn't let you leave till ten last night, I'm sure he can't argue against a long lunch today."

"Yes, he can." It was a grumpy response.

"Do I need to storm the battlements and steal you away from his clutches?"

"Ha-ha." Charlotte bit down on her lower lip before blurting out, "He scares me because of the way he makes me react. Sometimes I want to grab that tie of his and—"

"Do the kind of things I've been doing with my rock star?"

Charlotte's blush was adorable. "Only in my more insane moments." She pushed up her glasses in a quick, nervous movement. "Have you *seen* how big he is?"

"Sexy big." All wide shoulders and heavy muscle, though he had nothing on Fox as far as Molly was concerned. "Also, you shouldn't expect rational advice from me—I brought a man home after meeting him in an elevator."

Charlotte's shoulders shook, eyes gleaming. "Now you're about to head off with him for a dirty, dirty weekend."

Molly dropped her head in her hands. "What am I doing, Charlie?"

"I told you," her friend said softly, "being the brave one." She jumped as her cell phone rang. "It's His Carnivorousness," she muttered after glancing at the caller display, then answered in a professional tone. "Hello, Charlotte speaking."

A pause, Molly watching in interest as Charlotte's eyes sparked fire.

"Yes, I realize that," her best friend said, still in that polite tone. "However, I did work well beyond my contracted hours yesterday."

Another pause. Charlie's teeth gritted as her fingers clenched on the phone. "Yes, I am," she said in response to whatever she'd heard. "In fact, we're about to check into a hotel."

Molly squeaked, slapped a hand over her mouth. "Did you just tell your boss you were about to check into a hotel with Ernest?" she asked when Charlotte stabbed the End key.

Charlotte's eyes went huge. "Oh *God!*" she wailed, as if only now realizing what she'd done. "I told you he was driving me insane."

Molly nudged Charlotte's head between her knees when her friend began to hyperventilate. "Breathe, Charlie."

It took several minutes, Charlotte's face bright red even after she'd sat up for another couple of minutes. "I can't go back to the office now. I'll have to quit."

"No, you don't." Delighted that dealing with T-Rex was forcing Charlotte out of hiding, Molly dragged her to her feet and walked her to her office. Charlotte's breathing was choppy again by the time she stepped through the automatic doors.

"Be brave," Molly mouthed when her friend paused in the open doorway and looked over her shoulder.

A shaky smile, then Charlotte squared her shoulders and mouthed the same thing back at her. *Be brave.*

CHAPTER 15

HAVING TAKEN TWO DAYS OFF work, Molly stepped out of the Arrivals gate at Sydney Airport early afternoon the next day to find a driver waiting for her. He held a sign that said only SC Crew. Already in her roadie disguise, complete with jeans, cap, and a long-sleeved, checked shirt, she followed him to the car and got in. No one seemed to pay her any special attention—either at the airport, or when she checked into the hotel—though according to Fox, she had the room that directly connected with his.

His room wasn't booked under his name, of course, but that of another roadie. The other man was having a luxurious time up on the penthouse floor with the other members of the band while Fox and Molly had the invaluable gift of privacy.

As she walked into her room, having brought up her own luggage—a single wheeled suitcase—she couldn't help but think how smooth the whole operation had been to this point. That, of course, led her mind to wonder how many times Fox had done this type of thing before and with how many different women. She'd grown up with a man who juggled women like multicolored balls, knew how—

"Stop, Molly!" She cut off the hurtful train of thought the instant she realized where she was headed, annoyed with herself for doing her best to ruin the weekend before it began.

Fox wasn't her father.

In fact, the two men didn't even belong to the same species. Her father had been a particular kind of slime, and it wasn't the fifteen-year-old girl he'd been discovered with who'd been his first victim. Thea's mother, Lily, had been an innocent and trusting nineteen-year-old when he'd seduced her after convincing her that his marriage was about to end, only to arrange for her deportation when she fell pregnant.

Linking Fox to Patrick in any way was an insult to Fox.

With that mental reminder, she dumped her luggage on the stand in the corner, then pushed aside the curtains to expose an incredible view of Darling Harbour. The water glittered under the bright sunlight, the restaurants and cafés around it busy with locals and tourists both, while yellow water taxis bobbed at the nearest edge.

"This is the life," she murmured, shaking her head.

What in the world was she doing here?

A glance at the connecting door gave her the answer. Beyond it lay the room and the bed of a man who'd become her addiction. He made her come alive in ways she'd never believed she could, had taught her she had the capacity to feel with a wild passion she hadn't thought existed inside her. What would she do when he left?

The stab of pain in her gut was answer enough.

Walking over to the connecting door before the promise of future agony could paralyze her, she undid the lock on her side and tried the handle. It turned easily and while the room beyond was empty, she knew without a doubt it was Fox's. His aftershave lingered in the air, one of his T-shirts was thrown across the bed, and a blue-green guitar pick lay on the bedside table. It was the one he'd used when he'd come to her house, the one that was his second favorite.

Smiling, she picked it up from the pile of papers on the bedside table. Blank sheet music, she noted absently, then realized not all the pages were blank. The one partially sticking out at the bottom had notations made in the light blue ink of the hotel pen that had rolled to lie against the lampstand.

She touched her fingers to the notes, feeling as if she'd glimpsed a secret. She'd known Fox had written a number of Schoolboy Choir's songs, the majority in concert with David, but she hadn't realized he had formal musical training. It simply made him more fascinating, made her wonder how many more facets of him she hadn't glimpsed... would never get the chance to know.

She only had him for three more weeks, a blink in a lifetime.

Breathing past the melancholy thought, she tidied up the pages, then walked back into her own room, leaving the door open. Since the flight had only been a quick three hours, she wasn't tired, and the idea of sitting in her hotel room didn't appeal. She was considering heading down to grab a coffee at one of the harborside cafés when there was a brisk knock on the door.

Opening it, she found herself facing not a member of the hotel staff but a bearded man dressed in a Schoolboy Choir T-shirt, the black fabric stretched over a significant beer gut and tucked into faded blue jeans. On his head was a battered New York Yankees cap, and around his neck hung a nametag that identified him as part of the band's crew.

"You Molly?" He grunted, then looked down at his clipboard. "Yep, you're her." With that, he thrust a lanyard and attached nametag at her. "Make sure you don't lose that. It's your passport backstage—without it, security will throw you out."

Molly placed the lanyard around her neck, the photo on it a shot Fox had taken with his phone one night after dinner. "Got it." She turned and grabbed the small backpack she'd carried on the plane.

Grunting again, the man scratched at the salt and pepper of his beard, then nodded at her to follow him. "So, you actually know any shit or are you just here to fuck Fox?"

His tone was so matter-of-fact that Molly answered before embarrassment could steal her tongue. "Fox must trust you a lot."

A narrow-eyed look. "Hmm. Brains." He stuck out his hand. "I'm Maxwell. Don't call me Max."

"Nice to meet you, Maxwell. Are you the roadie in chief?"

"Roadie in chief?" He let out a deep laugh, slapping his beer belly. "Yeah, that's me. I think I'm gonna put that on my business cards. Maxwell, Roadie in Chief."

Laughing along with him, his amusement good-natured rather that mocking, she said, "Where are we going?"

"Out to where the band's performing tomorrow night." He stuck his pencil behind his ear, scowled again. "Never done anything this big this fast before, but it's sick babies. Whattaya gonna do?"

"You flew down for this?" Molly had expected the band to just turn up on a temporary stage with borrowed equipment... but of course not. They had a reputation for the caliber of their concerts, would certainly not shortchange the charity or their fans by putting on a mediocre show.

"Boys flew our whole team down," Maxwell told her. "Impossible to set up a show this big with a new crew, even with things stripped down to the basics." Adjusting his cap, he led her out through a side entrance that exited into an open-air parking lot. "Today's all about fine-tuning things, making sure the setup will work with the boys when they get going."

Molly paused when Maxwell slid open the back door of a van and placed his clipboard on top of what looked like electronic equipment. "You know," she said after he slid the door shut, hoping he wouldn't take offense, "I don't really know you and you want me to get in a black van with tinted windows."

Booming laughter. "Yep. Brains." Pulling out his phone with that pleased statement, he brought up the band's website and took her to the Photos section. "Here."

There was Maxwell with his arm around a sweaty post-concert Fox. Underneath were the words: *Fox and Man-In-Charge-of-Everything, Maxwell, after the Chicago show.*

"Convinced I don't plan to drive you into the outback and feed you to the kangaroos?" Maxwell asked, a twinkle in his pale blue eyes.

Grinning, she said, "Can I look at the other photos?"

"Sure." He handed her the phone. "If it rings, answer it for me—and by the way, you're meant to be the roadie version of an intern, so nobody's going to expect you to know much anyway."

Molly waited until she'd belted herself in and Maxwell was pulling out before saying, "That's clever." She thought she'd kept her voice light and nonconfrontational, but Maxwell shot her a sideways look.

"Yeah, Fox's clever." A short pause. "Hasn't ever used that brain of his to get a woman backstage incognito before though. Never snuck around with any woman, as a matter of fact. Always liked that about him—he doesn't mess with women who aren't free to play."

Molly wanted to squirm and avoid the issue, but the fact was, she was the one who'd put Fox in this position with someone who was clearly important enough to him that he'd trusted the other man with the truth, and she had to own up to it. "I'm free," she said quietly. "I just don't want to be famous."

Maxwell nodded. "Fair enough. Can't escape being famous if you're with Fox, though, so you better get used to the idea soon."

Molly didn't say anything to that—it was obvious Maxwell thought this was a long-term relationship given the effort Fox had gone to for her. Her fingernails dug into her palms, the idea of having Fox as her own a powerfully seductive one. It didn't matter that she knew the relationship would never last in the hothouse atmosphere of a rock star's life; this was her fantasy... at least for a short while longer.

It made her stomach hurt to imagine opening a magazine one day in the future and seeing him in the arms of another woman. A woman who would be right for him because she could survive in the environment in which he thrived, the roar of the crowds and the glare of the lights electricity in his blood.

Staring out the window until she could breathe again, she finished going through the photos on the band's website. They told a story—of friendship, camaraderie, music, and parties. So many parties. So many beautiful women. All of them in skimpy clothes worn over taut, toned bodies, bodies that were usually draped over one member of the band or another.

Including Fox.

She closed the browser and put the phone in the cup holder. The photos hadn't shown her anything she hadn't already known—the fantasy was wonderful, but the harsh reality was that their lives and worlds were poles apart, would never again intersect after this month was over. Again, that stabbing in her abdomen, sharp and brutal, her throat thick.

"Here we go." Maxwell drove through metal security gates after waving at the guards, and into what appeared to be a massive playing field or park with an unexpectedly solid-appearing temporary stage set up on one end.

Hopping out once they'd parked, Molly put on her fake glasses and helped Maxwell carry some of his more delicate equipment to the electronic nerve center of the concert, all of the audio and lights controlled by technology Molly had as much hope of understanding as she had of flying a fighter jet. That was when she saw Fox—he was on the stage with one of his bandmates. The blond one.

Noah.

The other man had recently been featured in a magazine article about the world's most beautiful people, but it was to Fox alone that her eyes were drawn. Even dressed in one of his ubiquitous black T-shirts and a pair of old jeans, he exuded

143

strength and a lazy sexuality as he and Noah apparently tested the sound system using electric guitars. She'd known he played one but had never had the chance to watch him perform live, was fascinated by how he held and moved with the instrument.

The guitar was gleaming red, of course.

Her lips curved.

"Don't watch him like that if you want this to work."

Coloring at Maxwell's low-voiced warning, Molly turned away... just as Fox glanced at her. Her body responded to the touch of that smoky-green gaze as it always did, but aware of how many other people moved around them, she pinned her eyes to Maxwell's back and became his shadow for the rest of the afternoon. While it was difficult to keep her attention off the man for whom she'd come here, she didn't have to feign interest in the work it took to set up a big show—even a "stripped down" one.

There was the big stuff like setting up the stage and any pyrotechnics, but all that had been done already. Today, it was about going over the myriad tiny details, from making dead sure each of the speakers around the grounds was functioning as it should, to checking the individual lamps in the light system, to ensuring catering staff knew what to bring in for band and crew both, to confirming that there was a fridge backstage for the water and sports drinks.

Maxwell had every one of those thousand-and-one things on a mental checklist and he used Molly like she was a real intern.

Dropping her bag to the floor when she returned to the hotel room, Molly took off the black-framed glasses she'd worn for the past hours and flopped down on her back in bed. "I hope you pay Maxwell what he's worth," she said to the half-naked man who'd come to lean in the doorway between their rooms.

"Why do you think he's still with us?" Prowling over, Fox straddled her supine body, the top button on his jeans undone to reveal a hint of dark hair.

Oh, but he was beautiful.

With that mental sigh, she placed her hands on his abdomen and shivered at the flex of all that gorgeous muscle as he leaned down to nibble at her lips.

"Sorry I left you to Maxwell's devices." Whiskey and hard rock, his voice had her nipples beading against the cotton of her bra, the heat of his body another kiss.

"It's part of my cover." Her breath caught at the sensation of his mouth on her throat. "I could hardly leave with the band when I'm meant to be learning the ropes."

"Are you telling me you're too tired?" Raising his head from her throat, he settled his lower body more heavily against her.

"I," she somehow managed to say, her breasts swelling and lower body clenching, "am telling you I need a bath and a massage."

A deeper smile, the dimple lean against his cheek. "Since they both involve your naked body"—words punctuated by kisses that made her smile even as they made her want—"I'm willing to make the arrangements." Petting her breasts with bold possessiveness, he pushed off her and the bed. "Stay there."

Since he'd turned her limbs to jelly, Molly had no trouble obeying. She heard him turn on the water and then he walked back into the room. "Let's get you naked while the bath's filling."

"You know," she said, teeth sinking into her lower lip and her mind blaring a warning she ignored, "we spend a lot of our time together naked."

Fox's expression was pure sin as he tugged off her sneakers and socks. "Are you complaining?"

"I'm not insane." Being naked with Fox was the experience of a lifetime, but part of her wished they could do things like the market more often, like any ordinary couple. Her chest ached at the idea of it.

She knew it was her fault that they couldn't. Fox hadn't ever wanted to treat her like a dirty little secret. *She* was the one who'd made that choice, decided to hide what was becoming a relationship she knew she'd never forget, even if she lived to be a hundred years old.

One month. Don't let the pain to come steal your one glorious month with him.

Swallowing her tears, she held out her hand to the rock star who kept slicing away pieces of her heart.

CHAPTER 16

FOX SLID INTO THE BATH behind Molly, luxuriating in having her here. He knew it was a big step for the woman whose smile had captivated him and whose heart, intelligence, and honest, generous sensuality now held him prisoner. He intended to do everything in his power to make her see his life through a less aggressive and less terrifying lens. Being a roadie wasn't the same as being his, but it provided a gentle, easy introduction to his world—because he wanted, *needed* her with him, and he'd do whatever it took to convince her to take a chance on him.

The hard stuff… yeah, that could wait until she'd committed to him.

Turning her face, she kissed his jaw. "I missed you last night."

He'd missed her, too, hating the cold loneliness of the hotel bed. Now, cupping the heavy warmth of her breasts from behind, he took her mouth in ravenous demand, soothing the ragged edges of his need enough that he could take this slow. "How was dinner with Thea and Charlotte?" Meeting her best friend was on his agenda—Charlotte was clearly important to Molly, and so the other woman was important to Fox.

"I made a Thai mango-chicken salad. It was a success." She softened against him as he moved his hands from her breasts to massage her shoulders and arms, aware how hard Maxwell could work his people.

Molly sighed and closed her eyes, the quiet expression of trust his undoing. "Can I just stay here?"

Grabbing the loofah she'd fished out of her toiletries case, he squeezed some liquid soap onto it. "No," he said, smoothing the puffy, girly thing over her body for the simple pleasure of touching her. "I fucking hate cold water."

Her laugh was startled, her eyes sparkling when she looked up. As she sassed him about being a tough-guy rocker, he thought of the wistfulness he'd sensed in her when she'd spoken of the amount of time they spent in bed and promised himself they'd do something silly and touristy and fun together in Sydney.

He wanted to take his Molly on a date.

MOLLY SLEPT IN FOX'S ARMS. The first time she woke, it was to the thick heat of him sliding inside her; the second time, she found herself alone, though the pale morning light told her it wasn't yet time to go to the site—and Fox would've woken her for that anyway. Sitting up, she pushed her hair out of her eyes and looked around for a note. It was scrawled on a slip of hotel paper thrust under the radio alarm clock.

David fucked up. Gone to see what I can do.—Fox

David? The one the press called the Gentleman of Rock?

Frowning, she pushed off the comforter Fox must've covered her with before he left, his body heat more than sufficient to keep her warm when he was with her. She had to have slept through a phone call. Or Fox had already been up and grabbed it before it could wake her—her rock star, she'd learned, was a surprisingly early riser. Hoping David wasn't in too much trouble, she showered and dressed for the day before calling Fox. It went straight to voice mail.

"It's Molly," she said. "Just wanted to say I hope it's nothing serious. Talk to you when you get back."

Since she didn't know if Fox would return before she had to meet up with the crew, she decided to go down to the hotel's breakfast buffet. "Mind if I join you?" she asked when she saw Maxwell sitting alone at a table in the relatively empty dining room.

"I never say no to a pretty girl."

Smiling, Molly went to get a bowl of cereal and some toast. There was fresh coffee waiting for her at the table when she returned, as well as a glass of orange juice. "Seriously," she said, "this is the life."

"Not after you eat the same crap weeks in a row." Maxwell's heavy black eyebrows drew together in a scowl. "When we're on tour, sometimes all I want is a bowl of grits or old-fashioned oatmeal."

Molly hadn't considered the situation from a long-term perspective, and as soon as she did, she saw his point. It was nice to be waited on and to have so many options at the buffet, but she'd be hankering for her own cereal within days, as well as her favorite brand of tea. "Do you carry things from home to make it easier?"

"Yep. What you're drinking, it's the best damn coffee in the universe—I had the hotel restaurant brew up a pot from my stash." He took a sip, sighed. "Different folks bring different things, but most everyone has at least a couple of items."

Molly tried to think of what it must be like to be on the road weeks or months at a time and couldn't quite comprehend it. It made her understand some of the "diva" requests occasionally reported in the media—for what often seemed an odd thing about which to throw a star tantrum. Food, though, was only the tip of the iceberg.

"You must miss your family," she said, having learned yesterday that the crew boss had a wife he adored as well as two teenage children.

"Yeah, it can be tough, but the boys pay me well enough that both *my* boys go to a fancy private school where they rub shoulders with the children of diplomats." Pride in his smile. "At least my kids think my job is awesome since I can get them and their friends into concerts now and then, so I don't have the hassle of having to deal with resentment. As for Kim and me, we have phone sex down to an art."

Molly choked on her coffee, heard Maxwell laughing that deep, chesty laugh as she tried to catch her breath. She mimed scrubbing the image from her mind, which furthered the laughter on his end, then said, "Do you know what happened with David?"

Sudden remoteness, the smile wiped away as if it had never existed. "Figure you'd best ask Fox."

Coloring, Molly looked down at her breakfast. "Sorry," she said quietly after realizing what she'd done. "I didn't mean to put you on the spot."

The friendly man sighed and reached out to pat her hand where it lay on the table. "No, I'm sorry for snapping at you—

we've all been bitten so many times that we don't trust anyone until they're blood. Takes time to become blood."

Molly met his gaze so he'd know there were no hard feelings. "I understand." It wasn't as if she was any different in the trust department.

Male voices sounded in the doorway a couple of seconds later, Fox walking in with David and a slender man she didn't know. Spotting her and Maxwell, they headed over, grabbing food along the way. Fox put his plate down on her left, while David took her other side, and the unfamiliar man slid into the chair beside Maxwell. In a few minutes, the table was covered with more food than Molly could eat in a week.

"Don't even ask," David muttered when she glanced at his black eye, the bruise vivid against the golden brown of his skin.

Molly poured him coffee from the fresh carafe the waiter had just placed on the table. The drummer clearly needed it—it was obvious he'd spent the night in the long-sleeved, formal white shirt and black pants he wore, his jaw darkly stubbled. "Did you put ice on that eye?"

"That's what I told him to do, but he's too pigheaded." The stranger stuck his hand across the table, his skin a warm, deep teak against the blue-gray of his suit. "Justin Chan, attorney for these idiots while they're in the region."

"Molly," Fox growled, "stop looking at David like you want to give him a hug and smack him upside the head instead. If we were in New York, I'd call his mother and have her do it."

"Don't worry," Justin said cheerily, "his folks will hear about it soon enough, and then he'll have to explain if this is the kind of example he intends to set for his brothers." A glance at David. "Wouldn't want to be you, dude."

"Oh, fuck." David banged his head against the table. "I should've stayed in jail."

Uh-oh. "Did you do something Thea's going to have to wrangle?" Her sister had flown in late last night to be on hand for media interviews the band was doing today.

Lifting his head, David groaned. "Yes. Mary, Joseph, and the saints combined, yes."

"She's been working since genius here called me." Fox bit into a piece of toast. "He was too chickenshit to call Thea himself."

"Shut the fuck up." Strong words, but the drummer's tone was morose. "God, could I have screwed up any worse?"

Molly thought about it, then leaned in to whisper in David's ear. "You might as well tell me your side of the story so I can spin it for you when Thea calms down."

Shooting her a considering look out of a bloodshot and blackened eye, he slugged back his coffee and blew out a breath. "I decided to walk around the city last night. It's something I do night before a concert." He rubbed his hands over his face. "On the way back, I ducked into a bar to have a drink. It never crossed my mind that I'd be recognized. I'm the drummer—nobody ever pays attention to the fucking drummer."

Fox snorted. "Bullshit. I've seen the stacks of fan mail." Thigh pressing against Molly's, he reached for the pats of butter beside her plate. "Mind?"

"Of course not." Feeling playful and happy to see him, she closed her hand over the muscled strength of his thigh under the table, close to the zipper of his jeans.

It earned her a warning look that told her he'd get his revenge. Stomach tight, she stroked her hand lower down, leaving

152

it there in an intimacy that coiled around her heart, and returned her attention to David. "So, someone recognized you?"

"Yep. The fuckwits decided they didn't want a 'pussy rock star' in their fine establishment." The insult was rife in his voice. "Like I was an airbrushed pop star, not a real goddamned musician." Snarling at his toast, he bit off a hunk. "I had to defend my honor, didn't I? Not my fucking fault the fucking bartender decided to call the cops just 'cause we broke a cheap-ass fucking table."

Molly had never heard David swear before this morning, not even in interviews or going up against pushy paparazzi. "Hold on," she said, wondering how much of that was leftover anger, and how much frustration at what this would do to his chances with Thea. "You were on your own, and you only came out with a black eye?"

David shrugged. "I was consistently the shortest guy in my grade until I hit seventeen. Shrimps get picked on—and my dad, he's old school. Decided to teach me how to kick ass. No one ever picked on me a second time."

His physicality something she would've never guessed at, Molly might have followed the conversational thread, but David fell to his breakfast with the concentration of a man who was done talking. She looked across the table to Justin. "Are you on call all the time?"

"That's why I get paid the big bucks." The lawyer's teeth flashed bright. "Good thing David's victims were too embarrassed to press charges—I mean, what hard man gets beat up by a pussy rock star?"

Giving him the finger, David stayed focused on his bacon and eggs.

Fox, his thigh continuing to press intimately against hers, jerked his head at Maxwell. "You feel good about tonight?"

"Setup's tight," the other man said, and the conversation drifted in another direction.

It was maybe ten minutes later, while Molly was having her second cup of coffee, that she ended up alone with David, the others having gone to pick up more food from the buffet. "You don't seem like the kind of man who gets into bar fights."

No response.

"You're crazy in love with her, aren't you?" she said softly, having grasped the depth of his feelings yesterday when he'd oh-so-casually asked her about Thea when they were backstage. The painful need in his eyes had resonated with the emotions growing inside her.

David paused with his fork against the plate, his eyes staring out into nothing. "Until I can't think. I need to get over it."

"Did you—"

"I asked her out. Had this whole argument worked out about how we'd be perfect together, but she never even gave me a shot." Fingers turning white on the metal, he said, "She cut me off so smoothly it was like being sliced off at the knees. Professional smile, distant eyes, gentle hand on my arm as she ushered me out of her office." He shook his head. "It was such a kick in the teeth that I just went."

Thea, Molly thought, was a smart woman who'd grown up cherished by two people who loved her and each other. The man Thea's mother had married when Thea was two had always treated Thea as his eldest daughter, "and no damn 'step' about it," as Thea had once quoted, love bright in her expression. Her two "baby" sisters, fourteen and fifteen respectively, saw her as their big sister and that was that—complete with teary phone calls about boys and complaints about being grounded.

Molly had met Thea's family over video calls and thought they were wonderful.

However, Thea had also had the bad luck to fall into a long-term relationship with a man who hadn't been able to handle her strength and growing success. Thea's ex had cheated on her, then blamed her for it, saying she wasn't woman enough to satisfy his needs.

Molly didn't know if David was or wasn't the right guy to help her sister get over that awful hurt, but any man sweet enough to be in love with her sister after such an icy rejection would at least treat her right, remind her that not all men were swine.

"Write a memo," she said before any of the others returned to the table. "About all the reasons why you'd be perfect together, then e-mail it to her."

David gave her a look that said he was questioning her sanity.

"Thea is surgically attached to her e-mail." Molly had figured that out the third time she and Thea had coffee together. Her sister had been on her best behavior the first two times.

Molly had actually been happy to see Thea taking quick glances at her phone—it had felt like they were both relaxed enough to be themselves for the first time, bad habits and all. "She'll read the memo because she can't help herself," Molly continued, "and if I know my sister"—which Molly thought she did, at least when it came to this aspect of Thea's personality—"she'll send you back a point-by-point rebuttal, so you'd better have your arguments ready."

Having twisted to face her, David shook his head. "That is either the worst or the best advice ever."

"Trust me." Molly took another sip of coffee. "Thea likes brains and she likes determination." Molly thought about it and decided to give him one other tiny piece of advice. "If you send her 'I'm sorry I messed up' flowers, steer clear of white roses." When David raised an eyebrow, she gave him a succinct answer. "Ex."

His jaw tightened. "Got it."

Maxwell and Justin returned to the table then, Fox waylaid by staff and guests.

"Damn." David put down his fork with a sigh as he too was spotted by a tableful of young men who, from their uniforms, looked like they were part of a high school sports team.

It wasn't until twenty minutes later that they could both eat again. Justin and Maxwell left soon afterward to take care of other matters, but Molly stuck around, promising to meet Maxwell in the parking lot in a quarter of an hour.

"That's why we mostly order room service," David said after he'd cleared his plate.

Fox leaned back with a glass of freshly squeezed orange juice. "We tend to have suites next to one another, and since Noah's always up before dawn, anyone else from the band who's up for breakfast turns up at his suite. Maxwell and some of the other crew usually find their way there as well."

"It's like a family, isn't it?" Molly snuck a strawberry from the bowl of fruit one of the men had brought back to the table.

"Depends on the people," David said, "and how long we've worked together. Maxwell, he's been with us since the first tour—most of the time, he treats us like his kids. Should piss us off, but he's got some weird voodoo going on where none of us can get mad at him. Or if we do, we feel so ashamed we end up giving him a raise."

Molly laughed when Fox nodded, his expression solemn. Then his cheeks creased and she had to dig her nails into her palms to resist the urge to kiss his smile right into her own mouth. "I better go." She cleared her throat, her voice husky. "I have to grab my stuff and meet Maxwell."

Fox squeezed her thigh under the table. "You're mine after tonight." It was a low murmur of sound that made David's face fall.

Bending down to the drummer's ear once she was on her feet, she said, "Memo," and left, her heart slamming a rapid beat and her nape prickling in awareness of Fox's gaze all the way to the door. She'd have to tell him to stop that or everyone would think he was hot after a roadie... but another part of her wanted to turn, to lock her eyes with his, tell the world he was hers.

Molly could barely breathe at the idea of being able to walk up to Fox in public, kiss him, smile with him. It made her lips curve, her body already turning to send him a last look when a flashbulb went off. Startled, she blinked to see that a fan too shy to go up to them was shooting photos of Fox and David from just inside the doorway.

Stomach queasy at that tiny exposure to the spotlight, she hurried out, the ugliness of the past a shadow she couldn't escape. *Damn her father!* She blinked back tears, angry with Patrick Buchanan for the damage he'd done, with herself for not being able to forget the pain, with fate itself.

CHAPTER 17

MOLLY HAD NEVER ATTENDED A live concert. By the time she was old enough to be interested and would've been permitted to go with her friends, the scandal had broken, permanently altering the course of her life.

To have her first experience be backstage at a Schoolboy Choir concert while the crowd thundered out front and Fox belted out lyrics that made her want to dance and drag him off to bed at the same time... wow

Halfway through the show, he and Noah were both shirtless and sweaty under the lights, their T-shirts thrown into the delirious knot of fans who'd paid a premium to stand in the mosh pit right in front of the stage.

Fox's had been caught by a young woman who'd screamed and clutched it to her chest before pulling it on over her sparkly top, Noah's by a guy who'd held it up like a trophy. The two fans were part of an enormous sold-out crowd. It was exhilarating to be buffeted by the roar of that crowd, feel the beat of the music under her feet, hear the growl of Fox's voice, then the raw ferocity in it as the band slowed down to play a ballad about loss and redemption that had been penned by the keyboardist, Abe.

The brutal tenderness of it brought tears to her eyes where she leaned against one of the supports at the back of the stage, concealed in the shadows but with an amazing view. Winking at her when she'd admitted this was her first live concert, Maxwell had said she was off for the night unless something went wrong and he needed all hands on deck. So she was free to just stand there and watch Fox move those magic fingers over an electric guitar while Noah took the microphone to belt out a rock anthem that had the crowd raising their arms and joining in.

The tattoos on Fox's arms and back shimmered under the lights, his muscles defined by the sweat that gleamed on his skin. She wanted to lick it up, the impulse warring with her desire to keep on watching him forever—he was hypnotic, beautiful, and talented. Noah leaned in close to him right then, the two playing their guitars off one another in a rhythm that was immediately picked up on and echoed by Abe and David. It made it clear exactly how long the four had been friends and musicians together.

God, they were good.

Molly hadn't truly appreciated the amount of sheer skill it took to do what they did until she'd seen them practicing yesterday and earlier today. The lights and the fireworks, that made for a good show, but behind it all was music, solid and pure. The four of them had been goofing off this afternoon, with Abe taking the mike, Fox on the drums, Noah on keyboard, David on guitar—all out of their comfort zones, and they'd *still* made great music.

Maxwell came to stand beside her. "So much naked talent," he said in her ear, as if he'd read her thoughts. "First time I heard them, I knew they'd be legends someday if they managed to stay together through the bullshit that comes with fame."

"It'd be a tragedy if they ever broke up." The four members of Schoolboy Choir created a stunning unit that truly was more than the sum of its parts. "Have they ever come close to it?"

"Won't lie, been some rough times—booze, women, drugs, notoriety, it takes a toll." Maxwell passed her a cold soft drink. "Any one of them could've dumped the others and struck out on his own when it got too hard, but even when they were fighting, they didn't walk away." A pause. "Drugs aren't as dangerous as women."

"It's all right, Maxwell," Molly whispered, rubbing a fisted hand over her heart. "I only have him for a little while—I'm no threat."

To her surprise, the big man put his arm around her shoulders and tucked her close to the comforting bulk of him. "Maybe you should try to change that." Startling words from the protective crew boss. "Boy's never been this happy—and I like you." He bussed her on the cheek in a paternal way, his beard scratchy on her skin.

David was right, she thought after he walked away—Maxwell had some weird voodoo going on.

Her pulse kicked as Fox turned his back to the audience and looked right at her. His mouth curved in a smile she knew was for her, and then he was taking the microphone once more. She exhaled, her abdomen taut. It was becoming clear she'd never become immune to Fox's smile, his touch, his kiss, the ferocious power of his voice.

When her phone vibrated in her pocket as he started in on one of the band's biggest hits, she ignored it before realizing she hadn't heard from Charlotte today. They stayed in daily contact, even if it was only a short e-mail or text message to touch base. It was a habit Molly had begun after Charlotte's mother first got sick and that was now so much a part of both their lives they rarely gave it a thought.

Pulling out the phone without taking her eyes off Fox, she glanced quickly at the message and burst out laughing. The music was so loud that there was no risk she'd interrupt the band, but she bit down on her lip to stop herself anyway. Tears in her eyes, she looked at David where he was making magic on the drums, wanting to hug him. Because the message wasn't from Charlotte.

David sent me a memo. WTF?!

In the year and a half that Molly had known Thea—after Thea decided to do some research on her biological father out of curiosity and discovered she had a sister—Molly hadn't seen anyone discombobulate her. "Good on you, David."

It'd be interesting to be a fly on the wall at Thea and David's next meeting, which was at least a week away as Thea was now officially on vacation. Not that her sister ever actually stopped working, but she was currently at the airport, waiting for her plane to the Indonesian island of Bali. The trip to see her parents had been organized well before the Sydney concert had come up, and with the local interviews now all done, Thea had decided not to cancel it.

"If you want me to continue putting out fires for you," she'd told the band before she left, "do *not* do anything that interrupts my vacation." The terse words had been directed particularly at David, whose black eye had been spectacular by that stage. "And next time someone tells you to put ice on a bruise, you listen!"

Molly had found the tone of that last pithy comment intriguing to say the least. Now, vowing to keep her nose out of whatever might end up going on between the drummer and her sister, she crossed her fingers for them both and typed a short reply: *Was it a good memo?*

Thea's response was quick-smart. *Bullet-pointed! With an introduction and a conclusion.*

Are you memo'ing him back?

Of course I am. I have to see what he does next.

Stifling her laugh again, Molly said, *Keep me updated. And have fun in Bali.*

I will—after I write this memo.

Leaving Thea to her rebuttal memo, Molly messaged Charlotte. *Hey, what's happening? I'm backstage at a rock concert. Surreal.* As surreal as the fact the incredible lead singer would be in her bed tonight.

I'm at work. Yes, on a Saturday night. The good news is, T-Rex hasn't yelled at me once in the past eight hours. I think he might be depressed.

Caught by the primal power of Fox's voice, it took Molly a few minutes to reply. *Ask him to dinner. Or dessert.*

T-Rexes only eat raw meat. But I ordered him takeout from a restaurant he likes. Now I'm going home. Enjoy the concert—and Fox. xoxo

Sliding the phone back into her pocket, Molly let the music sweep her away into a wild jungle of a world, passionate and furiously beautiful, just like the man who held the mike close as a kiss.

WHILE MOLLY HELPED THE CREW pack up sensitive gear after the concert, Fox and the rest of the band came out to sign autographs and take photos with the die-hard fans who'd stuck around well after the show ended. Though she tried not to, she couldn't help but notice the number of adoring women in the group—the one about to take a photo with Fox was a raven-haired knockout with a beaming smile.

"Oh, I can't believe I get to meet you!" she squealed when Fox put his arm around her waist for the shot.

He wasn't the only one being showered with female attention; all four men had their own groupies. Suddenly, Molly wasn't so sure she'd done the right thing in encouraging David's pursuit of Thea. "Damn it," she said as she broke a nail while rolling up one of the cables that crawled across the back of the stage.

Forcing herself to pay attention, she tried to keep her eyes off the tableau out front, but it was no use. This time when she looked up, it was to see Fox exchanging fist bumps with a tattooed biker type who turned around to have Fox sign his back with a black marker. Next to him was a brunette who tucked a piece of paper into Fox's jeans pocket, blatant invitation in her eyes and her assuredly collagen-enhanced lips.

The bitchy thought would've normally made Molly feel bad, but not tonight, with the woman licking her tongue around her pouty lips in a message a man would have to be comatose to miss.

Gritting her teeth against the urge to stride over there and slap her straight, Molly took the wound-up cable to where another one of the crew was putting them neatly into a gear truck. The charity volunteer crew was handling the big items, all of which had been hired, but much of the more delicate equipment was the band's and needed to be handled with care.

"Here you go, Jen."

"Thanks." The model-tall and slender black woman took the cable off her hands. "You want to schlep some water out to the guys? It looks like these fans aren't leaving."

Joining the cluster of fans was the last thing Molly felt like doing, but since she couldn't exactly say that, she stalled. "They always go the extra mile?"

"Depends on how tired they are, how far along in the tour it's been." Jen nodded at the crate of water that had just come out of the portable fridge now being loaded for transport. "Go on."

Reluctantly grabbing four bottles, Molly made her way through the small crowd after tugging down her crew cap and was soon at David's side. He was talking music with an eager young male and smiled his thanks at her for the water. When he leaned in close to whisper, "I sent her the memo," she decided her first instincts about him had been right. A guy who was still thinking about her sister, even surrounded by copious amounts of near-naked female flesh, was seriously gone.

Noah took his water with his usual charming smile, while Abe nodded quietly. Heading toward Fox, she found herself stopped by an exquisitely made-up blonde in skinny jeans and a plunging black top. "Are you like one of Fox's assistants?"

Molly nodded.

"Oh my God! I would *die* for that position." The blonde pressed her hands together and jumped up and down. "He is soooo hot."

Realizing the woman was a girl despite the illusion created by her makeup, Molly gave her a gentle smile. "I better get him this water."

"Oh, sure. Tell him to call me! I put my number in his left back pocket."

Molly touched Fox on his lower back through the white T-shirt he'd pulled on and was surprised by his frowning look when he turned his head. It changed into a smile the instant he saw it was her. "Is that for me?"

Nodding at the straightforward comment that sounded like a caress, she gave him the water just as another woman, this one definitely an adult, laid her hand on his chest, her turgid nipples plainly visible through her spaghetti-strap top. "Hi"—a breathy sound as she pressed those nipples against his arm—"I've been waiting to talk to you *all* night." Her eyes dropped to his groin. "Do I get a reward for my patience?"

Stomach churning, Molly walked away before she punched the groupie's lights out.

It was hours later before the crew's work was finally done. Fox had left with the rest of the band a while ago; it would've looked suspicious for Molly to go with them when the breakdown was only halfway complete. The truth was, she wasn't sure she was in the right frame of mind to be with Fox just then. When the other crew members invited her out for a drink afterward, she went.

"Is it always like that?" she asked Jen as they sat at the bar, Molly with a pretty virgin cocktail, Jen with a margarita. "The women I mean?"

"That was nothing." Jen sighed at the first sip of her drink, the salt from the rim of the glass a shimmer on her lips before she turned them inward to lick it off. "Rock star equals catnip for a lot of women."

Molly couldn't exactly argue, though it was only one particular rock star who was her personal catnip. "I guess that's why real relationships don't work in that life," she said, and it hurt to speak the words.

Jen shrugged, her slender shoulders graceful against the black band T-shirt. "I dunno. There are plenty of long-term relationships in the business. Some of 'em the woman looks the other way, but a rare few are solid to the core. Depends how hard you want to work and how much you love, I suppose."

Molly imagined living with a man—with Fox—knowing thousands of other women would be happy to crawl into his bed should he so much as crook a finger, and knew she couldn't do it. The jealousy would eat her up. As it was doing now. "I think I'll head back," she said, conscious she was the one who'd created the distance tonight. Stupid, when she had so little time with him anyway. "I'm exhausted."

"You did good for a rookie." Jen finished off her margarita and swiveled off the stool. "I'll come, too. Maxwell and I want to go see the opera house tomorrow."

They walked back across the road and into the hotel, the crew having deliberately picked a place nearby so no one had to worry about driving. Molly was crossing the lobby when she spied Fox inside the small hotel bar; he was leaning against the bar itself, the sex-kitten who'd wanted a "reward" in the seat right next to him.

It felt like being punched in the stomach.

The ding of the elevator had her snapping her head away from the cozy tableau. Punching in the number for her floor,

166

she tried to keep her face from crumpling, Jen thankfully too tired to pay her much attention. "Good night," the other woman said one floor down from Molly's. "If you want to check out the opera house, too, meet us downstairs at eleven."

Molly nodded. "Thanks."

Managing to keep herself together with the same furious will that had allowed her to survive that year of hell in high school, she entered her room and, striding across to the connecting door, locked it on her side. Only then did she give in to the urge to kick at the wall. It didn't help.

Damn him. Damn him. *Damn him!*

She ripped off her Schoolboy Choir T-shirt, toed off her sneakers and, leaving a trail of clothes on the carpet, walked into the bathroom. Choosing a water temperature so hot it was almost unbearable, she was about to step inside the shower cubicle when there was a banging on her door.

CHAPTER 18

MOLLY'S HEART LEAPT, BUT SHE knew it was likely a guest who had the wrong room. Wrapping herself in the hotel robe and switching off the shower, she frowned as the banging came again.

Not about to make herself vulnerable if the person was a drunk or otherwise aggressive, she padded out quietly and put her eye to the peephole—to see the last person she'd expected. Wrenching open the door when Fox went to pound again, she said, "What are you doing?" through clenched teeth. "You'll wake everyone on the floor."

Striding inside, he watched her close the door, then imprisoned her against it by slamming his hands palms-down on either side of her body, six feet four inches of pissed-off male. "What the fuck, Molly? You blow me off after the show and now you lock me out?"

Instead of being intimidated, she shoved at his chest. The fact it was a futile effort only ratcheted up her anger. "I didn't think you'd notice." Her eyes burned with furious tears. Blinking them back, she said, "You looked plenty busy at the bar!"

"Seriously? A groupie sneaks into the hotel with the intention of getting into any bed she can, and you—"

"And I what?" She thudded her fists against his shoulders. "I shouldn't wonder what the hell you were doing the hours I was at the site?"

Grabbing her wrists, he pinned her arms above her head with one big hand. He gripped her chin with the other, the green of his irises violent and his breath hot against her skin as he said, "You trust me, that's what you do!"

Kicking out at him, Molly tried to wrench away but he pressed his body so close that she couldn't move. "Trust you?" She sucked in ragged gasps of air. "Why? What do I know about rock stars?"

"I don't fucking care. You know about me!" It was a growl. "I made a promise and I don't break my promises." His kiss was a wild storm, his mouth demanding her response.

A red haze across her vision, she bit him on that luscious lower lip. Hard enough to hurt. Pulling away with a hiss, he shook his head. "That was not a good idea, baby."

Dark and low and rough, his warning rasped over her skin. "What," she said, hating that she was still so susceptible to him, "your little playmate didn't scratch your itch?"

His fingers tightened on her wrists, his other hand curling around her throat. "Don't push me."

She could almost see him throttling back his temper, and it infuriated her that he could remain in control while she was falling apart, hot, angry tears rolling down her cheeks despite her every attempt to rein them in. "I'm not the one being pushy!" Twisting in his hold, her chest heaving, she was angrily aware of his jean-clad cock shoving against her abdomen.

"If you think I'll let you in me after you've been inside *her*—"

His temper snapped with a snarl, his mouth slamming down on hers and his hand shifting to hold her jaw so she couldn't bite him again. Molly sent her knee up between his legs instead. Blocking her by pressing his body against hers, he thrust his hand into her robe, palming her breast with blunt possessiveness—as if he had the right to handle her however and whenever he liked. "Why didn't you answer my calls?"

"I didn't want to talk to you, that's why." Molly twisted again but only managed to open her robe even more. "You let her *touch* you!" Images assaulted her of that woman's fingers on his chest, her skanky breasts rubbing against his arm.

"Shit, Molly, people think they can touch us all the time." Tugging the loosened belt of her robe all the way open, he ran his hand down her otherwise nude body to squeeze her hip. "If I'd wanted her, I wouldn't still be in the clothes I was wearing after the show, and I damn well wouldn't have been at the bar keeping an eye out for you. I'd be in my room feeding her my cock."

Giving an aggravated scream, she managed to wrench a hand free and slapped it on his chest, shoving hard. "You think that's going to make me feel *better*?"

He released her all at once. Picking her up in an effortless move before she could take advantage of her freedom, he dumped her on her back on the bed. The robe gaped around her and when he came down over her, she felt him on every inch of exposed flesh. And his raw, masculine scent, it was pure Fox, no hint of the groupie. Her body surged to erotic life. Shoving his hand between them, he began to undo his

170

fly. "Say no, Molly." Harsh words. "Say no right fucking now if you want me to stop."

Thrusting her hands into his hair instead, she pulled him down to her, ravaging his mouth as he ravaged hers. Teeth and tongue and fury, it was as much a fight as a kiss. The fact her body was liquid for him only enraged her further. Sucking on her tongue, his knuckles brushing against her clit before the blunt head of his cock did the same, Fox pushed up her thigh and shoved inside her in a single push.

She screamed into the kiss, her hands clawing at his back through his T-shirt while her body rocketed out of control. His mouth dropping to her neck, the lip ring grazing her skin, he bit down hard enough to leave a serious mark... and Molly's orgasm tore her to pieces in a violent pulse that had her muscles locking around his cock. One hand tight in her hair, Fox pulled out and shoved deep again, and then he came and came inside her.

THE FIRST THING FOX DID after his brain started functioning again was push up and look down into Molly's face. "I lost my temper. Tell me if I hurt you." The idea that he might have was a chunk of ice inside him. Never had he spun that out of control with a woman. That it had been Molly who'd borne the brunt of his temper? *Fuck.*

"No," she said, and tried to turn her head aside, but he cradled her face with one hand, forced her to hold the agonizing intimacy of the eye contact, their bodies still locked together.

"Tell me the truth, baby."

171

"You didn't hurt me." Naked vulnerability, confusion, the remnants of anger in those brown eyes that couldn't lie, but no pain. "I was with you all the way."

Blowing out a shuddering breath, he pressed down on his forearms, his hair falling across his forehead. "Now we're going to talk."

Fine tremors ran over Molly's skin, each a kick to Fox's gut. "This isn't my world," she said. "I don't know the rules."

"There's only one rule you need to know with me." The embers of his temper glowing to life again at the reminder she'd doubted him, his voice came out a growl. "I won't fuck around on you while we're together. I told you that at the start and nothing's changed."

"I believe you." Her long, dark lashes lowered, rose again, her pupils deep ebony. "If I didn't, I would've said no. I was just..." Right when he thought she'd finally admit that there was no way in hell this had ever been, or could ever be, a temporary affair, she said, "I'm sorry I overreacted."

"Don't be sorry you let me see you." Fighting with Molly wasn't his favorite thing in the world, but he'd damn well take her anger over icy distance. "Don't you ever apologize for that."

Molly broke the eye contact once more, her throat moving as she swallowed. "We should shower. We're both sweaty from today. You need to..." Cheeks flushing, she shifted her hips in a silent reminder that he remained buried in her.

He could sense her pulling away emotionally in spite of their sexual entanglement, shaken by the visceral power of the minutes past. "I'm not done with you yet." Possessive fury continuing to thunder through him, Fox opened his mouth over hers, slid his tongue between her lips, and began to use his intimate knowledge of her body to seduce her.

If sex was all she'd give him, then he'd damn well use it to tie her to him until she could never again think of walking away. Fingers clenching on the rucked-up sheets, Molly moaned in the back of her throat as he flexed his hips in a lazy movement. "Not nearly done."

WRAPPING HERSELF TIGHTLY IN THE robe again after they finally had that shower, Molly ordered room service for them both from the twenty-four-hour hotel kitchen. She was still wrecked from the smoldering heat of their second time together that night. Fox had wanted to make a point, and he'd made it with a relentless concentration that had left her shuddering in ecstasy, his body her only anchor.

He hadn't liked being locked out, being distrusted. But even in his anger, he hadn't hurt her. What he'd done was worse—he'd taken her, branded her, driven himself into every cell of her body. She couldn't survive a month of this, of becoming further and further intertwined with a man who could never be hers. The thought of ending up an empty, broken shell like her mother was a nightmare... but even worse was the thought of losing Fox, of never again inhaling his scent, hearing his voice, feeling his touch.

"Room service."

Jumping at the knock on the door, she glanced at Fox where he lay on her bed.

Jaw clenched, he went into his room and closed the door while the waiter dropped off the food. His dark expression had grown heavier by the time he walked back in, his jeans low on his hips and his upper half bare. She didn't have to be a mind reader to know he was angry about the continued secrecy of their relationship, but he kept his silence as the two of them ate the food while sprawled in bed.

Molly picked at a plate of fruit, then set it aside on the bedside table, not really in the mood to eat. "How did that woman get past security?" she asked, knowing she was revealing too much of what she felt for him but unable to stop herself.

"How groupies always get past security." Fox shrugged and continued to eat his burger, but his voice held an edge that said his temper was still simmering. "Don't waste any more time on her. She's nothing."

Molly winced, wondering if that was how he'd think of her once their month was past. Then she wanted to slap herself. "I'm really not cut out to be a rock star's g—" She caught herself before she said "girlfriend," the word a knot of painful emotion in her throat. "Lover."

"Since I can still feel you hot and wet around my cock, I disagree." With that forthright statement, Fox finished off his burger, then picked up the beer he'd had her order and half-emptied the bottle before suddenly frowning. "You mind if I drink?" he asked, reaching out to tuck her hair behind her ear. "I never asked."

The tenderness shattered her. He remained angry, that much was clear, but *still* he thought about her. Cuddling close, she laid her head against his shoulder and felt the tension in her spine ease when he wrapped his arm around her without hesitation, his fingers closing over her nape.

"No," she said in response to his question. "It's my choice, doesn't have anything to do with anyone else." The golden silk of his skin an invitation to her senses, she stroked his side, petted his chest. It felt so right to just be with him. "Each time I turn down a drink, I remember why I made this choice and who I am. Does that make sense?"

Fox brushed his lips over the top of her hair. "Perfect sense. Was your mom a drinker or was she just drunk the day she got behind the wheel?" he asked, and she knew then that he'd read through articles not only about her father's fall from grace but also about what followed.

Molly could remember every detail of that fateful hour when she'd lost what little remained of her world: the fine yellow paper of the note calling her to the school counselor's office, the echoes created by the soles of her school shoes in the otherwise empty corridors, the Wet Floor sign where the custodian had wiped it clean of a spill, the kind face and sad eyes of the veteran cop who'd told her both her parents were dead. It was as defining a moment in her life as the day she'd watched televised images of her father being arrested.

"My mom was a high-functioning alcoholic for most of the last eight years of her life... then she was just an alcoholic," she said through the agony of memory. "But," she added, eyes gritty and throat dry, "from the things I picked up over the years, I know she began drinking years before, when she learned of my father's first affair."

Fox lifted his hand from her nape to run his fingers lightly over the side of her face. "Bastard has a lot to answer for."

About to respond that her mother held half the responsibility for choosing to stay with Patrick Buchanan despite knowing what he was, Molly's heart suddenly hiccupped, a wave of ice crawling over her skin. What was she doing speaking to Fox about things that made her feel as if she were that beaten, broken girl again? She knew how dangerous this was, how far she'd already fallen, how bad it was going to hurt when it ended.

She'd bleed the day Fox walked out of her life.

"The concert," she said in a stumbling rush of words, "it was amazing. I've never experienced anything like that."

It was about as subtle an effort to change the subject as a sledgehammer, but Fox let her retreat, maybe because he, too, didn't want to go that deep. "Yeah? It's a rush, isn't it? I love performing, especially when the crowd is that pumped."

Heart rate smoothing out as the ice eased its grip, she traced her fingertips over the ridges of his abdomen. "That teenager you let onto the stage to jam with you—he was so excited, I think he's probably not going to sleep for a month."

"Me, Noah, Abe, and David, we were all that kid once." Bracing one arm on a raised knee, he said, "You really had a good time?"

Surprised at the note of hesitation, she pushed up so she could look into those gorgeous eyes, his lashes lush and thick. "Yes! It was my first rock concert and I think I'm addicted." Fox's slow grin was the reward for her honesty. "The energy, the primal power of it, and most of all the music... my God, Fox, you four make the most incredible music." It pulsed in her veins even now, compelling and haunting.

"In the end," Fox said, "it's about the music. That's why we've stuck together—the money, the fame, it's peripheral. All the four of us ever wanted to do was make music."

Filching one of his fries when he put the little basket on his lap, she crunched it. "I was talking to Maxwell and he said you guys stuck through everything."

Fox nodded. "We've had a couple of really bad patches. Right back at the start, when we were young and stupid and didn't know how to handle the pressure, and a year ago, when Abe's divorce had him trying to drug himself into an early grave." He fed her another fry despite her scowl. "Your mad face is cute."

"You could get murdered for saying stuff like that," she muttered, charmed regardless.

His dimple flashed at her, and she was expecting the way he drew her down for a lazy kiss. Her palm flat on his chest, she sank into the pleasure, her earlier fear tangled with a poignant tenderness that urged her to continue being brave, continue hoarding the memories. Because now that she was thinking rationally again, she knew she wasn't her mother, would never be her mother—as tonight's fight had shown.

Karen Webster had never screamed at her husband. No, she'd been the perfectly coiffed and poised political wife, drowning her pain in alcohol.

If Fox actually had slept with that groupie, Molly would've slammed the door in his face. She had enough respect for herself to never allow any man, even one who was her personal addiction, to treat her in such a way. It would've brutalized her, but she would've eventually picked up the broken pieces of herself. What she would've never done was crawl into a bottle, just as now she wouldn't scurry back into the claustrophobic box in which she'd existed for so long.

Molly was going to *live*.

Even if it smashed her heart to splinters.

CHAPTER 19

THEY ENDED UP SLEEPING IN till noon, which wasn't surprising given the late night. Molly woke to find herself tucked into Fox's body, her breasts pressed to his chest. One muscular, tattooed arm was locked around her waist while the other lay under her neck, his thigh—heavy with muscle and dusted with hair that rasped deliciously against her skin—thrust between her own. Yawning, she snuggled deeper and just wallowed in the feeling of warm safety, the emotional storm of the previous night having left her raw.

Fox had told her they had the whole day free to do whatever they liked, and what she liked was cuddling in bed with her rock star. At least until he woke up. Feeling him stir almost ten minutes later, she pressed a kiss to his shoulder. "Hey."

"Mmm." It was a deep, sleepy sound before he tugged her impossibly closer to his body.

With both of them naked, the sensation was sensual, but right then, it was also just *good*. He felt strong and solid and protective around her, as if he was cherishing her. Though he was clearly aroused, it was the lazy arousal of morning, and he seemed far more interested in cuddling her to his body than in sex.

It made her melt, the idea that her hardcore rocker might not be against cuddling on a weekend morning in bed. Rubbing her nose lightly over his skin, she pressed another kiss to his chest, licking out with her tongue to taste him.

That initiated a sleepy rumble. Deciding to behave, she stayed snuggled up against him in silence, her bones lax and her sense of well-being incredible. No one had ever held her like this, ever made her feel so protected and anchored.

It was more than fifteen minutes later that he stirred again, his jaw moving as if in a yawn. Smoothing his hand in a slow circle on her back, he nuzzled his chin in her hair. "I like waking up with a soft, sexy librarian."

His sleep-roughened voice made her nerve endings vibrate. "I like waking up with you, too." Nuzzling him after the honest confession, she said, "What do you want to do today?"

"See some koala bears."

Molly laughed, thinking he was joking.

"No, I mean it." He tapped her playfully on her butt. "I've been to Australia so many times, but I've never seen a koala. It's fucking embarrassing."

Giggles bubbling in her blood, Molly wriggled out of his hold to get her phone from the bedside table. Propping herself against the headboard after tugging up the sheet to cover her breasts, a pillow at her back and Fox sprawled on his front by her side, she searched for places to see koalas. "There's a wildlife park about a forty-five-minute drive away," she said, skimming down the search results to tap on what looked like the best option. "It's open today and their website says you can get close to the animals."

Fox squeezed her thigh. "Come 'ere first."

Her body one big languid sigh, Molly leveled a mock scowl in his direction. "The park's only open until five, and it's already"—a quick glance at the clock—"almost a quarter till one. If I slide back into bed, we won't have much time there."

Fox wanted to tug her down, kiss that adorable scowl into his mouth, but she was right. If he had her under him, they wouldn't be leaving this room anytime soon, and he wanted a date with his Molly. "I'll take a rain check." Shoving off the sheet, he got out of bed. "Half an hour."

Twenty-five minutes and rapid fire showers later, the two of them having eaten a quick room-service breakfast despite the fact it was technically lunchtime, Fox pulled on jeans and a plain white T-shirt, then sat down on Molly's bed to finish lacing up his sneakers. In front of him, Molly was bent over, looking for something in her suitcase. He grinned. She had an incomprehensible woman thing about her ass, but he liked the view fine. Way better than fine.

Before he could give in to the urge to walk over and stroke the sweet curve of it, his phone rang. It was Noah, asking if he wanted to check out a music shop the guitarist had heard about.

"No, man," Fox said with a wink at Molly, "I'm going to go get my photo taken with a koala bear."

Lips twitching, Molly sat down beside him to do up her own sneakers. Wearing a casual but fitted pink shirt with fine white stripes and elbow-length sleeves teamed with jeans, the top three buttons of the shirt undone to reveal the white tank she wore underneath, she looked pretty and young and bitable. Her hair was in a ponytail, the tail fed through the back of one of his baseball caps, her creamy skin vulnerable to even the fall sun.

"Seriously?" Noah said into the phone. "I've never seen one either. Can I come?"

Fox thought about it. This was meant to be a date... but Noah rarely sounded excited about something as innocent as this, the world he lived in a dark place that often threatened to suck him under. Abe might appear the most dysfunctional of the four of them, but Noah was far more seriously fucked up. "Yeah," he said, "but you have to be ready in ten. Underground garage, level two."

Hanging up, he tugged on Molly's ponytail, delighted with her. "Noah's coming. He's never seen a real koala either."

"Ah, the debauched rock star life." Molly leaned in to kiss his dimple, and yeah, he grinned, loving the little things she did that told him what they had, it was special, was way more than sex.

"That was nice of Justin," she said afterward, "to take out a hire car in his name for you."

Fox snorted and pulled on his own cap, having asked the lawyer to do the favor yesterday, then drop off the keys. "Nice, my ass." Rising, they headed to the door. "I bribed him with the promise of a bottle of single-malt whiskey."

Once outside in the hallway, Fox waited for Molly to pull the door shut before taking her hand in his. Her eyes were startled when she looked up, but then her fingers curved shyly around his and it slammed all the air from his lungs. If he had his way, he'd walk through the hotel lobby with her hand in his so no one would make any mistake about who she was to him—but Molly wasn't in any way ready for the glare of the limelight.

So he satisfied himself with holding her hand until they stepped out of the elevator and headed to the black SUV Justin had hired. Unlocking it, he nodded for Molly to get into the front passenger seat. She shook her head. "Noah's much taller than I am. He'll have more legroom in front."

"Push your seat forward." Fox looked at the space behind her once she did. "He'll be fine. Bastard's the one horning in on our date," he said with a grin as Noah exited the elevator… with Abe and David behind him.

"Well, fuck." Fox groaned. "Damn it to hell, guys! How are we supposed to be anonymous if we go en masse?" Two of them could've skated under the radar if they were careful, but no way would that work with all four members of the band together.

"Hey, you don't own the koala bears." Abe folded his arms over a dark gray shirt with short sleeves, muscles bulging under the rich mahogany of his skin. His head was bare, his hair cut close to his skull and an intricate pattern razored in on one side—that pattern was dyed a vivid purple with jagged slashes of white and orange.

"You're about as inconspicuous as David's goddamn T-shirt." Fox scowled at his other bandmate's screaming tee. "Jesus. It looks like someone threw up a rainbow on you. You'll scare the koala bears away before we get near them."

David gave him the finger. "It was for charity." A wink at Molly from his uninjured eye, the other one ringed by a deep blue-black bruise. "Also, koalas aren't bears, you genius, they're marsupials."

"Shut your trap, Rainbow Boy." Fox pointed a finger at Noah. "*Explain.*"

Shoulders rising under the black of his sleeveless sweatshirt, the hood flipped up to conceal his hair, Noah spread his hands. "What was I going to do? They saw me sneaking out."

Fox thought of these men as his brothers, but they'd just ruined his one chance to be with Molly like a normal guy on a date with his girl. Before he could snarl at them, Molly stepped forward. "I have an idea," she said with the smile that had hit him like a roundhouse punch that first night and showed no sign of decreasing in potency. "I'll be your assistant." She hefted the little multi-zip travel bag she'd slung across her body. "I'll buy all the drinks, tickets, etcetera, and everyone will see what they expect to see."

"She's smart," Abe said to Fox. "You should try not to fuck it up with her."

Fox narrowed his eyes. "Just for that, you get to sit in the back. All three of you. Molly gets the front passenger seat."

Much whining and complaining later, the three men somehow folded themselves into the back of the SUV. Then it began. The one-liners, the zingers back and forth, the insults, the jokes. Molly laughed until she protested that her stomach hurt, and Fox had to forgive the others then, didn't he?

"Christ," Abe groaned when Fox brought the car to a stop at the wildlife park. "I think my joints are permanently frozen in place." Stepping out, he began to stretch his heavily muscled body.

Fox turned to Molly after they got out, held out his credit card. When her lips parted, he dropped his tone. "Don't argue with me. I might've agreed to let you play assistant, but you're not paying for anything today."

Those clear brown eyes, so beautifully expressive, told him the instant she decided to listen. "Does it have a PIN code so you don't have to sign for it?"

"Yeah." He gave it to her, eyes on her lips. One day soon, he was going to have the right to kiss her anytime he pleased, in daylight and in darkness. "You look so pretty, Molly. Like sunshine."

Her blood alight in joy, Molly began to walk toward the ticket booth, aware of Fox falling in behind her with the other men.

It was a fun, lighthearted afternoon.

The men had more privacy than they'd expected—the park was spread out, and with the majority of the clientele being families, even when people recognized them, they only requested an autograph and a photo, then let the band be. Molly took many of those photos, and each time she did, she marveled at the men's patience. Clearly, this was an unusual day, an unusual circumstance, but they were in a great mood and didn't turn anyone down.

She could understand, however, why Abe had punched out a reporter during his divorce, and why Noah had once infamously smashed a photographer's camera. It must get wearing to be constantly under scrutiny, never able to let down your guard.

"We have to remember most people aren't out to tear us to pieces," Fox said when she shared her thoughts with him. "Fans like this," he continued, "they don't have a hidden agenda. No comparison to the tabloid reporters who want to make money off our backs by manufacturing gossip."

They reached the koalas a few minutes later, and Molly watched as all four of the big, hardcore rockers fell in love with the shy animals. She took more photos, this time with her personal camera and those belonging to the men. Her favorite was of the four of them, arms around one another in front of a eucalyptus tree on which sat two koalas nonchalantly snacking on the leaves.

Fox was at one end, Noah on the other. They had their faces turned toward each other, laughing at something that had both David and Abe grinning.

"Hey!" Fox called out when Molly would've put away the cameras. "Our lovely assistant needs to be in this shot."

"I'll do it if you like," said the middle-aged woman next to Molly who'd stood by indulgently while her teenage son and daughter snapped pictures of the group.

"Thank you." Molly stepped into the space Abe and David had made for her between their bodies and was immediately enclosed in a heated wall of male flesh. Laughing as David whispered the word "memo" to her, she caught Fox's dimpled grin, and then the camera clicked.

The resulting photo, Molly thought when she looked at it, would live forever on her bookshelf.

A NUMBER OF THE AMATEUR SHOTS from the park were already online by the time they took their seats in the Chinese restaurant they'd ducked into for dinner, several of the photos part of an article that had made the front page of a local news website.

"It says," David read out for the other men after Molly pulled it up on her phone, "we were 'refreshingly devoid of bodyguards and shepherded only by a cheerful local guide.'"

"And"—Noah's golden hair glittered under the restaurant lights as he scrolled through several other sites on his own phone—"Molly's face isn't in any of the shots posted online."

Relieved, Molly was able to enjoy the delicious dishes served by waitstaff too harried to worry about who was famous and who was not. Sitting sandwiched between Fox and David, she felt very much a part of the group as they talked and has-sled one another in the way only good friends can do. Fox kept his hand on her thigh throughout the meal, and it wasn't sexual. No, it felt as if he was touching her because she was his.

Such a dangerous thought. Such a wonderful thought.

CHAPTER 20

RETURNING HOME THE NEXT AFTERNOON was a harsh reality check after the fantasy of the weekend, a fantasy that had lasted to the final minute she'd spent with Fox.

She'd woken beside him for the second day in a row, snuggled and warm, then hot and gasping, could still feel the blunt power of him inside her as she got into the shuttle for the ride to her apartment. Their morning loving had been slow, achingly tender, but he'd taken her again against the door just before she'd left for the airport, and that time it had been hard, rough, deep.

Her fingers brushed her emerald-green cardigan, over the mark he'd left on the upper curve of her right breast. "I'll be back as soon as possible," he'd all but growled, pinning her to the door with his strength, her legs around his hips and the thickness of his cock buried to the hilt inside her. "Think of me."

As if she could do anything else.

Her apartment felt lonely and too quiet when she walked back into it, Fox's scent missing from the air. He hadn't been happy about the separation, but Justin had asked David to stick around while he sorted out some unexpected issues resulting from the bar fight. Fox, Noah, and Abe had decided to stay behind in support until David was cleared to leave the country.

Stomach knotted and ribcage crushing her lungs at the strange emptiness of her surroundings, she checked her answering machine just to hear the sound of another voice. Nothing, as she'd expected. Everyone close to her had her cell number, and it was the cell that rang twenty minutes later.

"Hey!" Charlotte's voice was ebullient in welcome. "I was wondering if you were back. Want to have dinner together? I need to hear *everything*."

"Come over." Molly didn't want to be alone. "I feel like staying in. We can get takeout."

"No, I'll bring my special pasta sauce and we'll have spaghetti."

It was so good to have Charlotte there, to sigh with her over Molly's memories of the amazing live show, smile at the photos from the wildlife park. But for the first time since their friendship began all those years ago, Molly didn't tell her best friend everything. Especially not about how the night of the concert had ended—in angry passion and a terrifying tenderness that had smashed her defenses. Her vulnerable, scarred heart was now brutally exposed.

AT WORK THE NEXT MORNING, she smiled when her colleagues asked her how her long weekend had gone but didn't elaborate beyond a few words. Nothing could come close to describing the intensity of the past few days. She'd never been as happy, as angry, as scared, or as pleasured.

When Fox had messaged her last night to say he was out with the guys to celebrate Abe's birthday but that he missed her, she could've taken the chance to protect herself, backed away. Instead, she'd drawn in a trembling breath and told him what was in her heart: *I miss you, too.*

The resulting exchange of sweet, sexy messages had left her with a goofy smile on her face, especially when he ended with: *Abe just called me pussy-whipped. I told him he was a jealous fucker and he agreed. He wants a Molly now, too.*

The joy continued to hum in her blood this morning, even though she hadn't heard from Fox again. Conscious of the time difference and not wanting to add pressure in case there was a real problem with the David situation, she decided to wait till early afternoon to check in. As it was, she barely had time to glance at her phone all morning.

Clearing her e-mails when she had a half hour to spare at last, she flicked over to the website of the country's biggest newspaper, her plan to scan the day's news before knuckling down to write up an after-school program they'd decided on at the midmorning meeting. The big headline was about a politician who had an interesting way of getting herself into the media for someone who professed not to value self-aggrandizement and work only for the people.

Rolling her eyes, she skimmed over the rest of the page, then clicked across to another news site more irreverent in tone. It often had at least one article that made her smile. Glancing at the updated feature links on one side of the page as she began to flip open her handwritten notes from the meeting, she was about to close the browser when her eye caught on the third link in the list: *Fox Partying it up with Mystery Redhead in Sydney!*

Her blood went cold, then hot, then cold again. Feeling as if she were watching someone else, she clicked on the link. It brought up a full-color image of a shirtless Fox with his arm around a stunning, voluptuous redhead who had her hand on his chest, the eyes she'd turned to the camera screaming her claim on him.

Molly attempted to read the text but her vision was blurred, her heart thundering in her ears. Swiveling in her chair to stare out the window behind her, she tried to breathe through the agonizing pain in her chest. It was hard. A long, gut-wrenching minute later, she forced herself to turn back to the screen and read her way through the article. According to the reporter, "superstar rocker Fox" had met the woman at a private party hosted by the hottest club in Sydney.

A source at the hotel confirmed they'd last been seen heading into his room, his mouth "devouring" hers.

Numb, Molly closed the page and got to work typing up the proposed program. Her fingers moved on autopilot, as did her body when it came time to move on to other duties. She was grateful the library continued to be hectic as the hours passed. So long as she didn't have time to think, she was fine. The only person who would've immediately guessed something was wrong was Charlotte, and her best friend had flown down to the capital this morning with T-Rex for a big meeting.

Fox messaged her around three p.m. *David's in the clear. Be home tomorrow. xx*

Where the *xx* and the use of the word "home" would have made her melt last night, today it seemed a mockery. Numb still and not knowing what to do, she ignored the message. Around four came another: *In area with bad cell coverage. Talk to you when I return to the hotel.*

Molly had no intention of talking to him. When she finally made it home, having opted to stay late to help a colleague with a project, she took off her clothes and stepped into the searing heat of the shower... only to collapse into a shattered ball on the floor. The block of ice within her chest bled a shivering chill through her veins and tears wracked her body, her throat lined with broken glass. It hurt, but nothing hurt as bad as knowing Fox had slept with another woman.

"Stupid, stupid, Molly," she castigated herself, continuing to shiver under the white-hot spray. She'd known who he was from the start, and still she'd allowed herself to fall for his promises, to *trust* the rock star who'd just driven a knife through her heart.

FIVE HOURS LATER, SHE STUMBLED out of bed and walked to the living room to see the message light blinking on her machine. She'd turned it on before crawling under the blankets after her shower, having also switched off the ringer on the phone. Her cell phone, too, was off. Staring at the machine as if it might grow fangs, she reached out and pressed the Play button.

Thea's smiling voice cut through the silence. Fox, Molly thought on a wave of blinding fury, likely had other priorities. She allowed the embers within her to simmer as she listened to Thea's message. Better to be angry than to return to the heartbroken mess she'd been earlier. And if the anger was only a paper-thin crust covering devastating pain, it was enough to keep her going, keep her functional.

Leaving the machine on after the message had played, she walked into the kitchen and deliberately focused on the salad fixings in her fridge, well aware of her tendency to comfort herself with food. But her eye caught on the cheese and wouldn't let go. One toasted cheese sandwich isn't going to kill me, she thought mutinously and grabbed the block of cheddar.

Turning on her mini countertop toaster oven, she popped in the prepared sandwich and glanced at the clock. Three a.m. Great. She had to be up in less than four hours. Then again, it wasn't as if she was going to get any sleep with her mind running the photo of Fox with the redhead in a continuous loop.

When the answering machine clicked on without warning, she jumped before realizing she'd never turned the ringer back on.

"Baby, it's Fox. I know it's late, but I wanted to hear your voice. Just got back into the country after hitching a ride on a friend's jet. Call you later."

Molly reached out to shut off the toaster oven when the cheese began to burn. Removing the sandwich, she put it on a plate and went to the table. She finished it with slow, deliberate focus, drank a huge glass of water to wash it all down, then replayed Fox's message. He sounded so carefree, so normal. As if he hadn't kicked her in the teeth, then stomped on her heart. How *dare* he!

Grabbing the phone, she began to stab at the keys, inputting the number for his cell phone... and paused halfway through, his declaration from their last fight blazing into her mind.

"You trust me, that's what you do!"

Her fingers clenched on the phone. What if the paper was wrong? It was the first time her mind was clear enough to consider that, consider the fact that if Fox *had* slept with someone else, it meant he'd lied to her face when he'd told her he was hers for the duration. Not only that, he'd have had to have been with the redhead while he was messaging Molly, while he was telling her he was planning to stay late at the party because he didn't want to go back to the hotel room without her.

Fox was too blunt, too honest, to play those kinds of games.

Or was he, another part of her asked. After all, what did she know about him? She'd known him for under two weeks.

He told me about his family, about his grandparents.

Yes, the cold facts were public knowledge, but the emotions he'd shared weren't.

And he'd held her, comforted her, come to her on a boat in the middle of the night when she'd told him about her father. Could a man like that so recklessly trample on her heart? She wanted to say no, but the truth was that Fox's lifestyle was a world apart from her own—he existed in a world where friends had jets and life was lived in the fast lane. For all she knew, he might not think it counted as cheating if she was in a different country at the time.

"God." Sinking into the chair again, she shoved her hands through her hair, elbows braced on the table.

Maybe it was pointless to try to figure out any of this when she'd have lost him in just over two weeks in any case. "But he was supposed to be *mine* till then," she said to the air, the words torn from her bleeding, wounded heart. She was too emotionally raw to any longer avoid the tiny bubble of hope that had bloomed inside her in Sydney. Hidden deep, deep inside her, that fragile hope had whispered that perhaps her and Fox's relationship didn't have to end; it was too powerful, too beautiful, too *honest.*

A sob caught in her chest.

She had to know the truth, good or bad. Fingertips as cold as her skin, she called Fox. He answered at once, his voice a low, masculine murmur. "I woke you, didn't I? I'd say sorry, but I wanted to talk to you." A rustle as if he was moving the phone to his other ear. "Hold on a second. I'm just getting in the elevator—the call might drop."

When it didn't, she said, "Did you have a good flight back?" unable to immediately ask the question that might end them here and now.

"Smooth and quick. Stroke of luck that James was in the country and heading back to New Zealand—his jet is a beauty." She heard the ping as the elevator arrived at its floor. "Not as fast as I would've liked though."

Her insides twisted at the warmth in his tone and she knew he was talking about her, about getting back to her. Before she could respond, there was a quiet knock on her door. Heart slamming into her ribs, she rose shakily to her feet. "Fox, is that you?"

"Unless you have other strange men who stalk you."

Phone abandoned, she ran to the door and opened it to jump into his arms. He held her tight, walking in far enough that he could shut the door behind himself. "You did miss me," he murmured against the side of her face.

It was music, his voice, edgy and dark, and it infiltrated her bloodstream, made her want to forget the world. Except she couldn't. Not today. Not until she knew. Because she couldn't ever look the other way.

TAUT MUSCLES RELAXING AT THE unmistakable warmth of Molly's welcome, a welcome that made him feel he was home, erasing his worries that the distance might make her question what was happening between them, Fox went to kiss her but she pushed away, disengaging from him. Instincts on immediate alert, he slid off the small pack that held his clothes without looking away from her. "You missed me, but you don't want to kiss me?"

"I have to ask you something." Breaking the eye contact, she played with the bottom of the T-shirt she wore over flannel pajama pants. "It has a high possibility of making you angry."

Closing the distance between them, he backed her against the wall, bracing his hands on either side of her head. "You telling me we're about to have a fight?"

"Yes."

He could deal with a fight. What he couldn't deal with was Molly pulling away from him. "Ask."

"Wait," she whispered and, ducking under his arm, walked into the living room to grab her phone.

Following, he forced himself to leash his impatience as she pulled up something, the moonlight that seeped in through the partially closed blinds bathing them both in shadows.

"Here."

Fox swore the instant he understood what it was he was seeing. Setting the phone down on the coffee table, he dragged her into his arms. "Why didn't you call me?" He hated the fact that she'd been so badly hurt, wanted to eviscerate those responsible.

Burying her face in his chest, she fisted her hands against the leather of his jacket. "It was like getting beaten from the inside out." The confession scraped over his senses. "I lost my breath, couldn't think. I just kind of went numb."

Fox tightened his hold, his voice harsh as he fought to temper the fury in his blood. "That girl asked me for a photo—her friend's the one who took it. I don't know who she is, except that I bet you she's the fucking 'source.'" He paused. "Wait." Pulling out his own phone, he made a call while keeping her locked to him with his other arm; Molly needed to be held tonight.

"Noah," he said when the call was answered, the guitarist wide-awake despite the late hour. "Talk to Molly." He thrust the phone into her hand. "Ask him."

"No." She tried to give the phone back. "This is between us—"

"I don't want you to have any doubts, Molly. You *ask* him." He wasn't angry at her—she'd come to him instead of shutting him out, and that meant everything. But he refused to allow any room for even the tiniest worry, would not permit the users and the liars of the world to poison their relationship. "Go on, baby." When she continued to hesitate, he pressed his forehead to hers, his hand clasping the side of her neck. "For me."

It slayed him when she patted his chest and accepted the phone at last. "Noah?" A slight pause. "Can you look up a website on your phone?" She read out the web address of the article and went silent.

A second later Fox heard Noah swear with vicious ferocity before his bandmate lowered the volume on his voice. Fox knew the other man was telling Molly the truth. That Fox had been by his side the entire night. Noah had bad nights and good nights, and last night had been a bad one. So Fox had made sure he wasn't alone.

"Thank you," Molly said to the guitarist and returned the phone to Fox.

Taking it, he said, "Go to sleep, Noah." The phone thrust into a pocket, he slid his hand around to grip Molly's nape, bending his knees so they were eye to eye. "We okay?"

The shocked hurt that killed him was gone from her expression, but her jaw was now a hard line, her body stiff. "Why aren't you wearing a shirt in that shot?" she snapped, her hand closing over his wrist.

"Because when Abe uncorked the champagne, he sprayed David and me." It came out a growl. "Honestly, I didn't think anything of it. I'm shirtless onstage all the time."

"Well you should have!" she ordered, color on her cheekbones. "You should've thought of—"

Oh no, Fox thought when she bit herself off, Molly didn't get to stop there. Not when she'd come so damn close to claiming him. "I should've thought of what?" Having risen to his full height, he tugged back her head with a hand in her hair when she would've lowered her eyes.

"Nothing." Mutinous denial. "We should go to bed."

"No." He ran his thumb over her lower lip. "Should I have thought of you?"

CHAPTER 21

HER SKIN BURNED UNDER HIS fingertips, but she held her stubborn ground. "Ignore me. I've had a hellish day. I should really catch some sleep."

Fox didn't budge. "You were very clear on the rules," he said. "If you want to change them, tell me."

A long, tense silence before she said, "You're leaving in two and a half weeks."

His pulse turned into a drumbeat. "That's not an answer."

Breaking his hold without warning, she walked into the bedroom, her movements jittery as she stripped off her T-shirt and kicked away her pajama bottoms to reveal the white lace of her panties. His poor Molly was running to the safety of their scorching physical connection, a connection that required no words, no arguments.

His body reacted as always to the lush sight of her, his erection pushing against the zipper of his jeans. But this was too important to allow himself to be distracted. Shifting to face her, he ran his knuckles down the centerline of her body. "Tell me what you want."

Eyes huge and stark, she angled her face away, went to cover her breasts with her arms, but he enclosed her in his embrace before she could complete the action. Never did he want Molly to feel ashamed of her nakedness with him. She didn't struggle, but neither did she speak. Fighting his impatient fury to have her belong to him, he reminded himself that the scars that marked Molly were brutal and had been caused at a time in her life when she was incredibly vulnerable.

His temper simmered again, directed at those who had mauled an innocent young girl with such ugly savagery. Nuzzling a kiss to her temple, he cuddled her close, her creamy skin holding a shocked kind of coolness. "Molly?"

"Yes?"

"You can always ask," he said at that wary sound. "I'd rather you get pissed at me, scream and yell, than let suspicion stew inside that smart head of yours."

Trembling, she splayed her hands over his T-shirt. "You said I should trust you." A soft reminder, her head bent, the curling darkness of her hair in his vision.

"You should." He couldn't keep the demand out of his voice. "But until you do, I'll take questions." As long as she came to him, he could handle anything; all he needed was a chance to fight for her. "We agreed on that?"

She nodded, her fingers playing with the edges of his jacket.

"Molly?"

Clear brown eyes holding his own without blinking. "I'll always ask," she said. "I don't have it in me to stay quiet—not about something like that. I'll try to be an adult about it, but I can't guarantee no screaming and yelling."

"There it is," Fox murmured, his dimple appearing as his smile lit up his eyes. "There's my Molly's mouth."

The affectionate caress of his words broke Molly. Rising on tiptoe, she wrapped her arms around him and kissed him, hating that she might've hurt him. She *wanted* to trust him without question, wasn't sure the capacity for such faith hadn't been crushed out of her in childhood.

The fact Fox hadn't berated her for her need to ask, had instead done what was necessary to ease her worries, it meant more than he could ever know. Her father had always belittled and made her mother feel stupid on the rare occasions when Karen Webster had even mildly questioned his behavior.

Swamped with what she felt for Fox, she poured it into her kiss. And when the smooth metal of his lip ring invited her to play, she did. His responding chuckle was sexy, was Fox. "And that's definitely my Molly."

She wanted to be his Molly. So much.

Taking control of the kiss, he nudged her into a seated position on the bed. When she lifted her hands to his jeans, he shook his head. "I'll take care of you tonight, baby. I think you need it."

Molly grabbed his hand, shook her head. "This hurt you, too." Kissing his palm, she pressed it against her cheek. "Let's take care of each other."

Fox's eyes flashed, and she was flat on her back in bed a split-second later, his body big and heavy on her own.

"The things you say, Molly," he said in that whiskey-and-sin voice, his bristled jaw rasping over the palm she lifted to his jaw. "I'd planned to seduce you, coax you, and now all I want to do is push my cock into you, your skin touching mine, your heart beating against mine."

"Yes," she whispered, pushing his jacket off his shoulders.

The action made him exhale harshly and then he rose off the bed to strip down to the skin. Always he'd been her beautiful rock star. Today, his body was no less beautiful, but all she saw was the potent emotion in his eyes, an emotion that echoed the painful, hopeful thing inside her.

Needing him, she slipped off her panties and held out a hand. "Fox."

He came to her in a storm of masculine heat and blunt sexual words that made her feel adored. Breath lost when he entered her, she blinked back tears at the sheer rightness of their intimate connection, skin sliding against skin, breaths mingling.

Then Fox intertwined his hands with her own, pressing them on either side of her head, and she lost the battle. Kissing away her tears, Fox attempted to pull out, but she held him too possessively, her legs locked around his hips.

Shuddering, he said her name, buried his face against the side of hers. Rolling with his shallow thrusts, she turned her face to kiss his jaw, any part of him she could reach.

He lifted his head, met her kiss, his hair tumbled across his forehead and his fingers locked with hers.

"My Fox," she whispered, and then there were no more words, only the searing ache of a bond new and vulnerable and with the potential to break them both.

FOX BRUSHED MOLLY'S HAIR GENTLY back from her face as she slept curled up against his chest, shaking inside at the glory of what had passed between them tonight.

"My Fox."

No one had ever claimed him in such a way, a way that had nothing to do with obligation or money or fame. No one had ever cared enough to be possessive of him. Not of Fox, the rock musician who made a nice accessory or trophy to brag about, but of Fox the man. The fact Molly had been pissed off about the shirt thing? He fucking loved it, even if it was an uncivilized reaction. He wasn't exactly civilized where the woman in his arms was concerned. But he had to pretend he was, at least for a little while longer, give his lover time to come to terms with the violent beauty of what lived between them.

If she took the ultimate risk, if she came to him despite the fears that haunted her, if she chose Zachary Fox as no one else had ever done... she'd fucking *own* him, whether she knew it or not.

CHAPTER 22

MOLLY HAD TO HAVE TWO cups of tar-strong coffee to wake up the next morning. Still not quite human, she decided to wear a shirt with an old-fashioned tall collar edged in lace. A little Victorian with its long sleeves plus the white ribbon and lace in the detailing, the vintage find always made her feel pretty. She paired it with a simple calf-length black skirt that came with a wide belt, and her trusty black leather boots, the heel barely there to allow for easy walking around the large and busy library.

The rock star in her bed whistled when she exited the bathroom after pulling her hair into a neat twist and putting on her basic work makeup—nothing much more than a lick of mascara and gloss. "I want to tempt you back into bed," he said, "except I think you've worn out my cock."

Knowing she was being teased and not ready to think about the passionate power of the previous night, Molly decided to respond to his earthy sexuality in the same vein. "Wasn't I the one who woke up with something long and impatient sliding inside me?" she said through her blush.

His dimple came into view. "I like this naughty side. Show me more."

God, he made her feel so young and happy. "I wouldn't want to spoil the surprise." Picking up her purse and fighting the urge to kiss that dimple because she wasn't sure she'd stop once she started, she pulled out her spare apartment key and set it on the bedside table.

It was the first time she'd given a key to anyone other than Charlotte, but Fox was already so deep inside her, it made little sense to keep him out of her apartment. "Lock up when you leave. Though," she added, the "naughty side" in fine form this morning, "I won't kick you out if I come home to find you naked in bed."

Completely unconcerned by his nudity, Fox walked over to kiss her his way, his lips curved in a smile that hit her sideways. "Have a good day." A bold, petting stroke of his hand over her butt. "I'll see you tonight."

There was, Molly thought as she walked up the steps to the main entrance of the library, something to be said for having her day start with a kiss and a smile from her gorgeous, talented man. It only got better when said man had an extravagant bouquet delivered to her: two dozen roses in his favorite color, arranged in a clear crystal vase. There was no card, but she didn't need one—not with the adorable stuffed koala sitting in the sea of scented red.

She knew her grin had to be foolish, but she didn't fight it, picking up and setting the koala beside her computer before turning to face her colleagues, all of whom were agog. Charlotte had the same reaction after Molly showed her a photo of the bouquet at lunch. "I think you should keep him," her best friend said solemnly as they sat in the vibrant international food hall they'd chosen for today. "Also, find out if he has a twin brother."

Grinning, Molly sipped some of the miso soup she'd ordered to have with her sandwich. "Won't T-Rex mind if you run off with a rock star? He seems to be unable to do without you."

Charlotte stabbed at her sushi. "T-Rex can go bite himself."

Startled at the hostile statement from her sweet friend, Molly pushed at Charlotte's practical little black heel with her foot. "Spill."

"That meeting in Queenstown?" Charlotte ate a piece of sushi with grim-eyed focus before continuing. "Afterward, he made me go with him to every single jewelry store in the city to find the perfect bracelet for some woman he's dating."

"Oh." Molly winced, feeling awful she'd encouraged Charlotte in that direction. Luckily, Charlotte seemed more mad than sad. "That must've sucked."

"Yeah." Charlotte stabbed at her sushi again. "Every time I pointed one out just to end the whole excruciating experience, he questioned me in that Spanish Inquisition way of his until I finally gave him my actual opinion."

"What did you pick?"

"Here." Charlotte pulled up an image on her phone. "I was sneaking a photo of it when he caught me."

The bracelet was a stunning delicacy of diamonds and emeralds set in platinum, the design evocative of tiny flowers and spring leaves. It was made for someone as fine-boned as Charlotte, would accent rather than overwhelm.

"Isn't it beautiful?" A soft sigh, hazel eyes melting before a self-satisfied smirk curved her best friend's lips. "It also put a significant five-figure dent in his wallet."

Laughing, Molly thought hmm and considered the fact T-Rex had bought the one piece Charlotte had truly loved. Either he was an insensitive jerk or he was displaying the cool, strategic intelligence that made him a feared opponent in the business world. Molly wanted to believe the latter for Charlotte's sake, but it was hard to say when she'd never seen the two of them together. Still…

"Forget him," she said and saw Charlotte's fingers tighten on her chopsticks. "I think we both agree that Ernest is never going to be lover material, not for you"—a twist of Charlotte's lips, followed by a reluctant nod—"but what about Derrick? Didn't you say he sent you a flirtatious e-mail a couple of weeks ago?"

"Yes, but he didn't follow it up in person. Figures. He's a wimp."

Molly's mouth dropped open. "Charlie!" Her friend was never unkind.

"If *I* can stand up to T-Rex," Charlotte said with an adorable hint of pride, "I can't exactly respect a man who goes off with his tail between his legs each time the boss snarls."

"Okay, you have a point." Even if T-Rex was an idiot who couldn't see what was right in front of him, he was doing fantastic things for Charlotte's confidence. That alone put him in Molly's good graces.

"Anyway," Charlotte said, "I'm not the one with the exciting life." She looked pointedly at Molly's shirt. "Funny how that helpfully covers your neck."

Molly felt her skin heat. "It's one of my favorite shirts."

"Oh, please. You have a love bite, don't you?"

"Yes." Fox had left his mark on her and each time she thought about it, her stomach fluttered. "He's…" She bit her lower lip. "He asked me if I wanted to change the rules." And then he'd loved her with a tenderness that made her heart ache.

"Do you want to?" No lingering amusement in Charlotte's eyes.

Molly swallowed the single word she wanted to say, the declaration she wanted to make. "Where can it lead?" She put down her spoon, the soup forgotten. "He has a life on the other side of the world." A life lived in the glare of media attention, something it made her nauseous to even consider. "Mine is here. My work is here. You're here."

"I love that you put me on your list." A vivid Charlie smile. "But I can and will always visit you wherever you are." She closed her hand over Molly's. "The real question is—can you live with 'what ifs' for the rest of your life if you don't try to see if it *could* somehow work?"

For such a sweet person, Charlotte had a way of asking the most difficult questions. Could she walk away from the promise of a life with Fox? If she did, Molly knew her cowardice would haunt her for the rest of her life. But how could it ever work? "Charlie, I..." Breaking off, she just stared at her friend, lost and scared and fragile with hope.

Charlotte squeezed her hand. "Come on, let's treat ourselves to fancy coffees, then we can discuss *that* scene in the book you lent me."

Molly's emotional equilibrium was no longer so shaky when she and a smiling Charlotte arrived at the entrance to the building where her best friend worked... just as someone else was about to stride up the steps, having appeared from the other side of the street. "Ms. Baird. Good, you're back," said T-Rex, his black hair lifting slightly in the breeze. "I need you with me at a meeting in ten minutes."

Her free hand clenched by her side, Charlotte sipped silently at her frothy mochaccino as the six-feet-five stone wall dressed in a flawless Italian suit who was her boss glanced at Molly. She went to introduce herself when he said, "You must be Molly. I'm Gabriel."

"It's lovely to meet you," Molly said, wondering how he knew who she was.

"Likewise." Steel-gray eyes shifted from her to Charlotte. "You have foam on your upper lip."

Then he was gone.

"Yes, he's hot," Molly said consideringly, though inside she was dancing a delirious jig. No man noticed such a tiny fleck of foam on a woman's lip unless he was paying careful attention to those lips. "Kind of big for you though."

It was like poking a hornet's nest.

"Just because I'm not an Amazon doesn't mean I can't handle T-Rex!"

"Aha! So you admit you want to handle him?"

Charlotte growled at her, threatening to tip her drink all over Molly's white shirt. "You're an awful friend. Go away."

Molly's laugh bubbled out of her. "Do you think he's built in proportion?"

Charlotte pinked and avoided her eyes as she said, "I have to go before he decides to fire me again today."

"Wait," Molly said, not taking the teasing any further because if, despite all evidence to the contrary, T-Rex *wasn't* interested in Charlotte and she put herself out there, the rejection would crush her friend. "How does he know who I am?"

"Because he thinks my business is his business." Turning at the automatic doors, her best friend held Molly's gaze, a deep caring in her expression. "Think about what I said."

Molly did think about it. And knew Charlotte was right—she couldn't live with the "what ifs," couldn't watch Fox walk away because she was too scared to reach for him.

Her nerves were in knots by the time she returned home after work, but she wasn't about to chicken out in her decision to talk to Fox, standing forever in place, caged by the grief and anger of the fifteen-year-old girl she'd once been. He wasn't in the apartment, but his scent lingered in the air. Hugging a pillow to her chest for a minute, she breathed deep, then got moving; giving herself too much time to think would only ratchet up her nerves.

She was in the middle of preparing dinner when the sound of a key in the door had a smile breaking out over her face. "Thank you for the flowers," she said and walked into his arms, the material of his black T-shirt soft against her cheek.

Duffel sliding to the floor and guitar already propped up beside the door, Fox massaged the back of her neck as he kissed her slow and deep. "I had images of you naked on a bed of petals when I picked out the roses." He stroked his finger down the shell of her ear with that sinful confession, his lips curved. "What are we doing tonight?"

She'd intended to suggest they stay at home and talk, but all at once, that felt too confining, too claustrophobic for what she needed to say. "I thought dinner, then maybe we could drive up Mount Eden?" The volcanic cone offered sweeping views of the city, the vista breathtaking at night.

"Sounds good."

AN HOUR AND A HALF later, Molly realized she shouldn't have delayed, her nerves so frayed that Fox had watched her with careful eyes throughout dinner. However, he hadn't said anything, and now he parked the Ferrari at the top of the mountain she'd suggested, in front of the huge, sloping crater that told of a massive explosion millennia ago.

Getting out, he whistled at the view of the city spread out around them in every direction, thousands of lights glinting against the silky black of the night. "Damn. It's three hundred and sixty degrees."

His pleasure fed hers. "It's one of my favorite places in the city." Sliding her hand into Fox's when he held it out, she walked with him along the path that led to another vantage point on the other side of the crater.

And in his touch, she found her courage. "My mother," she began into the silence broken only by the whispering of the long grasses moving in the slight breeze, "loved my father." It had been a toxic love that meant Karen Webster couldn't walk away, even when loving Patrick Buchanan was a cancer on her soul.

"After the scandal broke," Molly continued, Fox's hand strong and warm around her own, "she resigned her board positions with various charitable organizations and stayed home with my father. I think she was waiting for him to dust himself off as he'd always done before." Patrick Buchanan had been like the proverbial cat with nine lives. "She didn't seem to understand how serious the charges were, that he'd certainly end up in prison."

Arriving at the vantage point, the spot otherwise empty tonight, Molly gave herself a break and pointed out the glittering lights of the cars snaking over the Harbour Bridge, Auckland a city surrounded by water.

Fox wrapped his arms around her from behind, a tall, strong wall of protective heat. "Nice view, but you know the view I like better." He bent to kiss her throat.

Shivering, she angled her neck for another.

"You figure people are making out in those cars where we parked?" Fox asked after fulfilling her silent request.

"I saw steam on the windows of the hatchback." A long, quiet minute as she luxuriated in the feel of being held under a starlit sky while the city sparkled like a jewel-bright carpet below them. "Do you want to hear the rest?" she asked when she felt strong enough to face the past again. "It's not particularly unique."

"It's about you." Fox spread his legs, drew her even closer. "I want to know."

Holding on to his forearms where they crossed her chest, Molly drew in a trembling breath. "When they granted him bail, my father came home and literally never left again until the day he died. He became an apathetic shadow of the brilliant, manipulative, controlling person I'd always known."

To this day, Molly didn't know if his withdrawal had been driven by shame, or simply disbelief that *he*, Patrick Buchanan, had been caught and held to account. "My mother... it was like she couldn't function on any level without his orders." Molly could still remember the bewildered look in her mother's sky-blue eyes.

"After I came home and found her passed out drunk every day for a week"—Molly's stomach churned at the remembered smell of alcohol drenching the air—"while my father sat staring at his computer, I began opening the mail that had piled up. That's when I saw what he'd been doing."

CHAPTER 23

"**D**RUGS?"

"Close." Her hands had begun to shake as she looked at the bank statements and final notices for bills. "Online gambling. He'd bankrupted us in a matter of weeks." Worse, he hadn't paid any of the insurance premiums since the day of his arrest, invalidating all the policies.

Fox's voice was harsh when he spoke. "No man has the right to do that to his family."

"I confronted him—I think part of me was hoping I'd misunderstood." Like a child wanting to be assured the bogeyman wasn't real. "When he stirred enough to yell at me to get the hell out, I waited for one of my mother's sober days and showed her the papers. The way she looked at me... I broke her heart into a million pieces that day." Molly would never forget that instant, never forget the unvarnished agony that had sent Karen Webster to the floor in a fetal curl.

Molly had begged for her mother to talk to her, said sorry a hundred times, but she'd continued to lie there, mute and fractured. "I don't think she was ever sober again."

"That is not on you." A ruthless declaration as Fox turned

her to face him. "Baby, you have to know that." He crushed her against the strong planes of his chest and only then did she realize she was crying.

Wrapped tight in the protective circle of his arms, she felt so safe that she couldn't fight the crashing wave of shattering emotion—feelings she'd hidden away for so long that she'd almost convinced herself they no longer existed. That none of it had the power to hurt her any longer.

Her nose was stuffy, her throat scratchy, and her eyes wrung dry when Fox spoke against her ear, the whiskey and sin of his voice an addiction—and that was the greatest irony of her life.

"You're telling me this so I'll know how bad you're messed up?"

Molly leaned back enough to meet his gaze, the smoky green black in the darkness. "Yes." He'd read the newspaper reports, knew what had happened next—the loss of their family home and everything else not already consumed by escalating legal costs, her parents' deaths in a car crash on the way to a court appearance, her mother later discovered to have been five times over the legal limit.

The only miracle was that Karen Webster had taken only her husband with her, her car smashing not into another vehicle but into a concrete pylon. When it came out that there had been no skid marks on the road, the media had called it a murder-suicide. Molly wasn't sure they were wrong.

"I've worn the coat of being a well-balanced, 'normal' person for so long that I almost believe it myself most days," she confessed, "but I'm not. I have stuff inside me that chokes me up until I can't breathe. I'm *really* messed up."

Fox rubbed his thumbs over her cheeks, wiping away the remnants of her tears. "I got plenty of fucked-up parts inside me, too. Yeah, they kick my ass sometimes, but I wouldn't be me without those parts, and you wouldn't be you." His voice dropping, holding her captive. "That's the Molly I want, the messed up, smart, sexy one standing right in front of me."

Passionate and edgy and starkly romantic, his words kissed the torn-up places inside her. "This," she said, her voice husky, "us. It's not working."

Molten fury, Fox's skin pulling taut over his cheekbones. "Hell it's not."

"Wait." Molly pressed her fingers to his lips. "That didn't come out right." She swallowed, blurted out the words that had been building inside her since the moment he asked her if she wanted to change the rules. "I don't want a deadline." Her heart ripping open, the exposure terrifying. "I don't want to pretend like my mother did, that my life—our relationship—is something other than what it is."

Fox's heart staggered at hearing the words he'd been waiting for since the instant he'd first realized she was his. Parting his lips to speak, he suddenly became aware of a large group of energetic and giggly teens racing down to the lookout. "Shit."

Grabbing Molly's hand, he led her back up the rise, head angled to avoid being recognized, and drove home as fast as legally possible. This was one night he definitely did not need to be pulled over. Backing Molly against the closed door of her apartment the instant they were inside, one hand on her hip, his other arm braced over her head, he said, "Let me get this right." His heart ricocheted inside his ribcage. "You're saying you want us to go on for longer than a month? No limits?"

Molly nodded.

When he simply watched her, she wet her lips, spoke in a throaty whisper. "Yes. I want to change the rules."

"You sure?" No doubts, there could be no doubts in her mind. "Because once you take that step, I won't allow you to back away."

"Yes." The single word was potent with emotion. "I'm sure. I want to be with you in every way... I want to see who we'll become together."

A dazzling kaleidoscope exploding in his mind, Fox thrust his hand into Molly's hair, unraveling her ponytail to fist his hand in the silky black strands. "No more hiding," he ordered. "You're *mine,* in private and in public. Do you understand?"

"Yes." It was a thready sound, her throat moving as she swallowed. "You want the same thing?"

"Baby, I never had any intention of letting you go at the end of the month." Fox's words shattered everything Molly thought she knew. "You're like the perfect song and I knew that the first night we spent together."

The perfect song.

No one had ever said anything so beautiful to her. Already-gritty eyes burning, she said, "H...how do we do this?" Her fingers curled against his back. "Will you fly down to spend time with me after your tour is complete?"

"No half measures, not ever," was his unbending response. "You come with me."

Again, he'd hit her with the unexpected. "I can't." Breathless words, her pulse in her mouth. "My life, my friends, everything is here."

"I'm not."

It was a simple, absolute fact. Shaken, she gripped at him to keep herself upright. "If I choose to stay here?"

"I told you, no half measures." His expression was brutal, all the niceties stripped away to reveal the strong, determined man at the core of him. "If you don't come with me, what'll we have? A few weeks a year?"

"We could make it work," she argued, so overwhelmed by the careening speed of this that her mind scrabbled to find steady ground.

"No." A flat rejection. "I want to take you out to dinner. I want to walk with you down the street. I want to pretend not to be bored while you shop. I want to kiss you before I go on-stage. I want you in my bed every damn night."

Each word he spoke, it echoed her own secret desires.

"So you decide, Molly, once and for all, if you want me enough to take the chance."

"That's not fair." She adored him, but he was asking her to alter the course of her life in a way that could never be un-done. "I want to be with you more than I've ever wanted anything—"

Kissing her without warning, his mouth hot, his tongue stroking deep, the slight abrasiveness of his callused fingertips familiar on the side of her face, he whispered, "Say that again."

"I can't bear to think of being alone in this apartment again," Molly said, her voice shaking, "of watching you leave… of hearing that you've found someone else. You're *mine.*" A raw claim.

Fox shuddered. "Fuck, baby, I got no argument with that." One hand continuing to cradle the side of her face, his thumb brushing over her cheekbone, he said, "Why the hesitation, then?"

The stark, unconditional honesty of the moment demanded she speak the truth. Finding another strand of courage, she gave voice to the fear that had a clawed grip on her heart. "What if we don't last in the real world?" The pressure of the media, the constant barrage of attention, it could wear a person down to the bone. "What if I'm not strong enough?"

"I know it'll be hard." Fox's breath hot against her skin, his body a wall of muscle. "But you've faced hard before and kicked it to the curb." Green eyes violent with a pride that tightened the chains around her heart. "Delaying the decision won't make it any easier."

"No." The only way to know if they had what it took to make it under the unforgiving glare of the world stage or if it would smash them into jagged shards was to step into that life.

Ever since she'd been old enough to understand the poisonous nature of her parents' relationship, Molly had promised herself she'd never make the same mistake, never become addicted to anything or anyone. Except here she was, addicted to a rock star who lived in a world that was the diametric opposite of the staid, suburban existence that had been the goal she'd set herself as a devastated and heartbroken teenager—the lights, the cameras, the intrusion, the cruelty, it was her personal nightmare.

No matter what happened, the instant she made this decision, she ended her chance of ever having an ordinary life. It hurt to think of the death of a dream she'd held on to for so long, but nothing hurt more than the thought of losing Fox.

"Yes," she said on a whisper of sound. "I'll come with you."

Fox's eyes held her own, a passionate, possessive fire in their depths. "No half measures, no regrets."

"No half measures," she vowed, her pulse a staccato beat and her heart on her sleeve. "No regrets."

Fox's kiss branded her, his body imprinting on her cells.

PART
TWO

CHAPTER 24

MOLLY'S FIRST IMPRESSION OF FOX'S home in the Pacific Palisades area of Los Angeles was of gleaming glass and shimmering blue set back against an unexpectedly green backdrop of spruces and other foliage. The light-filled modern structure, situated on a slope, was all square angles and floor-to-ceiling windows that provided a magnificent view of Santa Monica Bay in the distance, while the water from the infinity pool on the second floor fell in a cool waterfall to a lower pool.

"It's beautiful," she said, standing in the sunlit living room that overlooked the infinity pool. The sun beat down outside, but inside it was cool, the air-conditioning soundless. "It's not what I expected."

"What?" That lean dimple appeared in his cheek. "Some messy bachelor pad?"

"Um, yes," Molly admitted, wanting to kiss him but feeling oddly shy in this new place a literal world apart from everything she knew.

Laughing, Fox slid open the doors to the patio around the pool and tucked her to his side. His kiss was slow, the way he rubbed his nose against hers heart-catchingly sweet. "I have a cleaning service—they come in once a week unless I tell them not to. I don't like anyone in my space when I'm working on a new song." A playful bite to her lower lip. "I'll make an exception for naked Molly, however."

Scrunching up her nose at him, she said, "Can you ask them not to come this month?" She needed time to settle without having to deal with strangers. The one good thing was that she wouldn't have to stress about work—the copy-editing certificate she'd completed last year in order to earn extra income, before her promotion at the library put that on the back burner, was now going to be part of her new life.

It would take time and a lot of hard work, but she planned to build herself a career as an independent editor and researcher with the emphasis on the latter. Never did she want Fox to think she was with him for his money—and more, she needed to be her own person, needed to be the Molly who was Fox's perfect song. That Molly stood on her own two feet. "The house looks clean anyway," she added.

"Whatever you want." Fox nodded toward the kitchen area that flowed off from the large living space. "Their number's on the fridge if you want to make the call yourself."

Molly smiled, liking the idea of jumping right into their life together. "I will." Her jaw cracked on a huge yawn before she could say anything else. "I'm exhausted," she said when it passed. "Let's go take a nap."

Fox's eyes gleamed. "A nap?"

"A nap." She made her voice stern. "After we shower. Even flying in a fancy-pants private jet doesn't make me feel any less icky after twelve hours in the air."

Running his hand possessively over her body in a way that had her rethinking her priorities, Fox led her deeper into the house and to a sun-drenched bedroom. Centered in the sprawling space was a king-size bed made up with crisp white sheets, an electric guitar leaning against one of the walls. Seeing the guitar eased the nerves in her stomach—that this house was worth millions didn't alter the fact it was Fox's home.

And now hers.

The attached bathroom, she saw when Fox tugged her inside, was enormous, the shower full of jets, the bathtub a huge square thing. "Wow, I could go swimming in there."

Fox ripped his T-shirt over his head and dropped it on the shimmering gray of the floor tiles. "Get naked."

A sigh leaving her at the male perfection of him, Molly wriggled out of her clothes. Fox was already in the shower, all jets on and body soapy when she stepped inside. He hauled her close, his mouth firm on hers, his cock long and thick against her abdomen. "How about a little exercise before that nap?"

Hitching her up onto his hips with easy masculine strength, he pinned her against the tile. "Are you sticky and damp for me, Molly?" he murmured, reaching behind her to run his soapy fingers lightly over the cleft of her buttocks. "Say yes, baby, because I want in."

His words, his actions, they made her thighs clench around his hips, her mouth opening for his on a breathy "Yes."

He played his tongue over her own, confident and demanding, as the blunt head of his cock nudged at her, and then he was pushing inside. Shivering as he stretched her to aching pleasure, she wrapped her arms around his neck and used her teeth to tug at the ring that had been her temptation into the sexiest of sins.

"Fuck, I love it when you do that." Gripping her under her thighs, he began to move, the rhythm fast and deep, her breasts rubbing against the taut muscle of his chest with every thrust.

She kissed him again as he pushed his cock in to the hilt, then pulled out almost the entire way… only to thrust his way back in. The relentless pressure, the erotic friction, the feel of his powerful body moving in her, around her, it made her shudder and come without warning, her inner muscles convulsing on the thickness of him.

"Christ!" Fingers tightening on her thighs, he increased the depth and force of his thrusts until he came, the wet heat of his seed inside her a reminder of the primal nature of their intimacy.

THEY DID NAP AFTER FOX soaped up her lazy-limbed body, the pleasure heavy in her blood, while she shampooed her hair. Rubbing her dry with a big fluffy towel once they were clean, he nudged her toward the bed, murmuring, "Reflective glass," when she hesitated to walk naked into the bedroom.

It still felt incredibly naughty to cross the room nude, since *she* could see through the glass. She slid under the sheets, snuggling into Fox when he followed her to bed, his body cool from the shower, his hair damp. Above them, the wide skylight showcased a vivid blue sky, but her body thought it was five o'clock in the morning.

They slept in a tangle of limbs, Fox's body curved behind her own, his thigh thrust between hers, one of his arms under her head. It was a position she'd become used to, the warm strength of him lulling her to sleep within minutes. She didn't wake until three hours later, according to the bedside clock.

Fox wasn't in bed, but she rolled over just in time to see him coming out of the bathroom. He was as naked as when they'd gone to bed, and just as gorgeous. Noticing she was awake, he smiled that slow Fox smile that made her heart skip a beat. "Hello, sleepyhead."

"Mmm." Yawning, she stretched. "Come back to bed."

But Fox was already pulling on a pair of gray sweatpants. "Insatiable." Closing the distance between them, he pressed both palms on the bed, one on either side of her head, and bent to speak against her lips. "I'm starving."

Molly tugged him down. He didn't resist, lying on top of her, the sheet between them a thin barrier that did nothing to block the wild heat of his skin. "Kiss me," she said, her arms around his shoulders, "and I might make you that omelet you like."

His hand curving over her bare breast after he pulled down the sheet, he said, "Kisses as bribery?" Then his smiling mouth came down on hers, the kiss playful, his mouth sucking on her lower lip, her teeth nibbling at his in sensual retaliation.

Neither of them was in a hurry, content to just be together.

"I think you've earned your omelet," she said some time later, shaping the breadth of his shoulders with her hands. "Show me your kitchen."

Fox brushed her hair off her forehead, the tenderness in his expression intermingled with unhidden possessiveness. "I'm happy you're in my house, in my bed." He palmed her breast again. "Where you belong."

No woman, Molly thought, could question Fox's commitment when he was so blunt about it. "I'm happy to be here," she said, then gave him a rueful smile. "Also a little scared and nervous, but underneath it all, happy." And that happiness? It scared her, too... because it seemed too passionate, too wonderful, to last.

Fox's gaze was intent, his eyes dark. "Let's make this town ours, Molly."

THE FIRST THREE DAYS WEREN'T much different from the life Molly was used to living. By unspoken agreement, she and Fox stayed home except for short visits out to get groceries and pick up a couple of things she discovered she needed after she unpacked. By some stroke of luck, the paparazzi didn't seem to have realized Fox was back in the country, so he was able to show her around without anyone dogging their heels.

The area around Fox's home was lovely, it and neighboring houses set on large parcels of land that ensured privacy. There was also a park, complete with hiking trails, only a short drive away. Molly loved their walk along a canyon trail early one balmy evening, the two of them laughing as serious hikers passed them by with sniffs of disdain for their strolling pace. But his neighborhood was only a small part of a sprawling city, and Molly quickly realized she'd need a car if she wanted to get anywhere on her own.

"I'll take a few driving lessons," she said as Fox showed her the sights in his black SUV in place of the highly recognizable red Lamborghini that was his pride and joy. "Get myself used to staying on the wrong side of the road." Seeing they were on the highway that ran parallel to the coastline, she rolled down the window to take in the sea air, the view breathtaking along what her research told her was one of the most scenic routes in the country. "Let's do the entire drive one day."

"We'll take the Aventador," Fox said. "It hugs the road like you do my cock when I'm inside you."

"Fox." She pushed at one muscled arm, to his wicked grin. "I cannot believe you just compared me to a car!"

"No, I compared the car to you," he pointed out, one hand on the steering wheel, the big SUV moving so smoothly it appeared an extension of his body. "She gives me a sweet ride, but nothing comes close to my Molly."

Her heart turned to goo.

"As for your driving," he said, while she fought the urge to crawl over and distract him from the road, "I'll set you up with a car and a driver until you're comfortable on your own." Reaching out, he tapped her cheek. "I don't want you feeling trapped."

Molly's instinct was to say no, but she knew that was pride talking.

"I take care of what's mine," Fox said when she didn't answer, his tone uncompromising as he pulled off the highway and into a parking spot that overlooked the beach. Switching off the engine, he turned to brace his arm along the back of her seat. "Don't make an issue out of this."

Molly hadn't been about to until that last statement. "I'll make an issue out of anything I please," she said, the sound of the waves splashing to shore a gentle contrast to the tension in the vehicle. "Giving orders isn't the way to get me to agree to anything."

Fox's scowl didn't fade. "You know what I'm like. Did you really think I'd leave you to navigate a new city alone? Especially when you're going to be dealing with all the other crap that comes with being with me?"

She dropped her head back against the seat and into his hand. "No, of course not, but"—turning, she poked her finger into his chest—"you can't talk to me like that. I won't take it."

Fox curled his hand around her nape. "Then you can't fight me on everything." It was a snarl. "Jesus, Molly, let me take care of you. It won't steal anything from you if you let me make life easier for you."

Her breath caught at the ferocity of his words. "Am I that bad?"

"Yes." Direct, furious. "I've never had to fight so hard to give a woman so little. You even wanted to pay for the goddamn groceries!" Blowing out a breath, he tugged her closer with the grip he had around her nape, his kiss a stamp of possession. "I make millions. I don't have anyone to spend it on. I will damn well spend it on you."

Heart thudding, Molly pressed her hand against his chest. "Yes to the car and driver, but—"

"Always a fucking but," he growled. "No buts. I told you—I take care of what's mine, and you are *mine*."

"I am not a piece of property!"

He squeezed her nape. "And I'm not your fucking lapdog." Releasing her without warning, he put the car into gear and peeled out of the parking space to head back to the house.

He didn't say anything else until they were almost home,

when he slammed both hands to the steering wheel and shot her a fuming look. "I'm a man. If that's not what you want—"

"What?" Molly spoke through clenched teeth, the scream built up inside her. "I should go back to my old life? I quit my job, gave up my apartment—"

"You also promised to trust me!" Fox pulled up in front of the gate to the house, pushing the remote attached to the dashboard to open it. "Remember that?" He powered through the barely open gate and up the winding drive bordered by trees. "What do you think I'll do? Abandon you penniless and broken like your parents did?"

"You bastard!" Molly fisted her hands, eyes stinging at the brutal emotional slap that shoved her right back to the most horrible year of her life. "I did trust you"—with her deepest pain—"and you—" Unable to continue, she unsnapped her seat belt the instant they entered the garage and, shoving open the door, almost ran into the house.

Dragging her suitcase from the walk-in closet where she'd stashed it, she flipped it open on the carpet and began to throw her things in it as she fought not to cry. When Fox's hands landed on her upper arms, she wrenched violently away—or tried to. He wouldn't release her, tugging her back against his chest and wrapping his arms around her upper body in a steely embrace.

She kicked back at him, but her position left her at a disadvantage, her foot barely scraping his shin. "Let me go!"

"I'll never let you go." Spinning her around too fast for her to get her bearings, he clasped her to him again.

When she shoved at his chest, he didn't resist. "I'm sorry," he said.

"I don't care!" He'd used her deepest vulnerability to wound her. "I *trusted* you!"

Unbalancing her by hooking his foot around the back of her calf, he tipped her onto the bed behind her. He'd come down on top of her and pinned her wrists to either side of her head before she could catch her breath, his weight crushing her to the mattress. "I'm sorry for the way I said it," he gritted out, his pupils jet-black against the rich color of his irises, "but I'm not sorry for what I said."

"Get off me! I don't want to be anywhere near you!"

"Too bad." It was a growl of sound. "You're mine," he said again, "and I'll take care of you if it's the last thing I do. That includes making sure our fucked-up pasts don't mess up the best thing that has ever happened to me!"

CHAPTER 25

"**Y**OU REALLY NEED TO MOVE." Molly didn't want to hear the care in his tone, didn't want to see the unyielding commitment on his face. "I can't breathe."

Fox released her wrists and pushed himself up onto his elbows. "Better?" Touching his fingers to the side of her face, he went to run them down to her jaw, but she pulled away.

"Molly." The hard edge was back in his voice. "I'm no shrink, but it doesn't take a bunch of degrees for me to realize why it's so important for you to remain independent."

She flinched. "So you had to throw it in my face?" Returning her to a past that had almost destroyed her.

"You want me to ignore it instead? It's the big goddamn pink elephant in the room." Fisting his hand in her hair, he forced her to meet his gaze, the smoky green stormy. "I will *never* abandon you, never put you in a position where you have no choices." Shoving off her and the bed in a sudden move, he went to the nightstand to pull out a black leather document holder.

"Here." Throwing it on the bed beside her when she sat up, he strode to the door. "I know it'll only piss you off, but I was trying to do something to make you feel safe." He was gone a second later.

Shaken and feeling as if something precious was slipping out of her grasp, Molly picked up the document wallet. Unzipping it, she slipped out the page on top. It was a letter from an attorney, summarizing the complex legal documentation behind it. That summary was concise and to the point and it stole her breath.

Fox had set up an irrevocable trust fund in her name with a fifteen-million-dollar endowment. The money was being managed by a reputable financial firm, with the income from the principal accessible to her at any time: *income that could never be cut off by Fox or anyone else.* A generous percentage of that income would be automatically deposited into her account every month in any case.

The multimillion-dollar principal, on the other hand, would only be accessible to her after she spent at least two years with Fox, the clock having started the day she landed in Los Angeles. The payout would be doubled if she stayed five years, tripled if she stayed ten.

Hands trembling, she dropped the documents to the bed and thrust her fingers through her hair. She wasn't a shrink either, but she could see what he was doing and it broke her heart. Rubbing the heel of her hand over the organ, she got off the bed and went to find him, eventually tracking him to the gym downstairs. He'd changed into cutoff sweatpants and was lying on the bench press, having just lifted what looked like a ridiculously heavy set of weights.

Not wanting to risk disturbing him mid-press, she waited until he'd successfully cradled the bar, then straddled his body. "Look at me," she said quietly and, when he went to lift the weights again instead, closed her hands over the bar. "I won't allow our pasts to mess us up either."

Expression grim, he said, "You read it?"

"I read it." Releasing the bar, she cupped his face in her hands, her throat thick and her anger at the hurt done him a feral wildness within. "You don't have to pay me to stay with you, Fox."

A shake of his head, his jaw clenched tight. "That's not what I'm doing."

"If I have to face up to my demons," she whispered, "so do you." Somewhere inside her gorgeous, strong, talented rock star was the boy who'd been abandoned by his mother, left to the care of strangers for whom it was a paid task.

The brutal rejection had scarred him in ways she was only now beginning to see—but Molly had no intention of permitting that hurt to fester inside him. "We do this together," she said. "Don't you make me walk alone."

Rising into a seated position, he ran his hands down her back. "That's the one thing you never have to worry about."

This time it was Molly who initiated the kiss, Molly who rubbed her body over his, and Molly who demanded. Her pretty blue sleeveless shirt was on the floor in seconds, her bra gone the next instant. It frustrated her that she had to get off him to rid herself of her jeans and panties, but that only took a few heartbeats, long enough for him to kick off his sweats.

Then she was straddling Fox again, reaching down to grip the silk and steel of him, position him at her entrance before he took over, his other hand on her nape.

"Don't make me wait," she whispered and, heart trembling, spoke words she hadn't said to a single person since well before the day her world imploded around her. "I need you."

"Molly." Fox pulled her down over his rigid erection, going so deep she felt branded, his fingers digging into the soft flesh of her backside.

Molly cried out, found herself kissed with a rough tenderness that devastated her.

"We'll do this." Fox's voice, deep and harsh against her lips. "We'll make it." One hand stroking her hair. "Together."

"Together."

Into this scary, wonderful journey that had destroyed so many others. *Not us,* she vowed as Fox's kiss drew her under. *Not us.* Fox was hers and she would fight for him.

THEY WERE LYING ON THE bench press, Molly on top of Fox, his semi-hard cock still inside her and her breasts pressed against his chest when the woman in his arms stirred. "Beautiful and hot, and mine," he said, nipping at her jaw, fucking adoring her for claiming him with such sweet fierceness. "Not like property."

"Sorry." She shifted to rub her cheek against his, her movements making Fox groan as ripples of lazy pleasure rolled over his body. "I know you don't think of me that way—and I don't consider you a lapdog."

Taking a page out of her book, he ran his hand over her hair. "Sorry. You might have noticed I have a temper."

He felt her lips curve against his skin, and her response had him smiling even before she said, "I can handle it."

"I'll never say no to being handled by you, Miss Molly."

"How's this?" Rising to sit up on his body, she ran her nails over the flat disks of his nipples, a mischievous light in her eyes.

He arched into it. "More."

She gave him more, her expression telling him she was indulging herself as much as him. "Thank you," she said after he drew her down to demand a slow kiss that elicited a very female, very delicious sound from her throat.

He chuckled. "I'm that good?"

Sticking out her tongue at him, she tugged playfully at his lip ring. "You do have serious moves"—another tug when his grin deepened—"but I meant for the trust fund. I probably won't use it for my day-to-day life, but it means a lot to know it's there."

She pressed her fingers to his lips when he would've spoken, his scowl heavy. "I'll use it for things like dresses for going to industry shindigs with you, stuff I could never afford on my own and that I'll need as your date."

Fox wasn't happy, but he also knew his woman. "Yeah, okay, but you should know I plan to spoil you. Let me." He'd never had anyone to lavish with his attention, no one who was *his*.

Molly bit down on her lower lip. "I've never been spoiled before." A soft confession. "I'm willing to permit it on a trial basis."

He caught the hint of a smile, knew he was being teased. "Come here, Miss Smart-ass Molly."

Kissing and petting her when she laughed but obeyed, he knew that though they'd managed to survive this test, there'd

235

be others that cut deeper, threatened to do more damage. The only thing that might take them through to the other side was the fact they were both proving to be stubborn as anything, willing to fight claw and tooth for what they wanted.

IT WAS ON THE FOURTH day that Molly found herself on her own for the first time since her arrival in the country, Fox heading off to attend a meeting about the band's upcoming tour. "I'm picking up David along the way," he told her in the garage. "His place isn't too far from here—we'll walk over to it one of these days, force him to cook us a gourmet meal."

"Deal." Smiling, she fixed his baseball cap so it didn't shadow those incredible eyes. "Have fun and don't worry. I'll be fine."

"You have my number, and the numbers of the other guys?"

"Yes."

"Wait, I don't think I gave you Tawanna's." He took out his phone and sent her a message with the number. "She's my assistant." A grin. "My real one."

"Ha-ha." She kissed him simply because it made her happy to touch him, to taste his smile. "I'll probably stay in and go through my e-mails, work on the test pages for my first possible clients." They'd learned about her via the ads she'd taken out in a few places, then contacted her through the website Charlotte had helped her set up.

So now Anne Webster was (almost) no longer unemployed, Anne being her middle name. If Molly Webster did end up in the media, she didn't want people to start contacting her for prurient reasons. Anne would quietly go about her work while Molly lived in the spotlight with the sexiest man on the planet.

She kissed that man good-bye, then went up to the poolside patio and knuckled down to work—after first sending Charlotte an e-mail asking her best friend to message her when she was awake and free so they could catch up.

She was just finishing the second set of sample pages when the intercom chimed. Startled out of her thoughts, she walked over to the security panel after realizing someone had pressed the buzzer out by the gate. The chime came again before she'd figured out whether or not to answer. Noah, Abe, and David were all at the meeting with Fox, as was Thea, and Molly didn't know anyone else in the city.

"Hey, Fox!" came a husky female voice through the speakers. "It's Kit. I know you're back! Wake up!"

Molly's hand froze in front of the Answer button. Who was *Kit*?

"Hurry up! The damn paps are on my tail." An infuriated sound. "Dammit, now I'll have to find the remote you ga—Got it!"

Molly saw the security light turn green as the gate opened, a black sports car with its top down zipping up the drive to halt in front of the house a short time later. Whoever this woman was who had a remote to the gate, she was about to hit the front door—and she might well have a key for that, too.

Taking a deep breath and hoping against hope she wasn't about to surprise a former lover Fox hadn't yet told about his new relationship, Molly walked downstairs to open the door. The gorgeous woman on the other side, her skin a deep golden bronze, had a tumbling mass of midnight hair and a flawless body encased in a sleek emerald sheath.

Pushing her Audrey Hepburn sunglasses to the top of her head to reveal striking amber eyes, she blinked. "You're not the cleaning service." Lines marring her forehead. "If you're a stalker, you're a very not-crazy-looking one." The statement was followed by the most miniscule pause. "Love the top." The other woman gestured at the peach top with a softly-tied bow at the throat that Molly had paired with white capris.

"Are you a stalker?" Molly managed to interject. "A very fashion-conscious one?" The words were meant to give her time to think—because there were few people who wouldn't recognize the woman on her doorstep.

"Fox wishes." A snort. "I'm Kathleen Devigny."

Molly smiled through the nerves going haywire inside her. "I know—I saw *Last Flight.*" The low-budget adaptation of a heartbreaking novel set in the war-torn Congo had become a global blockbuster, catapulting the actress into Oscar contention. "I'm Molly."

Kathleen gave her a dazzling smile, perfect and false. "So, Fox isn't home?"

"No." Unsure what claim the A-list actress had on Fox, Molly felt acutely uncomfortable—but this was her home now and she had to claim it. "Would you like to come in?"

Kathleen's hesitation was slight. "Fox's science-fiction machine does make good coffee."

"You know how to use that thing?" Stepping back, Molly closed the door behind the other woman. "I haven't managed to turn it on yet."

Kathleen laughed, and it was a rich, warm sound, but instinct told Molly the actress was faking it. Not that Molly blamed her. If she and Fox— Molly cut herself off before she could obsess too far in what might be the totally wrong direction, and showed her size-zero guest up the hanging spiral staircase to the second level, Kathleen's heels clicking on the honey-colored wood.

Since she'd set up her laptop and notes outside, there was nothing in the sprawling open-plan space that flowed from kitchen to dining to living areas to give Kathleen any clue as to Molly's purpose here. "So," she said, wondering if the other woman would ask, "shall we try this machine?"

Setting her small purse on the counter, Kathleen walked around to the gleaming steel coffeemaker. "Is that a New Zealand accent?"

"Yes." Molly watched the astonishingly beautiful actress use the coffee machine with the ease of someone who'd done the same thing multiple times. "I've only been in L.A. a few days."

"What are you into?" Expression polite but distant, Kathleen passed across the first cup of coffee, made another. "My side of the business, or music?"

"Neither," she said, beginning to believe Kathleen's standoffishness had nothing to do with seeing Fox in a romantic way. "Come on, I'll show you what I'm doing at the moment."

Leading the other woman to the wrought-iron table that sat in a shaded area by the crystalline blue waters of the pool, Molly waited for her to take a seat before angling the laptop so the other woman could see the screen. "Words"—she smiled—"that's what I'm into."

Kathleen took a sip of coffee. "What's your screenplay about?"

Still not fully certain about Kathleen's place in Fox's life, Molly thought about how to respond to that cool question, went for honesty. "Are you always this suspicious or only when it comes to people you care about?" When the actress's expression became even icier, Molly shook her head. "I have no desire to be in any way famous."

Putting down her coffee, Kathleen took her sunglasses off her head and slid them back over eyes critics were calling "breathtaking in their expressiveness." "Yet you're with one of the most famous men in the world."

"It's funny how life works out." That, Molly thought, had to be the understatement of the century.

CHAPTER 26

KATHLEEN LEFT TEN MINUTES LATER, and five minutes after that, Fox called. "Whatever you said to Kit," he drawled, "she's convinced you have evil intentions toward my millions."

Her entire body warmed at his tone. "She's very protective of you." Molly understood loyalty; it was why she'd online-researched the heck out of T-Rex behind Charlotte's back weeks ago.

"We've been friends a long time," Fox said. "I've invited her back for dinner tonight—you two will be best buds as soon as she realizes you break out in hives at the idea of my millions."

"Smart aleck." Any uncertainty about who Kathleen was to Fox erased by his easy words, she luxuriated in the pleasure of talking to her man. "How's the meeting?"

"No big stress." The sound of voices in the background. "Gotta go, baby. I'll see you this afternoon."

He brought the entire band home with him, the four of them setting up shop in the state-of-the-art and fully sound-proofed basement studio. When Molly carried down snacks and cold drinks, she got two offers of marriage and a declaration that she was a goddess.

"Don't spoil the bastards." Fox scowled, grabbing one of the iced bottles of water. "They'll start following me home every day."

Hugging Fox from behind where he sat on a chair, guitar on his lap, she looked at David. "I hear you can cook."

The others hooted as David groaned. "Only for you, Molly."

Three hours later, the drummer took over the kitchen, with Molly acting as his assistant, while the other three men hung out around the big screen in the living area, talking and watching football. When Kathleen arrived, Fox threw her a beer and Abe asked her about a play in the game.

The actress disagreed vehemently with Abe's interpretation.

"Kathleen knows football," Molly said to David, popping some rolls in the oven to warm.

David stirred the pot of stew he had on the stove. "She used to be a cheerleader, but I think she would've rather played."

Hearing Kathleen roar at a touchdown, Molly agreed. "Written any new memos lately?"

A blush colored his cheekbones. "Your sister is determined to drive me insane."

Biting back her grin at how adorable he looked and sounded, she said, "You know you love it."

"Clearly, I'm a masochist." He added some pepper to the stew as Fox wrapped an arm around Kathleen's neck and dragged her into the kitchen area.

The other woman was dressed in skinny jeans and a plain white T-shirt, her hair scraped back into a ponytail and no makeup on her face, but she was no less stunning than she'd been earlier that day.

"Kit," Fox said, "you know Molly. Be nice to her. She's on the fence about dating a musician as it is."

Molly met the green of Fox's eyes, and suddenly it didn't matter that they were surrounded by others. Barely aware of Kathleen leaving his side, she placed her palms on his chest and, rising on tiptoe, kissed him soft and sweet and with all the scary, powerful emotions she felt for him. "I might be on the fence about this life," she whispered for his ears only, "but I'm not and will never be on the fence about you." He was it for her. Forever. "I will *fight* for you."

Fox's arms came around her, his head bent over hers. "You sure know how to pick your moments." One big hand against the side of her face, lips moving over her own as he spoke. "Should I kick everyone out? We'll keep David's masterpiece though."

"I think you'd have a mutiny on your hands." Stepping back with a silly, happy smile, she saw the drummer and Kathleen had moved to the other end of the kitchen to give them privacy.

Fox stroked his hand down her back with a deep, playful smile of his own. His dimple tempted her to steal another kiss—but the oven timer went off right then.

Leaning against the fridge, Fox watched her take the rolls out. "I'm starving." The ink on his arm was delineated exquisitely in the light as he caught the roll she threw him, tore off a piece to eat. "David—you letting your creation age or what?"

"I'm not the one who can't keep it in the bedroom," came the whiplash-fast retort. "Grab some bowls and tell the other wolves it's time to feed."

"I HAD FUN," MOLLY SAID to Fox several hours later, her sleep T-shirt soft around her thighs as she finished rubbing moisturizer into her face in front of the bathroom mirror and considered whether or not to tackle her hair with a brush. "I think Kathleen is thawing."

Dressed only in a pair of sweatpants, Fox cupped her breasts from behind, nuzzling a kiss into her neck, his stubbled jaw a delicious abrasion. It made her shiver and lean back into him, her arms raised to wrap around his neck as he petted her, kissing her neck the entire time.

When he stroked his hands down her body to tug up her T-shirt, slide underneath, she sighed in anticipation. The callused heat of his touch on her bare breasts was a raw shock of sensation. Shuddering, she found her eyes drawn to the mirror and to the way Fox's hands moved under the T-shirt as he fondled her, but mostly, to Fox.

The look of him as he touched her, as he kissed her... it made her feel *so* beautiful, until she could see what he saw in her. A sensual woman with creamy skin and curves that were as soft as Fox's body was hard. She didn't resist when he pulled the T-shirt off over her head and continued to pet her as he'd been doing, his tanned hands cupping her breasts, his fingers tugging on her nipples, the sinew and muscle of him apparent beneath the tats.

"Push down your panties, baby." Whiskey and sin and pure hard rock.

Shivering, she rolled them down as far as she was able to in this position, the lace tangling low on her thighs. Fox slipped one hand between her legs from the front the next instant. The erotic shock of seeing him do that had her breathless, her hips moving restlessly against him as he caressed her to a deep, pulsing orgasm.

"I love watching you come." Hand still between her legs, he nuzzled her neck again, waiting until she'd gained control of her boneless body before saying, "Lean forward and brace your hands on the counter."

Molly had no desire to argue, but instead of the fast penetration she'd expected, he was slow and tender, kissing his way down her spine to nip playfully at her butt.

"Ouch," she said without heat, his chuckle making her thighs clench.

Tugging her panties fully off, he waited until she'd stepped out of them—keeping himself busy by kissing his way back up her spine—before kicking her feet apart. One hand gripping her hip, he cupped her again from the front, using his middle finger to stroke lightly over her damp flesh.

"Hurry," Molly said, pleasure, intoxicating and rich, shimmering to new life inside her.

"You want me in?" he asked, the blunt head of his cock pushing into her, slow but relentless.

"Yes, please." She loved having him inside her, loved the feeling of possession, of belonging. "Don't go fast today."

"Anything you want, polite girl." His mouth hot and wet on her throat, he rocked into her, the words he spoke in her ear dark, carnal.

When Molly, her inhibitions lowered, murmured certain things back, he rewarded her by tugging on her engorged clit just enough to make her moan but not come. Sensation a sultry wave across her skin, she reached one arm up and back around his neck again, his skin hot against her own. "I adore you, Zachary Fox." *Adore* wasn't the only word she wanted to use, but Fox, she knew, would accept this word as he wouldn't the other.

Smoky, sexy eyes locked with hers in the mirror, his smile telegraphing an open delight. "I like being adored by you, Molly Webster."

Smiling, she continued to hold him close as he drove her to another luxuriant orgasm. A kiss to her shoulder before he pulled out—to her moan—and turned her around, hitching her up into a seated position on the black granite of the bathroom counter. It placed her at the perfect height for him to tug her forward and slide into her once again.

His cock rasped against her pleasure-swollen tissues, made her gasp. Leaning forward, she kissed him, playing with the ring in his lip. "This thing is the architect of my doom."

Cupping her butt, his smile sinful, he pulled her tight against his groin. "Ever think about a ring of your own?"

"Me?" She ran her hands over the lithe muscle of his shoulders, dropping her head to kiss her way across the ink on one side, the hot, masculine taste of him an intoxication. "No way can I pull off a lip ring. It just wouldn't look the same on me as it does on you."

Fox thrust a hand into her hair, holding her to him as she sucked on his neck. "I wasn't thinking about your lip."

"Hmm?" she murmured, blowing out a breath on the skin she'd wet.

His fingers clenched on her butt, and then he was pulling out of her, shoving up her thighs with a grip under her knees, and slamming back in. *Oh God, it felt good.* Bracing her hands behind her on the cool stone of the counter, she watched her man find pleasure in her body. His muscles bunching and releasing, his cock sliding in and out of her, slick with their mingled passion, his heavy-lidded gaze locked on the place where they joined.

It was the most incredibly erotic thing she'd ever seen.

It didn't surprise her in the least when her body wound tighter and tighter, only to come apart on a small scream.

"That's my Molly." Dragging her close, Fox took her mouth with his, one big hand on her nape. He always held her close during sex, made her feel unbearably cherished even in the most rawly sexual moment. And he always, *always* made eye contact.

Heart aching, she locked her arms and legs around him and watched him go over, her lover who was her everything. All her life, she'd fought never to be tied so absolutely to anyone, but she loved Fox until she couldn't breathe. The irony was that he was a man for whom the words "I love you" meant only abandonment, pain, and loneliness.

A HALF HOUR LATER, HER feelings for him a pulse in every cell of her body, Molly sat curled up in Fox's lap in bed, her T-shirt and panties back on and her lips cool with butter-scotch ice cream. "The ring," she said after he drew the spoon back from between her lips. "Were you serious?"

He ate a bite of the decadent dessert. "I was just think-ing"—a wicked smile—"since you have so much fun with mine, I might enjoy playing with one."

"Where?"

"Here." A tap of the back of the spoon against her left nipple.

Molly flushed, the ice cream he'd fed her before speaking that single word sliding down her throat. "Never going to happen." The idea of a nipple ring was so outside the realm of anything she'd ever considered that she could feel herself turning redder with every second that passed.

Setting the ice cream on the bedside table, Fox cuddled her close. "You are so cute." His chuckle vibrated against her. "I was teasing. Not that I wouldn't fuck you silly if you turned up with a nipple ring—but since I do that anyway, it wouldn't make any difference."

"You're awful," she muttered, threatening to pull his hair. "Maybe I'll get a piercing one day just to see the look on your face."

"You know another place women sometimes get pierced?" His voice was a gritty purr that touched her in her most private places.

"Yes. I read *Cosmo*." Grabbing the ice cream, she shoved a spoonful into his grinning mouth. "That particular piercing is never, ever, *ever* going to be a possibility."

Swallowing the ice cream, Fox dipped a finger in the butterscotch and painted her lips with it before kissing the cream off. "I was going to say I hope you don't go that far. I like you all soft and lush down there."

Breasts swelling under the T-shirt, the "soft and lush" parts of her damp, Molly decided to give Zachary Fox a taste of his own teasing medicine. "You know what else I read in *Cosmo*?"

"What?"

"That guys get certain lower-body piercings, too. Apparently it can be very pleasurable for a woman."

A look of pure horror on his face. "Jesus H. Christ! Feed me more ice cream to get that nightmare image out of my head."

Shoulders shaking in laughter, she did as ordered. If a few drops "accidentally" fell on his chest and she had to lick them up, well they both had a good time. Especially after she managed to drop the ice cream on the part of his anatomy he had no intention of piercing. Fox "complained" about her very bad aim and took over, only for Molly to find herself turned into dessert.

They fought for the spoon, laughing and cheating by any possible means, the sheets so tangled by the time a truce was declared that they had to get out and remake the bed.

It would hurt so much if he wasn't in her bed and her life one day in the future, Molly thought as she watched Fox leave the room to get rid of the ice cream carton. The fear was enough to choke her, make her want to turn and run, save herself from the pain. But the Molly who hid was gone, replaced by this wild Molly who loved a rock star named Zachary Fox... and who was considering the benefits of a nipple ring.

CHAPTER 27

KATHLEEN TURNED UP AGAIN TWO weeks later, while Molly was working at her computer. She'd had a bite from a nonfiction writer looking to hire a research assistant for a short-term contract. Since being able to make a living doing that type of work was Molly's ultimate goal, she was in the midst of preparing a detailed outline of her proposed research path when the other woman rang the doorbell.

"Hi." A long, false Kathleen smile when Molly opened the door. "Look, I was wondering if you wanted to do lunch? Since Fox is a good friend, and you're in his life, we should get to know each other."

"I'd love to, but can we do it tomorrow?" Molly said, unsurprised Kathleen remained skeptical about her—trust couldn't come easy in this town. "I'd really like to send an e-mail off to a potential client in the next couple of hours," she added so the other woman wouldn't think she was blowing her off for no good reason.

Kathleen's expression was odd for a second before she said, "Sure, I'm between films at the moment, so my time's flexible. I'll pick you up at one?"

"Sounds good."

Conscious Kathleen would select a nice restaurant, Molly dressed with care the next day, choosing a slim black skirt that flattered her body and a pretty mint-green top. To her surprise, the actress took her to a park in what appeared to be a suburban neighborhood where everyone was too busy with their kids to worry about anyone else. "That guy makes the best burgers," she said, pointing to a silver food truck parked in the shade of the palm trees on the street. "You game?"

"Sure." Molly waited with the actress at a picnic table while Kathleen's bodyguard went to buy the food, the line long enough that it'd be several minutes at least.

"Does the guard go with you everywhere public?" Molly realized she'd unintentionally stepped on a nerve when Kathleen's expression went blank, shields slamming down. "Sorry," she said at once. "I was just trying to break the awkward silence."

Kathleen shrugged and thrust a hand through her hair. "It's no secret. I have a disturbed and obsessed fan who thinks we're married—the cops haven't managed to catch the fucker, even after he broke into my house and left a disgusting piece of himself on my bed."

Knowing exactly the toll stalking could take on a victim, Molly was horrified, then outraged. "At least you won't have any problem with DNA evidence."

Kathleen laughed, the frost thawing a fraction. "That's just what Fox said."

The bodyguard returned then. Leaving the food and bottles of water on the table, he walked off to stand by the car with the driver, their eyes scanning the picnic table and surrounding areas.

The scrutiny made Molly want to squirm. "Don't you feel bad when they just stand there?"

"Not at the wages I pay them." The pragmatic words were followed by a small smile that might even have been real. "It's okay—they're professionals. I tried to get Butch to eat with me once, but he was mortified. How is he supposed to protect me if he's stuffing his face? Casey, my driver, he's a bodyguard, too, so he thinks the same."

"I see their point." Molly took a bite of the burger and moaned. "Oh my God, does Fox know about this truck?"

"Yes, I showed him." Taking a bite of her own burger, Kathleen chewed and swallowed before saying, "Did you get that e-mail sent?"

"Yes." Molly took a sip of water. "I got the project. It's small, but it's a start in the right direction." Fox had opened a bottle of champagne to celebrate last night, his genuine happiness for and pride in her another arrow to Molly's heart.

Kathleen was silent for a long while. Wary of exploding another conversational mine, Molly watched the mothers pushing their toddlers on the swings and found herself thinking how much Charlie would've enjoyed a lunch like this. She missed having her best friend nearby.

"You're really real, aren't you?"

Molly angled her head at the other woman. "I don't understand."

An incisive look. "The way you look at Fox, the way you touch him, you care about him."

Befuddled by the statement of the obvious and a little annoyed at Kathleen's continued questioning of her and Fox's relationship, she said, "Why else would I follow him halfway across the world?"

"I didn't mean to offend you." Kathleen blew out a breath. "The thing is, in this business... let's just say I've learned to be careful who I trust. Fox's always been good at looking after himself, but then he turns up with you after a vacation."

Molly kept her silence, giving Kathleen a chance to talk.

"It made me wonder what your angle was. Only I don't think you have one." The actress looked nonplussed. "Either that, or you're a better actress than I'll ever be."

"Not a chance." Putting down the uneaten part of her burger, Molly took another sip of water. "Fox is the only reason I'm here—he's become my home," she said simply. "I don't need anything else."

"I'm beginning to see that." Kathleen rolled her own water bottle in her hands. "I should've twigged when Abe mentioned how the guys end up at your and Fox's place more often than not for a jam session these days. They used to alternate between houses a lot more. Now he says it feels like your place is home."

Molly had had no idea Abe felt that way, he said so little. "Thank you for telling me, and thank you for reaching out."

"I did it to get some dirt so I could open Fox's eyes about you."

Molly laughed at the other woman's disgruntled expression. "I know."

"Shit." Kathleen shoved her hand through her already tousled hair. "Now we have to be friends. You're going to need me to teach you how to navigate these shark-infested waters." She leaned forward. "Rule one—nice people get eaten alive."

"Should I take notes?" Molly asked lightly, even as her

stomach turned at the reminder she existed in a different world now, one run on rules she didn't understand.

Kathleen smiled, and this time, it wasn't as perfect, but was much more real. "Don't worry. I've got the guidebook." She held out her hand. "Hi, I'm Kit."

SEVEN DAYS AFTER THE TENTATIVE beginnings of her friendship with Kit, and Molly didn't know what she was doing at a swanky New York party filled with tattooed rock stars other than her own, award-winning actors, actresses, and directors, "money people," assorted plus-ones like Molly, and beautiful swimsuit models with boobs out to there and legs up to their ears.

"Stereotypes," she muttered under her breath.

Fox leaned close. "What?"

"I'm reminding myself I shouldn't judge anyone until I meet them." She brushed a speck of dust off the shoulder of his black shirt with intricate black-on-black detailing along one side—which he'd worn in place of his usual tee because he'd overheard her talking to Charlotte about how men in suits were hot. She'd been teasing Charlie about T-Rex, but Fox had been adorably jealous.

When she'd pointed out how cute he was being, she'd ended up naked.

Now he was as gorgeous and as charismatic as usual, his version of a "suit"—the fitted short-sleeved shirt worn over a pair of well-loved jeans—unbelievably hot. In Fox's case, she thought, the clothes very definitely didn't make the man, the man made the clothes. "Though," she added in a whisper, "it's really, really difficult to accept that the twenty-five-year-old stunner is with the seventy-five-year-old lech out of true love."

"What a cynic." Fox's lips curved, his hand sliding to her butt, possessive as hell. "A sexy cynic."

Feeling her face heat, she tugged at his wrist, though his smile had melted her bones. *"Fox."*

He kept his hand where it was, stroking her through the tight red pencil skirt he'd bought her, and which she had to agree made her body look smokin'. "I love it when you blush."

"I'm going to kill you," she threatened *sotto voce* as one of the besuited record executives came over. The man oozed oily sincerity, but for some reason, Molly liked him. Short and with a balding hairline, he reminded her of a friend of a friend—Ken was a sweet guy, but he wanted so badly to be liked that he went over the top with it.

Now Fox was noncommittal to the point of looking bored with this "Ken's" conversational overtures. Molly did her best, but the man slunk away with a big fake smile a couple of minutes after he'd arrived. "Fox, that was rude." It shocked her to see this side of him—the arrogant asshole star.

"Do you know how many guys like that circle around me and the others? Fucking vultures. They want us to jump labels or for one of us to leave the band, go solo, make money for them." Scowling, he took a swig out of the beer bottle in his right hand. "If I was just some poor schmuck who wanted him to talk to me, I'd be lucky to get a 'piss off.' I wouldn't even exist."

Molly closed her mouth before she could say the words that wanted to come out. Fox knew these people far better than she did. But the way he'd spoken, he didn't sound like the man she'd fallen for.

A squeeze around her waist. "Hey, sorry." He nuzzled a kiss to her temple. "Band got kicked around a bit back at the start. Men like that tried to cheat us into signing lousy contracts when it became clear we were developing a following. Guess it's a sore spot."

Leaning into him, she placed a hand on his chest, his body heat caressing her through the fabric. "It's okay." She could understand his disdain for people like those who'd treated him in a shoddy manner, but the unexpected glimpse of who he could be in this world planted a seed of worry in her mind about exactly how well she knew him, a sense of burgeoning unease in her belly.

So when a long-limbed goddess with mink-brown hair down to her butt and a dress that might as well have been painted on sashayed over after Fox left to grab them something to eat, Molly wasn't in the mood to pull her punches.

"I heard you're a librarian," the other woman said, her tone syrupy enough that it was noxious. "That's… charming." A flash of teeth so white, Molly wondered if they glowed in the dark. "And what a… sweet outfit." Cue faux laughter, eyes catty.

"Thanks, I'd return the compliment"—oh God, she was going to go to hell for this—"but you look like you picked up your clothes in the red-light district."

"This is a *ten-thousand-dollar* designer dress!" It was a screech.

"Really?" Molly shook her head, deciding she might as well give in to Evil Molly all the way. "That material is $2.99 per yard at my local fabric shop."

"You know nothing about fashion!" Spluttering, the brunette staged a quick comeback as Fox appeared with a plate. "Foxie, I was just talking to your little friend." A giggle.

Fox grabbed Molly's hand. "It's time to leave this zoo. Here." He shoved the plate of food into the other woman's hand. "Eat this. Don't throw it up later."

The look on the brunette's face was priceless. Fighting laughter as Fox all but dragged her out of the glamorous hotel ballroom hired for the party by a celebrity couple who were friends of the band members, Molly waited until they were outside to tug up her skirt past her knees so she could keep up with his pace. He took her down the hallway, through an emergency exit, and past two landings before going through another door and down the corridor to an elevator.

It arrived within seconds. The instant they were inside, he scanned his keycard, pushed the button for the penthouse, and pressed her against the wall, his mouth fused to her own. All she could think about was the security camera, but then Fox licked his tongue against hers, his hand squeezing her hip, and she forgot about everything except his body and her own.

It was as well the elevator was a fast one, arriving at the penthouse level just as Fox was fisting his hand in her skirt to pull it up. Shocked by the blast of cool air that entered the elevator when it opened directly into their suite, she pushed at him. "Cameras."

"Fuck 'em." But he tugged her out and pinned her to the wall outside the elevator.

A tearing sound, the force with which he'd pulled up her skirt causing it to rip. Her panties were gone a second later, and he was lifting her up. Locking her legs around his waist, she felt him reach down to release himself from his pants, his knuckles brushing her acutely sensitive flesh. Molly's gasp was short, ragged. Entering her in a single relentless thrust, he wrapped the hand not curved under her thigh around her throat, his mouth demanding on her own.

Barely able to process the sensations, Molly simply held on for the ride as he thrust in and out of her in a primal rhythm that made it crystal clear who was in charge. She couldn't move, couldn't do anything but kiss him, her hands locked tight in his hair while he pounded into her.

She came in a wild clenching that made him groan and rasp something so dirty in her ear that she was sure she was blushing even as her womb spasmed in pure ecstasy. Holding him close, she ran her nails over his nape. It sent him over the edge, his teeth gritted together as he buried himself to the hilt inside her, his pleasure harsh and beautiful to witness.

MOLLY FELT A TRICKLE OF sticky wetness along her thigh when Fox finally pulled out of her and set her on her feet. Her knees would've buckled if he hadn't been holding her up. Eyes slumberous, he pressed her to the wall and initiated a kiss as lazy as his earlier ones had been voracious, then reached down past her bunched-up skirt to cup one of her lower cheeks, fondling it with a possessiveness she'd come to expect. As she'd come to expect the way he was after sex.

Finding the willpower to throw her arms around his neck, she kissed him in turn, playing with the ring she loved. "That was nice." She had no idea what had set him off, but she was a very grateful beneficiary.

"Nice?" He spanked her lightly after zipping up his jeans. "Phenomenal would be a better word choice."

"How about splendiferous?"

"Is that a real word?"

"Yes. It's like splendid, only better."

"Then yeah, I'll accept that description." A pause. "You were splendid, darling."

Biting her tongue to still her laughter at his posh English accent, she put on one of her own. "You too, Foxie dear."

A pinch on her butt that made her jump before he smoothed over the punishment. "This," he said, his tone a softer version of the sexy growl that was his singing voice, "would feel better if you were naked."

"Oh?" Molly played her hands over his shirt. "What about you?"

"Trust me." He moved his own hand to undo the button and zip on her skirt.

She stepped out of it, nudging the puddle of fabric aside with her toes as Fox pulled up her fitted silk top and dropped it on the floor. Her bra took a second to remove and then she was naked, every curve exposed. Fox stepped back to take a good, long look. "You're so damn hot, Molly." Smoky-green eyes lingering on her breasts, the sensitive flesh straining as his look became a near-tactile caress. "The first time I saw you, I wanted to bend you over one of those tables at the party and do you right there—except fuck if I wanted anyone else to see what was mine."

The things he said… "I didn't think you even noticed me."

"Oh, I noticed you—especially this mouth." A single finger tracing her lips, his next words not the sexual ones she'd expected. "You smiled at Thea, and it was a punch to the goddamn gut."

It was such a romantic thing to say, and such a Fox way to say it. "I've never had a reaction to a man like I had to you," she admitted. "If you'd crooked a finger, I would've probably followed you into a dark stairwell."

Wicked delight in his smile. "Now you're putting ideas in my head." Lifting her up again, her legs around his waist, he initiated another lazy kiss, all tongue and wet heat. It was a stark contrast to the other textures that touched her skin. The well-washed denim of his jeans, the crisp cotton of his shirt, the hard angles of his belt buckle, the heat of his skin, the cool bite of his teeth.

She moaned. "Oh, I like this."

"You were right though," he said, nibbling and kissing at her mouth as he spoke. "This feels good, but skin on skin feels even better."

Running her fingers through the chocolate silk of his hair, Molly raised the topic she'd earlier shelved. "What happened downstairs?" *Something* had.

His jaw a hard line, he said, "One of the execs was about to put the moves on you."

"What?" Molly shook her head. "Fox, I only spoke to that brunette. No one else paid me the least attention."

Fox raised an eyebrow. "Like I didn't at Thea's party?"

Oh. "You know I'd never—"

"I know, but that doesn't mean I'm rational about it." One more kiss before he slid her oh-so-slowly down his body, the friction exquisite.

Molly rose on tiptoe to follow his mouth as he pushed off

the wall and straightened to his full height. Knowing what she did of his internal scars, she hated that he'd worried about losing her for even a single second. "Don't go."

"*Molly.*" Stroking his hands down her body, he palmed her ass and they indulged themselves in one another for long minutes.

Her lips deliciously kiss-swollen, she resisted when Fox took her hand to lead her to the living area of the suite. "I need to go to the bathroom."

His eyes dropped, a *very* satisfied, very male smile on his lips. "I think you should stay sticky."

Making a face at him, she ducked into the bathroom off their bedroom and had a lightning-fast shower, hair pinned up. She was just about to step back out clad in the plush hotel robe when she heard voices. Hesitating, she looked down at her robe. It covered her neck to ankle, but it was still a robe and she didn't know who was out there.

It only took a couple of minutes to find a change of underwear and a summery dress— *Underwear!* Her face burned as she realized her clothes from the party were currently in a puddle beside the elevator.

Chapter 28

MORTIFIED, MOLLY TOOK A BABY step outside the bedroom as soon as she was dressed, hoping no one would notice her in the large suite. The first thing she did was glance toward the elevator. No clothes. When Fox winked at her as soon as she turned in his direction, she knew he'd thrown the incriminating evidence somewhere where Noah wouldn't immediately see it.

The blond guitarist wrapped his arm around her shoulders when she got to him. "Why, you've changed, Molly." A sniff. "Showered, too. How *interesting.*"

Molly elbowed him, having learned by now that while Noah could be glacial and distant at times, he also had a wicked sense of humor around people he trusted. Sometime in the past few weeks, Molly had fallen into that category. Now, laughing, he pulled her close to plant a kiss on her cheek. "Fox's been telling me all about the benefits of having a girl of his own."

"I think you've had more than one girl," Molly said as Fox grabbed a seat in one of the midnight-blue armchairs by the large plate-glass windows that formed two corners of the suite, then held out a hand.

No longer shy around the other members of the band, she slid into his lap.

Noah grabbed the facing seat. "I may have had one or two"—dark gray eyes dancing—"but I've never had my *own* girl." The slightest hesitation before he continued. "Didn't seem worth the bother. No offense, Molly, but having a girl of his own is a lot of work for a man."

She arched her eyebrows. "Oh, really?"

"It's not like Fox can pat you on the ass and say 'nice ride, honey,' then show you the door when he's done." Grinning at her narrow-eyed look, the guitarist leaned back in his arm-chair. "No, he has to talk and *listen*, and when you get mad, he has to grovel and make it up to you."

"You might grovel," Fox drawled, spreading his fingers on Molly's back. "I, on the other hand, apologize manfully and sex Molly into forgiving me."

"You're both as bad as each other." Scowling at her rock star and his unrepentant friend, she got up off Fox's lap. "I'm going to order room service. I don't think my palate was re-fined enough for the canapés downstairs."

"What the hell were those orange things?" Noah kicked out his jean-clad legs after she'd passed by to grab the menu sitting on the lovely little carved table a few feet away.

"Fish eggs," Fox told him. "Expensive shit."

"Tasted like it, too." Both men laughed before Noah turned to her. "Can you order me a burger, Moll?"

"Sure." Glancing at Fox, she said, "They have pad thai."

A groan that had her digging her bare toes into the sump-tuous champagne-colored carpet, her body sensitized to the sound of his pleasure. "Order me two plates."

"Two?"

"One thing we've learned—the ritzier the hotel, the smaller the portions."

"Yeah, make that burger order a double, too," Noah said. "Throw in a couple of beers."

The elevator intercom dinged on that statement, and when Molly pressed the button to answer, it was to find Kathleen on the other end. After the way the band and Kit ended up at their place more often than not these days, Fox had predicted their suite would become the natural gathering spot after the party, the reason he'd pulled strings to make sure they ended up in the penthouse. Not only did it have a huge living area, it had a separate dining room. Molly hadn't even known there were hotel suites with dining rooms until she'd walked into this one!

Now, pushing the button to allow Kathleen to ride up, Molly waited until the stunning actress arrived, then held up the menu. "Want to add something to the order?"

Slipping off the mile-high heels she wore with her short and sparkly blue dress, Kathleen came over. "I'm starving. Those canapés looked so tempting, but did you taste any?" She shuddered, placing her glittering purse on the table. "I should know by now—A.J. always goes for pretty over edible at her parties." Having scanned the menu as she spoke, she pointed to an item on the second page. "The grilled swordfish with vegetables. Makes my mouth water just thinking about it."

Molly scribbled her choice on the notepad beside the phone and was about to pick up the handset to place the order when the elevator dinged again. Kathleen walked across to answer it, letting up Abe. Who wanted a steak, a big one. Grabbing Kathleen as he said that, he bent her over his arm and kissed her full on the mouth. "You realize your very nice tits are about to fall out of that dress."

"Please." Kathleen patted his ripped chest. "I'm sewn into this thing. Just like you are into your T-shirt." She tried to pinch the black fabric between her fingertips. "Could it be any tighter?"

It was interesting, Molly thought, how Noah's eyes had locked on that byplay, which, despite the subject matter, had held no sexual innuendo whatsoever. Abe might as well have been talking to a sister. "Did you all abandon David?" she asked when Abe dragged a chair from the bedroom and flipped it to sit with his arms on the back.

"He took off an hour ago." A shrug of Abe's heavily muscled shoulders. "Said he had to pick someone up at the airport."

Hmm... After placing the room service order, adding in a few extras because she knew how much the men could pack away, she ducked into the bedroom and sent a quick message to Thea. *Are you in the country? Did you get a flight?* Her sister had flown to London to handle a situation for a client there, become stuck in England when flights were grounded because of a storm.

Finally. Spending a couple of days in New York, was the return message. *Just waiting for my luggage now. Damn memos.*

Molly stifled her laugh. *Have fun. xoxo*

When she walked back out into the living area, it was to see Kathleen perched on the arm of Fox's chair, all toned legs and tumbling hair. The child of a pillow-lipped Venezuelan supermodel and an American tennis ace now considered a "silver fox," there was no doubt Kathleen had hit the genetic lottery, her parents' genes combining to give her a breathtaking and exotic beauty.

She was laughing at something Fox had said, and at that instant, they were the embodiment of the perfect celebrity couple.

Then Fox glanced Molly's way, held out a hand... and the look in his eyes, it was for her, no one else.

"Oops." Kathleen rose with a good-natured smile. "I'm in your spot."

"Here." Noah patted the side of his armchair, distinct challenge in his expression.

Kathleen smiled sweetly. "Thank you, but I'd rather cuddle a rabid dog." Pointedly skirting his seated form, she pulled out the executive chair from the desk in the opposite corner and rolled it next to Abe.

"What's going on with those two?" Molly whispered in Fox's ear, having noticed the slight edge in their interactions soon after she'd first met Kathleen.

"Later."

As it was, by the time they got to bed, she'd forgotten the question and Fox had other things on his mind.

MOLLY WOKE TO AN EMPTY bed, but she could hear Fox out on the small private balcony off the bedroom, strumming his guitar. Smiling, she simply lay there for a while, listening to her man. His talent was apparent even in what appeared to be a meandering dance through the chords, as if he were exercising his fingers. The breeze was soft, the sunlight coming through the open balcony doors languid and golden, its rays just kissing the bed.

Every so often, when the wind lifted the gauzy curtains a fraction, she caught sight of Fox seated in one of the outdoor chairs. He was shirtless, his feet up on the railing and his guitar held like a lover. Stretching luxuriantly, she decided to get up, make them both some coffee using the espresso machine that came with the suite. She liked doing these things for him, looking after him as he did her. Showing Fox just what he meant to her until he believed it deep within, that was her number-one priority.

It was as she was tying the belt on the hotel robe that she remembered her phone. As was her habit, she'd turned it to silent during the night.

Picking it up to check if Charlotte had messaged, she was surprised to see notifications for six voice mails and double that number of texts. Curious, she opened a text message at random—from a library colleague—and felt her eyes widen.

Molly! You're on the front page of G&V! And looking hot!

Mouth dry, heartbeat a drum against her ribs, she scanned through the other texts; they all said pretty much the same thing. She had somehow ended up front and center on one of *the* major gossip blogs in the world.

Not bothering with the voice messages and her fingers too shaky to work the small phone screen, she grabbed the sleek touchscreen tablet Fox had given her with a card that said "Spoiling has begun." She was ridiculously attached to the thing already, which pleased him to an adorable smugness that always made her want to kiss him silly.

Today however, she was too stressed to think about how very cherished he made her feel. Sitting down on the edge of the bed, she did a search for the exact site address—while she had a secret weakness for celebrity gossip, it was strictly in magazine format. She'd curl up in an armchair on a Sunday morning, tea in hand, and spend a couple of hours reading through the articles.

Now, fingers trembling, she clicked through… to see a full-color image of her and Fox in the elevator. His mouth was locked on hers, his hand pulling up her skirt, the tattoos on his arm taut over muscle, while one of her own hands was clenched in his hair. Her other hand was lost to sight, but the angle of the shot made it appear she was stroking him through his jeans.

Her heart roared in her ears, the brutal memories of her father's scandal smashing to the surface to tear shreds off her. Gripping the sheet in one bloodless fist, she took a deep breath, exhaled. She did the same again and again, calming herself before she could spiral any further into the night-mare. "It could've been much worse," she murmured and looked back down.

The photo was tame by most standards—two lovers who'd gotten a bit carried away with a kiss. Embarrassing, but of a nudge-nudge, wink-wink kind rather than anything that would lead to malicious attacks. Fox, after all, wasn't a mar-ried politician who'd run a campaign based on family values, and she wasn't an underage girl.

No, this was a shot of two adults enjoying one another. Yes, it made her blush, would do so for a while yet, but she'd live it down. Her thundering heart settling into a more controlled rhythm, she blew out another breath and looked at the photo again. Her lips curved slowly. Maybe the embarrassment was worth it to see the way Fox was so totally focused on her, his entire being concentrated on the kiss.

She should've left it at that, but she'd already scrolled past the photo to read the article—which wasn't much, just a couple of lines about Fox's "mystery date"—and caught the start of the comment thread. It was already over two thousand, though according to the blog's timestamp, the image had only been up for an hour.

At first she didn't understand what it was she was reading, then it hit her with the force of a body blow.

"I'd do her. I'd even bring the paper bag to put over her face."

"Ugh."

"I never knew Fox liked pork chops. Oink, oink."

"What a hot slut. Lol."

"Maybe he was drunk?"

"Or maybe she has a vacuum for a mouth?"

"Total thunder thighs. Gross. Fox, u can do better hunney!"

"Molly? Baby, you're shaking. What's the—" Fox bit off a vicious word and grabbed the tablet out of her stiff hands to put it on the bedside table. "Come here." Tugging her trembling body up into his arms, he crushed her to the heat and strength of him. "Forget those fuckers. They're nothing but two-bit losers who live to pull others down." Rage had turned his body rigid, his voice hard. "They're *no one* to us."

She stroked her hand over his back. "It's okay," she said, finding her feet in the fierceness of his hold. "I just... it reminded me of the hate page from when I was at school." Except back then, the mean and nasty comments had come from other teenagers, while the profile pictures on these comments had shown adult faces. "I can't believe people would say such ugly things about someone they don't know."

"Face-to-face with you, not one of them ever would," Fox ground out.

Molly swallowed, continued to stroke his back. "I'll be fine." It was a surprising realization—she'd wobbled a bit, but she hadn't crashed. "It was unexpected, you know? The shock of it." To innocently scroll down, expecting maybe the odd cheeky comment about getting carried away, and yes, even a number driven by envy... and see such vitriol directed personally at her, it had been a punch to the gut. "They called me fat."

"If you're fat, I'll eat my fucking guitar," Fox muttered, sliding down his hands to cup her butt. "You're exactly right."

A woman would have to be in a seriously bad headspace to argue with that statement from the sexiest man in the world, and while the online attack had shaken Molly, the knock hadn't dented the heart of her. Nuzzling at his throat and drawing the primal masculine scent of him inside, she said, "We were lucky to skate under the radar this long, weren't we?"

Fox's eyes were solemn when they met her own. "Cost of doing what I was born to do is that I lose my privacy." The edge in his tone was tempered by the protective heat of his hold. "I won't lie. If you're with me, you won't have any either." His chest rose as he drew in a breath, released it. "Soon as the vultures figure out we're serious, they'll dig up everything about you. And Molly"—one hand cupping her face—"you have to be ready for some of your friends to turn against you when offered a big payday."

Molly heard the pain he couldn't quite hide, wanted to *hurt* the person who'd betrayed him. "Biggest skeleton in my closet has to do with my father." The idea of the world salaciously picking through the ruins of her childhood made a stabbing sensation jab through her, but she'd already considered that consequence when she decided to be with Fox.

"Whatever happens with that," she said, turning her face into his palm, "it won't be any kind of surprise." Today's shock, however, had had one unforeseen consequence. "I was so nervous all this time about media exposure, but I forgot I'm not a vulnerable, scared girl anymore." Hadn't been for a long time. "I'm a strong woman, a survivor... and I have you." A man who would never let her fall.

"Thank you." It was a rough-voiced statement, his head bent, his breathing low and harsh.

"For what?" She stroked the side of his face, his stubbled jaw a familiar sensation against her skin. "Baby? What's wrong?"

CHAPTER 29

"I KNOW HOW PRIVATE YOU ARE." His fingers flexed then curled again around the side of her neck. "I was fucking terrified you'd turn and run in the other direction the first time you saw what being with me can mean."

"What kind of rock chick would I be if I allowed boneheads like that to scare me off?" Stroking her fingers through the chocolate dark strands of his hair, she petted him as he'd so often done her. "I was just hoping we'd have longer to be *us* before the outside world started poking its nose into something that isn't anyone's business but ours."

The instant the words were out of her mouth, she groaned. "I'm such a hypocrite. I have a gossip magazine in my bag for the flight home." It had always seemed like harmless fun to read articles about the lives of the rich and glamorous; she'd never equated those "fluff" articles with the kind of hounding the media had put her family through. "I feel so bad now."

Fox laughed, pressing an affectionate kiss to the curve of her jaw. "As far as vices go, that's a forgivable one."

"Still, it's one I'm going to kick," she vowed. "Otherwise, I can't complain about the people who violate our privacy."

"I'll let you in on a secret." Fox bent his knees so they were eye to eye. "A lot of the 'shocking' news articles and 'scandalous' photo ops are carefully choreographed."

She pretended to pout. "Don't burst my bubble."

Nipping at her lower lip, he rose to his full height. "It's not all fake. Some of us don't want to play the game"—a growl of sound—"but we're pulled into it regardless."

"We lucked out in New Zealand, didn't we?"

"Baby, you have no idea."

"It has to be a hotel employee who sold the pictures." Scowling, she curled her fingers into her palms against the taut muscle of his chest. "Has no one heard of confidentiality?"

"So innocent." Fox shook his head. "You'll be terrible for my bad boy image if this gets out." Cupping the back of her head in one strong hand, he opened his mouth over hers, his tongue and lips doing things to her that made her whimper and want to beg for mercy.

A leisurely parting, their lips slick, he ran his knuckles down her throat, along the valley between her breasts. "Clearly"—he began to undo the belt of her robe—"I have to corrupt you as much as possible."

The robe fell to the floor, Fox's hands on her skin. No nasty words, Molly thought before thought became impossible, could ever hold as much power as the passion and the tenderness of her lover's touch.

KATHLEEN CAME UP AROUND TEN thirty that morning. The actress was dressed with her usual pizzazz in a formfitting leather skirt the color of roasted coffee beans, her feet sheathed in five-inch designer heels in luscious raspberry—the color matched her sleeveless top, the prettily tied fabric bow to one side of the high neck keeping the outfit on the right side of sexy. "I'm doing librarian chic, see?" She twirled in those teetering heels, her hair smooth and shiny in a bun at the back of her head. "In honor of our new friendship."

Molly bit the inside of her cheek. "I'd like to see you survive eight hours on a library floor in those heels."

Cocking her hip, Kathleen placed a perfectly manicured hand on it. "I'll have you know I ran in heels worse than this for an action flick I did three years ago. Did eighty takes at least because my douche-bag costar had to be a prima donna." Fingers pressed between her high, firm breasts, she fluttered her lashes and, voice a piercing falsetto, said, "What do you mean she gets to be in front of me? *I'm* the lead, not this jumped-up soap 'star.'" Kathleen made air quotes with her fingers. "Dickhead actually did the air quotes."

"Bet he's sorry now."

"He sends me weekly bouquets and asks for introductions."

"Have you? Introduced him?" Molly made a coffee for the other woman, her own tea already sitting on the gleaming wooden table in the dining room.

"In his dreams." Snorting, Kathleen took the coffee and leaned against the wall rather than taking a seat at the table. "How are you doing?" It was a gentle question. "I saw that piece on *G&V.*"

Molly blew on her tea to cool it, thinking of the forty-five-minute phone call she'd had with Charlotte. "My best friend pointed out that if I had to have a 'debut,' then better I got caught dressed to the nines in full makeup than wearing sweats while having a fat day with bad hair."

Kathleen's laughter was full-bodied and vivacious. "She's right, you know," she said afterward, amber eyes drenched in warmth. "I'd *pay* to be caught so deliciously *in flagrante* with a hunk like Fox." A wrinkling of her nose. "Except not Fox. It would be like sleeping with my spiritual brother. Ew."

Molly's face must've given something away because Kathleen's mouth dropped open. "Oh no, you didn't. You thought Fox and I bumped our bits?"

"You're stunning, he's hot, your friendship's rock solid." Molly felt like she'd been called up to the principal's office when Kathleen glared at her. "We're talking about *Fox* here." Gorgeous, talented, wonderful.

Kathleen groaned. "Oh, it is sickeningly cute that you think no woman can resist him."

Scowling, Molly folded her arms. "Did you just insult the man I adore?"

"As only a friend can." Kathleen twirled one heel-clad foot, eyes downcast, before raising her head and pointing a finger at Molly. "You ever breathe a word of what I'm about to tell you, and I'll sell a story to the tabloids saying I caught you doing unspeakable things with and to a goat."

"Cross my heart."

It took Kathleen another minute to speak. "The sparks were there—but not with Fox—with My Dick is My Life Noah." One graceful hand clenched against her leather skirt, she blew out a breath. "We'd never been close, Noah and I, maybe because there was always this tension beneath the surface, but that changed eighteen months ago. The connection…"

The other woman took a long sip of her coffee. "We played chess together." Her smile was unutterably sad. "No guy had ever spent so much time with me without wanting sex—though don't get me wrong, the heat was there. *Seriously.* But we never so much as kissed."

It was a difficult idea for Molly to process, Noah the most promiscuous member of Schoolboy Choir.

"We talked," Kathleen said, voice quiet. "Hours and hours, until I felt as if I knew him inside out, as if I could tell him anything. He was the one who gave me the courage to try out for that part in *Last Flight.*" Trembling voice, jerky breath. "When I was afraid people would laugh at an ex-soap-actress auditioning for such a serious role, he told me I was gifted and perfect for it, then drove me to the casting himself."

"What went wrong?" Molly's heart ached at the poignant emotion in every one of Kathleen's words.

A brittle shrug. "I walked into his hotel room after a concert and found him screwing a groupie."

Molly had known something bad was coming, but hadn't expected anything this brutal. "God, Kit, I'm so sorry."

"The worst thing was," Kathleen added, eyes shining wet, "I'd been to see him after three previous gigs. He'd cleared it so the hotels would give me a keycard." She blinked rapidly as if to stave off tears. "We'd always do the same thing—order room service and watch an old movie together on the couch. The bastard knew I'd be coming in."

Molly wanted to hug the other woman, hurting for her, but Kathleen wasn't finished. Her fingers gripping her coffee cup so tight that her bones pushed white against the golden bronze of her skin, she said, "I got the message loud and clear. Fox ran into me as I was leaving, took one look at my face and wrapped me in his arms while I cried."

Kathleen put down her cup on the small counter that held the coffeemaker, flexed her fingers. "That's when I knew he was a friend I wouldn't give up, even if it meant I had to see Noah at times." Breathing deep, she straightened her shoulders and finished her coffee before shaking her head. "I can't believe I actually told you that. It was the worst moment of my life."

"Maybe Maxwell's voodoo is rubbing off on me," Molly said, sensing the other woman had had enough of heavy emotion for now.

Kathleen's laugh was surprised, the strain around her mouth easing. "I think it is." She held out her empty coffee cup. "Please? I think this is a two-coffee morning."

Molly had just pulled the second cup from the machine when Fox walked through the door, a bakery box in hand. Pushing off the hood of an old college sweatshirt he hadn't been wearing when he left the suite, he put the box on the counter and dragged Molly in for an unhurried and thorough kiss that made her toes curl and Kathleen whistle.

Releasing her after a smiling nibble of her lower lip, he went over to hug Kathleen with the familiarity of long friendship. Even knowing there had never been anything sexual between the two, Molly found herself envious, because she and Fox, they were still so young, so new. She wanted the stone, the permanent foundations that'd take them through life.

"You weasel." Kathleen elbowed Fox in the gut. "You told Noah my room number."

Fox winced, stepped out of reach. "Jeez, Kit, I know better. He probably charmed it out of a desk clerk." Returning to Molly, he reached back to pull off the sweatshirt to reveal his white T-shirt.

"Where did you get the sweatshirt?" Molly asked as he threw it over the back of one of the dining chairs. "And where's your Lakers cap?" He adored that cap, treated it like it was an irreplaceable jewel.

"My extra *non-signed* Lakers cap is on the head of a busboy who's around my height, and who is currently riding around in my limo," Fox said, opening the bakery box. "My real cap is safe and sound in the bedroom. As if I'd ever wear that where someone might try to rip it off for a souvenir."

"Obviously." Molly tapped him on the nose. "So silly of me not to realize you had a spare decoy cap."

"Not one," Kathleen whispered. "He has a crate full of them."

Fox shrugged and bit into a powdered donut. "When something becomes a trademark, you can use it to throw the hounds off the scent." He rubbed his bristled jaw with his free hand. "Though I don't know where I'm going to find extra Mollys so I can sneak out with my Molly through the service entrance."

My Molly.

Her heart did a flip. "So I'm going to become a trademark?"

"So much they'll give us one of those stupid joint names."

"Folly?" Kathleen suggested, already halfway through a donut of her own, the raspberry silk of her top dusted with sugar.

"Good thing you don't write lyrics." Fox scowled. "Folly? Are you serious?"

"You do better."

Grabbing a chocolate-glazed donut instead, Fox put it to Molly's lips. "Taste this."

She did, groaned. "You're forbidden from bringing these anywhere near my vicinity except on very, very special occasions."

"Yeah." Kathleen sighed, fingers waving over the box as she deliberated her next pick. "This'll cost an extra four hours in the gym with Macho Steve, the Evil Personal Trainer, but oh baby, every minute will be worth it."

"Four *hours*?" Molly swallowed her second bite of the delicious treat, Fox taking great pleasure in refusing to give her the donut so he could feed it to her himself. "You're tiny!" An entire box of donuts wouldn't make any impact on Kathleen's sleek frame.

"I live in the land of make-believe, sweetie." Kathleen licked at the pink glaze of her donut. "You can never be too rich, too skinny, or too famous."

Thinking of the ugly comments on the elevator photo, Molly knew the other woman wasn't exaggerating. "You are being healthy though?" she asked, worried. "I don't want you to get sick."

Distinctive amber eyes widened. "Yes, I eat a healthy diet and I exercise—I don't throw up or starve myself." A strange hesitancy to her, Kathleen said, "Thank you for caring enough to ask. Not many people would."

It made Molly aware once more of how many layers those around her kept between themselves and others. Kathleen called her a friend, trusted her enough to share some of her past, but didn't expect Molly to care about so simple and important a thing as her health. True friendship, the kind Molly had with Charlotte, would take far longer to form.

And a lasting relationship, Molly thought, her eyes on the rock star who teased her he'd trade kisses for donuts, would take strength and commitment enough to stand against everything the world would throw at them.

THAT BATTLE BEGAN WITH A vengeance the next afternoon, when they returned home. A phalanx of photographers had camped at the gate to the house, flashes going off in a blinding staccato as they attempted to capture Molly's image through the closed windows of the SUV. A grim-faced Fox ignored them to nudge the car forward, and when one of the photographers stepped brazenly in front of the car, blasted the horn and kept going.

The man stumbled out of bumper range barely in time, falling backward onto his colleagues, his gestures turning rude as the gates closed behind the vehicle. The police arrived less than ten minutes later.

"One of them"—the senior cop jerked his thumb over a beefy shoulder—"wants to file a complaint. Says you tried to run him over."

Swearing, Fox invited the officers into the house and, using a laptop, accessed surveillance footage from the gate. It showed the photographer in question stepping in front of the car on purpose.

The cop rubbed his face. "All right. You want to press charges?"

"No. It's exactly the kind of publicity the piece of shit is looking for." Pitiless words, but Fox's voice was calm. "They've already got photos of your black-and-white coming through the gates. Fuck knows what story they'll spin from it."

"Still," the cop said, "I'll have a talk with him, see if I can dissuade him from pulling a stunt like this again."

"Thanks, but it won't do any good. The roaches always rise again." Closing the door after the police left, Fox slammed his fist against the wood not once but twice.

"Fox!" Molly grabbed his hand, saw broken skin. "You've hurt yourself."

"Leave it." Pulling away, he strode past her. "I need to be alone."

CHAPTER 30

ALREADY SHAKEN BY THE SCENE at the gate and the resulting police visit, Molly felt every word as if it were a blow. Fox had never rejected her touch that way. Feeling lost, she made her way to her favorite spot by the pool and took out her phone. "Charlie?" she said when her best friend picked up on the other end. "Can you talk?" Her voice wobbled despite her best efforts to keep her emotions contained.

"I can always talk when you sound like that." A rustling, as if Charlotte was moving around. "Give me a sec to make sure we won't be disturbed." Her best friend was back on the line before Molly could begin to worry about having interrupted her at work. "Okay, what's the matter? Are you still freaked out about that photo?"

"No, that's not it."

"Good. Because I've decided to have it framed and put on the back of my front door. It's what I aspire to every day—looking smoking hot while a sexy, sexy man puts his hands on me."

Smiling through the shakiness—no doubt as Charlotte intended—Molly said, "Are you saying that to wind up T-Rex?"

"He's not here. Away in Taupo to finalize a property purchase for his personal portfolio—I swear, the man wants to own the entire country," she said, and Molly could almost see her rolling her eyes. "So, talk. What's happened?"

As Molly and Charlotte spoke, she thought back to the start of her relationship with Fox, when she'd worried about his ability to contain things within while appearing as if nothing was the matter on the surface... and realized she'd never come up against that roadblock.

He trusted her, let her *see* him.

The knots in her spine began to unravel at the realization. He would, she was certain, share the reason for the depth of his anger once he'd calmed down. But hours passed, and Fox remained in his studio, not even coming up for dinner. Until, for the first time since they'd decided on a relationship, Molly faced the prospect of going to bed alone.

"Enough," she said and, pulling on the robe of opulent black silk that Fox had bought her in New York, the fabric decadent against her skin, walked downstairs. The red light over the studio door was on, but Molly turned the handle and stepped inside.

Fox looked up with a scowl from where he was listening to something via headphones, his guitar propped up against the wall. Sliding the headphones down to his neck, he said, "Molly, you know you're not supposed to walk in when the light's red."

She propped her hip against the complex control panel, lights blinking across the board and waves of sound charted on the built-in computer. "You've been down here for hours."

"I'm working." Shoving a hand through his hair, he took the headphones totally off and put them on the table to his left. "Sometimes I spend days in here. Get used to it."

It was the way he said the last that had her eyes narrowing. "Fine"—she folded her arms—"then you should get used to a woman who cares about you. You missed dinner."

"I'm hardly going to fade away." Legs sprawled out and eyes glittering, he said, "Go to bed. I'll be up when I'm done."

"You're done now."

Rising to his feet in a sudden movement that sent her heart into her throat, he pressed up against her, hands on the panel on either side. "You don't want to be with me in this mood, baby. Get upstairs, *now*."

Molly reached between them to tug open the knot of her robe instead, letting the lush fabric slide off to pool on the panel, her body nude in his arms. Fox's own body reacted as it always did to her, as hers did to him, but his eyes continued to glitter. "Using sex to get your own way?" It was a hard question, his hand thrusting between her legs.

Already wet for him, she gasped and gripped at his shoulders. But he withdrew his hand and returned to sit in the chair, undoing his jeans just enough to release his cock. "Come here, then. Fuck me." A crude challenge.

If there was one thing she'd learned with Fox, it was to be confident about her sexuality. The man wanted her, and even in his anger, he made no effort to hide it, his cock rigid, the vein that ran along the bottom plump with blood. Nudging aside his hand where he gripped the base, she straddled him and used her own fingers to guide him inside her molten core.

His fingers dug into her hips as she sank down to take him to the hilt, his head thrown back. Kissing his throat, she didn't ride him but began to squeeze her inner muscles in a rhythmic pulse.

"What the—" His breath hissed. "Where did you learn that?" It was a dangerous question.

"I like to read." Licking along the tendon on one side of his neck, she scraped her teeth over his jaw, kissed her way up to play with his lip ring. "I read the *Kama Sutra*. Along with a number of very educational erotic romances."

Gritting his teeth, he ground her down onto him. "The practical application?"

"I guess you'll have to be my crash-test dummy. Now sit back"—she pulsed her muscles in a faster rhythm—"and take it."

The words that came out of his mouth were so blue she blushed even in the midst of the eroticism. Then she loved him, pushing up his T-shirt to pay exquisite attention to the flat disks of his nipples with her fingers and her mouth as she used her inner muscles to torment and pleasure him. And the kisses, so many kisses. All of them raw, deep, audaciously sexual.

The orgasm seemed ripped out of him, a quick and violent and merciless thing.

Chest heaving in the aftermath, he lay back, eyes heavy-lidded and hands possessive. When she leaned in to kiss him again, he took control with sated laziness, one of his hands rising to her nape to position her exactly as he liked.

Molly shivered, and this time when her muscles clenched on his cock, it wasn't on purpose. Semi-hard, he remained inside her as they kissed for long, long minutes, the material of his T-shirt rubbing against her nipples to leave them pouting. Rolling one with the fingers of his free hand, Fox tugged, then flicked his thumbnail against it.

She felt her body coat him in a slickness that only increased when he went for her throat. He hadn't shaved today, and the stubble scraped over her skin with a coarseness at odds with the wet heat of his mouth. Moving restlessly on him, she wove her fingers through his hair, holding him to her.

"You like that?" More lazy kisses, his head rising from her throat.

"Yes," she said, as he ran his finger down the line of her throat. "Take off your T-shirt, please."

"Hmm." Using his grip on her nape to bring her forward, he claimed another kiss, his lips firm, his touch that of a man who knew his lover would permit him anything. "I don't think a bad girl who interrupts my work should get what she wants."

"You weren't working." She bit down on his lower lip hard enough to sting. "You were brooding."

Slits of dangerous green watched her from behind lowered lashes. "Brooding?"

It was a purr that dared her to repeat the accusation, but Molly wasn't about to be intimidated, even by her rock star. "Brooding."

Dipping his head, he tugged one sensitive nipple between his teeth, licking his tongue over and over it until she tried to rock her body on his. He held her down. "No," he said, freeing her nipple with a last leisurely lick. "I think it's time I reminded you I like to be in charge."

Skin tight at the sinful warning, Molly played her fingers over his lips. "I've never forgotten." Kissing him her way, softness and heat and tenderness, she stroked both hands under his T-shirt to push it up again, hot skin over steely muscle beneath her touch. "Doesn't mean I can't take care of you when you need it."

This time he helped her get the black material off over his head. Dropping it to the floor, he sat up so she could press her breasts flush against him. "Did you think I needed some Molly-time?"

She heard the thaw in him, and it did things to her to know she had the power to reach him even through such stormy anger. If she hadn't been able to deal with Fox's temper, they'd have had a serious problem—but she could... because despite everything, he let her in. "Yes." Kissing the side of his neck, she luxuriated in the feel of him around her. "I needed you, too. The sheets are cold without you."

"Out comes the truth," Fox said, though Molly had just smashed right through his defenses to lay him bare. "You only want me for my body heat."

"Of course."

Running his fingers down the cleft of her buttocks to where she stretched so tight around his renewed erection, he watched in possessive pleasure as she arched her body back against the panel. The position thrust up her breasts and he took full advantage, grazing his teeth over the lower curves, rubbing his jaw against her delicate skin.

"You've soaked my jeans," he murmured to his Molly, who'd fought for him exactly as she'd promised, who hadn't flinched or looked away when the going got hard. "That reminds me—it's been a couple of days since I've licked you up."

"I have been feeling a bit neglected," she said on a rasp of breath.

"Poor pretty baby." Careful of her sensitized flesh, he shifted her gently until she was reclining fully on the part of the panel that had no raised switches. Creamy and lush, she was a work of art, one for his personal and very private perusal. "Did you know I have video recording equipment in here?"

Molly's chest rose and fell in an unsteady rhythm. "What?"

"Yeah, sometimes it helps to watch the way my fingers move on the strings." He rocked into her to her soft moan. "Maybe I should turn it on—it might help me refine my technique to watch my fingers move on you."

Molly's spine arched up in a sweet curve, her body caressing his in a rush of liquid heat.

"Beautiful," he murmured and used his forefinger to stroke the slippery nub of her clit exactly as his Molly liked.

Giving a shocked little cry, she came a second time.

"I think," he murmured after her eyes opened, her body honey in his arms, "you like the idea of making your own sex tape." He loved how she always cuddled up against him after sex, his personal armful of woman. "Naughty Molly."

"We are not making a sex tape." It was a breathless warning. "The next thing you know, it'll be on the Internet."

"What if I promise to erase it after a thorough viewing to review my technique?"

"Do I look like I was born yesterday?"

"I love it when you blush." The pink flush made him want to taste, and because she was his, he leaned down and laved his tongue over her shoulder. "I guess I'll have to practice my technique on you."

He would've touched her again between the legs, but she pushed away his hand. "Too sensitive."

Shifting his hand to her thigh instead, he petted her slow and easy until she didn't repudiate his next caress of her clit. He kept each stroke featherlight, his kisses on her throat unhurried, building a song, note by carefully chosen note, until her body reached the right melody.

"My beautiful Molly." Who had *fought* for him.

PUTTING TOGETHER SOME FOOD AFTER their sexual play, Molly took the plate out to where Fox sprawled at the table by the pool. He'd changed into the cutoff sweatpants he often wore while exercising, his upper body gleaming under the moonlight, the sky midnight blue and scattered with stars.

"I like this robe," he murmured, rubbing the fabric between his thumb and forefinger when she put the food on the table. "I like what's inside it even more." His hand lightly cupping her breast, he drew her down for a kiss that felt as affectionate as it was sensual.

Body and heart both melting at the way he touched her, Molly took a seat opposite him, sipping at a cup of chocolate-mint tea while he cleared his plate. "More?" she asked, but he shook his head, his expression unreadable. "What's wrong?"

"Come sit in my lap."

Having missed him all day, she didn't hesitate to obey the order.

"Thanks," he said, his hand on the bare skin of her thigh.

"For cuddling?" She kissed his jaw. "Careful or your bad boy image will never recover."

"No, smart-ass." A squeeze of her hip. "For caring enough to hunt me down." He nuzzled the top of her head with his chin. "Kinda nice to know you'll come knocking if I go into a bad place."

Molly hurt for him that he hadn't expected his "girl" to come knocking. It told her far more about the damage done to him in childhood than any other words he could've spoken. "I don't know what your definition is of a relationship," she said, her tone gentle, "but mine includes not ignoring it when something's clearly eating at you."

Sitting up so she could look him in the eye, she stroked his nape. "Why did you blow up this afternoon? Talk to me."

"If I don't?" The balmy night breeze blew a few strands of darkest brown across his face, the moment capturing his wildness and rough male beauty so exquisitely she wished she had a camera.

"If you clam up"—she put on a severe expression—"I'll just have to tie you down and torture you with nefarious tricks until you spill."

The barest hint of a smile. "Nefarious tricks, huh? Give me details."

"Never." Tracing his jaw as she became aware he was absently tapping music against her thigh, she said, "You know how you're so protective?"

A gathering scowl. "You complaining?"

"I was going to say I feel the same way about you." It scared her how much he meant to her, but that fear stood no chance against the visceral power of the love in her heart. "Let me take care of you, too."

The silent music went still.

CHAPTER 31

"**Y**OU SHOULD BE SAFE in our home," he said at last. "You shouldn't have to fight to get inside, shouldn't have to deal with those fucking bastards screaming at you, watching you."

Molly wanted to kick herself—she'd just pointed out how protective he was of her. Of course he'd react badly to the idea that she might feel threatened in any way. "I feel so safe with you," she whispered. "More than I've ever felt, even before the scandal." To no one had she ever been this important, this precious, worth protecting. "Those photographers? They're annoyances; gnats. I know I get the deer-in-the-headlights look sometimes, but that's because it's all new. I'll get used to it."

Fox's hand clenched on her thigh. "Why should you have to get used to it?" It was a growl. "I want to make music—it's what I've always wanted. When did wanting that mean people have a right to invade our privacy?"

"It's not fair," Molly said, "but if we allow that to grind us down, we allow them to win. I'd rather we just live our lives, because one thing is for certain—you and I, we aren't going to break." It was a promise.

"No, we're not." Closing a strong hand gently around her throat, he ran his thumb over her pulse point. "But if one of those parasites ever pulls the kind of shit with you that they tried to pull with me today, all bets are off. I will destroy him."

"Don't do anything that'll get you thrown in jail," she said, looking directly into his eyes so he'd know she was dead serious. "You leave me and I will never forgive you."

Fox's thumb went motionless against her pulse. "You mean that."

"You know what my parents did," she said in answer, her mind roiling with memories of her father's ugly crimes and of her mother's alcoholism. "Their choices left me alone and nearly broken. I'm trusting you not to do the same thing to me." It was the biggest trust she'd ever given in her life, and her voice shook with the sheer, unrelenting weight of it.

Fox held the intimate eye contact as he spoke. "You're more important to me than any pap. I'll sic the lawyers on them—and I'll tell the overpriced sharks to bite hard."

Swallowing the knot in her throat, she touched her fingers to his lips. "Thank you."

"Don't thank me for not being an ass." He gathered her close, and they sat there for a long time, listening to the late-night wind whisper through the trees around the property, the waterfall of the infinity pool a peaceful murmur in the background.

"Tell me about Charlotte," he said some time later.

"Charlie? Why?"

"She's your family like the band's mine. I want to know her."

Yes, her rock star understood her. In ways no one else ever had. "We met on the first day of nursery school," she said, his heartbeat strong under her palm. "I remember her giving me her pail in the sandbox so I could build a giant sandcastle. Then she ran around and made sure no one disturbed my creation."

Her lips curved. "That's who Charlie is in a nutshell— sweet and generous and loyal." A woman who deserved a man who understood and cherished the treasure in his arms. "She's so honest and kind, I'd worry about her, but Charlie sees people for who they are." Though Molly wished her friend's innocence about the world hadn't been shattered as it had been.

Fox buried the fingers of one hand in her hair. "Were you good girls at school?"

"We weren't teacher's pets, but neither one of us is rebellious by nature."

"Yet you ran off with a no-good musician, and you keep talking about some guy called T-Rex with Charlie."

Molly slapped playfully at his chest. "You're not meant to listen in!"

A rumble against her as he laughed. "I can't help it. I'm fascinated by how you and Charlie can chat for two hours without running out of things to say."

"I could do that with you, too, though you'd probably ask for phone sex."

"Abso-fucking-lutely."

Bursting out laughing at the unrepentant statement, she nuzzled a kiss to his throat. "What was the worst thing you did as a student?"

Fox whistled. "That'll take some thinking. I made it my mission in life to be a problem—until I realized nothing I did

293

would make my mother want me enough to stand up to the prick." The acceptance in his tone was almost worse than the echo of old pain; Molly couldn't imagine how badly he must've hurt until the wound scarred over.

"Then," he said, "I became a model student. I think the teachers thought I'd been possessed, especially when I turned out to be freaky good at algebra."

"I hope you apologized to the teachers you drove crazy," she said, taking her cue from him and keeping it light; Fox didn't have to rip open old wounds, didn't have to bleed to invite her into himself.

"Naw... but I, uh, sponsor a program for kids like me."

The unusual hesitancy of his voice had her sitting up, her eyes locked with his. "A program?" It was a soft prompt when he fell silent.

"The ones who don't have anywhere to go for the holidays," he elaborated. "The program means they get to travel to another country, spend the time with a host family."

Her eyes burned. Blinking rapidly to fight it, she said, "That's wonderful," her throat thick.

Fox shrugged. "It's not the same as being with your own family, but I thought maybe the excitement of seeing another country would help blunt things. Anyway," he continued quickly, "the principal writes me now and then. He says most of the kids stay in constant contact with their host families and choose to go back to the same families year after year, so I figure maybe they've chosen new families like I did with Noah, David, and Abe."

There was so much she didn't yet know about this gorgeous, talented man. Each piece, each facet, he revealed, it tumbled her deeper and deeper into a love she knew would forever define her. "You're doing an incredible thing," she said, and when he looked uncomfortable, cupped his face. "Your girl is allowed to say mushy things like that about you. She's allowed to think you're wonderful."

"As long as you don't tell anyone." A scowling warning accompanied by a squeeze of the arm he had around her. "Let's go for a drive."

"Now?"

"It's a beautiful night. I want to show you my town under the stars."

Late as it was, the paparazzi had scattered and they were able to exit the property in the Lamborghini without stress. The drive proved to be romantic in a sweet, old-fashioned way, which she would've never expected of Fox. After a stunning moonlit half hour along the Pacific Coast Highway, the sea crashing to shore on one side, Fox circled back through Sunset Boulevard, stopping to buy her hot chocolate—complete with extra marshmallows—from a canny food-truck driver who'd set himself up within sight of night-shift workers on a road-repair project.

"Mmm, smells divine." She took a sip of the sweet liquid and settled in to enjoy the sound of Fox's rough purr of a voice as he gave her a personal tour, the tall palms on either side of the boulevard exotic to her eyes.

"Did you ever play in the clubs around here?" she asked some time later when they hit what he told her was the Sunset Strip, the area dazzling with spotlighted billboards and pulsing with nightlife.

"We had one of our first big breaks at that club over there." Fox pointed out a tiny doorway with a huge line.

"Owner's nurtured more talent than most in this town." He kept the car at an easy speed as they continued down the Strip, the gleaming black limo in front of them obviously cruising the sights as well. "You know that TV show you like? The detective one? Check out the convertible next to us."

Molly's eyes went wide when she did. A second later, she let out an "Eep!" and sat back while Fox started laughing. Shoving at his arm, she tried to scowl through her beet-red face. "I can't believe he... that she... at a traffic light! Where anyone could see." There was no way to miss the sleek blonde head bobbing up and down in the lap of the chiseled actor in the driver's seat.

"Pity"—Fox hauled her over for a hard, wet kiss before the light changed—"I was hoping it'd give you ideas."

It did, but Molly wasn't about to put those ideas into practice anywhere public. On a less populated stretch of road, however, and in a car that wasn't so low-slung... "Keep driving," she said, voice husky. "Show me Guitar Row. I read about it online."

"That'll be better in the daytime. We'll come back another day, have a real look around," he promised, pointing out a billboard up ahead that featured Schoolboy Choir and their upcoming concert dates. "When we first came to L.A., we used to walk up and down Guitar Row, salivating over all the instruments we wanted but couldn't afford."

Fascinated, she put the empty hot-chocolate cup in the holder and turned slightly in her seat. "Did you four meet at boarding school?" It was something she'd assumed but didn't know for certain.

"Yes, at an honest-to-God choir tryout. The music teacher forced us to go."

"No!" She grinned. "You were in the choir?"

"Hell, no." A growl of sound. "I sang flat and off-key on purpose. So did the others—Noah and I were friends already, but that's when we decided we were soul mates with David and Abe, too." A pause as he slowed the car to allow another limo, this one virgin white, to merge into traffic, a topless woman popping out of the sunroof to blow kisses their way before she was yanked back down.

"Was she wearing giant bunny ears?" Shaking her head, Molly shifted her attention back to the rock star who intrigued and compelled her far more than anything around them. "What happened next?"

"We made music together," he said simply, and brought her hand to his mouth for a kiss. "Starting out, we crashed in a cheap two-bedroom apartment, working every day job we could to make the rent and feed ourselves."

Molly could hear the passion in his voice, knew the dream of music had driven him. "How old were you?"

"Eighteen. Right out of high school." He placed her hand on his thigh as he shifted gears. "Noah and Abe, they both come from heavy-duty money, but it was an unspoken rule that we did this on our own. Best decision we ever made— money's never come between us, and the band? It's *ours*, no one else's."

Molly loved the insight into the band's friendship, into Fox, and kept urging him to continue. So engrossed was she in his stories of what it had been like to go from flat broke to filling stadiums with screaming fans that it took her a while to realize they'd left the lights of the city behind to prowl up one of the hills. "Where are we going?"

A sinful smile, the dimple lean and gorgeous in his cheek. "Best make-out spot in the city."

The row of cars at the top, complete with steamed-up windows, proved him right.

Pushing back his seat once he'd parked, Fox said, "Come here, Miss Molly," and maneuvered her into his lap.

She snuggled close. "This is so romantic." Los Angeles spread out in front of them like a twinkling carpet, the lights fireflies in the dark.

"Does that get me points?" Fox ran his hand under her unbound hair to touch her nape.

Skin taut at the tone of his voice, she said, "Depends."

"On what?"

"On what you intend to do with the points."

"Trust me?"

It was no longer even a question. "Yes," she said, "this earns you many brownie points." Nervous anticipation in her veins, she looked into eyes shadowed by the darkness inside the vehicle. "What do you want to use them for?"

Fingers trailing up her neck. "A little rope."

"You want to tie me up?" Molly's voice was husky, the sound a caress over Fox's senses.

"Yeah." He cupped the lush warmth of her braless breast through the T-shirt she'd thrown on over jeans, enjoying the simple pleasure of being able to touch her as he pleased. "I've always wanted to try it."

"You're telling me Zachary Fox, rock star named Reigning Sex God by a certain men's magazine three years running," she said, her breast pushing into his palm as she leaned closer, "has never tied up a woman during sex?"

"Even a Reigning Sex God has to develop his tastes." He rubbed his thumb over her nipple. "By the time I realized it was something I wanted to try, that girl I walked home from the bar had sold her story to the tabloids. I didn't trust anyone enough to play those games." Molly though... she could have every one of his secrets.

He was hers.

"Some people would say I'm being naïve believing that—"

Ice in his blood.

Screwing up her nose, Molly glared at him. "I said some people. I know you don't lie. You never have, not from the start." A pause. "Though you did let me *assume* you were perfectly happy for our relationship to end after a month."

Fox winced. "You ever going to forget that?"

"No"—Molly tugged at his lip ring—"I plan to hold it over you for the rest of our lives together." Shifting position to straddle him, she held his gaze with the clear brown of her own. "Thank you for never lying to me."

He heard the honesty, saw the vulnerability she didn't try to hide. "I never will, baby. Even if I know what I'm about to say will piss you off." Tucking his fingers under the edge of her T-shirt, he stroked the bare skin of her lower back. He'd always been a tactile man, but with Molly, it was more than that—it felt good deep inside to touch her, as if he was where he was meant to be. "Speaking of which... I got you something in New York."

"Other than the ridiculously expensive robe with which I'm madly in lust?"

"The robe was a present for me." She'd accepted that with open pleasure, but this next gift might slam up against her boundaries—it continued to frustrate him that she made no demands on him financially when he wanted to give her the world, wanted to make her happy. "It's in my front jeans pocket."

CHAPTER 32

WIGGLING HER FINGERS INTO HIS left pocket, Molly brushed something rigid and hot. "Is that it?" she asked, feeling sexy as only Fox could make her feel.

"That's for later." A wicked promise. "Try the other pocket."

Molly managed to get her fingers inside despite the way the fabric had pulled taut because of his seated position, touched velvet. Working it out, she saw it was a pouch from a high-end jewelry store he must've ducked into when he went to get the donuts yesterday.

"…you should know I plan to spoil you. Let me."

The memory of his words broke her heart as she considered what this gift meant to Fox. And it had nothing to do with money.

"Are you going to open it?" A fine tension to his body, lashes lowered to shade the expression in his eyes.

She could swear her commitment until she was blue in the face, she thought, but it would take him time to accept that she didn't need enticement to stay. Until then, she'd never turn down a gift, no matter how outrageous, never hurt him with what he'd read as a rejection. "I want you to show me," she said, handing him the bag.

Lips curving, he tugged open the little gold tie and poured a tumble of glittering gemstones onto his palm before picking up one of the earrings and holding it out. "I don't want to poke holes in you."

Aware she was handling thousands of dollars, she carefully hooked it on, then added its twin. "So?" She tucked her hair behind her ears to better show off the precious stones.

"You make them look beautiful." Sliding one hand under her tee and onto bare skin again, he cupped the back of her head with his other and smiled in the way that always made butterflies take flight in her stomach. "Want to make out?"

Molly had never made out in a car with a boy. Even the idea of it had nauseated her after her father was caught in his luxury sedan with his underage lover. "I might freak out," she warned, because while she felt fine now, the past had a way of biting when she least expected it.

Fox didn't ask for explanations; his expression told her he got it. "I can handle a freak-out. Especially if you let me get to third base."

They steamed up the windows, almost got busted by the cops, and there was no freak-out. It was the best date of her life.

"YOU LOOK HAPPY," THEA PRONOUNCED a week later when they met up at a sunny little café a couple of minutes' walk from Thea's office, the two of them choosing an outdoor table.

Molly took a sip of her passion-orange tea. "I am." She was starting to believe she and Fox would be okay, even in this hothouse atmosphere. "Is that stubble burn on your cleavage?"

Thea shoved her sunglasses up on top of her head to glance down, groaned. "Damn it. I thought this neckline was high enough." She pointed a finger at Molly. "'Fess up. You told David to write memos."

Molly gave her innocent eyes.

Snorting, Thea picked up her phone to check her e-mails.

"*So?*" Molly prompted, used to the way her sister multitasked.

"So... I guess we'll see if I can trust him while the band's on tour." A whisper of pain, an echo of the brutal blow her fiancé had delivered, the cheating, supercilious piece of crap.

Molly didn't know if her sister's heart could take another beating without permanent damage; she truly hoped David was the man she believed him to be. "I thought you'd be traveling with us?"

"No, it'll be one of my associates. I need to remain at base command for the most part so I can quickly stamp out any fires." Thea's eyelashes flicked up. "The other guys, how are they handling what's happening between David and me?"

"No one's making a big deal of it," Molly said, conscious Thea continued to worry about the possible repercussions of being involved with a client, especially if things didn't work out. "They mess with each other all the time, but not on this topic." Tight as the four were, it was clear Fox, Abe, and Noah understood exactly how important this relationship was to their bandmate. "We're all rooting for you." Smiling, she said, "As your sister, I hope that stubble burn is the first of many."

Thea laughed, her tension easing. "I'm considering flying in to meet up with the band during some of the tour stops, so you never know." Spooning up the foam from her cappuccino with one hand while typing a return message with the other, she turned the conversation back to Molly. "Are you looking forward to the tour?"

"Yes and no." Molly watched a bouncy, tanned woman walk by with two tiny dogs on leashes, each dog pure white with a diamanté collar. It wasn't until the woman had passed that Molly noticed she was wearing four-inch Perspex heels and had another fluffy white dog in the handbag slung over her elbow, her fingers curved to show off hot-pink talons. "Sometimes I feel like I've fallen down the rabbit hole."

"You'll be fine." Thea nibbled at her bran muffin. "Stay grounded, don't allow all this"—a wave at the flamboyance and wealth around them—"to taint what you have with Fox." She took a drink of her coffee before saying, "Why yes and no?"

"I'm excited because I get to travel with Fox, watch him perform." Molly would never get enough of watching him onstage. "But I'm worried about the pressure it might put on us—it's an intense environment." Pausing, she admitted, "I'm so possessive of him, Thea. I hate it when he poses with female fans without his T-shirt, even though I know it means nothing to him."

Her sister turned off her phone, gave Molly her full attention. "Have you spoken to him about it?"

"We fought about it after Sydney, but I haven't brought it up since."

Thea shook her head. "Do it, Molly. Otherwise, he'll end up hurting you without knowing it, and you'll become angry and resentful." She held up a hand when Molly would've spoken. "I've worked in this industry for a decade and the couples that make it are the ones who have no secrets. Because even a tiny thing can act like a grain of sand against skin, rubbing and rubbing until it makes you bleed."

TWO DAYS LATER, THEA'S WORDS circled in Molly's mind as she sat at home watching the live broadcast of a prime-time show: Schoolboy Choir was currently being interviewed by the witty, likeable host. The host's questions—which the guys were handling without problem, shooting back good-humored retorts—weren't what had Molly's nerves taut. That came courtesy of the other guest, a tall, curvy blonde in a dramatic, figure-hugging dress of deep blood-orange.

A major recording star in her own right, Carina had sung a chart-topping duet with Fox for Schoolboy Choir's most recent album, the rock ballad as hard as it was romantic. Molly had loved it. Until now. It only took her a couple of minutes into the interview to realize the other woman was intelligent as well as talented and physically blessed. She'd also clearly not been faking her enjoyment of the sultry kiss she'd shared with Fox in the music video for the song.

Molly would've had to have been blind to miss the flirtatious invitations Carina was sending Fox's way. And it wasn't just her imagination or jealous paranoia. The show had a tweet stream running along the bottom of the screen and the majority of the tweets had to do with the chemistry between Fox and Carina. Whoever was choosing the tweets to display had picked relatively tame messages, as opposed to the more sexually charged ones Molly knew had to be flooding the site, but that didn't matter.

So shipping Carina and Fox. #perfectcouple

She is totally hot for him. Love it!

OMG, most beautiful couple or what?

We saw it first! Foxina 4ever!

Molly's stomach knotted further with each second that passed. No one, she thought, seemed to remember that Fox had been spotted with a different woman in New York, Molly forgotten in the blink of an eye. The only thing that kept her from throwing something at the television screen was that no matter what the viewers believed, Fox wasn't returning the signals. And Molly knew every one of his signals intimately.

Forcing herself to breathe, she consciously relaxed her death grip on the cushion she'd hugged to her chest. Fox couldn't help it if he drew women like flies. The only way Molly would survive this relationship was if she trusted in their bond. "Doesn't mean I can't be a little irrational though."

Decision made, she put a piece of duct tape along the bottom of the screen so she couldn't see the tweet stream, and muted the TV every time Carina opened her mouth. The interview was suddenly enjoyable—enough that she didn't mute Carina's part in the live performance of the duet—but when the woman got too close to Fox, as if to recreate their kiss, she *did* throw the remote at the television.

Justifiable, she rationalized, just as Fox—strumming an electric guitar—smoothly deflected the attempt by leaning into Noah for an off-the-cuff jam session that had the audience rioting in their seats. In the interim, Abe grabbed Carina as if stealing her away. By this stage, the audience was wild, and they stayed that way as the host yelled out a good-bye message, the credits beginning to roll across the bottom third of the screen.

Molly didn't think, didn't give herself time to second-guess her emotions. Picking up her phone, she sent a message to Fox. *You were amazing. Smooth moves with a certain Miss Touchy-Feely.*

The response came quicker than she'd expected. She'd figured the audience had to be swarming the men for photos and autographs. *I thought so. Just so you know—these brownie points equal more ropes.*

Molly's teeth sank into her lower lip. *Promises, promises,* she sent, a deep happiness inside her at the unmistakable sign that though he'd just been publicly hit on by a superstar, he was thinking about her. *By the way, don't take off your T-shirt even if a fan wants it.*

Yes, Molly.

When his car purred into the drive an hour and a half later, exactly when he'd predicted he'd be home, a smile broke out over her face. Running downstairs, she opened the internal door to the garage and watched him park the Aventador, jumping into his arms as soon as he stepped out, her legs wrapping around his waist. "Hi."

A slow smile that was so *real* it stole her breath. "Hi, yourself, Miss Molly. I think you missed me."

Since the day she'd first understood she came last in her parents' lives, Molly had been protecting herself. Charlotte alone had broken through, but much as she loved her best friend, it was nothing as terrifying and as beautiful as what she felt for Fox. And her rock star needed to know that, needed to see she was in this for the long haul.

"Yes," she said, not hiding any of her emotions, though the exposure made her pulse stammer, her throat go dry. "You've been gone all day."

A hot tangle of a kiss, one of Fox's hands at her nape, the other under her butt. "I missed my Molly-time, too."

They just cuddled there for a minute before Fox turned to place her on the hood of the car. Pushing her down gently until she lay on her back on the metal, her feet on the ground in front of the low-slung vehicle, he ripped off his T-shirt. "So, I'm not allowed to be shirtless when I take photos with fans?"

Molly shook her head. "No. I hate it when other women touch you." He couldn't totally stop that, but at least this way, they wouldn't be touching his skin beyond the arm.

Leaning down, one hand on her breast, he suckled her upper lip into his mouth, his smile unhidden. "Then you'd better have spares backstage for me," Fox said, luxuriating in her possessiveness.

"I will." A firm statement, Molly watching him rise back up to his full height, her eyes following his movements as he dropped his hands to the studded black leather belt that held up his faded and ripped jeans.

"You want me, Molly?" he asked, sliding out the belt to drop it to the garage floor.

"No." Her fingers curled into her palms. "I think you need to come here and rev me up."

Nudging her thighs farther apart, he undid the button on her jeans, tugged down the zipper. "Want to take back what you said?"

CHAPTER 33

MOLLY STUBBORNLY SHOOK HER HEAD.

Stripping off her jeans, he settled between her legs again, so damn pleased with her that he'd play with her all night if she wanted. "Maybe it's the car," he said, undoing the buttons of the cardigan she wore as a top. "That's what has you so hot."

The fact she'd run into his arms, her need for him open and unhidden, it meant everything, his passion for her about far more than lust. He wanted to pet her, pleasure her, cherish her. "Seems like you're getting me to do this under false pretenses."

"It is," Molly said, tone breathy, "a very nice car."

"Just for that, I'm not going to put my mouth on you."

Molly flexed her fingers against the flawless red paintwork. "What if I ask nicely?"

"It'd have to be very, very nice indeed." God but he fucking loved that she trusted him enough to let her body be his favorite instrument.

Shivering as he peeled apart the sides of the cardigan to bare the lace-covered mounds of her breasts, his lover said,

"Please, Fox." A feminine whisper that wrapped him in silken chains tinged blush pink with the color on her cheekbones. "Please put your mouth on me."

Never had he talked this much during sex, but this was Molly and there were no rules. "Hmm, good start," he said, pressing a kiss to the delicate skin of her breastbone, "but I don't know if you really mean it."

"Maybe I don't want your mouth." Her hand gripping his hair, tugging him up with a scowl. "I can take care of myself."

Smoldering heat in his blood. "Oh, you'll be doing that one day soon. In front of me." It would be an erotic fantasy come to life. "But since you're being so uncooperative to-day"—he stroked his hand down one silken thigh, to her restless movement—"maybe you don't deserve an orgasm."

Chest heaving, she wrapped both legs around his hips to hold him to her, the denim of his jeans scraping against the cream of her skin. "You are a bad man and I adore you."

Ah fuck, but she knew how to cut him off at the knees. To-tally hers, he kissed her, one hand at her throat, the other on the plump curve of her breast. When she broke the kiss to gasp in air, he took his hand off her throat to run his mouth over the slope of it, continuing downward until he reached her breasts. It only took a second to push down the cups, bare her to him, her nipples lush berries in his mouth.

"Fox." A husky moan, her hands on his shoulders. "I want you."

That did it. The leash snapped. "Be a good girl for my cock"—he reached down to push aside the gusset of her pant-ies, undo his jeans—"and I'll use my mouth on you later."

Molly's skin tinged hot pink, but his smart, sexy librarian didn't back down. "I always am for you."

Pretty damn sure he'd spill then and there, he shoved up her thigh and pushed into her in a single thick thrust, both of them sprawled out on the hood.

"Fox!"

"I have you." Bracing his hands palms down on either side of her head, he looked into brown eyes drenched in pleasure, the pupils dilated, and found he wanted to hear the words Molly gave him, the ones that made him feel ten feet tall. But he didn't know how to ask for them, how to tell her how important those words were to his soul.

Then she raised her fingers to his lips, tracing the shape of his mouth. "My gorgeous, talented Fox. I'm so glad I wake up next to you every morning."

Shuddering, he stroked her thigh and found the patience to rock her slow and easy, his Molly who didn't only fight for him, but who gave him what he needed with a generosity that tore him to pieces. As the world splintered around them, he could only hope he gave her the same, hope that she saw no lack in her life.

He couldn't lose her. Not his Molly.

THREE WEEKS LATER AND MOLLY felt as if she was living in a dream world. The band was now officially on tour and had been for the past five days. Though they were surrounded by crew, and had—until an hour ago—been accompanied by a reporter from the most iconic magazine in the industry, Molly was the only one who was attached on a strictly personal basis.

She'd expected to be cornered by the reporter sometime during the fourteen days he shadowed the band, beginning with Schoolboy Choir's pre-tour preparations. She'd even worked out strategies to answer what she'd guessed would be intrusive questions, but the man had treated her with a kind of absent politeness, otherwise ignoring her existence. Molly had been delighted but mystified.

It was Maxwell who cleared things up for her.

"He thought you were flavor of the month," the crew boss said with his customary bluntness. "Since he's planning to write the definitive article on the band at this point in their career, he's not going to bother to include what he thinks is a bit of pussy."

Molly could feel herself turning bright red. Booming with laughter, Maxwell hugged her close to his bulk. "Don't worry about him. He'll kick himself later when he realizes his 'definitive article' has a hole the size of Alaska because he couldn't see what was right in front of his face."

"Damn straight," Molly said, tugging on her Schoolboy Choir cap when Maxwell released her.

"Good girl." His grin could've been of a proud father. "Boys don't have a concert tomorrow and we're not on the road, so get ready to paint the town red after tonight's show."

Molly might've been surprised at how circumspect the entire band had been the past five days, if she hadn't understood the demanding physicality of the concerts. Dedicated to their music as all four men were, giving a mediocre performance simply wasn't acceptable—it wouldn't only disappoint their fans, it would mean letting down the other members of the band.

As a result, they were more than ready to blow off some serious steam. "Wear the red skirt," Fox said, patting her on the butt after he'd showered off the sweat from the show. "With the sparkly top."

The "sparkly top" was a low-cut sequined halter in shimmering gold he'd bought her two days ago after spotting it in a boutique window across from their last hotel. Trying it on with a strapless push-up bra and the skirt she'd fixed after Fox tore it in New York, Molly whistled at her own reflection. She looked hot. Feeling confident and happy, she spent time straightening her hair before pulling it back into a sleek ponytail. A bit of careful makeup, with the focus on knockout red lips, and she was done.

"Oh holy hell." It was a harsh groan from the open bedroom doorway, Fox having slipped out to the living area of the hotel suite to raid the room service cart while she dressed.

Turning around on skinny black heels, she propped a hand on her hip, her stomach flipping at the heat in the smoky green of his eyes. "I love this outfit."

Fox, dressed in camo-green cargo pants and a white T-shirt that hugged his biceps, began to prowl closer. "Not as much as I do."

Molly held out a hand. "No way. I didn't go to all this trouble for you to mess me up."

Fox's eyes gleamed. "Bet I could change your mind."

"No bet. We both know I'm easy where you're concerned," she said, wrapping her arms around his neck and drawing in the clean bite of his aftershave. "You're all smooth." She rubbed her cheek against his. "Not that I don't like you rough."

Fox cupped her butt with possessive hands. "I know just how rough you like it, Miss Molly." Squeezing her curves, he ground his aroused body against her. "I'm absolutely going to mess you up."

"No, you don't." It took serious effort to break out of his hold, the flesh between her thighs already damp. "I want to see what you guys get up to on a night out."

"I sure as hell won't be getting up to the same things now that I have you in my bed. Which is where I'd like to be right now." Despite his frustrated growl, he held out his hand. "Come on, let's go watch the other guys' eyes pop out."

The smug satisfaction in his tone made her want to drag him to the sheets. "Wait," she said, fighting the temptation, "I have something for you."

He watched curiously as she picked up a little bag emblazoned with a shop logo and pulled out a black leather cuff. "I thought this wouldn't break rock star fashion protocol," she said and closed the cuff around his left wrist, the studded design an echo of the belt hidden beneath his T-shirt.

"When did you get this?" he asked, admiring the workmanship.

"Secret." Sliding her hands into the back pockets of his jeans, she kissed his jaw. Her glossy lipstick left a red imprint, but liking her mark on him, she didn't immediately wipe it away. "I get to spoil you, too, you know."

He echoed her position, his hands on her lower curves and his smile deep. "I'm already spoiled, but I could get used to this kind of a surprise." Eyes dropping to her lips, he went to kiss her, sighed. "Damn it. I'll ruin your pretty makeup."

"Come here." Lipstick or Fox's kiss? No contest.

NOAH WOLF-WHISTLED WHEN HE saw her ten minutes and a quick touch-up later, and suddenly she was being hauled to his side, one muscular arm around her waist. Startled, she landed with her hand on his T-shirt, the fabric black with silver detailing. The guitarist, she thought, could've stood in as a model for a fallen angel—beautiful and with an aristocratic look to him, his eyes holding a sardonic edge he made no effort to hide with people he didn't like.

"Forget about that schmuck," he said, motioning at Fox. "Don't you know blonds do everything better?"

Fox claimed Molly back. "Find your own woman. I'm not sharing mine." Nuzzling a kiss to her temple, his hand curving proprietarily over her hip, he glanced at David. "Car here?"

"Yep. Outside."

The "car" proved to be a Hummer stretch limo, complete with a full bar and tiny lights on the roof that looked like stars. Sliding onto the black leather seat that ran along the side opposite the door, Molly accepted a flute of sparkling grape juice from Abe. "Thank you."

He winked, thick lashes coming down over a dark brown eye, and turned up the music until it pumped through her blood. Soon afterward, everyone had a drink, the sunroof was open, and Fox's arm was around her neck as they cruised through the city en route to their first stop.

Molly had only gone clubbing that one disastrous time, never partied with a boy, never made out in the middle of a dance floor. Fox was no boy, but he absolutely made out with her in the midst of the pumping mass of bodies that was the hottest club in town. Molly knew there had to be cameras around, but the place was all but dark, and she was in too good a mood to ruin the experience by focusing on the outside world rather than her man.

As Charlotte had said, being caught in the arms of a sex god was hardly anything to be embarrassed about. So she danced flush up against Fox's hard body and when he demanded a kiss, opened her mouth for him, her hand curled over the warmth of his nape. The muscle and tendon of him moving under her touch as he kissed her was as hot as the weight of his hand on her ass.

Swaying with her under the pumping music, Fox scowled at Abe when the keyboardist cut in, but let her go. The members of the band were the only men to whom he'd surrender her. Soon as any other male even looked interested, Fox made it very, very clear Molly was off-limits. It was an intoxicating feeling, to be so publicly branded as his.

They went from club to club as a group, walking in at the front of every line. "This could go to a girl's head," Molly said, nuzzling at Fox's throat in the shadows to the side of the dance floor.

Bending closer to her ear, his breath hot and intimate, he ran his hand down her side, stopping to caress the curve of her breast. "Does that mean you'll suck my cock when we get back—after I tie your hands behind your back and bind your ankles together?"

Molly felt her skin blaze, wasn't ready for the kiss he laid on her, her ponytail wrapped around his hand. "You are so sexy when you blush." A delicious bite of her lower lip. "So?"

Molly somehow found the will to speak through the pulse of arousal low in her body. "If I say yes," she whispered in his ear, her lips touching his skin, "you'll have me on my knees in

the hotel room so fast my head will spin, and I'm having fun."
Not that she'd last long if he decided to persuade her. "I like
being out with you and the guys."

Hands on her hips, he squeezed. "I can be patient when I
know what I've got coming." Taking her hand on that low
promise, he led her through to the VIP section of the club,
no doubt leaving a generous tip with the bouncer whose hand
he shook on the way in.

"Do you always tip so well?"

"I waited tables when we were trying to make it," he said.
"Worked as a bouncer, too. You wouldn't believe the number
of big shots who never tip, the jerk-offs get so used to being
given everything for free."

Molly went to part her lips to reply when there was a holler
from the other end of the bar, and two seconds later, Fox was
being lifted off his feet by a big black guy in a flawless char-
coal-gray suit. David, who'd entered right behind them,
received the same treatment a few seconds later. "Damn!" the
stranger said. "You didn't tell me you were coming in!"

"That's why it's a surprise, asshole." Noah's laconic response had the older man grinning, the guitarist having just
joined them.

"Fuck you, pretty boy." Sharing a quintessentially male
hug, complete with thumping back slaps, the two drew apart.

Abe, the last one to enter, held up a hand. "I don't do
girly shit like hugs, man."

He was swallowed up an instant later and came out of it
grinning, the deep smile rare on his face. Slapping Abe's
cheek with hard affection, the stranger turned to Fox. "You
going to introduce us?" He was looking at Molly.

Startled, Molly found herself taking in the besuited man with new eyes. People had a way of ignoring her, appearing surprised when Fox introduced her. Seemed the "bit of pussy" wasn't meant to have a name. It would've infuriated her except that Fox always made it clear she mattered. So she was taken aback when he said, "Hell no," a scowl on his face. "You're not safe around women."

Flashing an undaunted smile at her, the stranger said, "I'm Shawn, but most folks call me Doc. A beautiful woman like yourself, however, can call me Shawn." He held out one thickly muscled arm. "Let me show you things Fox here didn't even know existed until I shared my wisdom with him."

Fox traded insults with Shawn as they walked up a spiral staircase and into a private section that offered a view over the entire club. Shawn, Molly realized, either owned or managed the club. From the confident way he moved in this space, she leaned toward ownership. Ordering them to settle in, he called up trays of finger food from the club's generous kitchen. Then, with food and drink flowing while the music boomed beneath them, Molly sat back and listened to the band catch up with a man who was obviously a trusted friend.

"This guy," Abe told her, "gave us our first big break."

Noah nodded, his beer held loosely between thumb and forefinger, the green glass of the bottle sweating with condensation. "He wasn't a big shot then—had a tiny place that was building a serious rep, and he put us center stage."

"Good business." Shawn ate a spicy spring roll before continuing. "They packed out the club night after night. Had lines out the door by the end of what was supposed to be their run—so of course I signed them up for another one."

Fox shook his head, fingers playing with Molly's ponytail, his arm along the back of the sofa. "We didn't pack in those crowds for weeks—not until word spread. Most people would've let us go, but Doc had our back."

David clinked his beer bottle to the club owner's. "Which is why he'd better have instruments for us."

Shawn whooped. "You gonna jam? Hell yeah, I have what you need!"

CHAPTER 34

MOLLY WATCHED FROM THE HIGH aerie that was Shawn's domain as the band brought down the house with a rocking set that had people screaming. "I don't think I'll ever get used to how amazing they are onstage," she said to the club owner where he leaned on the railing next to her.

"Some musicians," Shawn said, "they practice until they get good, others they have raw talent. Fox, Noah, Abe, and David, they always had the talent, but they had the drive too." Leaving for a few seconds, he returned with a cocktail glass filled with decadent-looking chocolate mousse, complete with an enticing red cherry on top.

Molly groaned. "You're going to kill me." He'd already talked her into a frothy, creamy nonalcoholic cocktail.

"Try a spoonful for me." He beamed at her shuddering moan when she gave in. "Good, yeah?"

"Divine." She spooned up another tiny bite. "Fox is right—you're dangerous around women."

That got her another deep smile before he returned his attention to the band.

"You're the first woman Fox's brought into my club," he said several minutes later. "Before, he might've picked up a woman here, taken her back to the hotel, but he's never once brought anyone with him."

Molly let the mousse melt on her tongue and tried not to think about those other women, but about the important part of Shawn's statement. "That's why you asked to be introduced."

"Nope. That was because I plan to steal you away from Fox—I have an old pinup calendar in my office." A low wolf whistle as he looked her up and down. "You'd fit right in."

Smiling at the blatant sweet talk, Molly scooped up a touch more mousse as the band gave in to the urgings of the crowd and began another number. "If we're going to be friends," she said to Shawn, "you can't tell me about the women Fox used to pick up and take back to his hotel."

"You know he wasn't a virgin when you met him, right?"

"Doesn't mean I want an action replay."

"Fair enough." He hollered along with everyone else at Noah's guitar solo.

Almost as if they'd timed it, Fox's growl of a voice rolled out over the last riff and David slammed down on the drums. Abe's keyboard joined in fifteen seconds later, Noah coming back in at the same time. "This is new!" she yelled to Shawn over the screams of the crowd. "Never before performed live!"

The big man's eyes sheened wetly. "Goddamn punks," he said, his pride clear.

Clapping and dancing along with the crowd as the band finished the song and walked offstage, she ran back to the door through which Fox emerged a few seconds later. "You were amazing!" Kissing the life out of him, she turned to the others. "That was incredible!"

"Do we get a kiss, too?" Noah drawled.

Jerking him forward by grabbing the front of his T-shirt, Molly smacked him on the lips. It was the first time she'd seen Noah thrown off balance. He recovered quickly. "Fox, sorry, man. I'm keeping her."

Fox wrapped an arm around her waist, his face holding the exhilaration of performing. "Not even in your dreams."

Then Shawn was there, hugging and backslapping his "punks." They partied with the club owner till after four in the morning. "I've never been out this late," Molly confessed to Fox as they danced to a slow song.

"You are such a good girl." A quick, hot kiss, her breasts crushed against his chest. "It turns me on like crazy—but what turns me on even more," he whispered in her ear, "is watching you be dirty only for me."

Drawing her aroused body off the dance floor when the house lights flickered, he took her back upstairs to say good-bye to Shawn. David had left much earlier, while Noah and Abe had both disappeared about an hour ago—Noah with a petite black woman *and* a pneumatic peroxide blonde, Abe with a statuesque, tattooed brunette, her skin pure cream.

"What's the deal with Noah?" Molly asked softly once they were settled in the far back of the limo, Fox having instructed the driver to take them on a night tour of the city. Now, with the opaque privacy screen up between the front and the back, it was as if they were in an intimate cocoon. "I could've sworn he was looking at Kit as if he wanted a second chance, but then he picks up women left, right, and center."

Fox shrugged. "Noah's got his demons. Frankly, it's better if Kit keeps her distance."

Molly shifted on the seat to look at his face. "That bad?"

"I think of him as a brother," Fox said, his voice quiet and his expression solemn, "but I also know he's not good for a woman who wants an actual relationship. We might not have partied the past few nights, but Noah was fucking a groupie or some other woman—probably women—he picked up." It was a nonjudgmental statement of fact. "I don't know if anything or anyone is capable of fixing what's broken inside him."

Saddened, Molly laid her head against his shoulder and didn't ask further questions. As she wouldn't betray Charlotte's secrets, she didn't expect Fox to betray Noah's. "The streets are so quiet and pretty this time of night." Rain had fallen not long ago, and everything shimmered, the lights reflecting off the tarmac. "Let's do this in other cities."

Fox ran his fingers lightly over the side of her face where she lay tucked up against him. "Just don't tell anyone I'm doing romantic bullshit."

"Tough guy." Snuggling into him, she said, "Can we ride around for a while?"

"Long as you want."

They stayed out almost to dawn, stopping to play barefoot in a deserted fountain and dance under the moonlight in an otherwise empty plaza. Held in Fox's arms, his cheek against her hair and the only sound that of their breaths, Molly drew in the scent of him and felt her heart overflow with love.

"Sorry 'bout the ropes," she said sleepily much, much later, cuddling up to him in bed.

"Nothing to be sorry about—I've never had a better night out." Fox stroked his hand down her spine, the callused pads of his fingers a delicious, familiar roughness, his words a gift against her skin. "I've decided to save the ropes for when we have hours to play. I wouldn't want to rush." A kiss to her shoulder as goose bumps broke out over her skin. "Good night, Molly Webster."

"Good night, Zachary Fox." *I love you.*

FOX WAS THE ONE WHO found Abe the next afternoon when the big keyboard player didn't meet the rest of them for a late lunch in Fox and Molly's suite. "I'll go wake him," he said with a grin. "Maybe I'll use this ice cube to do it." Plucking the cube from his otherwise empty orange juice glass, he wrapped it in a thick napkin.

Noah and David grinned, but with restraint. Both their heads had to be throbbing since it turned out that after Noah showed his women the door last night, he'd woken David up and talked him into another drink or five.

"The rock-and-roll life," Molly said sweetly, "is not healthy for your livers."

David groaned. "Fucking tequila. Never again."

"You said that last time."

"Shut up, you minion of evil."

Noah splurted his coffee. "Minion of evil? Last night you were declaring your undying love."

"I'm going to stab you in a second."

"For the record, Molly," Noah said, turning his attention to her, "we've been saints since we returned home. *Saints.* We didn't want Fox's girl to get the wrong impression about us."

Rolling her eyes, Molly took pity on the two males and was pouring them fresh coffee when her cell phone rang. It was Fox.

"Get in here, bring the others." He hung up after that terse instruction, and she saw why when they reached Abe's room.

The keyboardist was sprawled in his bed, reeking of alcohol, bottles strewn around him and the brunette from the club nowhere in evidence. This, Molly knew at once, was more than a few too many drinks. "He needs medical attention." She'd seen her mother like this, the memory an ugliness under her skin.

"It's on its way." Fox's jaw was a brutal line. "I called 911."

Thinking past her instinctive anger, the rage an old one, and back to the first-aid course she'd attended during university, she said, "We have to turn him to his side, make sure he has a clear airway." Abe had thrown up at some stage, that much was apparent, but he'd survived. They had to keep him that way until the paramedics arrived.

The men rolled Abe into the correct position while she checked to make sure his airway wasn't obstructed. His breathing did seem to steady after the change in position, but it remained shallow, the normally rich mahogany of his skin pallid. "Has he done this before?"

"No. He drinks, but nothing more than the rest of us." Noah's fists were so tight his skin had gone bone white. "Cocaine was his problem, but he kicked the habit. He *made* it."

Except it was clear to all of them that Abe had only switched addictions.

Five hours later, the keyboardist was conscious but in no state to get out of bed. "It was just a binge," he said when the others confronted him in his private hospital room.

Molly had stayed outside the room, knowing this was something the four men needed to discuss alone, but she remained within earshot. Noah's temper, from what she'd seen, was as hot as Fox's. Abe wasn't far behind. David was calmer, but he was furious today, white lines bracketing his mouth. If needed, she'd step in to defuse the situation before it got violent. None of the men were the type to raise a hand against a woman.

"A binge?" Noah shouted. "You were almost in a coma!"

"Shit, lower your voice." It was a groan.

"What the hell are you doing, Abe?" Fox asked through what sounded like clenched teeth. "You stopped snorting coke, so you'll kill yourself this way instead?"

"What I do in my own fucking time is my own fucking business."

"You want to go there?" David said, and he didn't sound like the calm one at all. "You really want to say that when we might have to go onstage tomorrow without you?"

"I'll be fine by then."

"Have you looked at yourself?" Noah demanded. "Your hands are shaking and you can't even get out of bed."

"Get back in," Fox said, then swore as there was a small crash. "Satisfied now? You can't do anything but destroy cheap vases."

Abe's response was too low for Molly to hear, but she could guess what it had been from Fox's response. "You don't get to pick and choose when we're your friends. We won't let you do this to yourself or to us again. Choose, Abe."

"What?"

"The band or the booze, the drugs, whatever shit you want to shovel into yourself."

A stunned silence.

Abe was the first to find his voice and it was a roar. "You can't kick me out!"

"You're kicking yourself out! How many times do you expect us to do this? Wait to see if you wake up? Get ready to call your mom to tell her in case you don't?" Fox's voice vibrated with unhidden fury. "Enough, Abe. You either want to live or you don't."

"I'm not trying to commit suicide for Christ's sake!"

"You think she'd want this?" came Noah's voice. "For you to wallow in a pool of self-pity because boo-hoo-hoo it's too damn hard to be alive? She fucking idolized you, man."

A charged silence, secrets hovering in the air.

"Enough," David said quietly. "We all need to cool off before we say things that can't be forgiven. I will not lose who we are together because of this." A grim silence. "Any objections?"

There were none, and the three men walked out a few minutes later. Noah strode past without spotting her. David nodded and was gone. Wrapping his arm around her, Fox called up the two bodyguards he'd told to wait downstairs. "Stay here," he ordered them when they arrived. "Watch him—and check everything that goes in and out. I find out he had any booze or drugs in that room, I'll have your heads."

Nodding, the two muscle-bound men took up position on either side of the door.

Molly kept her silence as she and Fox left the hospital via a loading dock not covered by the media. Everyone was whispering drug overdose, and the band had decided to let that stand. Abe's problem with cocaine was old news, would soon fade from the screens and papers if they didn't feed the story.

Given Fox's mood, Molly didn't think anything of it when he ignored a smartly dressed woman in the hotel lobby who said "Zachary" and made as if to walk toward him, her expression faintly supercilious. The elevator arrived before she reached them, and Fox nudged Molly inside.

"She didn't look like a groupie," Molly said, simply to break the strained quiet.

Fox's lips twisted in a humorless smile. "They all want something." He didn't speak again until they were back in their room. "You okay?" Knees slightly bent, he brought himself down to her eye level.

It startled her that he'd remembered her past even in his current frame of mind. "I had a couple of flashbacks," she admitted. "I guess it's something I need to learn to handle. This environment—"

"No." Fox's voice was harsh. "You do not need to get used to this shit because it will not happen again. And *never* with me. Got it?"

Molly nodded. "I wouldn't have fallen for you if I didn't believe that." Not after seeing up close and personal the damage substance abuse could do, emotional and physical.

"Good." A hard kiss before he spun away and grabbed his acoustic guitar.

She left him alone by the windows, having learned he worked out his emotions through music. It was over an hour later, when the music went silent, that she took him a cup of coffee. "You'd never really walk away from Abe, would you?" Molly was fighting her instinctive revulsion to addiction to be a friend to Abe and she'd only known him a short time; Fox had known him years. "He needs you more now than ever."

"I'm so angry with him, Molly. We worked so hard to get him clean—we never let him down. Not once." He set the guitar aside, the coffee forgotten on a side table. "Every time he called, day or night, we were there. Noah's the one who rode to the hospital with him last time, and David drove his mother there when the doctors weren't sure if he'd ever wake up."

Fox's voice was jagged as he continued. "She's this tiny, fragile thing, and she cried until I had to carry her out of the room, away from the sight of her son lying motionless on the bed." He shook his head. "Abe's sister died as a child, and that day, it was like she was reliving every instant of the agony."

A deep breath. "No mother, she said, should have to watch both her children die." Hands fisted, his eyes stormy. "After that, after the detox and the rehab, he promised her he'd stay clean. Then he goes and does this?" Pain combined with the fury. "I can't watch him go down this road again."

Molly understood in a way no one who hadn't lived with an addict could. At some point, the emotional drain snapped something inside you. "The third time I found my mother in a pool of her own vomit," she said, confessing a secret not even Charlotte knew, "I hesitated before calling an ambulance." It had only been a matter of seconds, but Molly would never forget who she'd almost become as a result of her mother's addiction.

The hesitation shamed her, but Molly had long since forgiven the worn-out and scared teenage girl who'd had to act the responsible adult at far too young an age. "I just couldn't take the cycle of remorse and promises, the one or two days of normality before the inevitable slide back into the bottle."

"Ah, baby." Fox stood to wrap her in his arms, his cheek pressed against her temple. "It wears you down until you start to ask, what's the fucking point?"

Molly nodded, tears choking up her throat. "With Abe, he

can't have been drinking all this time," she said, soothing him with slow strokes of her hand down the rigid line of his spine. "Close as we have to travel together, we'd have noticed. You'd have noticed."

"I hope to hell you're right." Exhaling a ragged breath, he tightened his hold and they just stood there, taking strength from one another in a brutal world.

CHAPTER 35

D ISCHARGED AFTER A NIGHT IN the hospital, Abe was
back onstage the next night. Tension lingered in the air,
but the band stuck together as the shows continued to go by.
When—out of nowhere—David was hit with news that threatened to tear down the foundations of his world, there was no
doubt in anyone's mind that Fox, Noah, and Abe had his back.

The laughter took longer to return, but it came in time,
with Abe going cold turkey on the booze. "I don't know if I'd
be able to stop," he said one night to Fox while Molly was in
the room. "So better I don't start."

Molly was hopeful he was telling the truth—that the de-
scent into alcohol had been a one-off thing and not the sign
of a new addiction. Determined to help in a way she hadn't
been able to help her mother, she cornered Abe before the
Manhattan concert. "Want to go shopping?"

He rolled his beautiful dark brown eyes at her, ridiculously
gorgeous lashes throwing shadows on his cheeks. "Don't you
have Fox for that?"

"Yes, but I want to buy something *for* Fox." He'd worn the
leather cuff at several concerts, a silent symbol of his pleasure,

and she wanted to find other small surprises. "You're his friend, you know what he likes."

"Take Noah. Fashion plate likes shopping."

"You're the fashion plate, not Noah," Molly pointed out. "Anyway, he's keeping Fox distracted while I go shopping. And David," she said, cutting off his next excuse, "is with Thea." Her sister had flown in this morning and disappeared into David's room; the two had gone through a tough time over the past week, needed alone time.

"What's up with David and Thea?" Abe narrowed his eyes. "They sort out the BS over that ridiculous claim?"

"Come with me and maybe I'll share what I know."

He still looked surly as he hauled himself out of the armchair he'd been sprawled in. "Now I have to put on my disguise."

Curious, Molly watched as the usually sleekly dressed male disappeared into his room and returned wearing an honest-to-God one-piece jumpsuit in black fleece with yellow smiley faces. He'd paired the monstrosity with sheepskin boots and donned a wig with knotted dreads that hung about his face. Each dread was capped off with a tiny pink barrette shaped like a butterfly.

Her jaw fell open. "No, seriously? You're going to walk out on the street in that?"

"People run when they see me coming. It's a repeller disguise." Grinning, he slipped his hands into the pockets of the one-piece no one should've *ever* made for a grown man. "Where's your disguise?"

"I don't need one." Thankfully, her elevator-photo notoriety had faded quickly, especially with the gossip sites and magazines focusing on the "secret" Carina-Fox relationship. *Grr...* "Ponytail, sunglasses, cap, and I'm set."

"Then I dare you to walk with me." Abe crooked his arm.

"I'm no chicken." Sliding her arm into his, she headed out into the noise and color and vibrancy that was Manhattan.

Abe was the band member she'd spent the least amount of time with, but he proved good company, even when a bus full of international tourists swarmed him for photos. Posing patiently, he told them he was a clown on his day off, his expression deadpan, while Molly attempted not to collapse in a fit of giggles. The photos she took were priceless.

It was on the way back to the hotel that he said, "You trying to become my friend, Molly?" A laid-back comment with a steely undertone.

"Yes." He was too smart for anything but honesty. "I know the band is tight, but you're guys. You'd rather shoot yourselves in the family jewels than talk about feelings, and sometimes even big, tough guys have feelings." As with her mother, Abe's problems seemed to result from an attempt to drown emotional pain.

"You got balls. No wonder Fox likes you." Slinging an arm around her shoulders, he held her to his side. "I had a shrink at the rehab center. Didn't talk to him. What makes you think I'll talk to you?"

"You don't have to talk to me, Abe. I just wanted you to know I'm here if you ever decide to acknowledge that you do in fact experience these mysterious things called feelings."

"You think that'll stop me ending up in the hospital?"

"Only you can do that," she said bluntly. "If you manage to mess up in spite of a rock-solid support network, then you're a self-destructive idiot."

"Don't hold back now." A hard-eyed comment as they snuck into the hotel through a back entrance.

"Lies don't help anyone."

He walked with her to the suite she shared with Fox. "I'll try not to be an idiot," he said at the door, no humor on his face. "Hey, Moll."

She stopped with the door partly open. "Yes?"

"Why bother?"

"Because you're my family now." She'd lost one already, couldn't bear to see this one fall apart too. Last time, she'd been young and scared and alone. This time, she was an adult who was learning her own strength—and she had Fox.

A MONTH INTO THE TOUR and three weeks after Abe's binge, all the tension had dissipated and Molly felt at home with the entire group. The crew teased her good-naturedly now and then about being an "intern" but said they'd have her back anytime. She did still pitch in around her own work—which was gathering steam, word of her skills spreading through the recommendations of satisfied clients.

It felt as if all was right with her world as she and Fox walked to their suite after the Chicago concert. She didn't think she'd ever get used to the feel of thousands of people singing along to the music, the thundering power of it indescribable. No wonder Fox remained wired up afterward, sometimes for hours.

"I want you naked the instant after we walk through the door," he said, his body heat kissing her skin. "On your hands and knees."

Her face flushed. Sex was always hard and fast the first time when he got like this. Then he'd go slow, every ounce of that untamed energy focused only on her as they explored one another and their fantasies. There'd been scarves involved last time, and he was playfully threatening to buy fur-lined handcuffs. But he was generous with his own body, too, letting her kiss and caress and pet to her heart's content—just not at the start. Wired as he was, he didn't have the patience.

Smiling hello at the private security guard assigned to monitor this floor, the other members of the band in suites just down from theirs, Molly walked inside. Fox paused for a second to say something to the guard.

Her fingers were on the hooks of her pretty, fitted black jacket embellished with lace panels on either side when she froze, the hairs standing up on the back of her neck. Having shut the door, Fox, his body primed as it pushed into her backside, went to reach for the button on the back of her skirt when he, too, went motionless.

"That's not your perfume," he said, pinpointing what had set her off.

It was too sweet for her, too opulent in its sensuality. "Maybe a housekeeper made a mistake?" The band had a standing order in all the hotels they used that no one was to enter their suites without a specific request.

"She'd have had to get past the guard." Stepping in front of her, he headed to the bedroom. "Stay here."

Molly followed at his heels, got a scowl, but he didn't order her back. A second later, they were at the open bedroom door.

The girl inside couldn't have been more than nineteen, every inch of her sleek and golden, her perky breasts tipped with pale pink nipples, the flesh between her thighs bare. Molly saw all that at a glance because the girl was reclining on the king-size bed on her elbows, her legs drawn up at the knees and thighs spread.

Black stilettos and a mane of glossy caramel-colored hair arranged artfully over one shoulder completed the look. "Hi," she breathed, after dismissing Molly with a single, contemptuous glance. "I thought you might want some company."

Jaw a vicious line, Fox's hand fisted. Slipping past him before he could give free rein to his temper, Molly grabbed the scrap of sequined fabric that was apparently the groupie's dress and threw it at her. "If you don't want to be arrested and thrown in jail for the night, put that on and haul ass." No way was she touching the G-string panties discarded on the carpet.

The girl pursed pouty lips painted a wet pink. "Fox wants me here, don't you, honey?" Her eyes went to the zipper of his jeans.

Molly felt Fox snap. Striding across the room, he would've taken the girl's arm and dragged her out if Molly hadn't stepped in front of him. "She's not worth the aggravation," she whispered, one hand on his cheek to force him to meet her gaze. "Touch her and she'll sue or sell her story to the tabloids."

Fox's eyes glittered but he didn't push past her. Reaching into his pocket, he grabbed his phone and made a call, barking a single order. "In here now!"

The security guard entered the room less than three seconds later, his face going ashen at the sight of the intruder. "I threw you off the floor."

The groupie, apparently understanding she truly was unwanted at long last, grabbed her dress and pulled it over her head. "A *real* man let me in." Her eyes slanted to Fox again as she picked up her purse. "Anytime, Fox darling. Just call me." She brazenly threw her panties and a scrap of paper holding a phone number on the bedside table.

"Sir, do you want me to contact the police?" the security guard asked as the intruder began to saunter out.

"Yes."

The girl spun around. "Fox!"

"Get the fuck out." With that, he turned his back on the guard and the groupie both, his breathing low and uneven.

Shaking her head at the guard when it appeared the other man might say something, Molly waved him and the screeching girl out. Not until she heard the front door close, locking out the sounds of the girl's continued disbelief, did she speak. "Fox," she said softly, "if you have her arrested, the story will—"

"I don't care." Reaching out, he began to tug open the hooks that held the lace-paneled jacket tight to her body. "Let them talk about it. We don't press charges, next time some woman's going to figure she has the right to walk into our home and our bedroom. They must think I'm a goddamn lowlife—that all a groupie has to do is flash her pussy at me and I'll cheat."

Molly realized he wasn't going to listen in this mood. She grabbed his wrists. "Not in this bed." No way was she about to lie on those sheets. "Take me bent over the sofa."

Fox's fingers halted in the act of undoing the final hook, the jacket having parted to expose the scarlet-and-black bustier she'd worn underneath for his eyes only, the pale globes of her breasts exposed by the half cups. "You liked it when I did that before?" he asked, the anger smoldering into passion.

Molly pressed her thighs together at the gritty sin of his voice, but she was aware he wasn't calm yet, the smoky green holding a hard edge. "Yes." Undoing the final hook herself, she shrugged off the jacket. "I *really* liked it."

Grabbing her hand, Fox pulled her into the living room and had her bend over the low sofa, hands braced on the back. The position made her arch her back, her butt higher than her head. "Don't move." With that harsh order, he went to the main door and threw the dead bolt.

FOX KNEW HE WAS IN the grip of a vicious temper, but he also knew he would never hurt a hair on Molly's head—and he needed to touch her. Brand her.

Stripping away her skinny black skirt but leaving her red heels on, he ripped off her panties to reveal the creamy curves of her body. The contrast of the silk bustier against her skin was so erotic he knew he'd make her ride him one day while dressed just like this. Not today. Today, he needed to be the one in charge, needed to know she'd accept him after the bullshit that had just gone down.

Hot with a combination of rage and lust, he tore off his own clothes without taking his eyes from the luscious sight of her bent over waiting for him, a flush of heat beneath the cream. At any other time, he'd have talked, have teased, further jacking up their arousal. Tonight, he gripped her hips and nudged at her with his cock.

Scalding heat, honey slickness.

Plunging in to the hilt to her gasp, he shifted one hand to her nape, holding her in position as he thrust hard and deep, his balls slapping against her with every stroke. It wasn't enough. He needed to feel her pleasure, needed to know she was his on this most elemental level, that her trust in him hadn't been damaged. Sliding his hand to her navel, he reached down and squeezed the succulent nub of her clit between thumb and forefinger.

"Fox!" It was a soft scream, her orgasm sweet and hot around him.

Bottoming out, he gritted his teeth as she squeezed him in possessive clenches, his own orgasm tearing down his spine. He hauled her up against him while his cock still twitched inside her. Breath jagged, he wrapped one arm around her waist, the hand of the other around her throat. "I will *never* fuck around on you."

CHAPTER 36

CHEST HEAVING, MOLLY REACHED BACK to cup the side of his face. "I know," she whispered, her voice breathless. "Baby, I *know*."

She wasn't sure Fox was calm enough to hear her even now, so she waited until after, when she was in his arms on the sofa, her bustier discarded beside her skirt and her body flush with his. Then, rising up on her elbow, she ran her fingers gently through his hair, petting him until he was no longer so on edge.

"I know you won't cheat," she said, looking into his eyes to make sure she had his attention, that he'd hear every word she said. "I might've worried at the start, before I truly knew you, but I haven't for a long time." He was too blunt, too honest to go behind her back. "You'd tell me to my face if you wanted out."

"Never going to happen." An unyielding statement, his arm steel around her back. "You're stuck with me."

"I like being stuck with you." Continuing to run her fingers through his hair, she leaned down to kiss him, sips and licks that were more about being with one another than sex. "You don't have to worry that things like this will make me doubt you."

"There'll be lies," he told her, one hand rising to curve around the side of her neck, his thumb grazing her jaw, "in the tabloids and magazines and online. I won't always have a way to prove I didn't do something."

"Fox, I trust you."' She turned her face to kiss his palm. Never had she thought she'd feel this kind of trust in a man, but Fox had taught her how—by being the man that he was. Temper, talent, and an unflinching loyalty. "As long as you talk to me, we'll be okay." Her lips curved. "Or you can sex me silly, then talk. I'm good either way."

The sinew and muscle and strength of him seemed to fully ease at last. "I like that last option." Shifting her so she lay on top of him, their bodies rubbing against one another, he pushed back her hair from her face, held her gaze. "Your trust means everything, Molly. I won't let you down."

"I know," she said, so content and safe in his arms that she couldn't imagine anyone or anything tearing them apart.

The world, however, had other ideas.

MOLLY WOKE WITH A JERK when Fox's cell phone went off in what felt like the middle of the night. Swearing, he let go of her to turn and reach for his discarded jeans. "Sorry"—a sleepy rumble—"I'll turn it off."

"'S 'kay." Already sliding back into sleep, Molly snuggled to his back... and felt the instant his muscles locked. She came immediately awake. "Who is it?"

"Thea." Turning to wrap his arm around her, he put the call on speaker. "Go, Thea."

"Is Molly with you?"

"Yes, I'm here," Molly said, knowing it couldn't be good news if her sister was calling at what the phone told her was four in the morning. "Has something happened?"

"Yes, and it's bad." Her tone made ice form in Molly's bones, her heart in her throat. "Before I tell you," Thea continued, "I want to say I'm so sorry, Moll. I'll do whatever it takes to bury this."

"Just spit it out," Fox ordered.

"Some sick fuck managed to sneak in and set up a video camera in one of your previous hotel suites." Thea's words were bullets in the silence. "It might've been motion activated, or just started and left to run until the digital card was full. From the angle on the still photos posted from the video, it looks like it was on a shelf."

Nausea swirled in Molly's stomach, skin flushing hot, then cold. She had a horrible feeling she knew exactly where the camera must've been—their last hotel suite had had an antique shelf against one wall of the bedroom, set up with old books in a way she'd found charming at the time.

"Where?" Fox demanded.

"Bedroom."

Molly jumped from the sofa and ran for the toilet, barely making it there before her stomach revolted. Throwing up so hard it felt as if her entire digestive tract was being peeled with a grater, she was barely aware of Fox coming after her and pulling her hair back so it was no longer in her face, his voice a low, rough murmur as he stroked his hand down her back.

When there was simply nothing inside her any longer, he carried her shivering body into the shower and, setting the water temp close to boiling, held her until she'd stopped shaking. "I'm sorry," he said, his tone raw. "I'm so sorry, Molly. I'll kill the bastard who did this. I pr—"

Snapping out of the shock, she pressed her fingers to his lips. "No, don't make that promise." Because Fox had never once broken a promise to her... and in that reminder, her world tilted back on the correct axis.

She had no illusions, knew the coming days and weeks would be brutal, even knew there was a high chance she'd fall apart again, but if and when she did, Fox would be there. He was always there and he was the most important person in her world, the one for whom she'd do anything. Even walk back into her worst nightmare.

Cradling his face in her hands, she said, "I won't allow this ugliness to destroy you, destroy us."

He crushed her to him, the water pounding over them until steam filled the small enclosure. Warm through and through, not from the heat but from Fox's embrace, she turned it off. Drying off and shrugging into a thick hotel robe while Fox stepped out to pull on his jeans over bare skin, she brushed her teeth to get rid of the last faint traces of her nausea.

"Come on." She took Fox's hand, her rock star having returned to lean in the doorway. "We need to talk to Thea and find out how bad it is, what she can do about it."

Fox pulled her back against him, his eyes furious but his voice gentle as he said, "This person will pay. I promise you that."

"As long as it's legal," Molly reminded him. "I don't ever want to visit you behind bars."

A grim nod. Instead of calling Thea back on the phone once they'd returned to the sofa, Molly used her tablet to connect face-to-face with her sister. Thea looked angrier than Molly had ever seen her, her cheekbones slicing against the smooth honey of her skin.

Her sister didn't waste time asking how Molly was feeling. Instead, she gave them the cold, hard facts. "The major news organizations aren't reprinting the still photos lifted from the videos, given that the images were taken in a place where you had an expectation of privacy. The blogs and online fan sites are also staying clear."

Still grim, she continued, "However, one extra skeevy tabloid has printed two stills with a promise of more, with the video to be uploaded on their site in just over twenty-four hours, and the publicity's gaining steam. Several other sites have scraped the photos for their own pages. It's trending on all the main social media platforms, and even the places that haven't printed the stills are carrying stories about them, so people are going looking."

Able to feel Fox's body vibrating with the rigid control he had over himself, Molly put her hand on his knee. "So," she said, "there's no way to close the gate, is there?"

"Fox's legal team can hit every single site that reprinted the stills with a lawsuit, but that horse has bolted." Her sister checked an incoming call on her phone, didn't answer. "I've already been in touch with them about getting an injunction to block the video, but the tabloid is based in another jurisdiction and I have a feeling they'll just move up the upload deadline the instant they get a whiff of legal action." She thrust a hand through her hair. "Only reason they haven't already uploaded is to maximize the publicity."

Molly wondered if she was in shock, she was so calm, but now that the first horror had passed, she didn't feel numb. No, she was becoming angrier with every second that elapsed—because this was *hurting* Fox, her protective, possessive lover, and no one got to hurt her man. "I want to see what they've already posted," she said. "I need to know how bad this is."

Thea didn't argue, just forwarded her the articles, then waited as she and Fox opened the file. It made Molly's nails dig into her palms to see an image of herself sitting up on her knees with Fox behind her, both of them nude. They were laughing, and he had his hands on her breasts. The tabloid hadn't blacked out that part, probably because Fox's fingers covered her nipples, but they'd put a rectangular block over her genital region, with the word "Explicit!" across it.

The second published still was a back view of Fox, nothing blocked out. In the background, she could be seen lying nude in the tumbled bed, her hair a wild mass around her head. In this one, they'd blacked out her breasts.

The text of the "article" was a collection of exclamation points: *Think these images are tame?! Well they are!! We have access to incredibly hot and explicit pictures of Fox and his current squeeze getting down and dirty!! Check back in two hours for a fresh fix as we count down to our upload of the original sex tape!! Exclusive!!*

"Only those two so far?" she managed to ask her sister through her fury, her mind filled with memories of that night, of the things they'd done. She was ashamed of none of it, would do it again, but only with Fox. The world had no right to violate the privacy of their bedroom.

"Yes." Thea guzzled what was probably tar-thick coffee. "It looks like the tabloid must've bought exclusive rights to the video and they're getting as much mileage out of it as they can."

"Shut the fucking company down." Fox's voice was so cold Molly felt her skin prickle. "I don't care how it's done—tell legal to throw everything we have at the bastards."

There was a knock on the hotel room door at that instant. Getting up, Fox walked over to open it. "You heard," he said to Noah as the other man walked in. He'd clearly been pulled out of bed and wore only low-slung jeans, his blond hair a mess and his eyes chips of ice.

"Yeah. Let's fuck the vultures up." Coming to sit next to Molly on the sofa, he reached up to rub his knuckles over her cheek. "You holding up okay, Moll?"

"I'm tough," she said, and it was, she was discovering, true.

Fox wrapped his arm around her waist again when he sat back down on her other side, his rage no less violent. "We're talking about how to take the tabloid down."

The guitarist nodded. "I might hate my old man, but the bastard is a shark," he said, a mix of admiration and anger in his tone. "I called him as soon as I found out about this. He says for you to file a criminal complaint as fast as possible."

"Right." Thea nodded. "So anyone who does anything with the video risks falling foul of the criminal justice system, not just civil law. I don't know if it'll work with the tabloid based outside the country, but it's better than nothing."

They filed the complaint. Meanwhile, Noah tapped his father's contacts to put a crack private investigator on the trail of the piece of scum who'd decided to use Fox and Molly to land a big payday.

"Someone in the security company either did this or was in on it," Fox gritted out. "Maybe the same 'real man' who let in the groupie, probably for a fucking blow job." Calling the head of the security firm, a former Green Beret he knew personally, Fox made no effort to hide his fury.

Apparently, that fury was shared—they had a name within the hour, after a check of the corridor surveillance footage from the hotel in question showed one of the guards walking into their suite during a concert. He was spotted going back inside minutes after Fox and Molly checked out, probably to retrieve the camera.

He hadn't been behind the groupie however; that was traced to a newly promoted guard whom his livid boss had just busted back down to mall patrol. The only people now in the band's security team had been with the firm for years, and all had also worked more than once for Schoolboy Choir. As for the man behind the video, he'd disappeared, but Molly knew he'd be found—greed this ugly didn't make for intelligence.

"This is your nightmare, isn't it?" Fox said hours later, once they were alone again, the suite having been swept for any surveillance equipment in the interim.

"Who does that?" she said, blood hot where she stood by the window. "Who thinks it's all right to spy on people in their most private space?" She fisted her hands on the sweatpants she'd pulled on—along with a zipped hoodie—for the visit by the cops. "Who thinks that way?"

"Scum." Fox walked over, eyes shadowed and voice taut as he said, "You gonna run?"

"No, I'm going to fight." Running out on Fox was simply not, and wouldn't ever be, an option. "Never again is anyone going to turn me into prey—and I refuse to allow them to hurt you. We'll kick their butts."

Fox's arms locked so tight around her that she couldn't

breathe for a second. Tugging back her head after easing his hold a fraction, he claimed her mouth. His kiss was wild possessiveness, unrelenting demand… but his body, it shuddered. Running her hands down his back, she held him close.

If she ever came face-to-face with the man responsible for putting that look in Fox's eyes, as if he was readying himself to lose her, Molly would beat the bastard bloody. "No running away," she said when their lips parted. "Not today, not tomorrow, not any day to come."

"My tough, beautiful Molly." His body shuddered again, his eyes dark. "I'm so fucking glad you're mine."

MOLLY HELD FOX'S WORDS BANG against her heart, her fingers locked bloodlessly tight with his as they stood ready to walk out the hotel's main door midmorning. She'd been running on anger and adrenaline since four a.m., had, until a few minutes ago, believed she had the tools to deal with the media mauling about to happen. Now, with the horde only meters away, she wasn't so sure. Her stomach churned, her chest painful beneath the peach top that she loved, the one with the softly tied bow at the throat.

"You sure we have to do this?" she asked Fox.

A squeeze of her hand. "We take the offensive," he said, his confidence and determination a powerful force. "We control the situation, and we damn well stand proud."

It was the same thing Charlotte had said when Molly called her best friend.

"Don't you dare let them shame you." Charlie's voice had been fierce. "Go out there and show the world that Molly

Webster is a force to be reckoned with. Also, try not to smack anyone—you sound like you'd really like to."

Molly realized the anger was still there, embers burning beneath the nerves. "Charlie told me not to smack anyone," she said to Fox, "but I'm not sure I'll be able to stop myself if a reporter gets out of line with you." Fox had focused only on her pain, shrugging off the exposure of his own body, but Molly was fuming over the way this incident had torn open his scars. "Don't let me do anything dumb."

His dimple appeared, her Fox back with a vengeance. "Follow my lead," he said, and hauled her in for a deep kiss, his free hand covering the side of her face in the hold that always made her feel cherished. "Ready?"

CHAPTER 37

"**Y**ES." THERE WAS NOTHING SHE wouldn't do for him. Looking over his shoulder, Fox nodded at Noah, David, and Abe, who were set to follow.

She'd thought the distance to the hotel entrance would seem endless, but the five of them were walking through the automatic glass doors what felt like a second later. David flanked Fox, while Noah and Abe stood next to her, a solid wall of friendship and loyalty. Charlie might not have been physically present, but Molly could hear her best friend's voice in her mind, telling her not to smack anyone. It almost made her smile.

The mass of reporters, photographers, and cameramen—corralled off the hotel steps by a wall of black-suited security—began to scream questions the instant they spotted Fox.

"Spin is everything," Thea had said to Molly and Fox in a call a quarter of an hour ago. "Make the world see you as an ordinary couple trying to have a relationship under the spotlight—and point out that this could happen to anyone."

Her sister had barely taken a breath before continuing. "Allow them to glimpse your anger but don't look hounded.

The scent of blood only makes predators hungrier—shrug and say you'll deal, but that the ones behind this will pay. No one messes with you and gets away with it."

Now, looking at Fox as he stood in front of the cameras, ignoring the screaming until the media people began to nudge one another to shut up, Molly thought Thea had been wasting her breath. He'd do exactly what he'd do.

"Fox! Fox!" One reporter's voice rose above the other fading ones. "Do you have a statement about the recent intimate photos of you and your"—the slightest pause—"lover?"

"Yeah, I have a statement," Fox said, his tone a growl.

The entire rabble went quiet.

"Being caught with a gorgeous, sexy woman having one hell of a good time isn't exactly something I'm going to apologize for." He paused as the reporters laughed, the tension dropping in a steep dive. "Especially when that woman is Molly."

Heads swung toward her, questions congesting the air.

"Are you going to introduce us?" another reporter managed to shout above the wall of noise.

"World, meet Molly." Gripping her jaw, Fox kissed her full on the mouth, complete with tongue. "Molly, world."

Blushing, she found herself half-laughing as she faced the cameras. "I'm going to kill you," she muttered under her breath when his hand landed on her butt.

His smile turned wicked.

"Molly! Molly! Are you as unworried about this as Fox?"

"Well, I did get caught in bed with a rock god. I'm real sorry." She didn't know where the words came from, but they were the right ones from the way the reporters began to hoot and clap.

351

Fox held up a hand when they would've shouted more questions, his other one hooked into the back pocket of her jeans. "One thing I want to say—Molly and I, we're never going to be sorry about what we do between the sheets."

Another wave of laughter and conspiratorial grins.

"But," Fox continued, "I'm the possessive type. I share my music, my voice, and I don't think anyone will argue when I say I've been more than open when it comes to interviews"—a round of nods—"but the one thing I will not share is Molly."

He waited to let that sink in before continuing, the ruthless edge back in his voice. "No matter how long it takes, I will crush both the voyeur who decided to get his pathetic rocks off by violating our bedroom, and the scum-sucking site that put the footage up."

He held up his hand again when the media would've asked more questions. "I have a request of Schoolboy Choir fans—we've always been accessible to you guys in every way we could be. Now I'm asking you to honor the years we've been on this rock-and-roll ride together by not sharing or reposting this content. This isn't about the music, it's about hurting my girl, and that is *not fucking okay.*"

Molly wanted so badly to kiss him at that instant that she almost didn't hear the question that floated into the air as they turned to leave.

"Molly! Is that a Kiwi accent?"

She knew there was no point in prevaricating; her whole life would soon be an open book to the media, the past she'd tried so hard to outrun thrown in her face. "Yes," she said, her fingers locked once more with Fox's.

"I TOLD YOU YOU'D HANDLE it." Fox closed his arms around her the instant they were alone inside their brand-new luxury coach.

As of now, Schoolboy Choir would no longer be staying in hotels during the tour. Aside from the driving section up front, which was sectioned off by a soundproofed wall, each coach had a furnished living area and bedroom, as well as a section for the facilities. It reminded Molly of the small apartment she'd rented right out of university, neat and functional, though without much extra space.

It would require some logistics to get the coaches to concert locations on time, with the band often having to fly ahead, but that was a minor issue compared to the guaranteed privacy. Each coach could only be accessed by a thumbprint scan.

"I thought you were incredible." Nuzzling her nose against his, she smiled. "You know how to play the media like you do an audience."

"I just laid it out like it is, no bullshit." Tender hands tucking her hair back behind her ears. "I would've come after you, you know. If you'd run. I wouldn't have been a good guy, wouldn't have let you live your life away from me. I'll always come after you."

"Hey." Rising on tiptoe at the words that sounded as if they were ripped from his soul, she kissed him, her hands cradling his face. "I told you, I'm in this for the long haul." Molly would repeat that promise until he believed her, until he stopped expecting her to give up on him. "You and me, we're a unit. They're going to start calling us Folly any day now."

"Smart-ass." A playful slap on her butt, the strain fading from his expression.

Stealing another kiss, she said, "Let's go into the bedroom and christen this hotel on wheels." Fox was a physical man and Molly was more than willing to use their intimate connection to show him how much he meant to her.

"No need to rush into the bedroom for that." He backed her against the wall, each word accompanied by a kiss. "We have to do a thorough job." His hands sliding up under her top to cover her breasts. "It's a very big coach."

"I guess"—Molly gasped as he fondled the lace-cupped curves with blunt masculine approval—"we'll have to take it one bite at a time."

"Perfect idea." Strong white teeth gripping the skin just above the pulse in her neck before he shifted his attention to divesting her of her top. Unraveling the pretty bow with a tug, he made quick work of the buttons, and the top was soon on the carpet.

Two more seconds and her bra of blush-colored lace met the same fate.

"You're far too good at that."

Dimple showing, he dropped a kiss on one pebbled nipple. "I practiced to get good just for you."

"Smooth, Zachary Fox, real smooth." Stroking her hands through the cool silk of his hair, she sucked in a breath as he took a leisurely bite of her right breast. "Do that again."

Fox's mouth curved against her skin before he did as ordered, licking his tongue over her flesh. "Want to play a little?" he asked when he raised his head.

Molly bit her lower lip, sudden bubbles of agitation in her blood. "This coach is secure?"

Steel glinted in Fox's eyes, his hand heavy and comforting on her lower back. "It came directly from the dealer and I watched the head of the security firm personally go over it with a fine-tooth comb. You're safe."

Her heart ached. Always, Fox thought of her, though the man who'd invaded their privacy in such a gutless way had harmed him just as much. "Yes," she whispered, wondering how she'd gotten this lucky. "I'd like to play."

Bracing his forearms on the wall on either side of her head, Fox pressed his mouth to her own, his body heat making her want to rub up against him like a cat. The kiss was wet, tangled, their tongues licking against each other until her breath was lost, her heartbeat a rapid stutter in her chest.

Fox wasn't in much better condition, his erection pushing into her abdomen and his breath harsh in her ear as he said, "Trust me, baby."

Bending at her nod, he picked up her blouse, but when he would've twisted it as if to make a tie, she gripped his wrist. "Don't you dare. I love that top." It was gasped out.

"God, you're strict." One big hand on her breast, he leaned in to kiss her again. "That turns me on." Nipping at her lower lip, he dropped her top back to the carpet and moved his hands to his belt buckle.

The funny, fluttery feeling in her stomach, ignited by watching him undo the buckle and pull the belt through the loops, only grew when he said, "Turn around, Molly."

That *tone*. Molly couldn't do anything but obey, the finely textured carpet that covered the walls of the coach deliciously abrasive against her aroused nipples.

"Hands behind your back."

She obeyed again, even knowing it would leave her at his mercy. Somewhere along the way, trusting Fox had become a bone-deep impulse. The leather was warm, strong against her skin. Again and again she felt the sensation of movement—he'd wrapped the belt around her overlapping wrists multiple times. A brush of metal, the buckle clinking softly for a second before he pulled the belt tight, rendering her arms helpless.

"Too tight?" His jaw grazed the skin of her shoulder. "Studs not pushing too deep where your wrists press against your back?"

Molly shook her head as he caressed her lower curves, her throat dry.

"That's good. Anytime you want out, just say so." Chest pressed to her back, he said, "You got it?"

"Yes." Molly curled her fingers against his zipper, his own hand slipping around to cup her breast before he ran it down her stomach to the waistband of her skirt, following it in a teasing line to the back.

Slipping the small black button there out of its hole, he brushed his thumb over the skin below. "You're so soft, Molly." The zipper being tugged down with those husky words. Shaped to her body, the skirt didn't sag but had to be pulled down—which Fox did slowly, so slowly, his kisses getting lower down her spine.

She shivered.

"Cold?" A breath of hot air against her skin as the skirt fell to her ankles, followed by a tender kiss to the delicate crease of skin where her buttock met her thigh. "Better?"

"More," she said, shameless.

But being shameless with Fox had its rewards. She got a second kiss, long caressing strokes of those rough-skinned hands over her thighs. "Lift your leg." Another kiss after she obeyed. "Now this one."

An instant later, the skirt was gone from around her ankles, leaving her clad in nothing but black heels and panties of blush-colored lace that matched the bra already on the floor. Fox had given her the decadent lingerie as a gift, as he gave her so many things. She truly was spoiled. Most of all because he was hers.

"Did I ever tell you I love taking you while you're wearing heels?" Kisses up her spine as he rose to his feet behind her.

Sucking in a shallow breath, she said, "You might have mentioned it once or twice."

His laughter low, masculine, intimate, Fox drew her hair over one shoulder and, sliding his hands between the wall and her skin, palmed her breasts. Her sensitive flesh was crushed against his hold by the heavy press of his body, but it wasn't painful—no, it felt wonderful. Especially when he drew one hand back to undo the button on his jeans, lowered the zipper what sounded like halfway and, taking her bound hands, tucked them inside.

Molly moaned. "You went commando before a press conference?" Hot and thick and erect, he felt too big to fit inside her, but he did. He always did, and the fit was perfect.

"Why the hell not?" Running the fingers of one hand lightly over her neck and shoulder, he rolled and tugged at her nipples with his other. "How would you like me, Molly? Like this." He ground himself against her lace-covered behind, her hands trapped in between. "Or should I throw you on your back, spread your thighs wide and pound into you while you lie helpless?"

Molly squeezed her fingers on the part of him she held, to his groan. "Whatever you want," she whispered.

"Oh, I like the things you say." A firm tug on her nipples before he caressed one hand down her body and into her panties from the front.

It was a bold, self-assured hold, that of a man who knew the woman he touched belonged to him. She could feel herself growing wetter against his palm with every second that passed, his mouth busy on her throat and shoulder, his free hand continuing to roll and tug at her nipples, shooting darts of sensation directly to her clit—which she tried to rub against his hand, but her position wasn't quite right, and she could only manage the most frustrating of brushes.

"Fox."

"You said I could do what I liked." It was a gravelly purr. "And I want to tease you."

Molly whimpered, tried to clench her fingers on him, but he'd already stepped back, her hands sliding away from all that rigid male heat. "You want me, baby?"

"Yes." Her fingers curled into her palms.

Sounds behind her—the light thud of shoes being kicked off, fabric rustling, a zipper moving the final few inches. "I'm naked," he told her a minute later. "I've got my hands on what you want. I'm stroking it hard and fast, rougher than you ever do." A quick kiss to her nape before he stepped out of reach once more. "That's not a complaint—I love your hands on me. Shit, I jerk off to the thought of you jerking me off."

A palm pressing between her shoulder blades when she would've turned. "Nu-huh. Don't make me tie your ankles too… or maybe I should."

358

"I'll fall."

He spanked her on one of her bottom cheeks, the ripple of sensation arcing through her flesh. "As if I'd let that happen." Hooking his fingers in the sides of her panties, he tugged them down and off.

She felt fabric around her ankles the next instant. "It's my T-shirt, not your top"—Fox's voice, low and with that gritty undertone that made him so powerful as lead singer—"so don't get mad."

Hobbled by the tie and in a slightly unbalanced position against the wall, she had to stay where she was or risk taking them both down, because Fox was right—he'd never let her fall.

"You have no idea how hot you look." A kiss to her nape. "My strong, smart, fucking perfect Molly."

Heart aching at the stark emotional power of his words, she drank in the sight of him when he stepped back and scooped her up in his arms. The words she wanted to say flirted on the tip of her tongue, words that meant everything to her, but that Fox could well reject.

CHAPTER 38

CARRYING HER TO THE BEDROOM with effortless ease before she could give in to temptation, Fox said, "I wouldn't want you to abrade your skin," and placed her carefully on her front, making sure her face was turned to the side and her hair out of the way. "Okay?"

His tenderness undid her. "Yes," she whispered, feeling something break inside her—old pain, old fear, the last hidden fragments crumbled into dust at the brush of his callused fingertip across her cheek. "*Fox.*"

"I have you, baby." Maneuvering her lower body until she was on her knees, her butt in the air and her face against the sheets, he ran his hands down her curves with unhidden pleasure. "Now this would make a pretty picture." His words turned the ugliness of what had happened into something beautiful, claimed it for their own.

An open-mouthed kiss on her lower back, his hand pushing between her thighs again, his fingers sinfully busy. Brought to the edge of what felt like a shattering orgasm, she screamed when he stopped... only to start again a minute later, after he'd eased her down from the high... then he repeated the cycle.

Until she was an incoherent pile of trembling woman, every one of her senses primed. That was when he drove into her. The fact her thighs were pressed together by the tie around her ankles made the thick heat of him feel like an invasion, hot and welcome. She was branded, she was owned, she was taken.

Molly came, sobbing her pleasure. And kept coming as he pounded into her again and again, his fingers digging into her hips and buttocks. When he gripped her hair in his hand near the end and tugged up her head, the pulling sensation on her scalp sent her over the edge.

She came so hard she passed out... but not before she heard Fox groan her name as he slammed deep into her one last time.

MOLLY ROSE TO CONSCIOUSNESS CRADLED in Fox's lap, her rock star sitting on the bed with his back against the headboard. Her bindings were gone, his heartbeat a hammer under her ear as he ran one hand along the curve of her spine, the other down her arm. Her own heartbeat not exactly steady and her skin sheened with perspiration, she snuggled closer.

"Hey." Fox tipped up her chin. "You okay?"

Seeing the concern in his gaze, she found the energy to reach up and kiss his jaw, his stubble coarse under her lips. "I can officially say that was the hardest orgasm I've ever had." The confession got her a deliciously male, flagrantly smug smile that wrapped another thread around her already claimed heart. "I used to read that in romance novels and scoff. I mean, who passes out from an orgasm?"

"My Molly."

"Your Molly." Her veins sluggish from the aftereffects, she ran her fingernails down his chest in a light caress. "Do you have to report in for anything today?" There might not be a concert tonight, but the band was constantly fine-tuning the show, part of what made them so good at what they did.

"Nothing that can't wait." He kissed the top of her head. "Do you want to sleep?"

Molly nodded, knuckling her suddenly heavy eyes. "It's been a crazy day." She'd expected to feel scared, humiliated and broken after what had happened, but instead she was content, happy… and proud.

"I survived the world seeing naked pictures of me and knowing they might see a whole heck of a lot more," she said, sitting up to look into Fox's eyes. When the green grew stormy, she shook her head and cradled his face in her hands. "I discovered I'm stronger than I thought. You know what else I realized?"

A shake of his head, his expression unreadable.

"That we don't blame and fracture when the going gets tough. We don't abandon each other." As her father had abandoned her mother in so many ways. "We stand together, and Fox, if we can do that now," she whispered, "can you imagine how strong we'll be in the years to come?"

His smile creased his cheeks, his gaze potent with emotion as he said, "I see you in every dream I have of the future."

"I love you." It spilled out, what she'd held inside for so long because she knew that for Fox, those three words in that particular order meant loneliness, neglect, and rejection.

He froze, but Molly wasn't about to allow her rock star to carry this hurt inside him forever. "I know that statement doesn't have good memories for you," she said, eyes locked to his. "That's why we'll make new ones together."

"Might take a hell of a long time."

"I'm not going anywhere." No fear, no regrets, no other always but Fox. "Just remember, this is me, Molly, saying it to you. And it means my heart."

He brushed his thumb over her cheekbone, his strained muscles easing beneath her. "Say it again."

"I love you," she said, understanding on a storm of emotion that this was the first time in his life he'd heard the words from someone he trusted not to kick him in the heart. "So much. Until it hurts and the hurt is one I want to feel forever."

THEY SLEPT INTERTWINED, WARM AND safe—and woke to another phone call from Thea, this time on Molly's phone. Molly immediately put her on speaker. "Thea?"

"You'll never believe what's happened!" The excitement in her sister's voice had them sharing a confused glance, especially when she continued on to say, "I mean, I'm looking at it and I can't believe it."

"Stop rambling and get to the point," Fox growled.

But her sister remained ebullient. "I always knew School-boy Choir had some dedicated fans, but this is unreal."

"Thea."

"Sorry, Moll." Thea laughed. "That tabloid site that published the photos? It's down."

"How?" Fox asked.

"Hacked, and a post on a major online bulletin board says it was done by the band's fans. Several other sites that scraped the images have also gone down." Thea sounded like she had the most gleeful smile on her face. "All of a sudden anyone else who reposted the photos is hauling ass to get them off."

"Will this blow back on Fox?" Molly frowned.

"No, I asked the legal team. Everyone heard what Fox requested of Schoolboy Choir fans—they did this on their own initiative."

The print version of the tabloid remained, Molly thought, but the worst they could do there was print stills with the explicit sections blacked out. Though, if the tabloid's management had any sense, they'd stay clear even of that. No paper could survive only on print; the tabloid needed to have an online presence, and printing the photos would no doubt be seen as an aggressive move by the band's fans.

"You haven't even heard the best part." So much glee Thea could've been a cat who'd found a whole vat of cream.

"There's more?"

"Get your tablet so you have access to a bigger screen."

It only took Molly a few seconds. "I have it."

When Thea told her to look up a major entertainment blog, she was leery. "Thea, I don't—"

"Trust me, this is a good one."

Arm around her waist, Fox pressed a kiss to her shoulder, and it gave her the strength she needed. The front page of the site blinked to life on her screen—and it was dominated by a photograph of a grinning Fox kissing Molly on the steps of the hotel this morning.

FOX'S TAKEN, LADIES!!

The accompanying article was relatively small, but it mentioned that Molly was from New Zealand, a librarian, and that her father had been a "disgraced politician." However, they'd spun the facts so instead of her family's past being a tawdry piece of gossip, Molly came out looking plucky and strong, her and Fox's romance a fairytale ending to a tough life.

Astonished, she said, "Did you do this?" to Thea, as Fox glanced at his phone, then stepped out to make a call.

"No, Molly, *you* did. The media, and more importantly the fans, are charmed by you—you couldn't have done better if I'd scripted everything." Open delight. "God, you were so *cute*. You even blushed!"

"I'm going to strangle you soon," Molly muttered.

"Like I care. Just keep on being yourself, being the ordinary girl who snagged a rock god." A pause. "Hmm, I'm going to feed that line to the press. Oh, if you want to get caught being adorable with Fox now and then, that'd be—"

Molly hung up on her laughing sister, then looked at Fox when he came to sit back down beside her on the bed. "The video's still out there."

"Yeah, but what dumbass will upload it now, especially when the man responsible has just been arrested and confessed." He held up his phone. "That's the message that came in." Running his hand down her back, he said, "Even if someone is stupid enough to touch it, the piece of shit told the cops he only got about ten minutes of usable footage."

"What?" Molly turned, heart thumping.

"Turns out he wasn't a technical genius. No motion sensors. He just switched on the camera and left it running."

"And"—Molly's eyes widened—"we came in super late that day." A tanker had spilled its load not far from the concert site, leading to traffic being held up for over two hours.

"The scum couldn't get back into the suite to reset the camera because his shift had ended." Fox closed his hand over her nape. "That's probably why the tabloid was building up hype—they were hoping for a big surge of initial customers paying to watch it before word got out about how tame it was."

Molly exhaled because Fox was right. Even if the video did leak one day, all anyone would see was a couple in love, cuddling and kissing and laughing. After surviving the exposure of the still photographs, photographs that could never be totally erased from the Internet, Molly knew she'd be able to handle that. "At least now," she said to Fox, "you have the compulsory rock star sex tape."

He squeezed her neck for the smart-aleck comment. "I can't have that video getting out." It was a snarl. "My reputation as a badass who does dirty, nasty things to women would be in shreds."

Giggling, she leaned into him, her hand on his ridged abdomen. "The media likes us now, but they could turn on us in a heartbeat, couldn't they?"

Fox looked down into her face as she looked up into his. "Yeah, so we don't live for them, we live for us."

"Us," she whispered, her lips parting for his kiss.

THE CONCERT THE NEXT NIGHT blew off the roof. Schoolboy Choir kept playing for two hours beyond the official end time, accepting screamed-out requests from the sold-out crowd. Noah and Abe took the mike a number of times and the crowd chanted "Da-vid, Da-vid" until the drummer surrendered and laughingly added his voice to one of the band's popular songs.

Molly was surprised to find that David *could* sing, and quite well. All the men could, though none had the ferocious power of Fox's vocal cords. But no one could pound a beat like David, caress the keys like Abe, or the guitar strings like Noah. Their diverse range of talents was what made the band so incredible as a unit.

"Thank you!" Fox yelled into the mike after what they'd announced as their final song. "You've been an amazing audience—and thanks for some other things I'll get in trouble for if I mention them too specifically!"

The crowd roared.

And the band did one more song, pure unfettered hard rock, before leaving the stage. Fox dragged her into a kiss the instant they were clear. He was sweaty and pumped and gorgeous.

"Fuck, man," Noah muttered with a scowl. "I really need a girl backstage."

Fox snorted. "You have about three hundred girls lined up outside your door every night."

"Yeah, yeah, but it's not the same as having a Molly." The guitarist swung his arm around Molly and smacked a kiss on her cheek before heading farther backstage.

"He's right," Fox said, dimple on display, "it's not the same."

She had to kiss it, to his chuckle. "You must be exhausted," she said afterward, exhilarated from having witnessed what she knew was a concert that would go down in rock history. "Starving, too."

"It hasn't hit yet—I'm riding on adrenaline." Wrapping an arm around her shoulders, his energy sky-high from the rush of performing, he headed toward his dressing room. The concert attendees who'd won a backstage pass through a radio contest hadn't yet been escorted up, so it was an easy walk.

David and Abe were standing outside their rooms, swigging on chilled bottles of water. Abe threw a bottle to Fox, who caught it one-handed. Noah appeared in his open doorway the next instant. "That might be the best concert we've ever done."

"I hope the crew got it all on tape." David glanced at Molly after she returned from Fox's dressing room with a fresh T-shirt for him, his own thrown out into the crowd as had become tradition. "What did you think, Moll?"

"Incredible, a legend in the making." The entire crew had stopped and listened as much as they could, not wanting to miss out. "Now what you need to do is get some food into your bodies, followed by a good night's rest."

Abe, David, and Noah grinned at her before saying, "Yes, Molly," in unison.

Well aware she was being teased, she made a face at them.

"Don't worry, boys." Fox tucked Molly to his side. "She'll be far too busy to hassle you tonight or tomorrow morning."

Molly elbowed him. "You are so not getting lucky tonight."

Noah hooted just as one of the crew called out a warning that the backstage fans were about to come in. Leaving the band in the corridor, Molly slipped out of sight. She had no problem with being known as Fox's girl, but she had no desire whatsoever to be a celebrity.

Fox winked at her as she entered the dressing room, and she knew he understood. Just as she understood that he thrived in the spotlight, in the surge of energy that came with performing live, and in interacting with the band's fans. If he'd needed it all the time, they would've never worked, but he was a musician at heart, liked the peace of home to create.

So they fit.

CHAPTER 39

HER ROCK STAR DID GET lucky that night—as if she had any chance of resisting him. She kissed his throat when he collapsed on top of her, tasting the salt and untamed masculinity of him, her fingers weaving through his hair.

On her wrist sparkled the white fire of a diamond bracelet he'd given her before the concert. Molly was almost afraid to ask what it was worth—she'd probably never wear it, she'd be so worried about losing a stone. "Don't," she murmured when he pushed himself up to his elbows. "I like you there."

A grin, his hand fisting in her hair to hold her in place for his kiss. "I need to get some more fluids into my body. Especially since you've just wrung me dry." Another slow kiss before he left her pleasured and sated body—to her shuddering moan—and walked out of the bedroom area of the coach. "You want a drink, baby?" he called out.

"Yes, please."

He came back with a sports drink for himself and a bottle of lime-flavored water for her, since she didn't like the taste of the sports drinks. Sitting up, she drank as he guzzled his standing up. Molly enjoyed the view, a smile on her face. Tattooed and muscled and all man, Fox could walk around naked as much as he pleased—for her eyes only.

Finishing off his bottle, he put it on the bedside table and opened up the safe built into the bedroom closet. "What're you looking for?" she asked, her attention on his gorgeous shoulders, and on the puzzle tattoo on his arm that she'd almost totally figured out.

It made her goofy with happiness that she knew him that well.

"This." Withdrawing the flat blue box, he got back into bed as her mouth dropped open.

"You didn't get me something else?" She put aside her own bottle.

"The bracelet's part of a set. I wanted to give you the necklace when you were naked so I could see it lying between your breasts."

Her lips twitched. "You are such a guy."

Grinning unabashedly, he hooked the necklace around her neck. "Oh yeah, I like this visual."

It was a simple pattern, two strands knotted together to hang along the line of her cleavage. Timeless, classic… and from the fire in the stones, each was of flawless clarity. "I'm going to pretend this is cubic zirconia," she said, "so I can wear it without freaking out."

A glint in his eye, Fox tumbled her onto her back. His hand was warm on the mound of her breast as he touched her in a way that said he was simply enjoying being with her. "Didn't I tell you? All your jewelry is fake."

"Liar, liar, pants on fire." She pretended to punch his jaw, then wrapped her arms around his neck. "It's stunning, Fox. Thank you."

"You're welcome." His thumb brushing over her nipple, the light in his eyes dimming as he said, "You can ask me for anything you know. I want to give you the world."

"I know." Molly caressed his nape, unsure what was wrong. "The fact is you're the best present I could've ever received. I'm not a greedy or possessive person, except when it comes to you—there, I'm afraid I'm awful."

"I like your kind of awful." An intense look, his voice rough. "Always be possessive and greedy about me, Molly."

"Something's bothering you." She could sense it with every cell in her body, had even before the concert. "Talk to me."

Bracing himself on his forearms above her, his lower body tangled with her own, he blew out a breath. "I got a call from Tawanna this morning to say my half sister Lauren's been trying to get in touch with me again." A hardness to his jaw. "You saw her right after Abe was hospitalized."

Molly connected the dots. "Linen shift, shiny bob, called you Zachary?" At his nod, she remembered what he'd said then, about everyone wanting something, and her protective instincts bristled. "What does she want?"

"She's trying to sell me some sob story about her husband losing his job and their house being repossessed by the bank." His expression was grim. "I checked it out the first time she asked months ago. They have enough money coming in from investments to live a stress-free, normal life, but she's used to luxury. Enough to lower herself to asking me to support them."

Aware of Fox's loyalty, his generosity, Molly knew his half sister must've done something horrible to cause the breach that clearly existed between them. She took a guess. "Has

Lauren ever made any effort to stay in touch except to ask for money?"

"Hell no." Fox snorted. "I reached out after she turned twenty-one, figured maybe she hadn't ever been in touch herself because it would create friction with her parents. I wasn't planning to mess that up, just wanted to know her."

Molly nodded, her heart aching. She knew exactly what it meant to find a sister; her relationship with Thea was an integral part of her life. So she could understand Fox's need to reconnect, hoped desperately this story would have a happy ending—even though Fox's tone made it clear the hope was a futile one.

"You know what she said?" Fox's shoulders tensed. "That she didn't associate with trash like me and she'd appreciate it if I didn't flaunt our relationship, as it might taint her reputation in the circles in which she moved."

"That bitch." Molly put one of her hands on Fox's cheek. "You don't have anything to feel guilty about then." When he would've argued, she pressed her fingers to his lips. "You do feel guilt—because you're a good man with a huge heart." A heart strong enough to have survived the rejection and neglect of his childhood. "But here's the thing: you might be related by genetics, but she's a stranger to you in every other way."

Fox's expression was intent. "You're not going to tell me to make nice with my family, all that stuff?"

"Lauren isn't your family. She's toxic, and you can't let her get to you." Weaving her fingers into his hair, Molly said, "I'm your family. Noah, Abe, David, and Kit are your family." She picked up his wrist, kissed the strange characters above his pulse point, which he'd finally confessed were from a made-up language he'd created as a lonely eight-year-old. "You told me this means loyalty. That's what family is, whether of blood or of the heart."

She kissed the characters again. "If Lauren has children later on, and you want to reach out to your nieces and nephews, I'll go with you." Molly wouldn't blame the children for the sins of their mother. "But Lauren doesn't deserve you."

He settled more heavily against her, the green of his irises rich against the jet-black of his pupils. "There's something else I haven't told you."

"I'll spank you later. Now talk."

It made him laugh, his shoulders shaking. "So fucking strict." Thrusting a hand into her hair, he kissed her the pure Fox way, all tongue and sex.

She was close to melting when he sat up and brought her into his lap so they were face-to-face. "When I was eighteen," he said, "I decided to give my mother another chance."

Molly's throat grew thick. She knew how much courage it must've taken for him to do that. Wrapping her arms around him, she held him as he spoke, but to her surprise, though she'd expected bleak pain, his tone was even, his eyes unshadowed.

"I walked up to her front door, knocked." He ran his knuckles down her back. "The maid who answered said my mother was in the park with Zachary."

"*What?*"

"Yeah, that was my reaction." Still no anger, no hurt. "I walked over to the park, and there she was playing with a little boy who called her Mommy. She redid her life, Molly. Redid me."

Molly had no words for the cruelty of it. "I'm so sorry," she whispered. "Your mother has no idea of the incredible man her son grew into, a son she'll never know, and that's her loss, Fox, not yours."

Fox kissed her throat, his lip ring brushing over her skin as he made his way back up to her mouth. "It was a kick to the guts then, and for a long time," he said. "It stopped hurting the first day you smiled at me and I knew you adored me just as I am. My sweet and honest and fucking sexy Molly who means it when she tells me she loves me and who comes knocking if I brood."

Lower lip quivering and eyes burning, Molly locked her legs around his hips, her hands on his shoulders. "I fall more in love with you each and every day," she whispered. "I will *hurt* anyone who causes you pain." If Lauren ever showed her face in front of Molly again, she'd better watch out.

Fox's lips curved, one big hand spreading on her lower back, the other curling around her nape. "No one can, not when I've got my Molly-love armor." Another kiss, his cock growing hard against her. "Enough of the bullshit. I want you."

"I thought I wrung you dry?" she teased, letting the subject of his mother and sister go. Fox wasn't the kind of man to worry things to death—what mattered was that he trusted her enough to tell her about something she had a feeling no one else knew. If he ever needed to talk about it again, he would.

Because she was his Molly.

"You did," he now said, tipping her flat on the bed and straddling her body. "I'm a broken man."

"Poor Foxie."

He narrowed his eyes. "Someone wants to be in trouble." Grabbing her wrists, he used his other hand to shake out a pillow from the case. She knew that case was going to be used to tie her wrists together before he shifted higher up her body and pinned her hands to the bed frame.

Excitement hot and dark under her skin, she looked down from his face as he knotted the fabric around her wrists… to realize his erection was within reach of her mouth. Since Molly Webster, good girl, was now Molly Webster, good girl with a naughty streak, she leaned up and sucked the blunt tip into her mouth.

"Christ!" Fox's hands slammed into the bed frame, the entire bed shaking. "That was not in the plan," he gritted out, one hand sliding down to cradle her head so she'd be in a better position to take more of him.

Unrepentant, she licked her tongue along the vein plump against her tongue. He thrust once, twice, each thrust shallow, before pulling out, his cock gleaming wet. "Your mouth should be illegal." Shifting down, he spread her thighs wide and bent to give her a taste of her own medicine.

A single minute and Molly arched up off the bed and against his mouth, her skin glimmering with perspiration. He showed no mercy, holding her spread wide as he continued to lick and suck until she was whimpering. Only then did he release her throbbing clit to flick his tongue almost delicately around her entrance.

"So," he said, lifting his head, "how should I punish you?" The lean dimple in his cheek invited her kiss, the ring in his lip her favorite plaything.

An ache in her heart, Molly didn't want to continue the

game all of a sudden. "Later," she whispered, her breasts rising and falling in a choppy rhythm. "I need to feel you inside me." Needed to hold him close. "I love you."

Expression altering to raw tenderness, he rose above her and tugged the knot in the pillowcase open. "You are such a bad girl. That's the second time you've messed with my plans." He dipped his head. The taste on his tongue her own, an erotic intimacy between them, he put one hand on the inside of her thigh and pushed into her, slow and relentless.

It drew a sound of acute pleasure from within her throat, her fingers buried in his hair and her legs locked around his hips. Fox kissed her throughout the loving, his forearms braced on either side of her head, his tattoos familiar and unique.

"My Molly." It was a guttural sound against her ear as he came in her arms.

WHEN MOLLY GOT A MESSAGE from Fox two days later to say he'd be out with Noah for a couple of hours, she didn't think too much of it. If he wanted to go off and do manly stuff with Noah, she didn't mind. Just like he didn't mind if she spent an hour on the phone with Charlotte or went out with Thea when her sister flew in.

Now she decided to e-mail Charlotte before getting to work at the little desk Fox had found for her; it fit perfectly in one corner of the living area of the coach.

It turned out Charlotte was online, so they video-chatted. Her best friend's life had become *very* interesting of late.

Molly ended the session with a smile on her face so wide it was probably blinding. "Go, T-Rex," she said with a little fist bump before forcing herself to concentrate on her work. Her eye fell on the bowl of strawberries on the desk as she opened her laptop and her smile grew impossibly wider. Diamonds were one thing, but Fox had a way of remembering the small things she loved.

Eating a couple of the juicy strawberries, she knuckled down. The work did eventually engross her, and darkness had fallen by the time she looked up. She got up, stretched, then decided to see if anyone was up for dinner—Fox's and Noah's afternoon out had apparently been extended.

Not that she was surprised, given what the men got up to, and it wasn't what people might expect. The last time Fox had disappeared—with David and Abe—they'd returned after drag racing around a special track built for speed. Gleeful as small boys, they'd been buzzed for hours.

The door opened in front of her at that second, Fox on the other side.

"Hey." She smiled, noting he didn't look any the worse for wear. "Dare I ask?"

A deep grin. "I got a tat," he said, jumping into the coach and pulling the door shut. "Noah came along for moral support, but he ended up with one, too. Not as amazing as mine though."

Proprietary of his body, Molly said, "Show me."

He took off his T-shirt, leaning back against the coach wall as she gingerly lifted the edges of the gauze bandage taped partway down his chest, just slightly to the left of center. "Fox"—she scowled up at him—"this is right over your heart." She knew a tattoo needle couldn't penetrate through muscle and bone, but still. "What if you'd been hurt?"

He squeezed her hip. "Worth it."

"It better be a work of sheer geni—" She froze as the gauze pad came off enough that she could see the ink, black against skin reddened from the recent work. It was shaped like a rectangular stamp, the kind businesses put on letters to say "Confidential." This one said something else.

Molly's Property.

Eyes burning, she pushed fisted hands against his abdomen as his arms came around her. "Idiot."

A kiss, his lips curved.

"What happens if we break up?" she said, so overwhelmed her mind was a mess. "They'll make fun of you, call you Folly's Property."

"Guess you better not dump my ass then or there goes my entire image." His dimple appeared. "Especially after I suffered hours of pain for you."

She touched her fingers delicately to the ink, leaning forward to brush a featherlight kiss over it as tears rolled down her face. No, he might never be able to say "I love you," those words yet hard for him, but he had other ways of making his point.

"Aw, hey baby, don't." Reaching down to cover the tat with the gauze again, he cuddled her close. "It doesn't hurt. I was just messing with you."

"Happy tears," she managed to get out.

"You like it, then?"

"I love it."

CHAPTER 40

WHEN FOX RIPPED OFF HIS T-shirt in the middle of the concert the next night to throw it into the crowd, realization slammed into her. God, she'd been slow. Fox hadn't just told her he loved her; he was telling the world.

Hugging her arms around her waist, she tried to hold the tidal wave of emotion inside, her breath rasping in her chest. Maxwell stopped on his way past her, patted her on the shoulder. "What did he do?"

"Be wonderful."

"Huh." Squeezing her into a hug, the crew boss said, "I thought you hadn't heard it."

"Heard what?"

He touched a finger to his earpiece. "Sorry, got to check out one of the speakers."

Forgetting his words when Fox turned to shoot her a grin before facing the roaring crowd once more, Molly just stood there. The man was going to kill her. Never had she thought she'd be so loved, so wanted, so cherished and adored. Taking out her phone, she texted, "I'm stupid in love with you," to his phone.

That phone was currently in her other jeans pocket, so he wouldn't see her message until after, but that didn't matter. What mattered was that it would be waiting for him whenever he checked. Sliding away her own phone, she frowned at the sudden silence in the stadium… and then the air filled with the pure sound of a single electric guitar. Even before lifting her head, she knew it wasn't Noah but Fox on the instrument.

He bent his mouth to the mike as he continued to play. "This song is for my Molly, who is the best fucking thing that's ever happened to me. Also, for those suicidal idiots sending her fan mail asking her to run away with them, I will hunt you down and rip off your nuts."

Laughing and crying as the crowd went wild, Molly wanted so badly to kiss him. Those words were so Fox. So her man.

He waited until the crowd quieted down once more before beginning the haunting intro to the song again, the ferocious power of his voice holding a rough tenderness as he began to sing. Noah, Abe, and David fell in gently in the background, Fox's voice and the guitar holding center stage until they slammed into a pounding beat as a unit.

It was hard rock and it was a love song, though the word "love" was found nowhere in the lyrics. The chorus was six words, a single voice, the music cutting off as if the band was one being.

My heart. My soul. My home.

Molly had tears streaming down her face by the time it ended, the crowd insane for a song she felt in her bones would become a classic. When Fox strode off the stage to drag her onto it, she went without argument, wrapping her arms around him and kissing him in front of the band, the crew, the audience of thousands.

He was hers, and she didn't care if the whole world knew how much she loved him.

Lifting her up against him, his arms steel, he spoke words for her ears only. "Since I'm already your personal and private property, will you be mine?" The dimple appearing. "It would really suck balls to be called Folly's Property."

It was a marriage proposal only Fox would make. "Yes, yes, yes." She punctuated each word with a laughing, crying kiss, uncaring of the flashbulbs and the lights and the eyes that watched them. "Always yes."

The smoky green exultant, his kiss a branding, he turned to grab the mike. "She said yes!"

The crowd thundered and screamed as the rock star who'd been meant to be Molly's one-night stand pressed his forehead to her own and whispered, "I'm yours."

I hope you enjoyed Molly and Fox's story! If you're curious about David and those sinfully enticing memos he's been writing to Thea, then turn the page for an excerpt from Rock Courtship, my follow-up novella! (Let's just say the Gentleman of Rock has some serious moves.)

For news about future titles in the Rock Kiss series, swing by my website: www.nalinisingh.com. *While at the website, don't forget to join my newsletter—I often send out free deleted scenes, short stories, and sneak peeks. The welcome newsletter has a special surprise for Rock Addiction fans!*

Any questions or comments? You can contact me at any time through the e-mail address on my website. You can also find me on Twitter (@NaliniSingh) & Facebook (facebook.com/ AuthorNaliniSingh) – xo Nalini

ROCK COURTSHIP

SINCE HE'D SACKED OUT FOR so long, he didn't have much time before he had to head to a downstairs conference room for the interviews. He'd steeled himself for the inevitability of coming face-to-face with Thea, but the sight of her still threatened to gut him.

Scowling, she strode over on sky-high red heels worn with a sleeveless and tailored black dress that ended just above her knees. "Did you put ice on that eye?"

He made himself speak, act normal—he'd become pretty good at that after the length of time he'd loved her. "Yeah, past few hours."

"What about last night?"

He shrugged.

Her glare could've cut steel.

Thankfully, the first reporter arrived a second later, and David spent the rest of the time making light of his new and hopefully short-lived notoriety. Interviews complete, he slipped away while Thea was talking to Abe, and once in his room, used his phone to do some research.

He had no idea how to write a memo, and if he was going to do this, he had to do it properly. The only question was,

was he going to do this? Putting down the phone, he got up and, going to the living area of the suite, got down on the floor and began to do push-ups. It was an easy motion for him regardless of his bruised ribs. Like most working drummers, he had to stay highly fit or he'd never last an entire concert.

He usually put in gym time every day, often went running with Noah or Fox, or did weights with Abe. Today, the familiar, repetitive motion of the push-ups cleared his mind, helped him think.

He only wanted Thea with him if she wanted to be with him.

Thea had made it clear his interest wasn't reciprocated.

But, as Molly had reminded him, Thea also had a first-class bastard of an ex. David didn't know exactly what had gone on between Eric and Thea, but he could guess, given that Eric had publicly flaunted a new fiancée within two weeks of the breakup. A silicone-enhanced airhead who simpered and giggled on Eric's arm and didn't have an ounce of Thea's feminine strength.

If fate had any sense of justice, the bimbo would divorce the fuckhead a year down the road and take Eric for every cent he was worth.

So, he thought, pumping down on his arms, then pushing back up, his body held in a punishingly straight line, it could have just been his timing that had led to her rejection. He'd waited six months after the breakup—until he'd thought Thea was okay, but what if she hadn't been at that point? He knew exactly how good she was at putting on a professional, unruffled face.

Hell, he'd once seen her handle a press conference with panache when two hours earlier, she'd been throwing up from food poisoning. What if she'd still been pissed off with the entire male sex that day in her office? Was it possible she'd have rejected any man who walked in and asked her out?

He paused, body tensed to keep himself off the floor as hope uncurled inside him. Because Thea hadn't dated *anyone* since the breakup. That wasn't just wishful thinking: he'd accidentally overheard her business partner at the PR firm, Imani, talking to another mutual friend on the phone a week before the band left L.A.—he'd been in a conference room early for an interview, the door open to the corridor where Imani was on the phone.

He should've called out and let her know he was inside, but he hadn't been listening at first; it was hearing Thea's name that had caught his notice. And then he couldn't not pay attention.

Imani, happily married to a surgeon, had apparently tried to set Thea up with a colleague of her husband's, only to be stonewalled. "I know Thea's over Eric," the other woman had said, "but whatever el slimeball did, he might have put her off men permanently." A sad sigh.

David wasn't sad about Thea not dating. He was ecstatic. Because it made it easier to believe that it had been his timing at fault. Like Imani, he didn't have any fears that Thea was still in love with the dickhead—no, she was too smart to put up with that kind of bullshit. That didn't mean the bastard hadn't hurt her; a woman as strong and as independent as Thea rarely allowed herself to be vulnerable, and David had a feeling her ex had used that rare, beautiful trust against her.

Fuck, but David wanted to kick the shit out of him. But more, he wanted to make Thea happy. Even if it meant taking a beating himself.

Getting up off the floor, he grabbed his phone and began to type out a memo on the tiny screen. It took him hours of drafting and redrafting to make sure it said exactly what he wanted it to say. He was still working on it when the band headed out to the concert location—where he saw the last person he'd expected.

Thea, now dressed in sleek black pants that hugged her butt and a soft, silky T-shirt of midnight blue under a dark gray blazer that nipped in at the waist, had come to say good-bye to Molly since the two women had missed each other that morning. Narrowing her eyes when she saw him, Thea ostensibly spoke to the entire band—but he knew the words were directed at him.

"If you want me to continue putting out fires for you," she said, "do not do anything that interrupts my vacation." A blistering look that was very definitely focused on David. "And next time someone tells you to put ice on a bruise, you listen!"

Then she was gone, her luggage already in the trunk of the car that was taking her to the airport for her flight to the Indonesian island of Bali, home to her parents and little sisters. He watched her step inside the car, its taillights fading far too quickly into the night.

Even then he didn't send the memo.

No, he waited until the minute before the concert was about to begin before pushing Send and turning off his phone. At least this way, he wouldn't be able to torment himself by checking for a response until after the show.

THEA HAD BARELY SUNK INTO the comfort of a cushioned armchair in a quiet corner of the airline's frequent-flyer lounge when her phone chimed. Putting down the glass of champagne she'd allowed herself in anticipation of the first real vacation she'd taken in over a year, she picked up her phone. It was impossible for her to simply ignore it—hazard of having a profession where a single leak or news report could change the trajectory of an entire career.

You never knew if it would be for good or for bad until it happened.

Seeing the message was from David, she felt her abdomen tense. He'd hardly spoken to her today, not that she could blame him. She'd been so worried about that eye of his that she'd snapped at him twice when all she'd wanted was to grip his jaw and check for herself that he was okay. He'd probably written her a nice, polite apology for not contacting her as soon as he was picked up by the cops... Only the thing was, Thea had had it up to here with David being polite to her.

He was polite to her when she had meetings with him and the rest of the band. He was polite to her when she called to ask him his views on particular publicity options. He was polite to her when she joined the band for dinner as a friend and not their publicist. He was *always* polite.

And nothing else.

Her hand clenched on the phone. If he'd been that way from the start, she wouldn't have known any different, but David hadn't just been polite to her when she came onboard the Schoolboy Choir team. He'd been sweet and funny and warm. So many times toward the end of her relationship with Eric, when her ex-fiancé had done or said something that hurt her, it was David she'd called.

She'd never told him the real reason why she was calling,

had always made it about work, but he'd made her feel better nonetheless. It had taken her several months to realize David was shy, but it wasn't the kind of shy that left him tongue-tied or lost. He just needed a bit of time to get to know people, warm up to them. When he did, his loyalty was etched in stone, his support unconditional.

That support had helped her deal with far more than he knew.

And now... he was polite and reserved and she *missed* him. So many times, she had to fight the urge to take hold of those strong, solid shoulders and shake him, tell him to stop it!

Even though he was meant to be a client and nothing else.

Bracing herself for the horrible, polite message to follow, she opened his e-mail. Her mouth dropped open.

He'd sent her a memo.

And it had nothing whatsoever to do with the bar fight.

REASONS WHY YOU SHOULD GIVE US A SHOT

Introduction: In this memo, I, David Rivera, explain why you, Thea Arsana, should seriously consider entering into a relationship with me.

First, let me address what I believe is your main reason for not dating me: that I am a client. This can be easily remedied. You own an agency in partnership. Your partner, or, if Imani has no space on her books, one of your senior associates, can take over the Schoolboy Choir account. If you'd prefer not to move the account, you can have Imani vet anything that has to do specifically with me. (Speaking as a member of SC, we want you, no one else.)

Second, while I admit I am a couple of inches shorter

than you and two years younger, I have absolutely no hang-ups about either. I don't think such a small age difference matters, and I'm fairly certain my maturity levels are acceptable. I point out that I, too, am an eldest child. As for the height thing—I seriously love those heels you wear. Never will I be so stupid as to demand you wear flats.

Not when watching you walk in heels is one of my all-time favorite things to do.

I'm also in good shape. I realize I'm not as pretty as Noah, or as built as Abe, or have a dimple like Fox, but I have been told I have good teeth. Therefore, I'm not physically deficient.

Third, I think you're hot. Extremely, combustibly hot. If I could, I'd keep you in bed for a week running, naked and mine, and I'd still not have enough. I think every part of you is hot, but I'm particularly turned on by your mind and your legs. You should see the fantasies I have of seducing your mind with my words while I stroke my hands over your legs, rub my fingertips along the inner skin of your thighs.

You don't mind calluses, do you, Thea? They come from drumming so intensely over a long period. All that physical work also means I have plenty of stamina. I can go as long and as hard as you want, or as slow and as deep, or any combination thereof. Hard and deep. Slow and long. Hard, deep, long? I can do that.

Your choice.

Or if you prefer it gentle and lazy, I can do that too. (Though we'd probably have to burn things down to a simmer with a hard, fast bout or three first.)

I'd be careful as I stroked you, but I'm afraid my touch would be a bit rough, a fraction abrasive, especially when I reach between your legs and use my fingertips to squeeze that pretty, plump, hard little—

Thea closed her eyes, took a deep breath. It didn't do much good, her chest heaving and her pulse a brutal thud against her skin. Mind filled with the potent erotic imagery he'd conjured up and thighs tightly clenched in a futile effort to contain the sudden throbbing ache in between, she stared up at the ceiling of the lounge.

All she saw was David's hand on her thigh, the small scar he had across the first knuckle of his right hand a slash of white against the dark gold of his natural skin tone. His arm was hard with strength and dusted with tiny black hairs, muscle and tendon flexing under his skin as he teased and played with her clit using those callused fingertips before thrusting a single finger deep into—

She squeezed her phone so hard that she heard the case crack, her body rigid and nerves gone haywire. When it was over, she collapsed into her seat in stunned shock, glad that the curved shape of it and her position in a seating arrangement right in back had hidden her from view of the others in the lounge.

He'd made her orgasm.

With nothing but the pressure of her thighs on her needy flesh and his words. The damn man had figured out her weak point and he'd aimed his missile right at it: her mind.

ACKNOWLEDGMENTS

A GREAT BIG THANK YOU to my beta readers for your brilliant feedback and encouragement: Sharyn, Jayshri, Nicole, Peta, and Rahaf – you are all awesome.

Thanks also to Nephele, for any number of things, not the least of which is driving me all over the Pacific Palisades area of Los Angeles so I could check out Fox's neighborhood.

To Jennifer. You rock hard. Thank you for everything.

A special thanks to my copy-editor, Anne, for her meticulous work, and to Jia, for all the help.

And to every single one of you: Your comments, reviews, e-mails, and smiles make this the best job in the entire world. Thank you for being so amazing!

ABOUT THE AUTHOR

NEW YORK TIMES AND **USA Today** bestselling author of the Psy-Changeling and Guild Hunter series **Nalini Singh** usually writes about hot shapeshifters and dangerous angels. This time around, she decided to write about a hot and wickedly tempting rock star. If you're seeing a theme here, you're not wrong.

Nalini lives and works in beautiful New Zealand, and is passionate about writing. If you'd like to explore her other books, you can find lots of excerpts on her website: www.nalinisingh.com. *Slave to Sensation* is the first book in the Psy-Changeling series, while *Angels' Blood* is the first book in the Guild Hunter series. The site also has a special section dedicated to the Rock Kiss series, complete with photos of many of the locations used in this book.

CPSIA information can be obtained at www.ICGtesting.com
Printed in the USA
LVOW07s2030230916

505968LV00001B/1/P